The Nymph's Heartwish

Heartwishes, Volume 5

Daisy Dexter Dobbs

Published by Department of Daydreams, 2022.

This is a work of fiction. Similarities to real people, places, or events are entirely coincidental.

THE NYMPH'S HEARTWISH

First edition. November 8, 2022.

Written by Daisy Dexter Dobbs.

Also by Daisy Dexter Dobbs

Heartwishes
The Viking's Heartwish
The Genie's Heartwish
The Firefighter's Heartwish
The Knitter's Heartwish
The Nymph's Heartwish
The Psychic's Heartwish

Watch for more at www.DaisyDexterDobbs.com.

Dedication

This book is dedicated to Margaret Evans Price (3/20/1888 – 11/20/1973) who wrote and illustrated wonderful books for children, one of which changed my life. As a frightened kid growing up in a dysfunctional environment, my method of escapism was reading. My absolute favorite book was Myths and Enchantment Tales. It belonged to my mother when she was a girl. The old, beautifully illustrated, hardcover book, published in the 1930s or 40s, was a collection of twenty Greek and Roman myths that took me on the most incredible journeys of the imagination. It was years later that I discovered Ms. Price, along with her husband, Irving Price, and Herman Fisher, co-founded Fisher-Price Toys in 1930. She became their first Art Director, designing a series of push-pull toys for their opening line, based on characters from her books. If you Google her name you'll find dozens of charming vintage illustrations that are utterly enchanting. I had framed some of them for my daughter's room when she was little. They made me smile with the fondest memories, no matter how many times I looked at them. I could fill pages with gratitude for so many fine authors and illustrators whose work has enriched my life.

Book Description

~<>~

Ask pub owner Nevan Malone anything about beer, wine and spirits and he's got the answers. But flowers? All he knows is they smell good, they're expensive, and women like getting them. So when his cousin, owner of Cupid's Headquarters flower shop, needs Nevan to watch the store for him, Nevan's completely out of his element. Plus he's stuck pet-sitting for his cousin's devious devil cat, which doesn't help lighten Nevan's grumpy mood. It's going to be one hell of a day.

To her horror, Aladee loses all her Cupid Academy class materials, including the map to Cupid's Earthly headquarters, during turbulence on her chariot ride to Earth from Mount Olympus. The capricious nymph fears she'll never be able to find Cupid, who'll be incognito. How will she ever make a positive impression on him before taking her final exam?

Nevan's dismal day starts looking up when a gorgeous, curvy, nearly naked blonde bounces into the flower shop, calling him Cupid and jabbering about nymphs, chariots and invisible wings.

Aladee's overjoyed. At last, she's found Cupid!

Nevan is cautiously captivated by the blonde, who's obviously a fruitcake, and probably a hooker. A nymph? The preposterous idea tickles him...right up to the moment her wings spread open.

The Nymph's Heartwish is book 5 of the Heartwishes series. This full-length contemporary romance novel is full of warmth and humor—with a very special touch of magic and a healthy dose of fantasy. It's inspired by the author's previously published novella, Finding Cupid. While all Heartwishes books are part of a standalone series, you'll enjoy them more if you read them in order. These are small town romances with happily-ever-afters, and no cliffhangers.

Chapter One

Friday Morning - Late Summer: Glassfloat Bay, Oregon
~<>~

"HALF POTATO PUB?" Drake Slattery mused while studying the new sign for his brother-in-law's establishment as it was being installed. "I don't get it. What's that even mean? What was wrong with Nevan's Irish Pub?"

"Nothing was wrong with it." Gazing at his pub's new sign with pride, Nevan Malone smiled. The signage was the crowning touch needed to complete the pub's renovation. The tedious work had taken so long, he feared at times it would never be finished. And now? It was everything he'd hoped for, and more.

Many of the pub's interior elements, from the furniture to the art on the walls, came straight from Ireland. Other artwork belonged to local artists. Unlike ubiquitous generic Irish pubs, Nevan included no shamrocks, Celtic typefaces, or images of leprechauns. They weren't a true representation of Ireland. He believed it was lazy to focus on tacky ornamentation people thought of as Irish, merely slap those elements up, and then call it an Irish pub.

The bar itself was huge and fabulous, visible from anywhere inside the pub. Like the hearth in a home, the bar area had a welcoming presence, an inviting vibe. He'd planned enough space around it to encourage movement and convenience, while also persuading people to stand and mingle. This wasn't your father's old-man style pub. This was a hip, vibrant spot, with an urban feel, meant to attract and satisfy young and old alike.

"I changed the name to reflect everything that's happened after the pub was nearly destroyed by the fire and smoke damage over a

1

year ago," Nevan told Drake. Recalling the memory was still painful. The minor financial settlement he'd received from his fire insurance was like a drop in the bucket. When he'd gone through every last penny of his savings and couldn't get a big enough loan to pay for the rest of the necessary restoration work for his popular family eatery, Nevan felt lost, and as gutted as the pub's insides.

Having exhausted all options, he'd considered accepting the meager offer he'd received from a real estate conglomerate to buy the historic brick building for less than half its value.

His family and friends stepped up, holding a fundraiser for him. They did it without telling him, using one of those online donation sites. Townspeople readily contributed, and hundreds of satisfied customers who'd enjoyed Nevan's hearty food and bustling bar chipped in as well. When Nevan found out, he was shocked, by the generous amount raised, as well as what all these people had done for him without him asking any of them for financial assistance.

"This town opened their hearts and wallets for me, so the new name is dedicated to them," Nevan explained.

Gazing up at the sign, Nevan's mother, Astrid, smiled. "I love the name."

"I had my doubts about the potato name at first," Nevan's cousin Red Devington said. "But once I heard the meaning behind it, I knew it was perfect." He draped an arm over his aunt Astrid's shoulder. "It came from one of grandpa's favorite sayings, didn't it?"

"It did." Silent for a moment, Astrid smiled. "Dear old Seamus Malone, with his thick, rich Irish brogue and addictive singsong sayings." She had a wistful, faraway look as she wrapped her arm around her nephew's waist. "He was a wonderful man. I couldn't have asked for a better father-in-law. You kids all loved Grandpa Seamus. The potato saying comes from an old Irish proverb he used to tell you kids. Considering all that's happened, the name couldn't be more perfect."

"And the meaning is...?" Drake questioned with a wry smile. "You just get half a potato with your order?"

Coming up behind her brother, Kady Malone looped her arm through Nevan's, got on her tiptoes, and planted a kiss on his jaw. "It means it's easy to halve the potato where there's love," she explained to Drake. "In other words, it's easy to share where there's love."

"Hey! You finally made it!" Nevan grabbed his little sister into a hug, swinging her around. "Please tell me you plan to be home for more than five minutes this time."

"I haven't seen you in ages!" Red gave his cousin a hug after Nevan set her down.

"Nothing could keep me away from your pub's grand reopening weekend—as well as the grand opening of your flower shop tomorrow, Red."

"It wouldn't be the same without you here, honey." Astrid gave her daughter a peck on the cheek. "Hey, remember the silly half potato song you kids all made up when you were little?"

"Wow, I'd forgotten about that," Red said.

"Half potato, no potato," Nevan started singing.

Red joined in, "Your potato, my potato."

"Mashed potato," Kady sang, "fried potato, baked potato, half potato!"

They all laughed and sang the full nonsense song together another three times, with each chorus louder than the last.

Astrid chuckled. "I remember the days when that's all I heard for hours on end."

Clapping his hands over his ears, Drake asked, "How did you put up with that awful racket, Astrid?"

"Ear plugs." She winked.

"I love the name you picked for your new business too, Red," Kady told him. "*Cupid's Headquarters* has just the right romantic panache."

"If you like flower shops named after a cat," Drake joked.

"Says the man named after a duck," Red quipped, eliciting a laugh from Drake and Nevan. "My baby, Cupid, loves his new namesake," he assured.

"Where is that mangy cat anyway?" Drake bent to look beneath the tables.

"Mangy my ass." Red gave Drake a playful whap as he bent over. "I'll have you know my fluffy white ball of fur was freshly bathed and perfumed this morning. He's fatigued from his spa treatment so I left him napping in my apartment, in his little bed with the satin sheets."

"Perfumed? And satin sheets?" Nevan rolled his eyes.

One of the sign installers called out, "Mr. Malone?" catching Nevan's attention. After getting Nevan's final approval, the workers packed up their gear and were on their way.

Drake stood gazing up at the new sign again. "Half Potato Pub...it's easy to share where there's love," he said thoughtfully, nodding slowly. "I like it. It really fits. It'll be a great conversation starter as well."

"Definitely," Red agreed. "Nevan should put a sign on the wall with the name of his pub and, beneath it, the saying," his hands spanned as if stretching across a movie marquee, "*it's easy to share where there's love.*"

"Great idea," Nevan said, with nods of agreement from the others.

Clapping Red on the back, Drake said, "You know I was just kidding about your shop name, right?"

"Puhleez, you don't even have to ask. Of course I do."

"Good, because I actually think it's spot-on. Flowers, love, Cupid, it all ties together. People will love it. In fact, did you know that in classical mythology, Cupid, the Roman god of love, also known as Eros in Greek mythology, was often depicted carrying roses, and—"

"Whoa!" Nevan's hand shot up. "Drake, you're morphing into professor mode again."

"Quick," Red said, "somebody turn Professor Slattery off before he rambles on for the next hour and we all start snoring."

"Okay, okay…" Drake barked a laugh. "I guess I do tend to get carried away now and then."

"Now and then?" Nevan rolled his eyes.

"Aw, stop picking on him, you two," Kady said. "I think the professor's stories are…interesting. You never know when something he's said might come in handy in some trivia game."

"Thank you, Kady." Drake beamed a smile which quickly turned tentative. "I think."

"Seriously," Red said, "I'm glad you like the shop's name. I still can't believe I'll finally be doing what I love for a living. Good God how I hated that banking job. I swear, I ate, slept and dreamed numbers, twenty-four-seven."

"You were always good at math, Red, but I agree, I'd take flower arranging over banking any day," Astrid said.

"Amen!" Red turned to Nevan. "Where's Buster? I haven't seen him today."

"I don't allow him inside the pub," Nevan answered. "Never have. I doubt customers would be too happy about dog hair all over the place. Buster's napping in my apartment…on denim sheets after the beer bath I gave him this morning." His smile morphed into a mischievous grin.

"You're incorrigible." Red gave Nevan's arm a playful slap, before turning his attention to Kady. "I hope you took lots of photos on this last trip. I want to see them all, especially your pictures of Ireland. God, I loved that place. Wasn't it amazing?"

"Absolutely," Kady agreed. "It's so similar to Oregon, lush, green and hilly."

"Because of all the rain in both places," Red said. "So are you here to stay or just making a stop between trips?"

"Reen's got all her fingers and toes crossed," Drake said, "hoping it's permanent."

"This time I'm home for good," Kady insisted.

"Or until the next travel urge grabs you." Nevan arranged tables and chairs just so, repositioning tabletop candles and condiments. Normally décor was low on his list of priorities, but tonight the town would see his renovated pub for the first time since it closed after the fire, and he wanted everything perfect.

"Nope, I did what I set out to do, backpacking overseas and seeing as many countries as I could the last few years. Hungary was my last stop. Just like I told you guys, I'm settling down to open my bookshop, right here in town." She pointed where she stood.

Astrid made a raspberry sound. "I'll believe it when I see it."

"Be prepared to become a believer, Mom." Kady laughed, shrugging out of her lightweight sweater and adding it to her tote bag. She did a slow 360, taking in the stunning carved wood bar, the new tables, chairs and booths, and the rich wood paneling lining the walls.

"Just look at all you've accomplished, Nev. This place was an empty shell the last time I saw it. If my bookshop looks half as good as your renovated pub, I'll be thrilled."

"Nevan's been working around the clock," Astrid said. "You know your brother. He's a workaholic and a real perfectionist."

"That's Mom's nicer way of saying I'm a control freak."

"Don't I know it!" Kady joined in the group's laughter. "I'm so proud of you, Nevan. It looks incredible, just like one of those grand old pubs in Ireland."

"That's exactly what I was going for. I was mesmerized by the family-friendly pubs on my trip there. The detail and depth in their carved wood was mindboggling. I had dozens of my own photos for reference, and a great book Drake found for me. It's over there on the bar." He gestured. "Take a look. It's filled with photos...and has a long title I can never remember."

"*A Pictorial History of Irish Pubs in Ireland and America*," Drake said from across the room at the bar, holding the hefty book aloft.

"Boy, that's huge, Kady noted. "Where did you find it, Drake?"

"In the trash." Nevan's lips curved into a teasing smile.

"No he did not," Astrid countered with a tsk. "Your brother-in-law found it in a thrift store at the bottom of a stack of books."

"Same thing." Nevan shrugged. "In any case, it was an excellent find."

"The esteemed Professor Slattery shopping in a thrift store?" Red arched an eyebrow. "I don't believe it."

"My sister basically twisted his arm." Nevan snickered.

"That's not true...entirely," Drake said. "I got the book before Reen and I were married, just after she broke her ankle when she had the cast on and couldn't drive."

"Reen begged Drake to take her to the grand opening of some junk store where everyone drops off their useless old junk," Nevan said.

"And yet, Nevan dear," Astrid pointed out with a smug smile and extensive wave of her hand, "you chose to do your renovations here using reclaimed wood and ornamentation from old Irish pubs."

"That's different, Mom." Nevan laughed.

His mother lifted one eyebrow. "Is it?"

"Where is Reen anyway?" Nevan asked, sidestepping his mother's question. "She said she was going to be here this morning, along with Gard and Sabrina."

"Reen will be here later," Drake said. "It was too chilly and rainy for the beach, so she and Sabrina took Lilly, Kevin, and Harry to the library for a couple of hours."

"Reen's crazy about Lilly and Kevin," Kady said.

"The kids feel the same about her too." Drake boasted a satisfied smile. "I think the main reason they wanted me to marry Reen was so they could spend more time with her." Gazing into the distance, his expression grew contemplative. "She's a great mom. So different from Janet it isn't even funny."

"Your ex was a real—"

"Nevan..." Astrid's cautionary tone matched her expression.

"A real piece of work. That's all I was going to say, Ma." Nevan offered a virtuous look, while exchanging knowing smiles with Drake. "Don't tell me my brother went to the library with them," Nevan said with a look of disbelief.

"I doubt it." Drake chuckled. "Gard said he'd be here soon, so I don't know what happened to him."

"Gard said he isn't on duty at the fire station this morning," Astrid noted. "Maybe they had an emergency and he got called in. I hope not." Her eyebrows pinched. "I get nervous when he has to go off to fight another fire."

"Gard's always careful," Nevan reminded his mother, drawing her close for a reassuring hug.

"Plus, don't forget," Kady said, "that Gard has an angel watching over him."

About to make a wisecrack about the angel, Nevan caught Kady's subtle warning look and shake of her head. He could be a dolt sometimes and was glad for his sister's signal. This wasn't the time for him to default to his usual joke cracking, especially if his mother was concerned about Gard's safety.

Releasing his mom, Nevan saw she looked less tense, which made him extra glad he'd kept his big mouth shut. Offering Kady a quick, furtive wink and smile, his gaze landed on her peppermint pink tote bag. Covered with rainbows, daisies and peace signs, both sides also had big block letters spelling out, *make love, not war.*

"Isn't that the same hippie purse," he pointed at his sister's bag, "Reen used for the donut pillow for her broken butt?"

"Yup." She lifted her bag high. "Reen returned it when she was finished using it."

"I can see why," Nevan teased, only to get another chastising look from his mother, which was well-deserved. But Kady took his teasing in stride. She'd always been a good sport and was used to his clowning around.

"I love that tote," Red said. "It's got such a joyful vibe."

"I think so. Wait until you see what I have inside for you two business owners." Grinning happily, Kady patted her tote.

Nevan eyed the cavernous bag, bursting with all sorts of stuff he didn't recognize. One thing looked like a bunch of skinny sticks tied into a neat bundle. Knowing Kady, it had to be some special hocus-pocus new-agey paraphernalia.

"I'm going to sage your newly renovated pub, Nevan, and your flower shop, Red." She carefully drew the tied bundle of scrawny twigs from the bag. "I brought my favorite mixture of white sage, lavender and cedar to make it more uplifting and relaxing. Nevan, would you please crack the pub's door open a few inches? Since your flower shop adjoins the pub, Red, you can just open the connecting doors. That way we'll provide a way for any bad vibes to escape to help clear the space."

Nevan screwed his expression. "Huh?" Her explanations were like listening to a foreign language.

Red chuckled. "Just do it, Nev."

Shrugging, Nevan complied with his sister's request. Kady's heart was always in the right place, even if he had no clue what she was doing when it came to her woo-woo stuff.

Pulling a small clay pot from her bag, she set it on one of the larger tables. "I can do my smudging in here."

"You're putting on your makeup here?" Nevan cracked and Kady laughed.

"You're hilarious, Nevan." Kady rolled her eyes.

Soon fragrant clouds of pale gray smoke wafted up from the pot. "I don't want any of you to worry," she assured, waving a small cluster of wide, long feathers through the smoke, spreading it. "I only use found feathers for smudging to ensure no animals are harmed. These are turkey feathers."

"Whew, thank heavens you cleared that up," Red teased.

"Yeah, I was really worried for a while," Nevan said.

Planting her fists on her hips, Kady glanced at Drake. "What, no witticism from my brother-in-law?"

"Nope." Drake shook his head. "I was too worried about those feathers to come up with anything witty."

In a futile attempt to conceal her laughter, Astrid covered her mouth. Kady and the others gave in to laughter too.

Walking through the expansive space as she spoke, Kady said, "Many people, myself included, like the smell of sage. It's said that people carrying unseen negative energy are repelled by it."

"Nope. I have zero unseen negative energy," Drake claimed.

"Well, I think the fragrance of sage is wonderful," Red said.

"Oh yeah, ditto," Nevan responded. "Who doesn't love the smell of Thanksgiving when they're sitting in an Irish pub?"

"You just keep on smudging with your sage, dear," Astrid encouraged. "We're all positively brimming with positivity and sparkly, positive vibes." She made a glittery gesture with her fingers.

"Wonderful! I love your upbeat, supportive attitude, Mom." Kady was seemingly the only one who didn't get that Astrid was joking.

Shaking a reprimanding finger at his aunt, Red told her just above a whisper, "Shame on you, Aunt Astrid." His smile conveyed his lack of seriousness.

Astrid gave Red a hesitant smile. It was all Nevan could do to keep from laughing at the rare sight of his mother looking guilt-ridden.

Fifteen minutes later, Kady had finished purifying the pub and Red's flower shop with her Thanksgiving-scented smoke.

"Thanks, Kady." Nevan pulled his sister into a buddy hug. "That was a great...uh, smoke cleaning ceremony." Nevan didn't have a clue about what she was trying to do but if it made her happy, he was fine with it.

"Much appreciated, sweetie." Red gave her a kiss on her cheek.

"Oh good." Kady's face lit with a smile. "I'm glad you're both pleased. Now your spaces will be safe and protected."

Taking a seat at the table, she said, "Let's sit together for a few minutes. I'm going to clear my mind and enter a meditative state. It would help if the rest of you did the same. Just offer some brief words of thanks, invoking the universe to help remove any unseen energies that don't serve your highest good. But we should wait a moment...until our visitor arrives with his happy news."

"Visitor? There you go again with your psychic mumbo-jumbo." Nevan laughed. Before he could say anything else, his brother Gard came bounding into the pub.

"Hey, bro, I've got great news!" Gard said.

Kady gave the drop-jawed Nevan a sweet *I told you so* smile.

"How do you do that?" Nevan held up a hand. "Wait, no, I don't think I want to know. It's downright spooky."

"I think it's very cool," Red said. "She's been like this since we were kids."

"She's my sweet little psychic." Astrid leaned over to clasp her daughter's arm, giving it a supportive squeeze.

Nevan wondered when his mother and the rest of the family would finally realize there was no such thing as psychics. Kady was simply more attuned to people and paid closer attention than most, which made her good at guessing what was going to happen.

"I see that look in your eyes again," Kady told Nevan with a teasing smile. "I know what you're thinking."

"Oh, so now you're a mind reader too?" Nevan countered.

"No, but wouldn't that be cool?" Kady laughed. "It's just that disbelief is written all over your face, Nev. I'm surprised you're not used to my psychic abilities after all these years. It's no big deal, really. I think most people are psychic to some degree. I just practice my ability more than the average person." She continued waving her feathers across the smoldering bundle she held.

"Um, no—" Nevan started before Gard interrupted him.

"Well, hello to you too, Gard. How've you been, Gard? It's so nice to see you, Gard." Gard said in a mocking tone after he failed to receive a greeting. "Especially because I'm here to change somebody's life."

"We're glad you're here, Gard," Kady said. "Your presence is always a welcome addition to any gathering. But you'll have to wait for a few minutes before you spring your surprise on Nevan."

"Me?" Nevan's hand flew to his chest.

Kady nodded. "Mmm-hmm."

"How does she always know?" Gard asked.

"Because she's psychic, just as I told you." Astrid's *I told you so* grin matched her words. "Hello, Gard, I'm glad you're here, honey."

"I'm glad somebody is," Gard joked. "Thanks, Mom."

"Since most people can't see negative energy," Kady said, ignoring the chatter around her, "it's important to trust our instincts to clear any lingering negativity. Mom, I'm sure you're on board with clearing your son and nephew's new establishments so they can practice their businesses happily and without the threat of—"

"Any bad mojo," Nevan said, muffling laughter.

"Call it what you will," Kady said kindly.

"Go ahead, honey," Astrid said. "I'm listening and ready to do whatever you need."

Several minutes later, Kady finished meditating and asked the universe for blessings for both the pub and flower shop.

"*Now* can I finally tell Nevan why I'm here?" Gard asked.

"As soon as I bring a flight of craft beers to the table for you to all test and enjoy," Nevan said, going behind the bar to pour 3-ounce samples in small taster glasses. "I need you to tell me what you think of these four new stouts."

"No argument from me," Gard said, and the others agreed.

"Okay, Gard." Nevan took a seat. "I'm all ears."

"You'll be making an already wonderful day even better," Kady told Gard.

Nevan's eyebrows knitted. After a long blink, he looked up at Gard. "I think I already know. You're here to pass your heartwish ring to me, aren't you?"

"Bingo! Now who's psychic?" Removing it from his finger and holding it out to Nevan, Gard said, "You don't seem very happy about it. I thought you'd be doing somersaults."

Clutching the ring, Nevan watched as its soft glow seeped from between his fingers. Offering a humorless laugh, he told Gard, "If this supposedly magical ring was the real deal, imagine what I could have done with it six months ago. But everything's already done now...finished after more than a year of blood, sweat and tears. What the heck do I need this hunk of pseudo magical metal for now?"

"I've got to take issue with you on that," Gard said. "Even you, Mr. Skeptic, can't deny what the ring did for my wife."

"The doctors did that for Sabrina, Gard, not a piece of jewelry," Nevan countered.

"What about the miracles Reen was able to achieve?" Drake said. "Everyone in the family has witnessed phenomena that were due to the power of the heartwish rings, Nevan."

"Everybody *thinks* the rings were responsible for so called miracles," Nevan refuted, "because you've all convinced yourselves it's true. The power of wishful thinking. That's how the mind works." He tapped his temple. "And why snake oil salesmen were so successful. And why people today fall for countless email scams, promising wealth if you provide your bank account and social security number." He gave a disgusted laugh.

Taking Nevan's hand, Kady gave it a tender squeeze. "Somewhere deep inside I think you know the magic is real, but you're afraid to accept it. That's okay, Nev, there's nothing wrong with being a skeptic or wanting proof. It just means it might take a little more time for you to come around and realize—"

"Realize what, Kady?" Nevan interrupted. "That the Malone family can cure the world of hate, financial hardship, grief, sickness, hunger, and death with a piece of jewelry? That we can just wish every problem away?" He looked from one person to another. "Sorry, I don't buy that."

"I remember Reen being upset that she couldn't heal all children sick with cancer," Drake said.

"Delaney was frustrated she couldn't eradicate all the illness in the world," Astrid recalled. She turned to Nevan with a warm smile. "I understand your annoyance, son. We'd all like to heal the world of all the awful, ugly things you mentioned. I wish we knew exactly how the heartwish rings work...or why. But we don't." Her shoulders lifted in a shrug.

"We just have to make the best of our turn to use the power of the rings wisely," Gard added.

"And do our best to make even a tiny positive change in the world," Kady said.

"All I know for sure," Astrid told him, "is that there's a very good reason the ring has come to you now."

Red rubbed his cousin's back. "Nobody's got more reason to be a little cranky and out of sorts after all you've been through, Nevan. We all know you've worked your ass off to restore this place. Hell, you practically rebuilt it from the ground up. You know what you're like?"

"Nope." A smile cracking his gloomy façade, Nevan shook his head back and forth. "But I'm sure you going to tell me."

"You're like the kid you were that one Christmas who was so damn disappointed when my parents gave you T-shirts, shorts and socks instead of the doll you really wanted."

Nevan let out a pop of surprised laughter. "For chrissakes, Red, how many times do I have to tell you that action figures aren't dolls?"

Huffing air over his fingernails, Red polished them across his shirt before glancing up at Nevan with a sly smile. "If you say so, cousin."

The mood in the room lightened as everyone laughed.

"Remember who got the G.I Joe you wanted that year?" Red asked.

After thinking for a moment, Nevan slapped the table and laughed. "Oh my God, it was you!"

"Yup." Red nodded. "I was the unfortunate one. It was one of my father's attempts to masculinize me. My parents also gave me a toy gun, knife, and construction set, complete with all the little tools. While I briefly considered dressing little G.I Joey in sarongs, and making him wigs from the neighbor's dog fur that I clipped, I wisely reevaluated that idea."

"Uncle Walter would have gone ballistic!" Nevan laughed, recalling Red's starchy, straitlaced father. "But you finally got the Barbie you wanted and I got your G.I. Joe. You promised Saffron, who detested math, that you'd do all her math homework for the next school semester in exchange for her Barbie."

The rest of the group sat there enjoying the craft beers Nevan had brought to the table, while listening to the cousins reminisce about that Christmas years ago. They were sampling a chocolate stout, a creamy bourbon-barrel-aged stout, a vanilla-espresso stout, and an oatmeal stout.

"I had to keep Barbie in Saffron's bedroom so my parents wouldn't catch on. In exchange for you teaching me enough about football and baseball so I could fool my father when he asked what games I was playing outside with the other boys, I gave you my soldier-boy doll."

"Action figure."

"Whatever."

As usual, Red had worked his special brand of magic, brightening Nevan's morose disposition. That was the kind of magic Nevan didn't doubt.

"Sorry I've been such a downer." Nevan ran his fingers through his thick hair. "I'm the luckiest guy in the world. Not because of this thing," he held up his hand, flashing the heartwish ring he'd finally slipped onto his finger, "but because I have all of you who put up with me. Who knows, maybe I'll even decide this ring isn't phony." He rotated his hand, watching the ring. "Thanks for being here with me this morning. Tonight and tomorrow night are going to be really special for me." He turned to Red. "And Red's got an equally big day tomorrow."

"Cheers!" Drake toasted them both and the rest joined in.

"We understand," Astrid assured. "You're just overtired and overworked, honey. And, as Red pointed out, crabby as hell." She winked and Nevan gave an acknowledging laugh.

"I'd rather give the ring to someone who could really use it," Nevan said. "Someone who believes it will do something for them." He looked at his sister. "Like you, Kady. That dilapidated old book shop is in sore need of updating. Hell, it's probably a fire hazard. If the ring's really magical, you could use it to get all the necessary work done."

"I appreciate that, Nevan." Kady gave her brother the sweetest smile. "But it's not my time to receive the ring." Her shoulders hiked in a shrug. "It may never be, and I'm fine with that. I've noticed the heartwish ring doesn't come to the recipients when they think they might need it most. It comes to them when everything seems fine."

"Each wish has been for something never even contemplated before receiving the ring," Astrid added. "I was just talking about that the other day with Delaney, Laila and Reen."

"Yeah, I get that," Nevan's sigh sounded more like a growl, "but shouldn't it at least go to someone who's sick, or in financial trouble, or someone really deserving of the ring?"

"Gard didn't want it when he received it," Astrid reminded him. "Neither did Reen. She wanted to give it to you instead. But we can't choose who gets the ring. The ring chooses the recipient. With time and patience, son, you'll know exactly what you're meant to wish for. I'm sure it will be something truly meaningful. Just look at the incredible miracles the ring made possible for Reen."

"But I'm nothing like my kind, goodhearted, do-gooder sister." Nevan gazed into the mirror across from him. Framed in lovingly carved wood leftover from the bar's reconstruction, the floor to ceiling mirror was nothing short of majestic.

Staring at everyone's reflection for a moment, he took in his cousin Red's inky-black hair and brown eyes. He and Red looked more like brothers than cousins. Nevan never had trouble getting women. He knew they found him attractive, and he used that knowledge to get exactly what he wanted. When they got too attached, talking about a future together, he ghosted them and moved on. That's the sort of selfish, uncaring jerk he was.

"Let's be honest here," Nevan said. "All I care about is me and my damn pub, while Reen would give someone the shirt off her back if they needed it."

"Bullsh—" Remembering Astrid was in the room, Gard stopped. "Bullshins," he said, inviting laughter from them all, even Astrid. "You'd do the same thing, Nevan. Stop selling yourself short. The ring thinks you're a deserving recipient. So do I."

"We all do," Drake said. "Reen would wholeheartedly disagree with your harsh self-assessment."

"Because Reen's convinced everyone is good and kind on the inside," Nevan said.

"She's right," Kady said with a reassuring smile. "You, dear brother, are one of the best."

"There, straight from your little psychic sister's mouth," Red said. "Now stop bellyaching and wallowing in your...whatever the hell it is you're wallowing in," he waved his hand in a clueless fashion, "and get off your sorry, self-deprecating ass so we can finish getting your pub and my flower shop ready for our grand opening celebrations!"

Opening his mouth to retort, Nevan was unable to come up with a single damn thing to say in response to Red's fitting diatribe. Instead, watching as Red elevated his chin, comically looking down his nose at Nevan, Nevan couldn't help dissolving into laughter. Determined to shelve his woeful, demoralizing attitude, he grabbed his very wise cousin into a buddy-hug, patting him on the back and whispering *Thanks, Red*, in his ear.

"Okay, everyone," a livelier, smiling Nevan addressed the group, rubbing his hands together briskly, "how about those reviews on the four new stouts?"

Chapter Two

Saturday

~<>~

AT THE SOUND of jangling, rapid footsteps, and labored breathing, Lonan crossed his arms over his chest, sending up a silent prayer to Jupiter. "You're late, Aladee. Again."

"I know. I'm sorry, Lonan. I had trouble finding my quiver of arrows, then it took me a while to locate—"

"The chariot has left without you."

"What? No!" Aladee blanched as she gazed around the near empty chariot boarding area. "It's my first trip to Earth with Cupid. I can't miss it."

"You already have." Lonan shrugged. Giving the disheveled blonde nymph a onceover, he tsked. "Look at your uniform. You're a disgrace to Cupid Academy." Why in the name of Pluto she always looked so tousled was beyond him. The young woman was a confection of bouncy golden curls, wide blue eyes, and a full lush body.

While most of the female students were forever primping and fussing over themselves, none were blessed with Aladee's allure. She was ignorant of her considerable charms, even to the point of disregard.

Glancing down at her knee-length white garment, Aladee smoothed her hands over the wrinkled pleats and adjusted the knotted gold cord at her waist. "I don't know why I'm so graceless."

A cluster of curls, almost the same shade as Lonan's hair, sprang loose from its confines at one side of her head, tumbling to her shoulder. "Oh dear..." Stuffing the locks back into place, she reaffixed the gilt-edged combs. "I was running late and didn't take enough time for my hair."

Lonan struggled not to laugh. It wouldn't do at all for his student to think he was amused.

"I lost track of time because I was reading the chapter on correct placement of arrows," Aladee explained. "I couldn't risk having one of my arrows strike the thymus gland when I was targeting the heart. Imagine the consequences if the poor person developed an unnatural affinity for domestic animals instead of their intended. It's wonderful to love cats and dogs because they certainly need care and attention from humans, but not in *that* way."

"Aladee—"

"I know I must avoid striking a male in his prostate when aiming for his phallus. The textbook devoted two pages to the possible disagreeable outcomes. Or what if I struck a female's pancreas instead of an ovary? Dear Jupiter, instead of getting pregnant, a woman could conceivably—"

"Aladee!"

Stopping short, she gazed up at Lonan with that naïve, trusting expression he'd come to cherish.

"Yes?"

"You're babbling."

"Oh...I have a habit of doing that, don't I?"

"Indubitably." Arching an eyebrow, Lonan smiled.

Aladee pouted. It was a look few grown women could manage without looking foolish and contrived. On Aladee's angelic features it was endearing, warming the cockles of his heart.

"What will I do, Lonan? Today's interactive love match exercise is part of my final exam. I can't miss it."

He hardened his features, striking a no-nonsense posture for Aladee's benefit. "You should have thought of that earlier. The rest of your class managed to get here on time without any problem.

Hopefully you'll learn a valuable lesson from this, and won't be habitually late in the future."

Lonan turned away from Aladee because she looked so forlorn he nearly drew her into a hug to comfort her. He made the mistake of glancing back when he heard a sniffle, only to see her bottom lip tremble.

"I-I've been practicing so hard all year. I know I'd do a superb job creating love matches, Lonan. Please, isn't there some way I can get to Earth?"

Uttering a cantankerous growl, Lonan stared at her. He had to be firm, couldn't cave in simply because he favored the girl. He was her teacher. It was his appointed duty, his responsibility, to ensure she learned a lesson from her mistakes.

"I'm sorry, Aladee..." He watched her features twitch and contort with distress. Frowning, Lonan motioned toward her with his hand. "Stop it. Don't do that."

"What?" Aladee sniffed and blinked, sending a fat tear coursing down her cheek.

"That! I hate to see a woman cry." *Especially you, Aladee.*

"I'm sorry." Aladee's chin quivered and a new set of tears escaped from her watery blue eyes. "I can't help it. Oh, Lonan, I'm such a hopeless failure. Every course of instruction I've taken at the academy has proven to be a disaster. No," she corrected herself, "*I've* proven to be a disaster." She broke into little hiccupping sobs. "I hoped Perfect Love Matches 101 would be different. I just want to help people find love. I want to make their lives richer, happier. But all I do is wreak havoc."

Her shoulders shook as she cried. Dropping her Cupid Academy paraphernalia to the marble floor, she covered her face, weeping so hard Lonan thought his heart would break. "You may as well just fail me, Lonan. I deserve it."

"There, there, Aladee. Don't cry." He drew her into a loose hug as she sobbed against his chest. The poor thing really did try hard. While she may be cursed with absentmindedness, a lack of organizational skills, and an innate naiveté, she was always attentive in class, did all her homework, and scored excellent grades on every test.

In Lonan's long career as a Cupid Academy instructor, he'd known few students as earnest, hardworking and devoted. Blessed with a good heart, the nymph was bright, willing, and highly intelligent. Book smart. But when it came to applying what she'd learned to real life circumstances, she inevitably fell flat on her face, unintentionally yanking others down with her.

"Gather your gear, Aladee. I'll take you to Earth in my personal chariot," Lonan heard himself say before groaning in frustration at his lack of restraint.

Aladee drew back, holding Lonan at arm's length.

Wide-eyed, she gasped, staring up at him. "Really, Lonan? You'd do that for me?"

He nodded with a sigh. "I'm making a one-time exception to the rules." He wagged a chastising finger. "You mustn't let any of the other students know. I don't want them thinking I'm showing favoritism. If they wonder how you arrived to join them, tell them one of the minor gods gave you a lift."

"I understand." Aladee's head bobbed with enthusiasm. "I promise to be careful and do my utmost to make you proud. You'll see, Lonan. I won't let you down."

Lonan winced. He didn't want to think of what sort of mayhem she might cause on this trip. Once she found Cupid, he'd no doubt be able to guide her, to keep her from inflicting serious disasters on unsuspecting mortals. "I won't be able to stay to help you, Aladee. I need to return immediately. You'll have to find Cupid's headquarters on your own. Can you manage that?"

"Definitely. I may be absentminded but I know how to read a map."

Giving her a patient smile, Lonan glanced at the bags and books she'd brought. "Yes, but did you remember to bring the map?"

Aladee retrieved her gear from the floor. "Yes." She gave one suede satchel a firm pat. "Along with the forgetfulness serum, the invisibility powder, the—"

Lonan groaned. "It's the other way around. Forgetfulness powder and invisibility serum. The forgetfulness powder simply needs to be inhaled to work, remember?"

Aladee nodded. "That's what I meant. Don't worry, Lonan, I brought the full list of precautions you gave us in class, all the things we should avoid. I brought my textbook too." She beamed a bright smile.

"I'm not sure that's a good idea." Lonan frowned. "On your last trip to Earth you left your class notes behind. Remember what happened when that unprincipled politician found your notebook?"

"Ooh...yes." Aladee bit her bottom lip and her cheeks flushed pink. "Fortunately we found it before he caused too much harm. Right?" She looked up at him hopefully.

"But if we hadn't, he could have gained political control over the world because the public suddenly found him to be irresistible." Recalling some of Aladee's other past escapades, Lonan ground out a monumental sigh, wondering if he was mad for releasing the well-meaning nymph on the unsuspecting world.

"I was foolish and much younger then," Aladee assured him.

"It was only two years ago."

"I've learned *so* much since then," she guaranteed, offering a persuasive expression of assurance. "Because you've been such a wise and *wonderful* teacher," she added with a smile.

"Indeed..." Lonan watched her juggling her belongings. "Perhaps it would be better if you used the schoolbag you were issued to keep everything together in one place. It's big enough to hold all of that."

Aladee's gaze dropped to her toes. "Um...I couldn't find it. That's another reason I was late this morning." Lonan moaned and she raised her eyes to his again.

"You can't flit around Earth wearing your academy uniform. You need to change into the traveling outfit you were issued."

"I didn't have time to change but I brought the garment with me." Glancing down at her tunic, Aladee frowned. "I know the academy's states wearing the travel outfit is important because it renders us invisible, but why is it necessary since the invisibility serum already makes us invisible to humans on the Earth plane? I'm much more comfortable wearing my light, airy uniform."

"The change of clothes is a necessary precaution," Lonan stated simply.

A frown line creased the area between Aladee's expressive eyebrows. "Why, exactly?"

Lonan's gaze flew to Aladee's ample curves, clearly evident beneath the airy silk fabric. He cleared his throat. "In case you forget to ingest the serum."

"But I wouldn't—" Aladee started again, only to be cut off by Lonan.

"The dual protection of the traveling garment as well as the serum doubly guarantees your power of invisibility won't fail for any reason." He didn't want to think of the chaos Aladee would cause if she were visibly prancing about Earth practically in the buff.

"Maintaining invisibility on Earth is crucial. It allows you to carry out your matchmaking tasks without unneeded distractions. It's not your school uniform that's the problem, Aladee, it's...what's underneath."

"There's something wrong with my body?" she asked in all innocence, glancing down at her bountiful physical attributes. "I thought my shape was pleasing. Are you saying humans wouldn't find me appealing?"

"On the contrary..." Realizing the rest of that sentence was better left unsaid, Lonan averted his eyes from her curves and took in a fortifying breath. "It's all in chapter eleven. Scanty silken garb isn't the norm for Earth's inhabitants."

"How peculiar," Aladee mused. "Why is it wrong to wear garments that enhance one's form?"

Lonan slanted her a dubious look. "Are you *sure* you read chapter eleven?" He felt a bit prickly discussing the subject with her.

"Yes, well...I think so. I'll reread it in the chariot, just in case. It sounds like a fascinating topic."

"People of Earth aren't as advanced as we are here on Olympus. As a rule, average human females don't dress in short toga-like garments that nearly expose their naked forms, unless they're...uh...unless they're engaged in a profession wherein they seek financial compensation for providing sexual favors."

"Payment?" Aladee looked genuinely confused. "When Earth women find their love matches, they expect an exchange of money before their unions can be consummated? I understood that a woman shares herself freely with the man she loves." Aladee's eyebrows pinched. "Why would women make a profession of sex, Lonan?"

"Well you see, Aladee..." Letting his words trail off, Lonan looked at her for a long moment, unsure of how to answer the too-trusting nymph's question in a short span of time. She clearly hadn't read chapter eleven, or didn't comprehend what she'd read. "On second thought, maybe you're not ready for this trip after all, Aladee."

Her eyes brimmed with tears again and Lonan cursed beneath his breath. "Very well, you may go, but be sure to study chapter eleven during the flight, and study the following chapter on Earth vernacular, including current slang, so you understand what's being said. And do *not* leave any of your class materials behind this time."

"Yes, Lonan."

"Be careful where you aim those arrows and at whom."

"Yes, Lonan."

"If you somehow do become visible, make sure not to let your wings show. And if—"

"I'll try not to, but if you recall, I don't always have control over my wings."

"Ah yes," he nodded, "I remember. Just do your best. Make sure you find Cupid immediately after we land. I don't want you doing *anything* until you find him, understand?"

Aladee offered a half-hearted nod. "You mean unless I come across poor lonely, lovelorn mortals desperately in need of my matchmaking skills on my way to finding Cupid, right?"

Hands braced on hips, Lonan glared at her. "Absolutely not."

"But if I can formulate a love match for them, then surely—" She stopped when she saw Lonan's eyes narrow. "Okay, I won't." Lonan arched an eyebrow at her. "I promise," she added quickly.

"Remember, Cupid will be incognito so you may not recognize him." Wiping the sweat from his brow, he gave a tired chuckle. "I'm getting too old to deal with the stress of fixing another Aladee-initiated calamity."

Standing on her tiptoes, Aladee kissed his jaw. "You'll never be old to me, Lonan. Ever. When the time comes for me to find a love match, I hope I find a man half as good, kind and handsome as you."

The look of admiration in Aladee's eyes warmed his soul, just as her words puffed his male pride. Shoulders back and chin elevated, Lonan escorted Aladee to his chariot.

~<>~

The chariot ride to Earth was magical. Aladee never tired of soaring through the clouds, anticipating the exhilarating adventure awaiting her once she reached her destination.

Interacting with humans was enjoyable because many of them seemed as ungainly and capricious as she was, which was a nice change from the diligence and seeming faultlessness of her fellow students. While she didn't yet understand many of Earth's strange customs, views and policies, she felt at home there.

While studying chapter eleven of her Perfect Love Matches 101 textbook, Aladee realized she must have missed reading it before. It was full of critical information, including Earth's backward stance on nudity and sexuality. Earthlings had turned the natural beauty of nakedness into a source of fodder for juvenile snickering and titillation. The section on prostitution was eye-opening, and the notion of rape made her shudder.

Lonan was right, people of Earth weren't as advanced when it came to the topic of sex as residents of Olympus.

Aladee used the long suede shoulder strap of the pouch containing her traveling garment, and vials holding the forgetfulness and invisibility concoctions, as a bookmark. She glanced up frequently from her reading to watch the changing skyscape. As Lonan's team of magnificent obsidian-black stallions galloped through the air, their jeweled harnesses glinting in the sunlight, Olympus became dwarfed in the distance, fueling Aladee's excitement. Soon, she'd be able to glimpse Earth.

"Look, Aladee, the Earth is coming into view," Lonan called with a quick glance over his shoulder. The chariot bumped and Aladee bounced. "Secure yourself well. We may encounter some turbulence as we descend."

"I will." Mashing her back against the curved sidewall, Aladee threaded her arms through two of the leather loops and held tight. At precarious times like this, she wished the chariots had backs and roofs.

On this trip Aladee was determined to restore Lonan's confidence in her by being a conscientious, model student, following his and Cupid's instructions to the letter.

Every arrow she shot would be perfectly aimed, striking its target at the exact point of intent. She'd wear her invisibility garment so as not to stand out among Earth's modest inhabitants, and she'd remember to use her forgetfulness powder and invisibility serum...or was it the other way around...as needed. She'd keep her textbook and notebook with her at all times so there'd be zero chance of leaving them behind.

She'd refrain from practicing her matchmaking skills before connecting with Cupid and the other students at his Earthly headquarters.

With those righteous, honorable oaths firmly in mind, Aladee yelped when she felt the chariot dip. Both she and her possessions bounced about. Freeing one arm from a leather loop, she scrambled to secure her scattered belongings.

To her abject horror, with the chariot's next sizeable dip Aladee watched her notebook, textbook, and suede pouch spring up and out of the chariot's confines, plummeting down through the air behind them.

All this before she'd even had a chance to finish chapter twelve detailing Earth vernacular!

"Are you all right, Aladee?"

Gasping as she endeavored to swallow a lump in her throat that refused to dislodge, Aladee felt the heat of a crimson blush blast her cheeks. By gods, she hadn't even reached Earth yet and already she was wreaking havoc. Jupiter only knew where her belongings would end up, who would find them, or what they might do with them!

If Lonan discovered what happened, he'd be beyond disillusioned with her for failing to keep her materials safe. But it had all happened so quickly. One minute she was making silent pledges to improve and the next—

"Aladee?" Lonan called again with a quick glance in her direction as he tightened his grip on the reins, deftly directing his team of horses through the rough air pockets.

Clutching the rest of her belongings to her chest, she swallowed a tortured sob. Her heart beating a rapid tattoo, she answered, "Yes, Lonan, I'm fine."

She wasn't sure how long after that the chariot touched ground. Lonan had initiated the veiling device before the chariot descended through the clouds, ensuring their invisibility.

"We're in North America," Lonan explained, "in the small seaside town of Glassfloat Bay in the state of Oregon. You'll clearly see this waterfront park marked on your map. Cupid's headquarters is within walking distance," he gestured across the large park with an outstretched finger.

"Return to this precise spot when it's time for the academy's chariot to bring you and the other students home in three days. Today is Saturday, that means you must be back here on Tuesday morning. Understand?"

"Three days. Tuesday. Yes, Lonan." Aladee felt so ashamed, so bungling, she could barely make eye contact with him. She could feel his gaze on her and for a moment, the merest whisper of time, she contemplated telling him about her lost belongings. But now wasn't the time. First she'd redeem herself by being a star student on this trip. Then, when Lonan was pleased and satisfied with her progress, she'd alert him about the unintentional slight midair mishap.

Once the academy dispatched a team of investigators to search for and retrieve the items, all would be well again. The thought brought a faint smile to her lips.

The smile faded when she thought about what might happen to her here on Earth, all alone and without her protective gear to keep her safe from harm until she found Cupid. Chapter eleven had outlined some frightening things that could occur to innocent, unsuspecting women at the hands of unscrupulous humans. She'd made notes about how to best protect herself should the need arise...but the notes were gone.

"You've been uncharacteristically quiet." Lonan had a concerned look in his eyes. "And you look a bit green. Did the chariot ride not sit well? I regret that it became rather bumpy toward the end and you were jostled."

"I'm fine. Your chariot driving was excellent." Gently resting her hand on his forearm, Aladee broke into a full smile. "My mind was just focused on locating Cupid and my classmates."

The genuine smile Lonan gave her in return warmed her to her soul. "I haven't told you this before because I don't want you thinking I'm praising you to get a better grade," she said honestly. "But you're a fine, dedicated teacher, Lonan. A truly good man. I'm so fortunate to have you in my life. Your support and belief in me means more than you can imagine. Please remember that, Lonan...no matter what happens."

"Thank you." Lonan tousled her curls and grinned. "That's nice to hear but you make it sound as though we'll never see each other again." He smiled. "I'm sure you don't have anything to worry about, Aladee. You're a good student and I'm sure I'll get a stellar report from Cupid detailing your excellent matchmaking tasks."

"From your lips to Jupiter's ears," Aladee muttered.

Chapter Three

~<>~

"AT LEAST ANOTHER hour? What the hell, Red?" Nevan bellowed into the weighty receiver of the ornate French provincial-style phone. "I'm in over my head here. I don't know what the hell I'm doing. It's eight o'damn clock in the morning. I only got an hour of sleep after the pub's reopening celebration last night. The only reason I'm even able to stand here talking to you is by the grace of mega-strong coffee—gallons of it. Which reminds me, you're going to need a new box of coffee pods."

When Nevan turned to pick his mug up from the machine, he found a fluffy white ball of fur sitting next to it, staring at him. Startled, for the umpteenth time since he got to the shop, he told Red, "I swear, that ghostlike cat of yours is going to be the death of me the way he keeps sneaking up on me. Are you sure I can't stick him in your apartment until you get back." The cat gave a sinister look while Nevan sipped from his coffee.

"It's not like he's going to hurt you, Nevan. Cupid enjoys being around the flowers. It makes him happy. He won't bother you, I promise. Just let him do his thing, and he'll let you do yours."

"If the flowers make him so happy, why does he keep giving me a menacing look...like he wants to swipe my face off with his claws."

"Oh, Nevan, I've always enjoyed your delightful sense of humor."

"No, you definitely haven't," Nevan countered. "You're just sucking up to me now so I'll stay and watch your shop."

"Humorous as well as perceptive. What a guy! Look, I'm sorry, Nevan. Truly. I know how tired you must be. The last thing I wanted to do was to drag you out of bed this morning but I had no choice.

It's my grand opening today and tomorrow. I need someone there I can trust when shoppers arrive."

"Isn't that what your employees are for?" Nevan didn't mean to bark at his cousin but he couldn't help being irritable. He knew this wasn't Red's fault, and that Red must be stressed, but Nevan's better side had a hard time emerging when he was hungover and exhausted.

"Poor Edwina's sick as a dog with a vicious head cold. That reminds me, speaking of dogs, Buster isn't there with you, is he? I'm afraid he'd stress out Cupid too much with his burly ways."

"Buster stress Cupid out? Ha! That's a laugh. No, he's not here with me, because I don't want to subject Buster to this flowery atmosphere or your demonic cat. What about Alfred and Laverne? Can't they be here?"

"Alfred has finals this morning, and Laverne, who's over sixty, is in the midst of a monstrous episode of sciatica. I feel guilty because her back is probably worse due to the heavy lifting she insisted on doing when we were setting everything up for this weekend."

"I know you didn't plan this, Red, but—"

"Exactly. It's not like I planned for my van to give up the ghost after I left Kenesack Farm out here in the boondocks. Do you honestly think I want to be stuck miles away when this is my shop's grand-opening weekend?"

"No but—"

"I made sure to get to the farm at four-thirty a.m. so I'd be back to Glassfloat Bay in plenty of time to get everything done before the shop opened. Henry Kenesack generally rises at three-thirty each morning and, sure enough, he had everything ready and waiting for me. Gorgeous stuff, Nevan. Wait'll you see it."

"So you got a craving for fresh-grown peas and carrots before the crack of dawn?" Nevan asked, aware his voice still had a decidedly grouchy edge to it.

"You're just being silly now. One of my employees would normally make the pickup. Henry cultivates unusual wildflowers on his property along with a multitude of beautiful organic produce. It's the only farm in the vicinity where I can get the right filler flowers for my arrangements."

"Filler flowers? I have no idea what you're talking about."

"You know, like astilbe, wax flowers, Queen Anne's lace, heather, blue thistle, and eupatorium."

"No, I don't know." Nevan rolled his eyes and downed the rest of his coffee. It was on the cool side and bitter, but double-strength caffeine, which is all he cared about.

"They fill, or puff out, the arrangement, enhancing the main flowers like—"

"Okay, okay, I get it." He had zero interest in flower facts. "Look, Red, I'm sorry but I can't—"

Red's tuneful, voluminous sigh interrupted Nevan's protest. "If you have to leave and lock up," he said haltingly, "go ahead. I'll understand. Even if..." He paused and Nevan knew damn well it was for dramatic effect. "Even if it means I'll lose an entire day's revenue. On a Saturday. The biggest, most important income day of my week. And since it's the first day of my grand opening, I'd lose an astronomical amount of business, as well as potential new customers who come to check out Cupid's Headquarters. But you just go on ahead and leave. I'll be fine."

"Come on, Red, I just can't—"

"All my loyal, paying customers," Red went on, "who are depending on me for the delivery of their promised floral arrangements today will be devastated, not to mention infuriated at what they'll perceive to be my gross incompetence and irresponsibility."

Nevan silently rolled his eyes skyward as Red droned on.

"Like the Wentworths," Red said. "It's their fiftieth anniversary. If that pricey floral delivery doesn't make it to Francine Wentworth today up on Beauregard Hill, it means moolah down the drain, and Martin Wentworth will do his big-bucks floral shopping elsewhere from now on. But I understand, Nevan, you're tired and suffering from a nasty hangover because you had a hugely profitable grand reopening celebration last night, so…"

Aw hell.

Nevan felt the weight of Red's guilt hammer descending on his head with a hefty *pound, pound, pound.* "You're putting a half-asleep, hungover guy who knows zip, nada, zilch about flowers in charge of your shop on its grand opening morning, Red. Seriously, do you really think this will end well?"

"I have full faith in you, Nevan. You know your mom's neighbor, Mrs. Jorgenson? It's her first birthday since she lost her beloved Pete. The poor dear's been grieving for nearly a year. Those flowers would really cheer her up. Remember how sweet and attentive she was after your grandma Bekka died, and how she kept you supplied in brownies, cookies and mystery casseroles?"

"Yeah," Nevan admitted, recalling how the frail old woman had fussed over the Malone clan, intent on easing their grief. "She's a sweet old lady."

"An angel. The very least we can do is send her a lovely arrangement as a birthday surprise."

"You still don't get it. Sticking a flower in a pot looks *lovely* to me," Nevan grumbled.

"I bookmarked a page in my catalog," Red offered. "Just copy what you see there. It'll be a snap. I know you can do it."

A memory nagged at Nevan. "Wait a minute…I thought Mrs. Jorgenson's husband died a decade ago."

"He did. Pete was her cockatoo."

Nevan barked a laugh. "She's been in mourning for a year over a damn bird?"

"Honestly, Nevan..." Red sighed. "Sometimes you can be so insensitive. Pete was more than just a bird. He was her companion and friend. Just like Buster is for you and Cupid is for me."

"Oh, sure, I understand," Nevan lied, not buying into the concept that birds or cats held the same importance as dogs. But he knew better than to take a ridiculous discussion about some dead bird any further with his cousin. It would just lead to another argument where he'd be accused of being mean, cold and heartless while Red came off as the kind, caring, sensitive one. Which was true but Nevan didn't want to waste time in another endless sensitivity discussion.

"Hey, cut that out you mangy furball!" Unsuccessfully shooing away the cat, he told Red, "That monster just swatted a bunch of yellow flowers off the counter onto the floor."

"That rascal. Let me talk to him," Red said. "Put me on speaker phone so Cupid can hear me."

"The cat? You want to talk to your cat over the phone?" With Red's affirmative response, Nevan switched to speaker phone, wondering how the hell he'd gotten rooked into this.

After ample baby talk, mixed with positive affirmations, Red finished with a round of kissy sounds. About to tell Red his ridiculous cat-talk did no good, Nevan watched Cupid jump down from the counter and go to his designated area. It looked like a cat version of a Barbie palace, with a sparkly pink fence and little castle building with an entrance and bed for Cupid. The damn cat went right inside, reclining on his satin sheets.

"Okay, I don't know how you managed that, but it worked." Nevan picked the yellow flowers up from the floor. "Look, it's not that I mind watching your shop for a while. I'm well-staffed now and the pub's running smoothly, but aside from the fact that I'm clueless about flowers, the stench in here is pretty hard to take. It's making me nauseous."

"Excuse me?" Nevan could hear Red bristle. "There is *no* stench. The flowers at Cupid's Headquarters are always fresh and in perfect condition."

"Fresh or not, they stink to high heaven. I feel like I'm a stiff in a goddamned funeral parlor, for chrissakes. I don't know how you can take that sickly sweet smell all day."

"Unlike the manly smell of the beer your customers slosh all over the tabletops and bar, you mean?" Red sniffed. "There's nothing like the inviting fragrance of eau de stale beer."

"I keep the pub clean. The smell of stale beer isn't an issue," Nevan argued. "Even if I *wanted* to be here I don't have the faintest idea how to put all this flower crap together to look like the fancy stuff in these pictures."

Nevan murmured a curse as he looked at the floral arrangement catalog and all the frilly stuff around him like ribbons, glittery things on wood sticks, green plastic chopstick things with fat red hearts at the top, and countless other doodads. There were endless types of flowers inside and outside of refrigerated glass-front cases, containers of all shapes, materials and sizes, spongy green stuff, and multicolored grassy-straw material.

"This is your area of expertise, Red, not mine. How about your sister, Saffron? Or Reen, she's real artsy."

"I already checked. Saffron's working extra hours at the real estate office because Monica and Hud are on their honeymoon. Reen's on an overnight with Drake and the kids in Astoria. Your mom went with Kady to her attorney appointment in Rainspring Grove. Laila's got a BOGO offer on scones at the bakery. Delaney's editor is breathing down her neck. She has to complete her manuscript today. Sabrina's helping Annalise at the café because two servers are out with the flu."

Nevan heard the deep breath Red expelled.

"Trust me, Nevan, if there was anyone else available, *anyone*, I would have called them instead."

"Well," Nevan couldn't help laughing, "that's pretty clear since it sounds like you tried everyone in town before settling on me."

"It's just you and Barry, the delivery driver. Just try to relax and let your inner woman come out. You'll be fine."

Nevan tsked. "For the umpteenth time, I don't have an inner woman."

"Of course you do. All men do."

In a near growl, Nevan said, "You're not helping your argument any. Can't you tell those mechanics it's an emergency and you need your van fixed right away?"

"Two men are working on it right now. I'm sure they're doing their brawny best. Alfred should be there in an hour...maybe two. You should have plenty of time before it gets busy at the pub with the lunch crowd."

Nevan cursed under his breath. His cousin was always there whenever Nevan needed him. He'd worked tirelessly helping Nevan get his pub ready while Red was busy doing the same for his own shop.

When they were kids, growing up in Chicago, Red dreamed of having a creative career. Being a florist was high on his list. He stubbornly clung to that dream, even though he knew early on that an alternate fate was sealed.

The thought of spending his life working in his father's bank diminished Red's spirit, but the foreboding Walter Devington demanded it. It was a tedious job, void of levity or pleasantries. Red looked stiff, starchy and uncomfortable in the custom tailored but dull three-piece vested suit his father insisted he wear.

"I'm exhausted," Red had confided to Nevan, "defeated, trying to please my father and never succeeding. It's like Einstein's quote about insanity, 'doing the same thing over and over and expecting different results.' With each battle I lose to my father, something inside me withers and dies."

When Red left his position at the bank, and came out to his parents, they disowned him, cutting off all contact. Red was crushed. Devastated. But Nevan reminded Red he now had a brand new lease on life. The deadened part of Red came alive again, blooming like one of his flowers. When Red shared his plans to follow his dreams and open his own flower shop, Nevan was sincerely happy for his cousin. He didn't know a soul more deserving than Red.

How the holy hell could Nevan rain on his cousin's parade after all Red had been through to get here—and after all he'd done to help Nevan?

He couldn't. The very least Nevan could do was man Red's froufrou flower shop for a couple hours without pissing and moaning about it. It wasn't as if Nevan needed to be at the pub in person until five or six, so that really wasn't an issue.

"All right, Red, I'll—" When the bell for the front door jingled, Nevan glanced up. "Holy shit."

"What's wrong?" After a moment of silence, an alarmed Red asked again, "Nevan, what's wrong?"

"You got a customer." Nevan did his best to keep his eyeballs from bugging while he scraped his jaw up from the floor. "Gorgeous...and practically naked."

"Probably not Mr. Wentworth," Red offered.

"Definitely not."

"The store's not supposed to be open until ten o'clock."

"I must have forgotten to lock the door after I came in."

"No problem. Just be cordial and ask if there's anything you can help with. And for God's sake, don't forget to smile, Mr. Grouchypants."

"Yeah, yeah...hey, Red," Nevan whispered into the phone, "did you hire a stripper for your grand opening?"

"A what?" Laughter came over the phone. "You mean to jump out of a flower cake and say *ta-da*? No, but—"

"Gotta go, Red. Talk to you later. And take your time." Nevan hung up the phone and locked eyes with the dazzling vision walking toward him.

Chapter Four

~<>~

"AT LAST! Cupid's Headquarters! I'm sorry I'm so late." Practically breathless, Aladee scurried to the front of the large flower-filled room to meet with the head of the academy. The room certainly had Cupid's artistic touch, with romantic blush colors of pink, peach and ivory enhanced by gold accents and scrollwork. She felt perfectly comfortable in this beautiful, fragrant space, although she couldn't say the same for Cupid, who looked as if he'd ingested a pickled bullfrog.

"Are you all right, Cupid? You look ill." When he didn't answer, Aladee snapped her fingers, bringing his gaze up from her chest to her eyes.

"Sonuvabitch," Cupid whispered, gawking at her.

"Son of who?" She slanted him a curious look, her ego deflating upon the realization he'd evidently mistaken her for one of the male students.

"No, Cupid, it's me, Aladee, daughter of Arrius and Venuvia, granddaughter of Quintus who rode with Odin in the Aesir-Vanir war. I'm a female." She straightened her shoulders, thrusting out her chest so he'd recognize her womanly attributes. She watched his gaze slide to her chest again, lingering there as if the god of love had never seen breasts before.

"Yeah, I noticed," Cupid responded in a most uncharacteristic tongue-lolling fashion.

"Oh, you're displeased that I'm not wearing my traveling garment, is that it? I can explain. While I was in the chariot, one of my bags accidentally flew off before I could catch it. It was the one with my traveling clothes, which is why I'm still dressed in my academy uniform."

She motioned to her short toga and Cupid followed her gesture with his eyes, leaning over the counter to get a better look.

Quite taken with Cupid's Earthly disguise, she paused for a moment. The youthful mortal form he'd assumed had black hair, deep brown eyes, and a tall, lean, muscular build. His golden tan was enhanced by the open-necked pale blue denim shirt he wore. Cupid was a breathtakingly beautiful man, no matter what his chosen disguise, but Aladee liked this rugged look most of all. He looked manly, strong and...famished.

"You seem to be drooling, Cupid. Are you hungry?"

"Hungry?" His eyes roved over her from top to bottom and back up again. "I'm suddenly starving."

"With all these lovely flowers to munch on? I'm surprised. Have you tasted them yet?" Cupid shook his head to say no. She snagged a crimson rose from one of the cool cases and munched on a petal. "Mmm, tasty. The quality is almost equal to the ones on Olympus. Here, try it." Aladee held the rose out to him.

"You mean Olympia? In Washington?"

"No, I meant Olympus."

He gave her a curious look. "I'll take a pass." Cupid pushed her outstretched hand away. "But you go right ahead and chow down on the flowers."

"Thank you. I'm hungry from the journey. My lunch was in the same bag as my traveling clothes. My invisibility powder...or liquid," she shrugged, "was in the pouch too. Along with..." Her teeth sank into her bottom lip and she hesitated. Trilling a deep sigh, she plunged ahead. "Along with my textbook and notes. I am *so* sorry, Cupid, truly I am. Please don't tell Lonan, he'll be terribly disappointed in me. You won't say anything, will you?"

Offering a peculiar smile, Cupid shook his head back and forth slowly. "Not a word. Not a single word."

"Thank you." She felt her posture relax at his assurance. "That makes me feel better, especially after the unusual time I've had since Lonan dropped me off at the park. Glassfloat Bay is such a lovely spot, so green, lush, and filled with interesting people. I can see why you chose it for your headquarters. So, naturally, I was quite surprised at some less than pleasant occurrences as I searched for you."

"Naturally," Cupid said.

"I was taken aback as a strange, grimy man proposed intimate, tawdry acts." Aladee rolled her eyes in disbelief as she recalled the unprovoked incident. "He forced me to accompany him against my consent."

"Wait...what?" Cupid straightened, gazing at her with concern. "Someone tried to hurt you? Where, outside the shop?"

Coming around the counter, he looked like a warrior ready to do battle for his lady fair. The fierce look in his eyes sent a bold ripple of pleasure through her veins, which made it an excellent time for her to remember that Cupid was a married man. Psyche was a lucky woman to have a man so brave and fearless, and yet as loving and intimately adept as Cupid for her husband.

"I'm fine. I met with no real harm." Aladee stilled him from action by taking hold of his arm, which felt strong, hard and sinewy. He was quite tall, and altogether far too appealing. "Fortunately, I remembered the lesson in chapter eleven on disengaging a male during aggressive behavior by causing intense, throbbing discomfort to his testicles with a firm, swift jab of the knee."

Cupid's mouth quirked into a wider smile. "You kneed some guy in the...eh, in his groin?"

"My apologies. I hadn't intended to cause harm to anyone on Earth but he gave me no choice. I was forced to incapacitate him. It wouldn't have been so bad if I'd been able to find your headquarters immediately after we landed, but..." She tugged a crinkled piece of paper from one of her pouches.

"It's not that I forgot to bring a map, I just brought the wrong one." She turned the paper toward him. "This one's for the gathering Saturn hosted last December on the planet Skrodoe. So, naturally, I had to stop and ask people for directions to your headquarters after I disembarked and the chariot took to the air again."

"Uh-huh. After Saturn's chariot flew away...back to the planet Skrodoe."

"No, back to Mount Olympus. And it was Lonan's chariot."

"Oh yeah...right."

Aladee squinted, studying the man closely. His tight blue jeans accented his muscular form. She couldn't help relishing a lingering gaze. Like most females, she'd always found Cupid attractive and desirable, but she'd never experienced this intensity of longing. The thought made her uneasy.

"You...you *are* Cupid, aren't you?" she whispered, leaning close.

"You're into role playing, huh?" The man smiled at her, a full, dazzling white-toothed smile. "If that's what you want, sure, I can be Cupid."

"Good." Breathing a sigh of relief, Aladee smiled. "I was worried because you've been eyeing me so strangely. Lonan warned me you might be..." She looked left and right before leaning forward and whispering, "*Incognito*. Now I understand why Lonan was concerned about my academy uniform. By the odd looks and comments I've received, it seems people believe I'm seeking payment for sex."

Cupid arched an eyebrow. "Are you?"

"Of course not." Aladee laughed. "You know that isn't the way of us nymphs."

"Soooo...you're not a hooker, you're a nymph."

Her eyebrows pinched and one eye narrowed. "Are you testing me?"

"Nope, just curious." Cupid appraised her. "How come I don't see any wings?"

Clearly she *was* being tested, but what a strange set of questions Cupid employed. "You know not all nymphs have wings."

"Uh-huh. And you're one of the wingless variety?"

"Not exactly. Mine only open at certain times," Aladee explained.

"And this isn't one of those times?" The too-handsome Cupid snickered.

Aladee grew increasingly uncomfortable. He seemed to be teasing her or, worse yet, flirting. That wouldn't do at all.

If Psyche suspected Aladee had flirted with her husband, Aladee would be expelled from Cupid Academy, and that would be just the beginning. She shivered at the thought of the fearsome vengeance Psyche might exact.

Again, Aladee narrowed her gaze. "Why do you ask all these questions, Cupid, when you already know the answers? Is this part of my final exam? I've worked terribly hard to pass this course. It's only fair to tell me."

"Look, miss, I don't know what exam you're talking about, and I don't care if you have wings or not. It's been a long time since I've seen a working girl who looked like you, or who had such a great line. Cupid, nymphs, chariots, Olympus. It's all very cute, and you're definitely hot, but, sorry, I don't pay for sex. It's been fun, but you should probably be on your way."

Aladee slanted him a curious glance. Cupid made no sense. He gazed at her as if she were a multi-course banquet, making her feel all hot and twittery. He was clearly making barefaced sexual banter...yet he spoke unkind things to her.

"While you may be physically beautiful, I would never entertain thoughts of coupling with you, Cupid. You and Psyche are joined for eternity. Woe be unto anyone who angers the major gods on Olympus. Yours is a cruel test to be sure, one I imagine other female students have endured as well. No, I will *not* be on my way." She felt her bottom lip tremble and fought back tears. "I traveled a great distance to learn everything about love from you."

"Love? From me?" Cupid clapped his chest, giving her a strange look. "Are you on drugs or something? Because I'm not into that."

"Why do you speak so strangely?" Aladee studied her mentor for a long moment before realization hit. "Ah, I think I understand. You're speaking in coded Earth vernacular while you're incognito. I would understand better if I'd had an opportunity to study chapter twelve before my textbook flew out of the chariot. It appears you're testing my ability to be clearheaded and exercise restraint even when frustrated and aroused. Because this certainly isn't the way you usually speak to me."

Leaning forward, she took a deep sniff. "Have you been partaking in the fruit of the vine, or perhaps something stronger?"

"Me?" Cupid laughed, clapping his hand against his broad chest again. "Hey, I'm not the one talking gibberish here. If I'm drunk it's only from the stench of all these flowers." He gestured around him. "What did you say your name was?"

"Don't you recognize me, Cupid? It's me, Aladee. Perhaps you're suffering a form of travel sickness from your chariot ride earlier. It's happened to others, causing a temporary state mimicking inebriation. Look at me well, Cupid. Remember me? I'm in Perfect Love Matches 101 at the academy. Lonan is my instructor."

"Okay, listen, Aladdin—"

"Aladee. Al-uh-dee."

"Right. The name's Nevan." He extended his hand. "Glad to meet you."

"Nevan? It rhymes with heaven. So that's your Earthly name for this trip?"

"It's the only name I've got, sweetheart."

"I don't understand. You told me you were Cupid."

"Nope, I didn't." He chuckled. "You assumed I was Cupid because of the sign." He gestured to the large three-dimensional pink cursive script lettering high on the wall behind them, in back of the counter. "It's a natural mistake."

She gazed at the gilt-edged words, reading them aloud. "*Cupid's Headquarters.*" Returning her gaze to him, she pointed at the sign. "It's right there in plain lettering."

Scanning her surroundings, Aladee felt certain this was the right place. There were pedestals topped with miniature statues of the gods and a lovely border around all the walls depicting the Roman deities, not to mention the generous representation of Cupid's form and likeness almost everywhere she looked.

"This *must* be the right place. The décor has Cupid's personal touch."

"That's because Red's really into mythology."

A distinct feeling of apprehension zigzagged up her spine. "Where are the other students?"

"Look, Aladdin or whatever your name is, I'm not into hookers, or call girls," the man called Nevan said, failing to address her inquiry. "Not even high priced ones. Don't have to. But, damn if you're not about the sweetest little thing to come my way since...well, since I can remember. And I don't even mind that you're nutty as a fruitcake."

He chuckled. *Chuckled!* This man was laughing at her!

"I'm on duty now. There's a bunch of flower arrangements I have to put together for, eh...Cupid, but I'll be free in a couple hours and I'll be glad to drop you off where you live, or at one of the shelters. Until then, you can either wait here in the back room," he gestured over his shoulder with his thumb, "or come back later."

Mustering all her bravado, Aladee stood her ground, refusing to break eye contact with this Nevan individual. "What have you done with him?"

"Who?"

"Cupid! Where is he?" She adopted a fighting stance. "If you've harmed him in any way, I'll—"

"Whoa! Take it easy, miss." Nevan stepped back, his hands raised in a gesture of surrender. "Red's fine, okay? He's waiting for his van to get repaired, that's all."

"His chariot is broken?" Aladee was thoroughly confused. Nothing made any sense since she disembarked from Lonan's chariot. "Who is this Red you speak of?"

"My cousin, Redmond Devington." Nevan shrugged his big meaty shoulders. "He's Cupid, the one who runs this place. I'm just filling in for him until he gets back. Well, technically, he's not exactly Cupid. You'll find the true Cupid right over there." He pointed. "Taking a cat nap."

Aladee walked toward the spot Nevan had indicated. Just as she reached the tiny pink fence, a precious ball of white fur emerged from a castle-like structure.

"Oh my goodness." Placing her hands on her knees, Aladee bent to speak to the cat. "When Lonan said you'd be incognito, I had no idea it would be to this extent."

"Red, the cat's owner, should be back soon. Since he's a mythology buff, he can answer all your Cupid-related questions."

"Such strange things you say." Aladee clasped the sides of her achy head, struggling to understand. "So for this trip Cupid has divided himself into two separate entities, using the name Redmond Devington, as well as posing as a cat while on the Earthly plane?"

"You're making my head spin."

"That's a counterfeit accusation. Your head is stable."

Nevan seemed exasperated. "Look, Red's been Red for as long as I've known him—and his cat, Cupid, has been his cat. Period."

"Are the other students with him?"

"Red mentioned Alfred had some exam this morning. Say, are you here to fill in for Edwina? Because I could use someone who knows what the hell they're doing here until Red gets back. Of course," he eyed her garb, "you'd have to wear one of the smocks."

"I'm prepared to work, yes, that's why I'm here. I have my bow and quiver of arrows with me. Just point me in the right direction and I'll get started." Aladee saw Nevan's jaw drop.

"You've got a bow and arrows?"

"Secured to my shoulder." She nodded.

Nevan craned his neck. "Don't tell me. They're invisible, right? Just like your wings." He had the audacity to smirk at her.

"You know the standard student issue is designed to be invisible to the eyes of mor—" Aladee gasped. "Oh my Jupiter, you're mortal!"

With spread fingers, Nevan examined his chest and abdomen. "Yup, last time I looked."

"That explains my arousal," Aladee muttered. Nevan's jaw seemed to drop again. "I was concerned when I thought you were Cupid. I'm not supposed to be sexually attracted to Cupid to the point of feeling feverish."

"So are, uh, are you saying you want to have sex with me?"

"Sexual intercourse?"

Nevan nodded, and this time it was Aladee's jaw that dropped.

"Most certainly not!" It was a necessary untruth. While this Nevan person made her have twirly feelings in her belly, she couldn't have him assuming she was a prostitute like those she'd read about in chapter eleven.

Planting hands on her hips, she advised him, "I am not a Cinderella sex professional."

"A what?" Scrunching his features, Nevan looked at her as if she were deranged. Shaking his head back and forth, he mumbled, "This whole thing is crazy."

"Indeed it is. I find myself quite befuddled. I speak of Cinderella Hooker. Do you know her?"

"I don't have a clue what you're talking about. Who's that, some stripper friend of yours?"

"Apparently she is a prostitute. One of the men I met in the waterfront park kept calling me Cinderella. He thought I was a sex professional. When he inquired if I am a Hooker, I explained to him that I am not related to the Hooker family."

Laughing, yet again, Nevan held his forehead, muttering, "This is just too much. You're making my head hurt."

"I'm sorry. It's not my intention to—"

The bell jangled as the door to the shop opened and a few people filed in.

Nevan gazed at the clock on the wall and Aladee's eyes followed. The time read eight forty-five.

"Damn, I forgot to lock the door," he said. Addressing the people who'd entered, he said, "The shop's not open until ten but feel free to have a look around and let me know if I can help you with anything."

Aladee watched as Nevan scooted behind the counter, grabbed a peppermint pink smock from a hook and tossed it to Aladee. The words *Cupid's Headquarters* were embroidered over a chest pocket embellished with little hearts. It was adorable.

"Put this on. *Now!*" he commanded, before returning his attention to the people who'd entered the shop. They told Nevan they were just browsing. Once they left, he locked the front door.

Aladee complied with his request to don the smock as soon as she shrugged out of the shoulder strap that held the bow and quiver of arrows against her back.

Nevan watched her with a baffled expression. "What are you going?"

"Removing my bow and arrows. I can't get into the smock until I remove them from my back, otherwise they'll stick out and I'll look like a hunchback."

Mumbling an oath, Nevan rolled his eyes toward the ceiling. Once Aladee slipped into the smock, she stood there looking around.

"Now what?" Nevan grumbled.

"I need a safe place to store my bow and arrows so they don't get into the wrong hands. Especially after I've already lost the other items I told you about."

She wondered why Nevan kept giving her odd looks. It was a reasonable request. Since he didn't offer to assist her, Aladee searched until she discovered the deep shelves beneath the counter.

"Can I store them down here on the bottom shelf? Do you think they'll be safe there?"

"Absolutely," Nevan said through choked laughter. "I guarantee it."

The weighty bow and arrow set clanked with a distinct thud, followed by a scraping sound as Aladee shoved them to the back of the shelf.

Nevan whipped his head down toward where Aladee knelt. "What was that?" He looked stunned.

"I told you." Gazing up at him, she did her best not to utter an impatient tsk. "My bow and arrows."

Nevan's clearly faulty loose jaw dropped once more. Such a pity. Sometimes the most appealing specimens of manhood were the ones most lacking in the intelligence department.

Chapter Five

~<>~

NEVAN FELT AS though he'd fallen down the rabbit hole, or something equally far-fetched. From the moment the luscious sexpot had walked into his cousin's flower shop, Nevan's life was turned upside down, inside out, and scrambled beyond recognition.

When the screwy dame knelt down, supposedly depositing her invisible archery set on the shelf, and Nevan heard that unmistakable clunk of metal, he worried that *he* might be the one who'd lost his marbles and not the little blonde doll with the body made for sin.

If he wasn't bonkers, then there had to be a logical, feasible explanation for the clunking noise. Maybe she'd just hit her head on the shelf above. Once she'd finished, Nevan got down on all fours. Peeking into the bottom shelf, he expected to find something there that might account for the thud and scraping he'd heard, like some of Red's flower arranging junk.

Nothing. The shelf was empty.

Still on his hands and knees, he glanced back up at her, not expective the view his position afforded. She wasn't wearing any underwear. His throat went dry. Tearing his eyes from the unanticipated view, he adjusted his gaze, focusing on her face instead. She eyed him curiously as he reached deep into the shelf. When his fingers connected with something that shifted beneath his touch, he yelped, yanking his hand out as if he'd been burned. He looked deep into the shelf's recess again. Nothing was there. Not a damned thing.

Shit. He could swear he'd felt leather and cylindrical rods like...like arrows. No. It wasn't possible. He must be going crazy. At some point, he'd had a complete nervous breakdown without being aware of it.

His sense of adventure abandoning him, Nevan decided not to explore the shelf any further. What he *thought* he felt was simply an illusion brought on because...because his mind was playing tricks on him since he was so turned on by the strange little blonde. That, combined with endless months of hard work and not enough sleep, had rattled his brain.

Or maybe it was due to the crushing hangover he was nursing after sampling all those craft beers from the new Portland microbrewery last night.

Further investigation of the shelf was a waste of time. If one of them was loony it was the one who thought she was a fairy, or pixie, or whatever the hell she'd told him.

He glanced at her again, briefly spotting the back of her smock lift and blouse out behind her shoulders, with Aladee quickly pushing down on the twin protrusions.

What. The. Actual. Fu—

"Oops, sorry." She gave an apologetic laugh. "My wings have a mind of their own sometimes."

Wings?

Doing a classic doubletake, Nevan slowly shook his head back and forth. No. He did *not* just hear her say that. And he didn't just see what looked like a pair of wings spreading beneath that smock. Just. Not. Possible. Swallowing hard, he knuckled his eyes, blinking the image away.

First invisible arrows and now... His eyebrows knitted as he studied her, wondering if sleep deprivation had caused him to hallucinate, simply dreaming her up.

While his thoughts joggled, he watched Cupid leap into Aladee's waiting arms, nuzzling against her as she cooed to the cat. The shameless creature shined up to her like he was some noble beast.

Funny, he looked more like a harmless stuffed animal in her arms than like Beelzebub when he was staring Nevan down.

Some people might think his whole family was nuts. One of his sisters believed her husband used to be a genie—the kind who floofed up out of a bottle in a puff of smoke. Then there was the guardian angel who saved Gard and little Harold while Gard battled the blaze in the building housing Nevan's pub and Red's flower shop.

On top of that was the heartwish ring itself, supposedly crafted from one stone, split in two by Odin, yeah, the mighty Norse god—*that* Odin, making a matching pair of magic rings, handed down in his family for generations.

Nevan's gaze dropped and he glimpsed a soft blue glow emanating from his ring. Instinctively he shook his hand, letting it drop at his side and wiping it on his jeans. He'd never get used to seeing that glow coming from a little piece of stone. He'd seen the light when others wore the rings too. Nevan knew there must be a scientific explanation, like a form of phosphorus in the rock.

While his family believed the rings had magical powers and had created miracles for those making wishes on the stones, Nevan had his doubts. There was a great deal to be said about the subject of wishful thinking and self-deception.

"It's odd that Cupid collects payment for selling flowers," Aladee noted, still holding the cat and stroking his fur...while the animal gave Nevan a dirty look. "Shouldn't flowers be free for everyone?"

Still dazed, Nevan scratched the back of his head, trying to focus on what she'd just asked.

"Maybe flowers don't grow as easily here as they do on Mount Olympus. We're fortunate to have every variety available there, free to everyone for the picking." She switched to baby talk. "Aren't we, Cupid?"

He could swear she was a flesh and blood woman, standing there mindlessly chatting to the cat the way women tend to do.

Without thinking, he reached out, clasping her arm. She was warm and soft. Skin, muscles and bone. If she was a hallucination, he'd dreamed up a damn good one. She eyed him as if he were idiotic, looking first at his hand, then up into his eyes in question. At the same time, Red's cat emitted a low growl. He snatched his hand back, surprised at himself for touching the woman who was a complete stranger. A *strange* stranger.

"Sorry, I was just checking to see if you're..." He stopped himself from saying *real* because she might think he was nuts. "Eh...warm enough. Red keeps the air conditioning on for the flowers and it gets cool in here."

"It's a wee bit chilly but I'm fine. Thanks for checking. So what exactly does a florist do?"

"People like to have flowers arranged in fancy-schmancy ways," Nevan said, "with all sorts of doodads and thingamabobs. If they can't do it themselves, they come to a florist, like Red, who does it for them."

"*Fancy-schmancy, doodads, and thingamabobs...* I wish I still had my textbook with the chapter detailing Earth vernacular. Do the people purchasing Cupid's flowers keep them or give them away?"

"Who knows?" Unable to concentrate, Nevan groaned, still wondering if he was losing his mind. "Look, Aladee, it's not my shop, it's my cousin's. I own the pub next door. Ask me anything about beer, wine, or spirits and I can tell you whatever you want to know. But flowers? I don't have a clue."

"While I'm here perhaps you can school me on intoxicating beverages and I can school you on pulchritudinous blooms."

"Pulkra-what?"

Her face lit up with a smile. "It means beautiful." Cuddling against her, Cupid the cat purred and Aladee kissed the top of his head.

Nevan decided her smile was the most pulchritudinous one he'd ever seen.

"Sounds good," he said. "I know what a rose, a daisy, and a carnation look like. That's about it. The rest are just a big, smelly hodgepodge to me."

He looked at the papers Red had neatly organized on the marble counter and groaned. They were the orders Nevan was supposed to get ready for Red's customers. They should have been completed and out for delivery by now.

"You are troubled, Nevan?"

"I need to get these flower orders done, fast." He wasn't sure if he was talking to himself or to Aladee. There was a good chance she was merely a figment of his imagination. Red was a great guy. He didn't deserve to lose customers because his cousin had gone bonkers.

"I'm happy to help. What can I do?" Placing the cat on the counter, Aladee smiled at Nevan.

Raking his fingers through his hair, he said, "I'm not sure. I'm fairly lost myself. I'm supposed to have these orders for Red's customers finished and out for delivery but, like I told him, I don't have a clue how to make flower arrangements." He moved the book Red had left open with bookmarks toward Aladee. "Here's his book with photos showing how to put the stuff together. It's all Greek to me."

"Poor Nevan, you look so pained. Don't worry, I'm well-versed in Greek, both ancient and modern." She covered his hand with hers. The cat put his paw on top, which kind of freaked Nevan out. "Nymphs are personifications of nature, so we work well with flowers." Massaging Cupid's fur, she added, "Nymphs also have a special connection with animals. It seems you and Cupid have been at odds, or so he tells me."

"Oh he does, does he?" No way would he believe she'd had actual two-way communication with Red's monster cat. Nope, nope, nope.

Listening to women jabber on, especially about silly stuff, wasn't high on Nevan's list of favorite things. There was something different about Aladee though. Until today, the only solid attraction in his life was his popular pub. Between operating it, then working like hell to restore it after the fire, and now devoting his time to running the newly renovated eatery and bar, he'd had little time for women or much else.

For the first time, his mind was on more than work, thanks to the woman claiming to be a cherub, or whatever. Maybe she was a little mixed up. Big deal. She seemed fairly normal in most respects, just a bit of a fruitcake. She probably referred to herself as a nymph the same way his sister, Kady, thought of herself as a psychic. Just a way to make herself feel special and unique.

"Where did you learn Greek, in high school or college?" he asked.

"I'm not familiar with those terms. I learned several languages when I was quite young, before I turned seventy-five."

Nevan returned her smile until he zeroed in on what she'd just said.

"Seventy-five?" She was in her mid-thirties at most.

"Yes. I'm proud to say I excelled in Latin before I turning ninety."

Nevan laughed. "Okay, now you're just yanking my chain."

"Oh no, Nevan." She raised both hands to show him. "See? I'm not yanking anything attached to you," she said with utter innocence while his dirty mind raced with enticing images.

"So...just how old are you, Aladee? If you don't mind me asking."

"Not at all. I turned three hundred fifty last week."

The poor woman was beyond the fruitcake stage. She was certifiably loony. A real wacko. But what about the invisible bow and arrow thing? Could lunacy be contagious?

"May I get to work on the flower arrangements?" she asked.

"Sure, go right ahead." His mind churned with concerns, emotions, and curiosity as he watched her build beautiful floral arrangements as if she'd been making them all her life.

Looking left and right, Aladee asked, "Is there a mirror I can use?"

Waving his hand, Nevan assured her, "You don't need one. You look fine."

The light laughter she tittered sounded like fine, tinkling glass.

"Thank you, Nevan, but I like to use a mirror in back of the flower arrangement I'm creating. It helps keep balance, proportion, and symmetry when I can see what I'm creating from both front and back."

Oh man, Red was going to love this flower-savvy doll.

"I'll see what I can scrounge up." Rifling around the back room he found a ten-inch high mirror on a folding stand and brought it to her.

"Perfect! Thanks."

Nevan tried not to think about her nearly naked body beneath that pink smock. Aside from her irrational talk about Cupid and being his student on Olympus, she came across as quite intelligent. Her mind just seemed...tousled, like her curly blonde hair.

"Would it be all right if I substituted some amaryllis, hydrangeas, tulips and ranunculus in a few of the arrangements? I think the colors and shapes would blend together beautifully, giving that little something extra." Picking up a small bushy bunch of tiny pinkish flowers from one of Red's metal buckets, she studied it a moment. "Using limonium for a filler would add the perfect touch of texture and whimsy, don't you agree?"

He was impressed that she was so adept at this floral stuff, right down to knowing the names of all the flowers and what matched with what. What she'd created looked great to him, even better than the images in Red's book. There's no way Red wouldn't be favorably impressed.

"I don't know anything about any of that. Everything looks great to me so go ahead and use whatever you think works. Knock your socks off."

"I'm barefoot today," she answered seriously. "But I can knock off my sandals if it pleases you."

"Uh, no...that's okay." Nevan drew in a deep breath, expelling it slowly. "Just create the flower arrangements however you think is best, as long as they look real nice when you're finished, because we have to please Red's customers. He's a great guy, always there for me, so I don't want to let him down."

"I'll make each arrangement as splendid as possible. Red won't be able to keep himself from giving me a high grade on this floral task. Oh, Nevan, I feel certain I'll make Lonan proud of me yet."

"Right, I'm sure you will." Nevan offered, watching her bustle around, humming some haunting melody as she worked. He didn't know what to make of it when she asked the cat if he wouldn't mind bringing her a few of these and a few of those, giving the flower names in Latin. The cat just up and complied, as if he understood.

"I have a dog named Buster. Do you think he'd understand you too?" Why not ask? It wasn't any crazier than anything else going on today. Besides, he didn't want Red lording it over him that his cat, Cupid, was smarter than Buster.

"I believe so. We'll see what happens when you introduce us." Aladee went back to work.

Pointing at the wall clock a few minutes later, she smiled. "I believe you said to open at ten o'clock." Picking up the cat, she brought it back to the pink-fenced castle, depositing it inside. To Nevan's amazement, Cupid stayed right where she put him.

"Right." He crossed the expansive room and unlocked the door, allowing several people waiting outside into the shop. If she hadn't been watching the time he would have forgotten all about opening up.

"Welcome to Cupid's Headquarters!" Aladee held her arms held wide as she slowly turned in a circle. She'd said it even better than he'd coached her. "You'll find Cupid has some amazing floral treats," she added in that same joyful tone.

The woman was astonishing. "Just ask if you have any questions," Nevan tacked on. "One of us will be happy to help." By *one of us*, he meant Aladee, because he was basically useless here unless someone needed heavy lifting.

People milled around and Aladee answered questions, took orders, and made one sale after another that Nevan rang up. At least he knew how to work a damn cash register and credit card swiper.

As she engaged with male customers, he realized Aladee brought out his protective instincts. Made him feel like a caveman. Made him want to beat his chest and howl.

He still wondered if she was a hooker, although she vehemently denied it. Maybe she was a hooker with a heart of gold. He watched and listened as Aladee flitted about, waiting on customers and making the shop feel alive with her dazzling smile and vibrant personality. The flowers didn't seem so smelly or bad to be around anymore. In fact, Nevan could imagine forking over a tidy sum to his cousin for a truckload of blooms just so he could toss Aladee in the middle of all that soft, fragrant color and—

"Do you know that man?" Aladee asked, interrupting his wayward thoughts, as one of the customers left the shop.

Nevan shifted his gaze, looking at the guy. "I don't think so. Why?"

"That's Ken Carlson. He's married, and has a mistress," she informed Nevan indignantly. "He bragged to me about it. Can you imagine? I believe if I would have encouraged him, Mr. Carlson would have proposed I become a second mistress."

"He got fresh with you?" Feeling that unfamiliar protective urge kick in, Nevan was a prepared to duke it out with the short, paunchy bald guy who just left.

"No. I asked questions about his wife and that slowed him down. I convinced him that whatever he bought his mistress should be dwarfed by the arrangement he chose for his wife. Then I signed him up for the flower of the month delivery program—for his wife only. It's the least he can do for her, considering his philandering ways, don't you agree?"

"Absolutely." Nevan felt a grin take hold.

"Do you think Cupid will be pleased with the way I handled Mr. Carlson?"

"By having him walk out of here after ordering two flower arrangements instead of one, *and* selling him a subscription to the flower of the month club?" Nevan chuckled as he thought of the euphoric whoop of joy Red would give when he learned about the pricey transaction. "Trust me, he'll be thrilled."

It was the first time Nevan found himself eager to learn more about a woman, not just what was beneath her toga, but also her curious mind and how it worked. If he believed in such preposterous things, Nevan could almost imagine Aladee really was from another planet, or Olympus, or wherever.

"All the flower arrangements are finished, tagged according to Red's instructions, and ready for delivery," Aladee said.

"You finished all those orders? While waiting on customers, answering their questions, and taking new orders?" She gave a proud nod. "I swear, Aladee, you're incredible."

"Thank you. Please pass your opinion on to Cupid when he returns."

"Definitely."

"Are we delivering the flowers ourselves?"

"No, Red has a delivery man." Nevan got out his phone and gave the driver a text, letting him know everything was ready to pick up.

"What's that?"

Nevan had no idea what she meant. "What?"

"That." Aladee pointed to his phone.

"This?" He turned it back and forth. "My phone."

"What does it do?"

He angled his head, studying her. "You've never seen a handheld phone before?"

She shook her head. "No."

She was either joking or she'd been living in a cave. "It's a personal telephone, a lot smaller that the old-fashioned kind," he gestured toward Red's fancy French provincial phone, "because those would be kind of hard to carry around in your pocket or purse." He chuckled at his own perceived humor, but Aladee had that same blank look across her face. "You know," Nevan continued, "for contacting people, like making calls and sending texts."

Her head slanted. "Instead of doing it telepathically, you mean?"

"Telepathically?" Her golden curls bounced as she nodded. Nevan hated being reminded that she was positively loony, which had him wondering if she'd run off from—

Oh shit...

"Aladee..." He paused to gather his thoughts. Keeping his voice calm, quiet, and making sure to smile so he wouldn't scare her off. "Did you come here from Wisdom Harbor Psychiatric Center? It's okay. You don't have to be afraid to tell me if you did." He attempted his best, most reassuring smile.

"No, Nevan. As I already explained, I'm from Olympus." She pointed skyward. "Lonan brought me to Glassfloat Bay in his chariot so I could find Cupid and my classmates. Remember?"

Aladee spoke slowly, as if addressing a small child. Or a nitwit.

Giving him the kindest smile, she touched his forehead with the back of her hand. "Poor Nevan. Today's stress must have taken its toll and impaired your memory. Don't fret. I too sometimes become rattled and forgetful."

She looked and sounded so normal. So knowledgeable.

Nevan had little time for reflection because several people entered the shop within minutes of each other. If it weren't for Aladee's speed and creativity when constructing striking floral arrangements, Nevan would have screwed things up for Red big time.

During the rush of shoppers, Red's delivery driver, Barry, arrived. Nevan and Aladee gave him all the particulars for the deliveries. After Barry left with the first half of the orders, Nevan helped out with the customers. Virtually clueless when asked questions, he referred people to Aladee. She was a natural at flower stuff, right down to which blooms were edible and which, like the azaleas and hyacinth, weren't. She happily furnished customers with the occasional demonstration, encouraging them to take a nibble on the gardenias, lavender and honeysuckle, while cautioning them not to ingest the honeysuckle berries because they were poisonous.

She was like a flower savant.

Hell, if Nevan had walked into Cupid's Headquarters looking for a bouquet, he would have walked out with tons of stuff he hadn't intended to buy. Nevan was so busy ringing up sales and writing up orders because of her savvy suggestions, he barely had time to turn around...or think about what it would be like to be in bed with her.

Okay, that was a damn lie. Lusty thoughts of holding an armful of naked Aladee was definitely the number one thought occupying space in his mind.

"You have an incredible knowledge of flowers," he told her, hoping to distract his errant thoughts. "Have you worked for a florist?"

"No, but I'm majoring in botany, studying plant science, and plant biology. Perfect Love Matches is actually my minor study subject."

"At the university?"

Aladee shook her head back and forth, offering an affable smile. "At the academy, on Olympus."

"So..." Nevan started, not quite sure how to proceed, "when you say *Olympus,* you're referring to a location in the vicinity of Glassfloat Bay, right?" He was so hoping she'd say yes. "This is a serious question so I hope you'll give me a serious answer."

Aladee laughed, making her eyes sparkle. "You have an uncommon sense of humor, Nevan. I am, and have been, quite serious about my origins and home on Olympus. I wouldn't lead you down a path of deceit."

Nevan's shoulders sagged. "Which means you're talking about the mythical place with gods and goddesses and Hercules and—"

"And Cupid, Apollo, Jupiter, Minerva, and all the rest. Yes. You may know it better as *Mount* Olympus." She finished placing a plump sprig of something she called baby's breath in a floral arrangement. "Check your geography books. Mount Olympus is more than a famed place of mythological lore, it's a very real location in Greece."

That was news to Nevan, although he'd never been a whiz at geography. He'd have to Google it to make sure it was true.

"So you're Greek?"

"No." She gave him a patient smile. "Residents of Mount Olympus have no regional identity. Where we live is invisible to mortal eyes, unless we grant a mortal the ability to view our home."

"Invisible...of course." Nevan was proud of himself for not rolling his eyes.

"The mountain has fifty-two peaks and deep gorges," Aladee explained. "The highest peak is called Mytikas, one of the highest mountain peaks in Europe. It's where the Greek and Roman gods live—usually in harmony, but," Aladee chuckled, "that's not always the case. The gods have a reputation for unpredictability."

Nevan enjoyed listening to all her imaginary facts. If school teachers had been this interesting, he would have paid better attention and got better grades.

He was about to pursue a further line of questioning when the door to the shop jangled.

"Cupid has returned!" Red announced with a grand flourish as he crossed the threshold.

Chapter Six

~<>~

WITH HANDLES of galvanized metal buckets lining his arms, Red traipsed toward the counter. "I've got more of these in my van, Nev, can you give me a hand?"

"Sure, but first—"

"Cupid!" Aladee shouted, bouncing in place and snagging Nevan's rapt attention. "I'm so glad you're finally here. I feared I might never connect with you."

Divesting himself of the pails, Red eyed Aladee over his shoulder. "Well, aren't you the little darling." He donned his personalized pink smock, turning up the collar and zhuzhing the sleeves to mid-forearm. "Nevan, wherever did you ever find this endearing little breath of fresh air? She's so unlike your other...*friends*." Red engaged in a snarky laugh.

"No, you don't understand, Red, I—"

"It's me, Aladee!" she said, as if that would explain everything.

"Aladee, hmm?" Red walked toward her. "Well, it's a pleasure to meet you, I'm Red Devington, otherwise known as Cupid."

He offered her his hand, which she clasped and shook with enthusiasm.

"And this," he made a broad gesture, "as I'm sure Nevan has already informed you, is Cupid's Headquarters, my humble little spot of floral heaven here in Glassfloat Bay."

Cupid the cat chose this moment to saunter over to Red from his doll-like castle setup. One leap and he was in Red's arms.

"He's usually not this attentive." Red stroked Cupid's fur while the cat meowed in his arms, nuzzling against Red's chest. "My poor baby, are you ill?"

"No, he's fine," Aladee assured. "He's just showing you appreciation. He says he feels bad because he rarely shows you the thanks you deserve for taking such good care of him."

One of Red's eyebrows arched with interest. "A pet psychic?" he surmised.

"No, just a nymph, able to communicate with animals," Aladee answered with a smile and a little shrug.

"Oh...well all right then." As if she'd just told him she was an ordinary, everyday woman, Red returned her smile before his attention was caught by the row of completed flower arrangements across the counter. He gasped, studying the striking, colorful arrangements. "These are sensational, Nevan. Exquisite. I'm amazed. Speechless! There, you see? I told you that you have an inner woman."

"It's all Aladee's handiwork," Nevan said. "Except for this." He reached beneath the counter and plopped a sorry looking vase with an even sorrier looking cluster of droopy flowers and leaves in front of Red, who recoiled in horror.

"Thank heavens for Aladee. Why didn't you tell me your new girlfriend is so gifted?" Red gave Aladee another admiring appraisal. "A pet psychic *and* a skilled flower arranger. Incredible."

"She's not my girlfriend, or a pet psychic," Nevan told him. "She's—"

"Pity," Red said. "Are these for delivery?"

"Yeah, they're the second half of the orders. Barry didn't want to smoosh them too close together in his van. He'll be back soon for these. As for Aladee," he sped on before Red could interrupt, "she's a nymph...from Mount Olympus." Nevan twirled his index finger at his temple indicating Aladee's lack of mental stability while she focused her attention on Red.

"I know how busy you are, Cupid," Aladee said, "so to refresh your memory, I'm in your Perfect Love Matches 101 course. Lonan is my instructor."

"Lonan's the guy who brought her here...*in his flying chariot,*" Nevan further edified.

"Is that so?" Red took Aladee's hands in his, giving her a warm smile. "Well, consider yourself hired until your chariot comes soaring back to fly you home again. Your artistry is extraordinary." He fingered one of her floral arrangements, marveling at Aladee's creative skills.

"I hope you don't mind that I took some liberties by adding wildflowers like this bit of cassiope mertensiana, some micranthes aprica, and a little clematis hirsutissima." Aladee gestured to the arrangements. "I also felt the delicacy of gypsophila and some spirea would be fitting as filler flowers for these." She motioned to other arrangements.

"White heather," Red translated from Aladee's Latin, "Sierra saxifrage, and..." He went on to say the English names of all the flowers Aladee mentioned. Looking up at Nevan, Red said with amazement, "Latin, Nevan. Your lady friend named each of these flowers in Latin."

"She knows Latin and ancient Greek," Nevan told Red. "She's like a doctor of flowers, or something."

"My major is botany," Aladee told him. "But that doesn't mean I don't feel a strong affinity for Perfect Love Matches. As you've stated in class, Cupid, a woman can do whatever she sets her mind to."

"That sounds exactly like something I'd say," Red told her. "I believe it wholeheartedly. Whoever you are and wherever you're from, you're hired." He gave Aladee a welcoming smile. Cupid the cat seemed to concur, by tapping Aladee's arm with his paw while offering a meow.

"Wonderful! I so enjoy working with flowers, Cupid. Oh!" Aladee's hand flew to her mouth as she scanned the area. "I'm sorry," she continued in hushed tones. "I forgot. I should be calling you *Red* while you're in your Earthly guise as a florist, shouldn't I?"

"It doesn't matter. You may call me whatever you like, as long as you promise to stay and work for me." Clasping Aladee's hand in his, he leaned over and kissed it.

"The chariot won't return for three days, so I'll be able to get plenty accomplished," Aladee assured him.

"Don't encourage her, Red," Nevan warned. "She honestly believes all that fairytale stuff."

"A little fantasy never hurt anyone," Red replied with an elegant shrug. "Besides, she doesn't seem depressed, suicidal, or harmful to others, does she?"

"Well no, but—"

"You're not any of those things," he asked Aladee, "are you?"

"Goodness, no." Aladee shook her head. "Aside from being somewhat absentminded, forgetful, and a bit disorganized, I'm emotionally well, and hoping you'll find my work worthy of a top grade."

"See, Nevan?" Red said. "She's just as normal as you or me."

"Yeah, she's just about on your level of normalcy," Nevan retorted. "But don't toss me in the mix, okay? Go ahead and ask her for her ID."

"We'll take care of details later." Red gave a dismissive wave. "All I need to do is look at these stunning floral arrangements and this fat stack of receipts to see how hard Aladee's been working." Turning his attention to her, he added, "Aladee, if this was a test and I was in charge of grading it, you'd get an A-plus and go to the head of the class."

Aladee sniffed and her bottom lip trembled. She looked close to tears—the happy kind women get. "Thank you so much, Cupid. You have no idea how happy and relieved that makes me. Will any of the other students be working with me here?"

"Alfred's the only other student currently in my employ. He'll think you're just yummy." Red winked. "Oh, for heaven's sake," he said to Nevan. "Get that vicious attack dog look out of your eye. Alfred's gay. I don't remember ever seeing you get jealous before."

Nevan blew out a stream of air. "I am *not* jealous," he lied.

Red returned his attention to Aladee. "How old are you, Aladee? Twenty-five? Certainly no more than thirty at most."

Aladee giggled. "Oh, Cupid, you flatter me. I turned three hundred fifty last week." She beamed a proud smile, telegraphing utter disregard for her supposedly advanced age.

"Get that, Red? She thinks she's three hundred fifty years old."

"I see," Red said, as if Aladee's absurd answer was an ordinary response when asking a woman her age.

"It's time my cousin spent some quality time with an older woman. I've heard they can do wonders, Nevan." Red gave a devilish smile.

"Your cousin..." Aladee's eyebrows pinched and she looked puzzled. "Nevan told me he's mortal. How can he be one of your cousins, Cupid, if he's mortal?"

Nevan crossed his arms over his chest, smirking. "Yeah, gee, Red, what's your answer for that?"

"It seems I've finally met someone who shares my enthusiasm for Roman mythology," Red told Aladee. "We'll have to do lunch so we can talk more about it."

"Thank you, Cupid. I would be honored to have lunch with you whenever you please." After a little curtsy, Aladee squinted at Red and then Nevan. "I see a strong resemblance. You're both beautiful men with your raven-black hair, deep brown eyes with thick black lashes, and lean, muscular bodies. You certainly do look enough alike to be cousins, except for—"

"Except for Nevan's utter lack of ostentation? His scarcity of charm or absence of style, perhaps?" Red offered helpfully, ignoring Nevan's grumble.

Before Aladee could respond, Red cupped his hand at the side of his mouth, speaking to Aladee in a conspiratorial whisper, "You see, Nevan's my *Earthly* cousin. Perhaps one day, with my guidance, he'll achieve godly status." Red glanced at Nevan. "Although that's doubtful."

Nevan shot his cousin a look.

"I understand," Aladee said, as if she actually did. "In the meantime, perhaps I can embrace Nevan from the outside if that might help."

The corner of Red's mouth quirked up. "Well, Nevan? What do you think? Would it help to have this little beauty wrap you up in her arms?"

Before Nevan could open his mouth, Aladee pressed herself against him, giving him a hug and rendering him speechless, as well as mightily turned on.

Letting go of Nevan, Aladee took a step back. "I believe Nevan and I would make an ideal love match, Cupid. Close to perfect. I've observed our attraction chemistry as we worked together. When he's close, there's almost an electrical charge passing between us, causing delightful sensations fluttering low in my belly."

Nevan stood staring with his mouth hanging open, wondering how he could be so damn turned on by a fruitcake.

"The only uncertainty," Aladee continued, "is Nevan's mental acumen. He has difficulty understanding or accepting ordinary truths. Such as when I informed him Mount Olympus is a factual place."

"Well of course it is." Red turned to Nevan. "It's a geographical location. You can see it on a map." His fingers flitted through the air. "Google it."

"And you should have seen Nevan jump when he felt my quiver," Aladee told Red.

"He felt your quiver? Right here in the store?" Red teased in mock horror. "Why, Nevan, you're no gentleman."

"She's talking about her quiver of arrows, smart ass. The ones she's supposedly got stowed under the counter. But don't bother looking for them because they're *invisible.*" His eyebrow vaulted high.

"*You* can't see them because you're mortal," Aladee corrected. "But since he's a god, Cupid can see them with no problem."

"Thank you for the compliment." Red smoothed his dark hair, and his cat snuggled closer, purring.

"I had to take them off my shoulder when customers arrived. Nevan said I must keep myself covered in this smock while they're present."

"Kudos to you," Red said to Nevan with some surprise, "for remembering that I like my employees to wear their uniforms." Red gave him a thumbs up.

"That's not why I told her to wear it." Nevan motioned toward Aladee. "She's practically naked under there, Red, plus," he glanced around before continuing in a near whisper, "she's not wearing any underwear."

"Under where?" Aladee asked, her head inclining to the side.

"Right," Nevan confirmed. "Nice girls are supposed to wear underwear."

"Under where do I wear this?"

"Yes you do," Nevan said.

"Do what?" Aladee asked.

"Put on underwear."

"Under where?"

"Exactly."

"I don't know where," the clearly frustrated Aladee said, her arms lifting and dropping to her sides.

Red broke into laughter. "Like Abbott and Costello doing their Who's on First skit."

"Who?" Aladee asked.

"Never mind," he waved his hand, "it's not important." Lowering his voice he explained, "Nevan's talking about panties, Aladee."

"What are those?"

"Underpants," Red further clarified. "You know, intimate garments women wear beneath their outer clothing."

"How curious. I've never heard of anything like that."

Red and Nevan exchanged dumbfounded looks.

"Stay right there," Red told Aladee, passing his cat to her. "Nevan, help me get the rest of the buckets from the van in here so I can get everything in the coolers."

Once outside the shop, Nevan asked his cousin, "What do you think's going on with Aladee? Is she certifiable? Just kind of ditzy? On drugs?"

"I don't think she's on anything," Red said.

"I don't either. She strikes me as being kind, sincere, and intelligent, even though she's convinced she's a nymph and you're Cupid."

"It seems she genuinely believes all this fantasy business she's telling us," Red admitted.

"I thought you said Mount Olympus is a real place," Nevan noted.

"It is. But she's talking about the mythological site, home of the ancient gods, not the geographical location in Greece where hikers climb and festivals are held. Believe me, Nev, I for one would *love* to learn that the mythological Mount Olympus exists but, regrettably, there's nothing to support that supposition."

Nevan studied his cousin through narrowed eyes. "How do you know all this stuff? I always knew you were a whiz at math, but you're a mythology expert too?"

"Mythology's always been a passion of mine. You should know. I've talked about it often enough."

Nevan laughed. "I don't necessarily pay much attention when you go on about stuff."

"Which comes as no surprise." Red gave a good-natured laugh. "A look around my shop with all the myth-related elements decorating the space should tell you it's something I love."

Nevan figured Red was right. Now that he thought about it, he recalled the shop definitely had a mythical atmosphere.

As they worked they watched one potential customer after another enter Cupid's Headquarters, and saw others coming out carrying packages and floral arrangements. No one left empty-handed.

"Ka-ching, ka-ching, ka-ching." Red mimicked the sound of an old-time cash register. "That girl's simply amazing."

"I agree," Nevan said. "Aladee's either completely off her cute little rocker, or she's—"

"A real nymph from Mount Olympus, here to connect with Cupid," Red finished for him, reaching into his van for another armful of buckets full of weedy looking flowers.

"That's not one of the options I had in mind." Nevan huffed laughter as he gathered the remaining pails. "There's no such thing as nymphs, mythological gods, or any of the absurd stuff she jabbers about. She also claims she can communicate with animals telepathically. We both know that's not possible. It's fantasy, pure and simple."

"Speak for yourself," Red told him, causing Nevan to tsk in response. "Seriously, Nev, we've witnessed some mighty strange goings on in this family. Who are we to say, unequivocally, that Aladee isn't exactly who she says she is?"

"Nope, not possible. Maybe she's super brilliant on the subject of mythology. Trouble is, I've never heard of a myth savant, have you?"

"No, but until we have this figured out and know what to do with Aladee, it might be a good idea to give your mom or one of your sisters a call. They'd be able to help Aladee better than we can when it comes to getting her appropriately outfitted for society."

"Agreed. I'll take Aladee to Bekka House after I leave here, and give Mom a call to see if she can stop by. She'll be a good one to assess our little *nymph*." Nevan hooked air-quotes over the word.

Bekka House was the Malone family's jointly-owned house, left to them by their beloved grandmother, Rebekka Eriksen, Astrid's mother. Bekka also happened to be one of the friendly spirits who frequently visited the seaside house, or so the family believed. Nevan was strongly skeptical about it.

"Is Kady still staying at Bekka House?" Red asked.

"Yeah, she's the only one staying there now. I'm sure she won't mind the company. I think she and Aladee are cut from the same kooky-patterned cloth." Nevan broke into a grin. "I'll bet she has some clothes she can lend Aladee. They look about the same size."

Red eyeballed Nevan, looking at his cousin's jeans and rolled-sleeve denim shirt. "Our appropriate apparel discussion reminds me," he said, and Nevan had a good notion what was coming next. "Why aren't you wearing one of the shop's smocks like I asked you to? You look like you're getting ready to solder something in all that denim."

"I knew you were going to ask me that." Nevan's mouth twisted into a half smile. "I told you before, Red...I don't do pink."

"Well," Red gave his cousin a second head-to toe appraisal, "I'll give you a pass, considering how you valiantly stepped up this morning, saving me on my first grand opening day. I really appreciate it, Nev. Thanks. You know I'm always here for you if you ever need a return favor."

As they approached the shop, their attention was snagged by Aladee opening the door for them, holding it wide. They deposited the pails of Red's floral stuff, which all looked pretty much the same to Nevan, regardless of all the fancy Latin names Aladee happily spouted as she pointed at each one.

"You see, Cupid..." she said with a quick glance around, positioning her back to the storefront, away from the eyes of curious customers. Then she unfastened the buttons of her smock and held it open, just like a flasher. "This is what Nevan meant. I'm still wearing my academy uniform. That's why he insisted I wear the smock. I'm afraid my invisibility traveling garment was lost during the chariot ride."

Nevan averted his gaze long enough to watch Red take in Aladee's form beneath the barely there tunic she wore.

"What, no wings?" Red asked with a smile, arching an eyebrow.

"That's exactly what I asked her," Nevan piped up.

"They're invisible most of the time," she said.

"Convenient, hmm?" Nevan gestured toward Aladee, as if to say to his cousin, *See, I told you she was nuts.*

"I see," Red responded to Aladee, offering Nevan a bland smile.

"Do you really think you should be encouraging her delusions, Red?" Nevan asked.

Red ignored his cousin, returning his gaze to Aladee's attributes. "Knowing what a lush bounty awaits beneath your rose-petal-pink smock, it gives me a sense of perverse pleasure knowing my cousin has been alone with you during my absence, working alongside you all the while and unable to have his way with you." With a quick glance toward Nevan, he added, "Which must have made him insane."

"Ha-ha, very funny," Nevan mumbled to Red, who offered a smirk in return.

Red glanced back and forth. "Where's Cupid...my cat," he clarified."

"Comfortably snug in his castle dwelling." Aladee pointed. Rebuttoning her smock, much to Nevan's dismay, she added, "I've been aware of Nevan's sensual interest mounting since I arrived, but he's been most honorable, a perfect gentleman."

"Well I guess I'll have to give him an A-grade too." Red winked at Nevan.

"In no way did Nevan attempt to seduce me or try to have his way with me, as the odious man in the park had attempted. In fact, I believe Nevan would have displayed bravery and heroism if he'd witnessed the attempted assault."

His playful façade gone, Red looked alarmed. "Someone tried to harm you in the park?" His attention shifted to Nevan, who gave an affirmative nod. "Good God, what happened?"

A bright smile stretched across Aladee's features. "You would have been so proud of me, Cupid, for deftly employing the tactics you've taught us in class. I loudly warned the assailant that, having studied chapter eleven of my textbook, I was fully prepared to take swift and appropriate action. I clamped my thighs together thusly," she lifted her smock to show them, "to protect my nether regions. Finally, I advised the man I am well versed in self-defense tactics and maneuvers, thanks to the detailed illustrations I'd studied during my chariot ride."

"And that stopped him?" Red asked, disbelief etched across his features.

"Well, no." Her cheeks pinked. "I believe it was kneeing the hostile man in his private parts that dissuaded him from committing his crime upon me."

"You poor thing. You must have been terrified." Red drew her into a hug. "You're right, Aladee," he held her at arm's length, "I'm very proud of you."

"Oh thank you, Cupid!" she gushed, beaming like she'd been awarded an Oscar.

"I see Alfred," Red said, watching his employee walking from his parked car across the street. "So you can leave any time you're ready. I'll be fine here without you."

"Ready for a visit to my family's house?" Nevan asked Aladee. "You'll meet my mother and one of my sisters. We'll stop at my apartment first, so you can meet Buster too. We'll bring him along. Bekka House is plenty big enough for you to stay until you're ready to go home."

"Thank you, I'd be honored to stay at Bekka House. I won't be a burden for too long since I'll be leaving in three days when our chariot returns to take us back home."

"To Mount Olympus," Red said as more of a statement than a question, and Aladee nodded. "Nev," he said, "many thanks for giving up your morning for me, especially after the long busy night you had, and the one you'll have tonight as well. I won't forget it."

With a pleasing glance at Aladee, Nevan smiled. "It wasn't any trouble at all, cousin...not at all."

Chapter Seven

~<>~

THE LIGHT CLEAN fragrance of fresh-cut flowers scented the air as Nevan and Aladee crossed the threshold into Bekka House. The Malone family kept the house fresh, clean, and presentable for anyone who might need to stay there, or use it for a gathering.

"Oh," Aladee breathed as she did a pirouette, taking in the spacious surroundings. "What a lovely, cozy, inviting place. There's a definite vibe of love here. There must have been some very happy times shared here."

With her talk of vibes, Nevan knew Aladee and Kady had a lot in common. When he'd called his mother before leaving the flower shop, she told him she and Kady had left the attorney's office in Rainspring Grove and would be there soon. He was eager to see what they made of Aladee and her bizarre story.

"Buster likes Bekka House too." Aladee watched the large dog meandering from room to room, sniffing. "He loves you so much. He's thankful you saved him when you found him two days after your pub was destroyed by the fire."

Nevan did a double take. "What?" She couldn't possibly know how he discovered Buster. Not unless someone told her. "What are you talking about?"

"About Buster being abandoned on the side of the road by his previous owners. When you found him he'd been without food and water for days. Ill and severely matted, he was preparing to die. Buster said his world and his heart sprang open," Aladee demonstrated with her arms, "with love and hope when you picked him up and brought him to the dog doctor."

Nodding, Nevan absently said, "The vet." He remembered the day well. While driving home from Rainspring Grove after meeting with his attorney, he spotted a big lump at the side of the road that had some movement. Unsure if it was a large bird, coyote, or maybe even a child, it appeared to be suffering, so Nevan stopped to check. What he saw shocked him. He liked to tease Red about his mangy cat, but there was nothing even remotely humorous about the poor, nearly lifeless, mangy creature he saw.

It took Nevan some time to realize it was a dog. Being so badly matted around his face and throughout his body, he was unrecognizable as a canine. Nevan called Red, telling him about the animal and asking about his cat's vet. Red gave him the address and met him there. He too couldn't believe the atrocious condition of the poor animal.

The vet and his staff had seen badly matted dogs, but Buster was the worst case they'd encountered. The sheer volume and weight of matted fur had to be incredibly difficult for him. From his appalling condition it was apparent the dog had been neglected for a long time.

After a three-hour grooming session, where nearly eight pounds of tightly matted fur was carefully shaved from his body, raw spots were visible all over his skin, due to the weight of heavy mats pulling at his body. His hugely overgrown nails caused Buster to move abnormally, resulting in him having to relearn how to walk. Buster was so weak he had trouble standing, much less walking.

It was a damn good thing Nevan couldn't find any information about the son-of-a-bitch who did this to Buster because Nevan gladly would have broken several laws making certain the bastard got exactly what he deserved.

As Nevan's gaze dropped to the scar on his hand, Aladee said, "Buster wants you to know he feels bad for biting your hand that day. After being so badly mistreated, he was afraid of all humans, which is why he snapped when you scooped him up."

Nevan would be furious if he found out Red or someone in his family was playing a cruel joke on him by having an actress pretend to be a nymph. But he couldn't fathom why anyone would go to that extent just to trick him.

"Aladee, tell me the truth. I need to know how you learned all this. You've said some things that I've never told anyone."

"Buster and I spoke telepathically. He hopes he was as much a comfort for you after you lost your pub in the fire as you were for him when you adopted him, bringing him back to health."

Nevan's shoulders slumped. It was impossible for her to know any of that. He'd been in a dark place emotionally after losing everything. Taking care of Buster had saved Nevan from sinking into a cavernous pit of depression. If he didn't have Buster to care for and worry about, Nevan would have been a basket case. Instead, his concern for the mistreated dog kept him strong and resolute. The powerful bond he and Buster forged while healing each other was unbreakable.

"It's too hard for me to believe, Aladee. I-I can't."

She smoothed her hand up and down his arm. "It's all right, Nevan. In time you'll come to accept it...and me."

Nevan remembered one thing he'd never shared with anyone—not a soul. Except for his dog. "Okay, tell me, why did I name him Buster?"

"Buster, come here, sweetie," she called to the dog, who pranced right over to her, tongue lolling. Placing her hands at Buster's temples, she closed her eyes for a long moment. "Hmm, interesting. Thank you, Buster. Good boy." She patted the dog's backside and he went on his merry way.

"When you were little you watched an old Danny Kaye movie called *Wonder Man*," she said. "Buster was the name of the twin brother. You decided then that if you ever got a dog, you'd name him Buster. He said he enjoyed watching the movie with you."

"Oh man..." Nevan held his head with both hands. This couldn't be real. Not a chance.

"Buster told me your friend, Annalise, chose the name for her dog, Choo-Choo Laverne from the same movie."

"*Buster told me*...those preposterous words just burned a hole in my brain."

"Oh dear...should we call a vet?"

Nevan laughed in the midst of his angst. "A vet is an animal doctor. For humans, it's just a doctor and, no, I don't need one. The sort of doc I need comes wearing a white coat and carrying a straightjacket." He looked at the woman who swore she was a pet-communicating nymph and gave her a crooked smile. "Better get ready because when the men in the white coats come, I have a feeling you and I will be going with them together."

"That sounds nice. Where will we be going?"

"To the funny farm."

"Excellent! I enjoy spending time with funny animals." Aladee strolled to a wall filled with framed family photos, asking Nevan to fill her in on the particulars. It was an excellent opportunity for him to push thoughts of her telepathic pet communication out of his too-cluttered mind. As they looked at the photos together, she was able to easily point him out in each picture where he appeared, even as a toddler. She was almost as good picking out Red.

"You have a nice family," she said after Nevan showed her his brother and sisters. "How many siblings and cousins do you have?"

"One brother and four sisters. Then there's my cousin, Red, and his sisters Saffron and Lorraine."

"I've always wanted to be part of a big family."

"Do you have any brothers or sisters?"

"Not anymore." She looked wistful. "My brother died along with my parents in an avalanche while mountain climbing. My aunt, uncle, and a cousin were with them and died too. So," she breathed a full sigh, "there's just me now."

"I'm sorry. How long ago did your family pass away?"

"Nearly fifty years ago, shortly after my three hundredth birthday. I'd caught a bad cold, probably from a guest at my party, so I stayed home the day of the hike. We'd done this hike many times before but this time—" Her eyes shimmered as the room's natural light reflected off unshed tears. "I miss them all very much."

"I'm sure you do. Sorry," he repeated because there wasn't a single damn thing he could come up with other than that. While he felt bad for her regarding the tragic way she said her family had been lost, he couldn't accept Aladee's fantasy about being over three hundred years old.

"Your mother must have been very busy with six children."

Nevan laughed. "We were a handful, but we all took turns helping Mom. She raised us on her own. That's her there." He pointed to Astrid in one of the photos.

"It's interesting that her hair is so light and yours so dark."

"Mom's full Norwegian and my dad was Irish, with black hair and blue eyes. The six of us kids took a little from both sides."

"Where do your dark-brown eyes come from if your mother and father both have blue eyes?"

Shrugging, Nevan cracked, "The milkman?"

"Oh I see." She gave him a sympathetic look. "You grew up with two fathers."

Nevan fell into easy laughter. "Oh Aladee, you really know how to tickle my funny bone."

"I never touched it, Nevan." She lifted both hands, palms out to show him. "I don't even know where it's located." That made him laugh harder. "Now show me, which one is your father Malone, and which one is father milkman?"

"You really do take things literally." After Nevan provided Aladee with a simple clarification of his joke that flew over her head, he turned back to the wall of photos and pointed out Sean Malone. "Dad was a firefighter. He died when I was a kid."

"I'm sorry." She touched his arm, surprising him at the simple yet pleasurable sensation of her fingers on his skin. Comparing Nevan to the photo of his dad, Aladee smiled. "You look like him."

Nevan nodded, "That's what I hear. He died saving children, including my older brother, Gard," he showed Aladee Gard's photo, "from a fire at the school when I was very young."

"How tragic. I'm sure the knowledge that your father's guardian angel was there with him at the time of his heroic deed and passing is a great comfort to your family."

Her words shook him to the core. When Gard had the heartwish ring, he was supposedly informed by his guardian angel, who also happened to be their great-grandmother, Helga, that she'd been with Sean when he saved the children in the school fire, and lost his life. She said she'd also been with Gard as he saved Sabrina's little boy, Harold, from the horrific fire in the building housing Nevan's pub.

It was a raw topic for Nevan—mostly because he couldn't bring himself to believe it really happened.

"Who told you that?" he practically barked at her. "Where did you get that information?" His harsh, accusatory words and demeanor startled Aladee, frightening her—he could see it in her eyes, which had grown saucer-like as she took a tentative step back, away from him.

Well hell...it was the first time he'd ever turned into an ogre and panicked a woman. "I-I'm sorry, Aladee. I didn't mean to—"

"No, Nevan..." Her tone was so delicate and gentle Nevan could barely hear her. She lightly rested her open hand over his heart. "There's no reason for you to apologize. I'm the one who must apologize for speaking to you of such a personal and painful memory. Please forgive my foolishness and ineptitude." Her bottom lip trembled and she lowered her head, looking as though she were about to cry.

God damn, he felt like the biggest imbecile on the planet.

Tenderly placing his hands on her arms, he spoke as kindly as he could. Not used to comforting women, he was determined to do his best after browbeating the poor thing.

"There's nothing to forgive, Aladee. I was just stunned when you mentioned the angel. I-I took it out on you, and shouldn't have done that. Can you tell me why you said that about a guardian angel? I promise not to jump down your throat this time."

Aladee's hands flew to her throat and she gave him that wide-eyed clueless look again.

"I meant that figuratively." He hoped his smile was reassuring.

Her smile in return was so sweet and comforting, Nevan wanted to wrap himself in its warmth and sincerity.

"That's how it happens for mortals," she explained. "You each have a guardian angel. While they aren't always able, or meant, to prevent bad things from happening, they help guide those they're assigned to protect through the situation...even when that situation is death."

Her head tilted to the side as she focused on something over Nevan's shoulder. Turning to look behind him, he saw nothing. With her gaze rising above them to a midway point between the floor and ceiling, Aladee smiled, saying, "You're very welcome," before returning her attention to Nevan.

Reminding himself to remain cool and unthreatening, regardless of Aladee's reply, Nevan calmly asked, "Who were you just talking to?"

"Helga. Your family's guardian angel. She told me she was your great-grandmother—your grandma Bekka's mother." Spotting Helga in some of the photos, Aladee pointed her out. "Here, the woman with the flowing white-blonde hair. She thanked me for explaining to you about guardian angels."

Nevan was thunderstruck. He had no clue what to say. How could Aladee possibly know about Helga? It was one more thing to add to the growing list of impossibilities.

Again, he wondered if he'd gone off his rocker...wondered if Aladee really existed. Fortunately for his family, Wisdom Harbor Psychiatric Center wasn't too far from Glassfloat Bay, so Nevan wouldn't be too much of a burden on them after the men in the white coats came to take him away.

"Are you all right, Nevan? You look..." her head tipped to the side, "strange." Still incapable of speaking, he gave a slow, affirmative nod.

"I forgot. Mortals don't necessarily believe in angels, or have the ability to see them. You've been nothing but kind to me since I arrived. I didn't mean to upset you, Nevan."

"You didn't," Nevan assured, finding his voice again. "It's just me...I'm not a guy who readily buys into woo-woo stuff."

"Woo-woo?"

"You know," he twirled his hand in the air, "magic, angels, psychic stuff...or nymphs." He attempted a smile, which probably came out lopsided. "So you actually saw Helga right here in this room?"

Aladee nodded. "We spoke telepathically before you heard me speak to her as she departed."

"So she's gone now?"

"Yes. She's beautiful. She wore a lovely, unique garment of crocheted squares. It was vibrant, multicolored, and full of intricate needlework."

Nevan remembered the multicolored crocheted coat Helga supposedly wore as an angel—it was her favorite item of clothing when she was alive.

"I can feel your grandmother Bekka here, Nevan. Oh!" Sniffing the air, her eyes went wide like a delighted kid at Christmas. "The fragrance of ginger!" Knowing what was coming next, Nevan just closed his eyes and shook his head. "I smell the cookies she used to bake for you. Can you smell it too?"

He didn't want to say yes, didn't want to admit it, but he had to be honest. "Yup. It's her pepperkaker." Nevan sighed. As long as he was nuts he may as well be full-fledged crazy.

"I'm honored that your grandmother offered me this warm welcome to the home she so dearly loved. Thank you, Bekka." As soon as Aladee spoke those words, the fragrance dissipated.

"Come on," Nevan gestured. "I'll show you the rest of Bekka House and fill you in on my family."

"Okay."

She wanted him to tell her about all the family photos lining the walls in most of the rooms. He did, answering all her questions and telling her of his favorite family memories.

"This is weird." He rubbed the back of his neck.

"What?" Aladee studied the photographs and pieces of artwork as they strolled through Bekka House.

"I never talk this much," he said with a laugh. "About anything, but especially about my family. When I'm with you I somehow turn into a regular ratchet jaw."

"*Ratchet jaw.* You use the most colorful words and phrases, Nevan. I have absolutely no idea what that means."

He gave a dismissive wave. "It doesn't matter. Never mind."

Something about Aladee put him at ease...made him want to tell her everything that popped into his head. He hoped the therapist they set him up with at the psychiatric center would be half as effective as talking to Aladee.

"I enjoy hearing you talk, Nevan. Good communication is crucial in a love match." Her eyes sparkled when she smiled. "The longer I'm with you, the more certain I am that we're destined to be together."

Whoa! Danger, Will Robinson, danger!

"Look, Aladee, I like you. A lot. You're nice, real pretty, and interesting, but I'm not in the market for a relationship, and I definitely don't believe in love matches, or love at first sight. Besides, I doubt it would work if I'm a regular Earth guy and you're up there living your invisible life on Mount Olympus."

"I've wondered about that too. If we're meant to be together, it will happen, regardless of the obstacles."

Changing the subject as far away from relationship talk as possible, Nevan said, "Sooo...as you can see, the entire house is full of artwork and crafts. Most of it was created by family and friends." He showed her the explosion of color from Red's dazzling artwork, consisting of bright, spirited paintings of flowers, otherworldly beings and mystical realms.

Aladee traced the edge of one of Red's canvases. "He so successfully captured the look and feel of Mount Olympus, I could almost imagine Red has visited there."

"He's always been artsy, and he's a big fan of mythology. Some of his artwork has had gallery showings. I don't have a creative bone in my body, but I appreciate my cousin's artistic flair. Some of Red's work is on display in my pub. If it wasn't for his artwork decorating the walls of my apartment, my minimalist, bare bones place would be pretty dull."

"Bare bones?" Aladee's eyebrow lifted. "You have skeletons on display? How...unique. I'm sure the bones must be...an interesting presentation."

Nevan couldn't help smiling. It was clear Aladee would bend over backwards to avoid insulting someone, or make them feel bad about themselves.

"There aren't any bones decorating my place. Except for Buster's rawhide bones. *Bare bones* just means plain and simple." Aladee looked relieved.

"As for your Mount Olympus reference regarding Red, stepping into his apartment is like being zapped to a distant galaxy. His place is as stimulating and full of life as he is. It's down the hall from mine, in the same building as his flower shop and my pub. I'll show you next time we're there."

"I'd love seeing both of your living spaces. I only got a brief, tiny peek at yours when we picked up Buster."

Nevan pointed to another row of artwork. "These paintings were created by my sister-in-law, Sabrina, Gard's, wife. I have her artwork in the pub too. She's had several gallery showings too."

"Beautiful."

He suspected Aladee would like the large but cozy family room with its supposedly magical retro aluminum Christmas tree. It was filled with an eclectic assortment of ornaments, and spotlighted by a rotating color wheel. His sister, Delaney, brought the tree with her from Chicago when she'd moved to Oregon a few years ago.

"Be right back," Nevan told her, heading to the family room to plug in the color wheel so Aladee could get the full effect when he brought her into the room.

A few minutes later, he enjoyed Aladee's oohs and aahs as she gazed at the hypnotic tree. Women seemed to be similarly affected by the decades-old tree. She wanted information about all the unique ornaments, many of which his sister, Reen, had knitted or crocheted.

She seemed to enjoy fingering the imaginative little ornaments as well as all the handcrafted items around the room. "Mmm...I can feel the love, the caring, the feeling of friendship here." Aladee hugged herself. "There's nothing like being surrounded by handcrafted items created with love. Everything at Bekka House gives me a joyful, welcoming feeling...a real sense of contentment."

The doorbell rang. It had to be his mother and Kady.

Turning to Aladee, Nevan patted the air with his hands. "Just stay right there, okay? Don't move from that spot. I'll be right back." He still wasn't convinced she was real. Now he'd know for sure.

While it appeared that Red had seen and spoken to Aladee, what if he really hadn't? What if Nevan had hallucinated the entire morning and Red hadn't even returned from the farm yet? What if Nevan was still in bed right now, dreaming?

"I'm losing it." Grabbing his head with both hands, he walked toward the door. Muttering unintelligible nothings, he thought about the two things most likely indicating he might be losing his mind—the invisible bow and arrows that he was sure he felt, and those twin protrusions at Aladee's shoulders beneath her smock—the ones she claimed were her wings.

Still mumbling to himself as he opened the door, Nevan watched his mom's usual smile sag as soon as she saw him.

"My goodness, you look awful, honey. Are you sick?" Astrid's hand immediately went to his forehead, checking for a fever. "What's going on?" She smoothed her hand across Nevan's cheek as she and Kady entered the house. "You sounded a little frantic when you called."

Astrid turned to her daughter. "Your brother looks little peaked, doesn't he?"

Giving him a narrow-eyed study, Kady nodded. "Like he's been shaken by something."

"Which is strange," Astrid said, "because Nevan's usually impervious to sickness or emotional troubles."

"Ma. I'm fine. I don't have a fever—and you're talking about me like I'm not in the room, when I'm standing right here in front of you."

Ignoring him, Astrid said, to no one in particular, "He's too tall for me to be able to tell. Bend down, son." After placing her hand fully against his forehead for a longer period, then inspecting Nevan's eyes and feeling both sides of his neck, she pronounced, "No fever or swollen glands. He doesn't appear to be ill. Probably the effects of a whopper of a hangover."

"Thanks, Doctor Mom." Nevan laughed. "Hey, when are you going to stop treating me like I'm five years old?"

Her concerned mom expression dissolving, Astrid smiled. "Probably never going to happen," she teased. "Well hello there, Buster." She squatted to accept the dog's enthusiastic greeting.

Petting Buster, Kady's eyebrows arrowed down. "I'm getting the sense that you're..." she looked up at her brother, sloping her head as she studied him, "panicked. But I don't know why because I get only positive vibes here in the house today. What's wrong, Nev?"

Nevan closed his eyes in a long blink before forging ahead. "Come on, I need to show you both something...eh, some*one*." A moment later, the three of them were in the family room, standing before Aladee.

"Oh, you're Nevan's mother, Astrid," Aladee said with a fetching smile, "and you're his sister, Kady. I recognize you from your photographs. I'm Aladee." She rested her hand on her chest. "I'm pleased to meet you both. Nevan has told me many wonderful things about you."

Nevan remained silent and unmoving, like a statue.

"It's very nice to meet you too, Aladee," Astrid said. "That's a lovely name."

"Nice to meet you, Aladee," Kady said.

"Aha!" Nevan nearly shouted, startling the rest of them as he walked back and forth, waving an extended finger. "So you two can see her?"

Astrid and Kady exchanged puzzled glances. "Well of course we can, dear," Astrid said. "She's standing right in front of us."

"Can't *you* see her, Nev?" Kady asked.

"Yeah, but that's not the point." If they could see Aladee it meant he wasn't totally off his rocker...just partially.

"What *is* the point, dear," Astrid encouraged.

"He probably partied too hard last night," Kady suggested, gesturing a drinking motion. "Still hungover."

"I was hungover early this morning but not anymore. Now I'm just worried about being ready for a straitjacket and a ticket to Wisdom Harbor Psychiatric Center."

"For heaven's sake, Nevan, you're talking nonsense," Astrid said. "Sit down, dear." She took a seat in one of the plump, oversized armchairs.

Kady plopped down on the sofa opposite the chairs, patting the cushion next to her. "Come sit next to me so we can talk, Aladee." As soon as Aladee sat, Buster jumped up to sit next to her. "Looks like you have a new friend." Kady chuckled.

"Buster," Nevan reprimanded, "you know you're not supposed to be up there, buddy." Buster dutifully responded by resting his head in Aladee's lap.

Looking from Kady to Astrid, Aladee said, "I think Nevan is concerned because he doesn't believe I'm real." Her eyes glistened as she smiled. "But as you can see," she held her hands, palms up, in front of her, "I do indeed exist." She went back to petting Buster.

"Ask her what she is and where she's from," Nevan said. "Go ahead, ask her."

Astrid shot her son *The Look*. "Nevan, it's not like you to be so rude."

"Yes it is." Kady laughed. "What's the story, Nevan. No, wait," she held her hand up like a stop signal, "maybe Aladee should be the one to fill us in."

"I understand my unusual situation may be challenging for you to accept," Aladee began, "but my story is entirely true." She paused long enough to study both of them before taking in a deep breath and proceeding. "I'm a nymph who has come to Earth from Mount Olympus, via my instructor Lonan's flying chariot, so that I can join Cupid and my classmates. When I arrived here in Glassfloat Bay, I—"

"Did you get that?" Nevan sat forward at the edge of his seat. "She's talking about Cupid, the guy on the Valentine cards, who flies around with his bow and arrows." He made a flying motion with his hands. "And did you get the part about the flying chariot?" This time his hand whooshed straight up toward the ceiling.

"Nevan, shush!" Astrid scolded with a wave of her hand.

Holding his hands up in surrender, Nevan kept his mouth shut. Astrid made it clear he was acting like a blockhead again. He needed to keep his wits about him. He didn't want to scare Aladee off in case she was in need of medical attention, or had family searching for her.

"Go ahead, Aladee." Astrid shot Nevan another warning look. "I'm listening."

"Okay." Aladee gave a relieved smile. "I was scheduled to meet with Cupid, the head of the academy, and with my classmates, but things went awry. You see, Red's flower shop has the same name as my intended rendezvous point, *Cupid's Headquarters*. At first I believed Red himself to be Cupid. Now, I'm no longer certain. I'm worried I may not be able to rendezvous with Cupid and the others for the flight back to Mount Olympus three days from now. It's a great concern—I don't want to be left behind."

Nevan watched his mother's smile stretch from ear to ear. Glancing at Kady, he saw Astrid's expression mirrored.

"Well, Aladee," Astrid slapped the arms of her chair, "that's got to be the best darned opening line to an introduction I've ever heard. *Ever*. I'm thoroughly intrigued, and glad to help in any way I can."

"Mom..." Nevan wanted to warn his compassionate, sympathetic mother to be careful and not get too involved in case Aladee was some sort of scam artist, but it was already too late. The same went for his empathetic bleeding heart sister. He didn't really have the impression that Aladee was out to scam them. It was more like she was a lost soul, in which case, she'd found the right people in his mom and sister.

"Aladee," Kady twisted in her seat to face her, "may I hold your hands for a moment?"

Nodding, she placed her hands in Kady's open palms, watching as Kady closed her eyes. Everyone was silent. When Kady opened her eyes again, she gave Aladee a warm smile before looking across the room.

"Aladee's telling the truth," Kady announced. "Either that, or she at least firmly believes that this is her truth. She's not deliberately lying."

"You're a psychic, Kady," Aladee said as more of a statement than a question. "I could feel the stimulating vibes from your hands as we connected. I'm glad you're here. It makes me feel better...more confident."

Aladee spontaneously wrapped Kady into a hug, with Kady immediately reciprocating.

"I knew it would be like this with the two of them," Nevan said to his mother. "It's been one hell of a day, Ma."

Astrid rose from her chair. "Don't anyone move a muscle. I'm going to put on a big pot of coffee, then I want to hear absolutely everything. But first..." She dug through her cavernous purse, drawing out her very old, very prized, Kodak Instamatic. "I want to take a few photos for posterity. Smile, girls!" Aiming her camera at Kady and Aladee, she snapped their picture. *click...click...*

While everyone else appreciated the ease of taking pictures with their phones, Astrid claimed it just wasn't the same as being able to hold a photo in your hands, touch it, and place it into an album with all the others she'd taken through the decades since she'd first gotten her beloved camera. She took care of that thing like car collectors baby their cars.

Checking his phone, Nevan noted he still had a few hours before he had to be at the pub for his Saturday night grand reopening celebration. He expected it would be bigger than the one last night. Saturday nights were generally the busiest for him. Fortunately, he'd already made sure everything was ready to go, including a fridge full of his popular Irish pork pie. With his mom and sister here now, hopefully they could watch Aladee, or find someplace to take her, before he got off work tonight.

"What's this big pot of coffee your mother speaks of?" Aladee asked.

Scrunching her features, Kady asked, "You've never had coffee?"

"No."

"It's a hot beverage people drink at breakfast...well, all day long if they're coffee lovers. Since you've never had it before, we'll add cream and sugar the first time. You should love it."

"Nevan, dear," Astrid called from the kitchen. "Can you give me a hand carrying everything into the family room?"

"Sure." He popped up from his chair, knowing full well this was his mom's way of saying she wanted to speak to him privately. Once he got to the kitchen she reminded Nevan not to be a jerk, to act like a gentleman, and not jump to any conclusions before giving Aladee a fair chance.

"Mom, the woman thinks she's a nymph. How can I not jump to conclusions?"

"Maybe she is one." She offered a shrug. "Our family's seen genies, angels and ghosts. Why not a nymph?" With a sweet smile, she carried her tray with the coffeepot and fixings into the family room, with Nevan following behind with a trayful of scones from his sister Laila's bakery.

"Mmm, what an enticing aroma." Aladee breathed in as Astrid placed the tray on the coffee table.

"I'll fix you a cup." Kady leaned forward, preparing a cup for herself and Aladee. "Thanks for remembering the non-dairy creamer, Mom."

"Of course. The scones on the right side with the pine nuts and cranberries are the vegan ones."

After giving her mom a thumbs up, Kady turned to Aladee. "Are you a vegan, Aladee?"

"I'm not sure what that is."

"Basically, it's someone who doesn't eat or drink animal products."

"Hmm, in that case, I'd have to say no, I guess. As much as I love all vegetables and fruits, and make them the mainstay of my diet, I do enjoy some meat now and then too."

"I've been guilty of lapsing occasionally," Kady confessed with a mischievous chuckle. "Just a little." She held her thumb and finger an inch apart. "Usually at holiday time."

"Like the Feast of Lupercalia?" Aladee's expression brightened.

"Well, I was thinking more Christmas, but any holiday food is good, right?"

"Right. Oh my goodness, Kady, I'm so happy I'm here. You Malones are wonderful. You and Red have made me feel so welcome, safe, joyful and...and..."

Rising off the couch, Aladee threw her head back, singing out a sweet, high-pitched jubilant note as a great, broad pair of butterfly-like wings sprouted from her back.

Chapter Eight

~<>~

"HOLY SHIT!" Nevan shouted in what sounded way too much like the voice of a scared little girl. Scrambling off the chair, he backed to a corner of the room, faster than he'd ever moved in his life. "What the...?" he muttered, plastering himself against the wall.

Hands splayed out at his sides, he blinked a few times, hoping what he thought he saw would be gone the next time he looked. No such luck. There they were. A big-ass pair of iridescent champagne-colored semi-sheer wings, as plain as day, fluttering just like...like *wings* for chrissakes!

"Wow!" Astrid said. "Holy cow!" *click...click...*

"Oh my stars!" Kady watched in awe. "How utterly magnificent!"

Gathering the courage to detach one hand from the wall, Nevan pointed accusingly at Aladee, who stood there looking calm and blissful.

"What the hell's going on?" he sort of screeched, which wasn't helping his male ego any. "What's going on?" he said again, lowering his voice an octave.

Aladee's wings flapped and fluttered gracefully until she lifted off the floor.

She *lifted* off the floor!

click...click...click...

She fluttered toward Nevan, He moved to the opposite wall.

"Don't come any closer," he warned, waving a cautionary finger at her. To Buster's credit, he just stayed where he was, gazing up at Aladee like this was an everyday occurrence.

96

"Calm down, Nevan." Astrid snapped picture after picture, but her voice wasn't nearly as tranquil as she'd probably expected. It was all warbly. "It's all right, dear. Just relax." He wasn't sure if his mother was trying to calm Nevan or herself. "I'm just glad I put a new film cartridge in the camera this morning."

"Don't be such a baby, Nev," Kady teased her brother, obviously finding this all fascinating. "This is wondrous. Amazing! Just let yourself enjoy it."

Aladee flew closer to him. "Oh, Nevan, you're so funny."

"I hate to burst your bubble, Aladee," he managed to say as she approached, "but what you see here isn't me trying to be funny. This is the real deal, okay?" He expelled a deep breath and inhaled another.

"Your words are strange, but I sense you're troubled by me all of a sudden. I'm the same Aladee, whether on the floor or airborne."

"Are you kidding? Those!" he said, sounding like a squeak toy as he gestured to her wings. "Those things growing out of your back, they're...they're..."

Aladee glanced at her wings as if they were something normal and mundane. "They're just my wings. I told you about them before. You spotted them protruding beneath my smock earlier, remember?"

"Yeah, but jeez, Aladee, they're *wings*. I mean, you've got wings! And you're...you're flying around. In the air!" Nevan slapped his hand over his face, shaking his head. "No. Uh-uh. This *can't* be happening."

"It's definitely happening," Astrid confirmed. "I see it too." *click...*

"Isn't this fabulous?" Kady said excitedly. "Aladee, you're remarkable. And your wings are majestic."

"Thank you, Kady. I'm glad you think so. It seems Nevan disagrees."

Calmer now, Astrid told Aladee, "You have to understand, dear. Here on Earth we aren't used to seeing wings sprouting from anyone's back, or seeing someone fly around. It's a bit...disconcerting."

"My apologies. I'm afraid I have little control over when my wings appear. They just do sometimes...especially when I'm overjoyed."

"No need to apologize, Aladee," Astrid assured with a smile that matched her calming tone. "It's just going to take us a while to get used to this, that's all." Her fingers were no longer digging deep into the stuffed arm of the chair.

Sliding his fingers from his eyes, Nevan looked up at Aladee again. She was still hovering, smiling at him.

"There's nothing for you to worry about, Nevan," Aladee assured him. "After all, I did tell you I was a nymph, didn't I?" She landed on the floor in front of Nevan, gathering him into a hug.

Nevan groaned as he melted into Aladee's embrace. First the whole invisible arrow thing, and now this. No question about it—he'd lost his marbles. Maybe some toxic flower pollen from his cousin's shop was eating away at his brain.

"Nevan?" Aladee said in a lulling tone.

"Yeah?"

"Look at me."

He did. Damn, she was beautiful.

"Please don't be angry. I'm sorry my wings sprout unexpectedly. It's genetic. It happened to my mother and grandmother too. They'll retract again soon, then you won't have to look at them anymore until the next time they appear."

Nevan's head snapped up. "Next time?" She nodded and all Nevan could say was, "Oh boy..."

Pouting, she gazed up at him. "I'm sorry you think my wings are ugly."

Nevan spotted a single tear trailing down her cheek and felt something inside his gut snap. Maybe it wasn't his gut...maybe it was his cold, cordoned off heart.

"They're not ugly." He brushed the tear away with his thumb. "I think they're beautiful."

"Really?" She planted her hands on his chest.

"Kady," Astrid said, "Why don't you come into the kitchen and help me doctor up this coffee with a little Kahlua while Nevan and Aladee, um, *talk*." The two of them picked up the trays, scurrying out of the room.

"Yeah, really," Nevan answered Aladee. "Can I...can I touch them? I don't want to hurt you."

"Yes." Aladee's demeanor calmed. "They're quite sturdy, not as fragile as they look."

Ignoring the notion of how impossibly weird and incredible all of this was, Nevan smoothed his fingers across one of her wings, enjoying the blissful look in Aladee's eyes as he did. Subtle shades of pink, blue, lavender and green mixed with the shimmery champagne color. It felt like silky butterfly's wings. When the wing fluttered beneath his touch, Nevan smiled.

"It feels like we're in a fairytale," he said. "So I guess you're really a nymph after all, huh?"

"I am." Aladee nodded. "Do you know what I've always wanted to do?" she whispered against Nevan's cheek while wrapping her arms around his neck.

"What's that?" God, he loved the way she felt in his arms.

"Kiss a handsome mortal man," she told him.

And she did.

~<>~

"How could I have lived so long without experiencing this thrilling sensation?" Aladee licked her spoon. "This...what did you call it?"

"Hot fudge sundae," Annalise Griffin, owner of the café answered, clearly enjoying the sight of Aladee relishing her ice cream.

"Hot fudge sundae," Aladee repeated with reverence. "By gods, it's sheer culinary perfection. The most delectable edible I've ever consumed." She sat back against the booth's red vinyl seat, smiling in a way Nevan had never seen her do before. He recognized the expression, having seen it on women numerous times. *The Chocolate Smile* was a look akin to a true orgasmic experience.

"That's about the best endorsement I've ever had!" Annalise laughed. "I'm delighted you're enjoying it so much. Let me know if you need anything else."

"Thanks, Annalise, we're good," Nevan said. "We'll take the check whenever you're ready."

"Sure thing." Annalise gave them the check. As she was leaving, Nevan stopped her. "Annalise, you undercharged us. You forgot to add on Aladee's sundae."

"I didn't forget." She offered a sunny smile. "It's on me, Nev. Watching the joy of a woman relishing her first ever hot fudge sundae is all the payment I need." She winked and took the credit card Nevan had dug out of his wallet. "Back in a flash."

"She's a real gem," Red noted and Nevan agreed.

Absently glancing at Aladee, Nevan couldn't help noticing how cheerful and content she looked—as if she was on the verge of breaking into song.

Whoa!

He reached across the table, stilling her arm before she brought the next scoop of ice cream to her lips. "Aladee, please, whatever you do, don't let your wings pop out while we're in public, okay? I'd never be able to explain it."

"I promise to be extremely careful. Although," she paused to tongue a fluffy dollop of whipped cream from her spoon, "it won't be easy." Her delighted, closed-eye moan drew the attention of diners at the next table.

Kady and Aladee had raided Kady's closet at Bekka House, looking for casual clothes until Aladee could get some at the mall. Kady was taller than Aladee, and had more meat on her bones, but they managed to find an outfit that worked...sort of.

She wore one of Kady's oversized unicorn rainbow T-shirts, with a large peace symbol patch centered on the back, and the words Make Love, Not War, painted above and below it with glitter paint. Too-long bell-bottom jeans with rainbow-hued rhinestones up the sides, had embroidered patches and hippie insignias all over the knees and back pockets. The jeans were belted at her waist with a bright pink polka dot scarf, and rolled at her ankles. An oversized pair of rainbow flipflops completed Aladee's Kady-ish look.

"You should have seen Aladee flying around the room," Nevan told Red in a cautious whisper. "Craziest thing I've ever seen."

"The universe is full of seemingly inexplicable things," Red said. Nevan wasn't sure why Red always seemed to have a calm of look of wisdom when he smiled, but he did. "It's all the curious and mysterious little moments along the way that make life so brilliant, so worth living. Hopefully I'll get to see Aladee's wings in action before she leaves us. I've always been particularly open-minded when it comes to the paranormal and supernatural."

"Is that what I am?" Aladee swiped the tip of her tongue across a speck of fudge sauce on her lips. "Paranormal and supernatural?"

"Well," Red patted Aladee's hand, "as far as we've known until meeting you, nymphs, Cupid, and the gods and goddesses of Olympus were purely mythological. Like something out of a storybook. A fantasy, fairytale, something mystical." He tossed off each word with a flit of his hand. "So to my way of thinking, yes, that qualifies you as being paranormal and supernatural."

"What are we going to do with her?" Nevan asked.

"Help her find Cupid, of course," Red said matter-of-factly.

"That would be wonderful." Aladee made satisfying little murmurs of pleasure as she licked the last vestiges of chocolate fudge from her fingers, setting Nevan's libido into overdrive.

"That's nuts, Red. How are we supposed to look for a guy who stars on Valentine cards?"

"It's the least we can do, Nevan, now that we've explained I'm not actually *the* Cupid."

Swallowing a melty spoonful of ice cream, Aladee got that far away orgasmic look in her eyes again. "If I don't find Cupid and my classmates in time, I may get a failing grade on this assignment."

"But there's no such thing as Cupid," Nevan whispered out of the side of his mouth to his cousin in protest.

"Just as there's no such thing as nymphs who sprout wings and flit around the family room," Red offered with a smirk.

His elbows propped on the table, Nevan dropped his head into his hands, groaning. He had a hell of a time accepting all this otherworldly stuff, while it just rolled off Red like a common, everyday occurrence. Of course, it might have something to do with Red supposedly communicating with plants and flowers.

Nevan glanced at his phone. "I need to leave for the pub soon. Kady and my mom will meet you and Aladee inside the mall at the west side entrance."

"Excellent!" Red rubbed his hands together briskly.

"Remember, she only needs a few simple things and some underwear." When Aladee opened her mouth to speak, Nevan told her with a smile, "Please don't start. Mom and Kady will explain everything you need to know about underwear, okay?" Aladee smiled and nodded.

"Just put everything on my credit card." Nevan handed it to Red. "But don't go spending a fortune and bankrupt me while I'm still paying off my debt for the pub reconstruction." He laughed, even while realizing Red could easily do just that if he got carried away shopping for clothes.

"Don't worry," Red assured him.

Nevan smirked at his cousin. "Famous last words."

"What is this mall I'm going to?" Aladee asked.

"You can't walk around Glassfloat Bay looking like a hippie reject from the sixties." Nevan motioned to what she was wearing. "And you sure as hell can't wear that skimpy toga. A mall is a big place with lots of different stores where you can shop for clothes."

He was glad he had to be at the pub, There were few things he detested more than clothes shopping. When he needed something, he ordered it online.

"What is clothes shopping?" Aladee asked and Red gasped.

"Don't tell me you're a shopping virgin," Red said in joyful disbelief. Aladee shrugged in response. Red looked to the heavens, mouthing what seemed to be a silent prayer of gratitude, and Nevan knew without doubt his credit card bill would be astronomical.

"Be still my heart. Trust me, Aladee, you're in for the time of your life. We'll get you all dolled up. After we meet with Aunt Astrid and Kady they'll start you on some lacy undies, then we'll shop for an LBD, a pair of high-heels, and..."

Nevan groaned, picturing dollar bills with wings like Aladee's, flying out of his bank account.

"What's an LBD and high heels?" Aladee asked.

A look of astonishment crossed Red's features as he gaped at Aladee. "You poor, deprived little thing. LBD stands for *Little Black Dress*," he explained, his expression full of sympathy and compassion, as if Aladee had just stated she was terminally ill. "Don't tell me you've never had one." She shook her head back and forth. "Good gracious, every girl needs at least one LBD in her closet."

Letting out a protracted groan, Nevan rolled his eyes.

Red leaned closer to Aladee, his elbows on the table, looking like he was about to divulge a great secret. "As for high heels," he looked heavenward, "just wait until you see what they do for a woman's legs. My cousin, who's already been drooling over you all day, won't be able to keep his eyes or hands off you when he sees you in your new LBD and heels."

"Number one, I haven't been drooling over her," Nevan lied, "and two, what did I tell you about getting all starry-eyed about clothes shopping, Red? This isn't supposed to be a whirlwind shopping spree. And Aladee doesn't need a little black dress, or any other color dress," he spat. "She'll only be here for as long as it takes her to find—" Nevan just couldn't bring himself to say *Cupid*. It sounded too damned insane. "Her teacher," he said instead.

"All she needs," Nevan went on, "are some conservative clothes that fit decent. Stuff that'll cover up all her..." Nevan gestured toward Aladee's curves and she looked up at him with those big baby blues, and that kissable mouth.

Damn, Red was right. Nevan was drooling.

"Just some inconspicuous stuff," Nevan said, "that she can wear while she's out there searching so she doesn't attract any more attention than she already does. Do you want to be responsible for some asshole attacking her because you've outfitted her like a high-price call girl?"

"Of course not. Whatever you say, Nevan," Red agreed, far too quickly for Nevan's comfort.

"I mean it, Red."

"Absolutely." Red flashed a broad smile. "A few drab pieces of utilitarian garb and we'll be done."

Nevan doubted his mom or Kady would be much help reining Red in since they were shopaholics too. Once they realized Aladee has never shopped for clothes before, Astrid wouldn't be able to resist the fun-filled opportunity to dress her up like a living doll.

Not that Nevan wouldn't enjoy seeing Aladee all dolled up too, but he'd rather see her without a stitch on...except, maybe for that pair of heels.

Chapter Nine

~<>~

"THIS FEELS just like the Feast of Lupercalia!" Aladee announced, giddy as she knelt at the center of her bed at Bekka House, whipping one article of clothing after another from the multitude of bags strewn across the bedspread. The shopping trip at the mall was extraordinary, more fun than she'd had in the last century.

"You mentioned this feast before. What is it?" Kady propped on the edge of the mattress.

"My favorite holiday." Aladee held up a lacy pink bra. "This is striking. So unusual. I'm glad you introduced me to this bra garment, Kady."

"Trust me, you won't be as thrilled once you've worn it for a whole day," Astrid joked. "So, tell us about this favorite holiday of yours."

"The Feast of Lupercalia originated in ancient Rome, before what you call Valentine's Day. There are similarities but Lupercalia can include animal sacrifice, fertility rites, and some sex too."

"Like a Roman orgy?" Kady asked.

"Oh no, the sex isn't lewd, and there's no debauchery." Reaching into another bag, she gathered the sheer black confection Red called a *nightie*. Smoothing her cheek across the silky material, she noted, "This is beautiful...soft and sheer as my wings. A nightie...is it meant to be worn at night while dining?" She held the delicate garment this way and that, examining it. "There's far less material here than in my toga."

She watched Astrid and Kady exchange glances. "No, it's meant to be worn when you're alone with..." Looking at Kady, Astrid gave a tentative smile. "Why don't you explain it."

"You wear it when you're with your lover," Kady explained to Aladee.

"Or your husband," Astrid added quickly. "Do you know what that is? A lover, I mean. Because, if not, I'd be glad to teach you some basics about the facts of—"

"Yes, I know what it means." Aladee felt her cheeks warming, probably turning as pink as the bra. "But I appreciate your kind offer of tutelage, Astrid."

"Well that's good." Clearing her throat, Astrid smiled. "Because it's been years since I had to explain about the birds and bees to my daughters...or my sons." Astrid's face bloomed with a telltale shade of crimson.

"Wait...no!" Kady's eyes grew wide as she sported a mischievous grin. "You told Gard and Nevan the facts of life?" Aladee found Kady's expanding grin infectious.

Her shoulders lifting in a helpless shrug, Astrid admitted, "Who else was going to do it? Your father was already gone by the time the boys were old enough to hear about it. I didn't want them getting God knows what sort of ridiculous misinformation from the kids at school. So," she elevated her chin, looking pleased with herself, "yes, I'm the one who told your brothers everything they needed to know."

"Wow." Kady giggled.

"This seems to have less to do with birds or bees than I originally imagined," Aladee mused. By *facts of life*, am I to assume you mean teaching your sons about procreation?"

"And puberty, safe sex, and consent," Astrid confirmed, "as in *no means no*."

"Did you teach them about how to do *it* when they're alone?" Kady's eyebrows jiggled.

"Aren't you supposed to be psychic...and mature?" Astrid sported a teasing expression. "Because if you really were, you'd already know I didn't need to teach them about pleasuring themselves because, apparently, boys somehow inherently know about that." Rolling her eyes skyward, Astrid said, "Thank God!" The three women laughed together.

Aladee enjoyed the interaction between mother and daughter. Though she'd only known them a short time, she already treasured them both. They made her feel wanted and accepted, as if she were a longtime friend or family member. As if she belonged.

"I want to hear more about Lupercalia." Astrid was clearly eager to change the subject.

"It's customary for young men to draw the name of a prospective lover from an urn." Aladee held the nightie, admiring it, swinging it back and forth to watch the fringe at the bottom sway. "The love matches last one year, until the next feast. Sometimes marriages result from the game."

"Have you ever been matched with someone at one of these feasts?" Kady asked.

Aladee shook her head. "No. I've never found anyone I wished to be united with for that long." As the words spilled from her lips, Aladee realized she wouldn't mind being with Nevan for an entire year. It could never be, of course. In two days, she'd be back on Olympus.

With a wistful sigh, Aladee told explained, "We begin the celebration on February fourteen, according to your Gregorian calendar, to honor Juno, goddess of fertility." She examined a pink garment they told her were called panties. "What an interesting item," she mused, spreading her hands through the openings and wiggling her fingers.

"Remember, you should always wear panties," Astrid reminded Aladee. "Well, except when..." Her face pinked again.

"Yes, I understand," Aladee told her. "The Feast of Lupercalia," she continued, "commences the following day, celebrating spring and Faunus, the god of nature and agriculture. There are fertility rituals, but I attend mainly for the array of specialty foods, the games, and to partake in the feast's special fruit of the vine. It's all great fun."

"So you're a wine drinker?" Kady asked.

Aladee wrinkled her nose. "I only partake occasionally. I've learned I must monitor my intake of fermented grape because it loosens my inhibitions. I also enjoy drinking brew made from fermented grains—"

"Beer," Kady said and Aladee nodded.

"When I imbibe too much of any intoxicating beverage, I end up feeling like a wild, wanton nymph." Chuckling, she offered an apologetic shrug.

"Nevan will love hearing that." Kady elbowed her mother.

"You mean because Nevan owns a pub?" Aladee asked.

"Um...not exactly." Kady winked at her.

Unsure what Kady meant, Aladee took the rest of the clothing from the bags. "This wondrous clothes shopping event was most enjoyable. I liked wandering with you and Red through the cavernous structure filled with assorted vendors. Thank you for taking me."

"It was fun watching you experience your first shopping spree," Astrid said. "Red was certainly full of energy as he ran about selecting one thing after another for you to try on." She smiled. "I must admit, he's got great taste. I just might bring him with me next time I go shopping."

"Will you both stay with me while I try on my new clothing? It would be so helpful if you'd offer guidance to let me know if I'm using any items incorrectly. Most aren't familiar to me."

"Absolutely," Astrid said.

"We didn't get a chance to see everything Red picked out," Kady said, "so we're eager to see it all on you."

"I'm eager too." Aladee felt self-conscious about putting on all the strange garments. "But nervous."

Offering an encouraging smile, Astrid made a grand flourish with her arms open wide. "On with the fashion show!"

"A show..." Aladee said thoughtfully, recalling films Lonan had shown the class of Earth entertainers performing magic. "Yes, I will perform my fashion show for you! *Ta-da!*" she added, the way she remembered the performers doing. They laughed together, making Aladee relieved and glad they enjoyed her attempts at levity.

"You can use the bathroom here," Astrid motioned to the bedroom's adjoining bath, "for privacy."

In the large bathroom, Aladee rifled through the bags of clothing, trying to remember which items were meant to be worn together. The garments were quite unlike the tunics and flowing gowns favored on Olympus. She selected a combination of black and pink for her first ensemble, coordinating colors and fabrics the way she'd seen them in the mall. Gazing at her reflection in the full length mirror mounted on the back of the bathroom door, she fussed and adjusted until she was satisfied with her appearance.

Grunting as she worked to get her feet into the shoes called heels, she called out, "Why do women of Earth choose to wear foot gear with such high heels and pointy toes? It's difficult to walk, my toes feel pinched, and my feet are prickling as if I were walking on a thousand tiny nails." Taking her first few steps was an ordeal. "I can barely maneuver on these oddly constructed contraptions. I keep falling off."

Astrid told her, "It's like Red said when we were in the mall...women will put up with almost anything if it means they'll look good. There's a pair of shorter heeled pumps, as well as a pair of flats in there too. You can try those instead."

"I will with the next outfit. Ready to see me?" She suddenly felt excited. "Close your eyes until I tell you to open them, okay?"

"Okay," they called back.

Aladee wobbled out of the bathroom and into the bedroom, doing her best to strike a pose as pleasing as the ones she'd seen on the store mannequins. "Ta-da!" she announced. The pleasant look of anticipation she first spotted on their faces soon turned to expressions of shock. She couldn't tell if it was good or bad.

"Oh my goodness." Astrid covered her mouth. It seemed she was trying not to laugh.

"Oh boy." Kady clapped her hands over her mouth and eyes, peeking out at Aladee.

"I'm sorry, honey," Astrid began, "we don't mean to laugh, but..." Her face grew red and her eyes crinkled and watered until she finally collapsed into open laughter with Kady following suit.

Aladee quit posing. Her expression, along with her shoulders, drooped. With a wobbly, tentative gait, she marched to the mirror, checking her appearance.

First there was the tight black denim leg gear called jeans. Over them she'd pulled on a pair of lacy pink panties because Astrid instructed her to always wear them. Torturous shiny black high heels completed the lower portion of her outfit. For the top, she'd put on a black V-neck sleeveless top, and over that, the pink bra that matched her panties.

To complete the look, she'd released her hair from its clasps, fluffing it and allowing her voluminous just-below-the-shoulder curls to flow through two of the three openings of another pretty pink garment that she assumed was a hat.

"I thought this looked nice." She studied her reflection. "What makes it humorous?"

"Oh, Aladee," Astrid wiped tears of laughter from her eyes, "if you only knew how incredibly refreshing you are." She got off the bed, coming to Aladee and giving her a warm hug.

"We're sorry, Aladee," Kady assured. "You look beautiful. It's just that the outfit you put together is...amusing." Kady joined them in a brief three-way hug.

"Before you start your search for Cupid tomorrow," Astrid said, once they'd separated, "we'll help you get dressed, to make sure the panties," she snapped the elastic waistband, "go *inside* your jeans, and that your shirt," she fingered the V-neck top, "goes *over* your bra."

"Oops." Aladee's hand flew to her lips.

"As for the heels," Kady said, "I doubt you'll be able to walk more than half a block with those on."

"I don't know what a block is, but I won't dispute that." Patting the two poofs of blonde spilling from either side of the headgear, she asked, "Did I at least get the hat right?"

Astrid and Kady exchanged a lengthy look, obviously on the verge of laughter again.

"We need to have a talk with Red about your, ahem," Astrid placed her hand against her mouth, "*hat.*"

"Those are crotchless panties," Kady explained, taking the pretty pink hat from Aladee's head and displaying it across the vee area between her legs. "The legs go through these openings, and the center, um, well that's to allow for...easy access." Her cheeks colored rosy as she provided her explanation.

Aladee scrunched her features, angling her head. "You mean for quick means of urination?"

Once again, mother and daughter exchanged curious expressions.

"No dear. Kady means for easy *access*," Astrid repeated the exact same word Kady had used. "You know, for easy, um, entry."

Taking the skimpy panties from Kady, Aladee examined them until their true purpose finally registered with her. She imagined her cheeks must have turned the same shade Kady's had a moment ago.

Aladee put her hands through the holes, one at a time. "If gaining instantaneous access is so important, why should the sex partner bother to wear these at all?" When neither of them offered an answer, Aladee shrugged. Cupping between her thighs, she asked, "So this part of me must be called the crotch?"

"Mmm-hmm," Kady confirmed.

With another gaze at her full reflection, wearing the lacy pink intimate garments outside of her clothing, Aladee pulled on the sex panties as a hat again, drawing her hair through the leg openings. Striking a purposely silly pose for Astrid and Kady now, complete with another *Ta-da!*, she burst out laughing.

"It's no wonder you couldn't restrain yourselves from laughing. It seems I've transformed from nymph to jester."

"You turned an already enjoyable day into a truly memorable, fun—and funny—occasion," Astrid assured.

"Earth clothing is confusing. It's much simpler on Olympus for both males and females."

Aladee paraded across the bedroom in each outfit. By the time she got to the last two outfits, she had a much better understanding of putting together an acceptable Earth ensemble.

"I'm only here for three days." She looked at the empty shopping bags. "That's not long enough to wear all these."

"You can bring the clothes you like back to Olympus so you can show your teacher and classmates some of what you learned about how we live and dress here on Earth. It'll be like an extra credit project." Kady beamed a smile.

"That's an excellent idea. Perhaps I'll gain favor with Cupid for doing an unassigned fashion project."

"If we have time before you leave," Astrid said, "I'd love to sit down with you over hot cocoa and learn more about Cupid and your life on Mount Olympus."

"Ditto," Kady said.

"I'd like that. I hope we have the time." Aladee clasped their hands. "Please explain hot cocoa and ditto."

"Cocoa is a chocolate drink fit for the gods." Closing her eyes, Kady licked her lips. "And ditto means *me too*, or *I agree*."

"Chocolate?" Aladee thought about the scrumptious hot fudge sundae she'd had with Nevan and Red. "Oh, I *love* chocolate!" Her delighted demeanor soon sank. "Regrettably, if it's fit for the gods then I must not indulge. It wouldn't be proper, for I am naught but a lowly nymph, not a god...not even a minor one."

Wrapping an arm around Aladee's shoulder, Astrid chuckled. "Don't worry, Kady was speaking figuratively. Fortunately, lowly nymphs and lowly mortals are permitted to enjoy cocoa whenever they darn well please."

"Okay, Aladee," Kady rubbed her hands together briskly, "there's one more item left for your fashion show. Let's see how you look in this." She held up the black dress Red had selected for her.

"Ah, the LBD," Aladee said with near reverence as she fingered the soft jersey fabric.

"If it fits, you can wear it tonight," Kady said, "for Nevan's celebration."

"Prepare for another of Aladee's famous fashion shows!" Spreading her arms wide at her sides, Aladee's mouth opened, but before she could say *Ta-da!* again, Astrid and Kady chorused it together, their eyes twinkling as they smiled. Aladee took the dress from Kady, and the undergarments Astrid held out to her.

The black bra and panties looked much the same as the pink except for the color, and the absence of any shoulder straps on the black bra. Red told her it was strapless because the dress had something called a halter neckline.

"Do you think it's too dressy?" Astrid asked Kady as Aladee stepped into the bathroom to put everything on.

"Since Aladee only has three days before she goes home, I say she should go ahead and get all dressed up," Kady answered. "She'll have a ball."

"Ditto!" Aladee called from the bathroom and they all laughed.

Aladee experienced the strangest sensation listening to Kady speak about the few days Aladee would be with them. Astrid reminded her so much of her late mother and Kady was the sister Aladee always wished she'd had. She already found herself growing lonesome for these women, as well as Nevan and Red, and thought about how much she'd like to extend her stay. That, of course was impossible. Cupid expected her to return to Olympus with her class.

Remembering to put the bra and panties on first, Aladee grew frustrated trying to get the dress on correctly and asked for help. Once Astrid showed her how to wrap the front across her breasts and waist, they fastened it. Astrid tugged the fabric into place, then stood back to look, offering Aladee a glowing smile.

"Oh honey, you look just beautiful," she said, which meant the world to Aladee.

Aladee thought the deep V-neck wraparound style of the halter dress showed her curves to their full advantage. The knee-length skirt portion flowed from the cinched waist in soft, smooth folds.

Standing in front of the full-length mirror, she hardly recognized herself. A satisfied smile stretched across her face.

When they returned to the bedroom, Kady echoed Astrid's compliments. She'd unboxed a pair of black pumps with a shorter heel, urging Aladee to try them on. They were so much more comfortable than the towering heels she'd had on earlier.

Walking with more ease, Aladee asked, "What did Red mean when he told me to *strut my stuff* when I'm at Nevan's pub tonight?"

"He meant you should feel confident about the way you look and have a wonderful time," Astrid said. "Granted, the translation may a little different than Red might explain it, but it's close enough." Giving Aladee a thorough appraisal, she added, "That shouldn't be difficult at all because you look stunning."

"Really?" Looking down at her dress and smoothing the dark material, she asked, "You don't think I look silly? It's such an unusual look for me. I don't believe I've ever worn anything black before, except for mourning clothes."

"Trust us," Kady told her. "You look amazing. I can't wait until Nevan sees you."

"I'm not sure if he'll like the dress...or me." Aladee held the skirt portion out to the sides. "His jaw keeps dropping when he looks at me, and he gets a curious look about him, as if I've upset or annoyed him."

"I guarantee you haven't upset or annoyed my son, Aladee. Nevan has something else in mind entirely."

"What would that be?" Aladee sighed. "I wish I understood more about the way mortals on Earth think."

She watched the women exchange perceptive glances again. "I suspect," Kady said, "my brother has the birds and bees in mind." She jiggled her eyebrows as she'd done a few times before. Aladee wasn't sure what that particular facial expression meant, but Kady lit with joy and levity when she did it, so it must be positive.

"Are you suggesting Nevan may have some interest in me of a carnal nature?"

Astrid and Kady laughed. "Yes, dear," Astrid said, "I'd venture to say you're on the right track."

"I wish I had longer than three days here to spend with you." She gazed around her with fondness. "I love the feel of this room.

Thank you for allowing me to remain in Bekka's lovely house until my departure."

"It's our pleasure," Astrid told her. "We keep the house ready and available for anyone who needs it, which is just the way my mother would want it."

"Bekka gave me a warm welcome with the gingery fragrance of her pepperkaker."

Astrid and Kady exchanged tender smiles. "That means Grandma Bekka really likes you," Kady said.

"I'm glad. I also had the opportunity to see Helga, Bekka's mother. You have two beautiful, loving beings guarding your family from the life beyond."

Her eyes glistening with unshed tears, Astrid reached out, touching Aladee's arm. "Thank you...I love hearing about my mother and grandmother. They were two of my favorite people. It's incredibly comforting knowing they still watch over us."

"You're able to communicate with spirits?" Kady asked with obvious interest. "Like a medium?"

"I'm able to communicate with people no longer on this plane, as long as they're open to it. In this case, both Bekka and Helga appeared and spoke to me as Nevan gave me the tour of this home. He was unable to see or hear them. They were full of praise about all of you."

"We definitely need more time together so I can pick your brain," Kady said excitedly. Aladee was aghast and apparently it showed. "It's the *picking your brain* part that kind of freaked you out, right?" Kady laughed. "Don't worry, that just means I want to learn all I can from you about connecting to the afterlife."

"I'd enjoy sharing my knowledge and experience with you, Kady. It's one of my favorite topics."

"Perfect!"

"I think you just made a friend for life, Aladee." Astrid chuckled.

The three chatted a while longer about all manner of things, including the awful time Red had when his family disowned him after he'd come out to them as being gay. It broke Aladee's heart to hear the details.

When Astrid checked the time on her phone, she gave a surprised *Oh!*, and suggested they get ready for the pub's celebration.

Chapter Ten

~<>~

NEVAN ARRIVED at the pub just before five o'clock, bowled over by the size of the crowd waiting to get in. His pub had always been popular with locals and vacationers but he'd never had a long line of people waiting outside before. Concern set in when he wondered if there might be a problem inside preventing customers from entering—a burst pipe, or maybe a kitchen fire. Once inside, he saw the pub was packed. When someone called out his name, people raced toward him, taking pictures, video, and asking questions.

His brother, Gard, broke through the crowd to Nevan's side, explaining what happened. The story of his pub being nearly demolished by the fire, the way the community rallied to support him, and why he'd renamed the establishment Half Potato Pub, had made the national news.

"Wow, must be a slow news day," Nevan joked, feeling both glad and overwhelmed. "This is amazing."

"I know," Gard agreed. "There's no way in hell you could afford advertising like this, and it all happened naturally."

After talking to the press, something he'd never done before, Nevan excused himself and headed to the large table where his family and close friends sat. Aladee was there too, sandwiched between his mom and Kady. She looked incredible.

"Can you believe this?" his sister, Delaney, said, clapping the back of the empty chair next to her, indicating Nevan should sit. Red was seated in the chair next to his. "It's a madhouse in here. I can barely hear myself talk."

"I've never seen so many people gathered in one place in Glassfloat Bay before," Astrid said, "except maybe for the annual Valentine's Day Fling. You've got a Chicago-sized crowd here, honey." The Malone family had all lived in Chicago before moving to the Pacific Northwest, so Astrid knew what she was talking about.

Astrid had called Nevan earlier, letting him know they'd explained to Aladee the importance of not telling anyone she's a nymph, or letting her wings pop open. They'd simply say Aladee was a friend of Kady's who'd come for a short visit. Tomorrow they'd tell the family about Aladee's true identity.

Nevan's attention centered on Aladee. He had to hand it to Red. He knew what he was talking about when it came to fashion. Nevan was glad Red insisted on getting her the LBD, as he called it, because Aladee was breathtaking tonight. She exemplified a perfect fusion of beauty, brains and sex appeal, enhanced by a quality of sweet vulnerability that set her apart from any other women he'd known.

"Your pub's filled with positive vibes," Kady told him, snapping Nevan out of his reverie. Closing her eyes and pressing her fingers to her temples, she added, "So many people here are hoping Half Potato Pub will succeed. I can feel it." She opened her eyes and smiled. "I did a tarot card reading for you before I came. Everything looked good. There's big success in store for you, Nev."

"Fingers crossed," Nevan said, appreciative of his sister's eerily accurate feelings.

"This celebration rivals that of Lupercalia." Aladee's eyes glistened. "I'm having a wonderful time getting to know your family and friends. I've discovered a delicious new drink too." She held up her glass. "It's called a mojito." She giggled.

Nevan could see she was already tipsy. "Careful," he told her, "those'll sneak up on you."

"What's Lupercalia?" Reen asked Aladee.

"Oh, Reen..." Turning to face his sister, Aladee bounced with excitement—and the effects of the mojitos, no doubt. "It's the most wonderful, grand celebration we enjoy each February on Mount—"

"In Olympia, Washington," Red cut in, "where Aladee lives. You said it's an annual family reunion, right, Aladee?" Leave it to quick-thinking Red to save the day.

Nevan watched Aladee's eyes widen as she remembered she wasn't supposed to let on about her real identity or where she came from.

"Right." She offered a nervous laugh. "Sorry, spirits jumble my thoughts." Her eyes darted from Astrid to Kady and Red, before she lowered them to her folded hands in her lap.

"Same thing happens to me when I have anything stronger than a little Kahlua in my coffee." Reen laughed, then gazed around the pub. "I'd say someone's raking in big bucks tonight, Nev." Her smile stretched wide.

"I just hope you've got enough beer, wine and booze to handle this throng," Gard said. "I came here with the intent of getting plastered and don't want to be disappointed." Feigning a reprimand, his wife, Sabrina, poked him while others at the table laughed.

"Running dry is one problem I don't have to worry about," Nevan said. "I ordered an excess from my regular suppliers, as well as a few new local brew pubs, and was worried I'd have no place to store it all so, drink up, bro!"

All the Malones and their close friends were present. Tables and booths were packed with familiar faces of loyal, longtime customers. The support and encouragement touched Nevan deeply, making him determined Half Potato Pub would live up to the meaning of its name.

Gard turned serious. "What about your Irish pork pie? Please tell me you're not in danger of running out." While Nevan's tall, flaky, lard-crusted pie was a favorite of his customers, Gard practically worshipped it.

"Well," Nevan rubbed his chin, "I guess that depends on how much of it you binge-eat."

"This is awesome tonight, Nev," his sister, Laila, said, scanning the crowded pub. "I'm so happy for you!"

"Thanks. I expected a good turnout but," Nevan scratched the back of his head, "this is unreal."

~<>~

"How did you and Kady meet," Laila asked Aladee as everyone at the table conversed.

Remembering her coaching, Aladee smiled. "Kady and I are *good friends*," she said, hooking air quotes around words just as Red had done when he'd helped coach her. Red had used the gesture several times when explaining how to answer questions, so she assumed it was important to include. "*Kady and I had lots of fun together while traveling.*" She followed that with a wink and a hearty thumbs up, the way Red had done.

"Oh my God." Kady dropped her face into her hands, laughing.

Aladee felt quite proud of herself until Kady's unexpected reaction.

"Oh boy." Astrid covered her mouth with her napkin as she laughed.

"Um, is there something you want to tell us, Kady?" Delaney asked with a smirk.

"Yes, do tell." Reen rested her elbows on the table, perching her chin in her hands.

"Whoa..." Squinting one eye, Gard held up his hand. "Since Kady's my sister, I'm not sure I want to hear this."

Leaning toward Red, who was also laughing, Aladee asked quietly, "Did I say something wrong? I tried to do everything just the way you instructed."

"You did just fine," he assured her. "But there's no need to add the invisible quotes." He demonstrated with his fingers. "They can give things a vastly different meaning." Waving a dismissive hand, he added, "It's my fault. I swear, if they cut off my hands, I couldn't talk."

Her gaze dropping to Red's hands, Aladee whispered, "Your hands have vocal chords?" Red's expression dissolved into laughter.

"Come on, guys," Kady broke into a grin, "it's not what you think. Aladee and I are just friends." One of her eyebrows boosted. "*Platonic* ones. We'll tell you more tomorrow, after Nevan's celebration is over."

"Well that was a chore," Nevan said, returning to the table after talking to a group of reporters. "Hopefully everything's under control now. You wouldn't believe some of the questions they come up with. I'm surprised they didn't ask whether I wear tighty-whities or boxers." Nevan laughed at his own joke. "Did I miss anything?"

"Nothing much," Gard said, "other than Aladee's revelation that she and our little sister are lesbians."

His eyes popping, Nevan's gaze flew to Aladee. "What?!"

"I'm sorry. I didn't know Kady's a lesbian." Aladee shrugged her shoulders. "I accidentally revealed it by using these." Her fingers made hanging quotes. "For some reason everyone thinks I'm a lesbian too, and Kady and I are lovers."

Scrunching his features in confusion, Nevan asked, "What the hell?" He shook his head. "I was only gone a few minutes and—"

"It's my fault." Red's hand shot up.

"Your fault? What are you talking about?" Nevan planted his fists at his hips. "What the heck's going on?"

"It's fine," Astrid said. "For heaven's sake, close that hanging jaw of yours and stop looking like a deer in the headlights, son, it doesn't become you." With a calm smile, she explained, "It has to do with Aladee taking everything so literal, that's all. We told everyone," she waved her hand around the table, "we'll talk more tomorrow after your celebration's over."

"Sounds like a discussion I don't want to miss," Drake said.

"Same here," the rest chorused in one form or another.

"Sunday brunch tomorrow morning at Griffin's Café," Astrid announced. "Be there if you want to get the scoop." Calling down the long line of tables pushed together, she said, "Annalise, you'll have a full house for brunch tomorrow." Annalise gave two thumbs up in response.

Aladee wasn't sure exactly what had transpired, only that something she'd said or done had created a problem. She felt stricken. The Malones had been wonderful to her, and she'd repaid them by creating havoc on Nevan's special celebration night.

She felt her chin tremble and got that funny feeling in her nose and eyes indicating she was about to cry. She couldn't allow that to happen in front of everyone. She'd already drawn more than enough negative attention to herself because she'd obviously made a mess of Red's instructions.

"Astrid," she began, "can you show me where the restroom is, please?"

Astrid's jovial expression shifted to one of concern when she turned to look at Aladee. "Of course. Follow me, dear. I need to go too."

As they walked through the still crowded pub toward the restrooms, Astrid took Aladee's hand, giving it a supportive squeeze. "You look like you're about to cry. I'm not sure what's wrong, sweetie, but don't worry, everything's going to be okay."

Aladee could only nod in response, afraid anything more would have her sobbing in the middle of Nevan's pub. Once they entered the sizeable restroom, Aladee couldn't hold the tears back any longer.

"I'm so sorry. Please forgive me, Astrid." She used the heels of her hands to wipe away tears.

"For what, dear?" Astrid grabbed some tissues, handing them to Aladee, who dabbed her eyes.

"For spoiling Nevan's important festivities and making everyone think Kady and I are lesbian lovers." Her tears fell harder and her shoulders shook. "I-I don't understand how I managed to do that. Apparently I misinterpreted Red's excellent instructions."

"Aw, come here, honey." Astrid drew her into an embrace, smoothing her hand over Aladee's back and muttering comforting words. She let Aladee cry for a short while before holding her at arm's length, smiling. The warmth of her compassionate expression soothed Aladee's heavy heart.

"First of all," Astrid said, "we know Kady isn't a lesbian, but if she was, we'd be fine with it and love her just the same. No one here would care if you were a lesbian either. Well, except for Nevan." Astrid chuckled. "So you see? There was no damage done."

A sense of relief washed over Aladee. "I'm so relieved to hear that. If I'd caused Kady the sort of problems Red has endured with his family, I couldn't forgive myself. Because of my misuse of Red's invisible quotation marks," she made the sign with her fingers, "I fear I may have alerted your family that I'm..." she looked left and right, ensuring they were the only two there before whispering, "*different.*"

"That's okay too. It'll be fun tomorrow morning when we tell them you're..." mirroring Aladee, Astrid looked around the bathroom, "a nymph," she whispered, her smile expanding. "Honestly, I can't wait to see their expressions when you tell your story about Cupid and Mount Olympus."

Aladee had lost her parents so long ago, she'd almost forgotten the supportive give and take interaction with family members. Like the Malones, Aladee and her family had shared a close bond with a similar sense of lightheartedness.

"Your family is as wonderful as Bekka and Helga told me they were." At Aladee's words, Astrid's eyes glistened with tears, which she blinked back. "While I'm here," Aladee continued, "I'd like to pretend you're all my family. Would that be okay?"

"Absolutely. We'd be delighted to have you as an honorable Malone. Now no more tears, okay?" She used a tissue to wipe beneath Aladee's eyes and nose. "I want you to enjoy the time you spend here with us, so just relax and have a good time this evening, okay?" Draping an arm over Aladee's shoulder, Astrid led her out of the bathroom.

"Okay." She gave Astrid her most appreciative smile. Being an honorary member of the Malone family made Aladee so joyful it was like winning a grand prize.

Halfway to their table, Aladee stopped. "Astrid?"

"Yes, dear?" She offered Aladee a warm, generous smile.

"Thank you for being so wonderful, so kind and understanding." Drawing Astrid into a hug, she said, "If I had found Cupid right away, I never would have met any of you, so it's turned out to be a perfect accident, hasn't it?"

"I think so," Astrid agreed.

"I've had such great fun and learned so much as you've introduced me to Earth culture, Astrid." Feeling richly cared for and blessed, happiness and gratitude coursed through Aladee's entire being. Closing her eyes, she sang out her most jubilant note of exultation. Before she realized what was happening, her wings blossomed fully and she lifted from the floor.

Overcome with elation, she'd forgotten where she was until she heard a mighty rumble of people crying out in astonishment. Opening her eyes, she gazed down at the crowd beneath her. Everyone was pointing up at her.

Oh no! What had she done? How could she let this happen? She should have known better than to imbibe the mojitos!

She looked at the people sitting at the Malone family tables. They were all slack jawed. Staggered, Nevan looked as though he was about to scream, keel over, or maybe kill someone—possibly her.

Beneath her, Aladee saw Astrid's dazed expression as her hand flew to her throat. She couldn't tell what the woman was thinking, only that she was flabbergasted. Aladee would be devastated if Astrid hated her for ruining Nevan's special night.

As people gathered closer, Aladee noticed them taking pictures and shouting questions at her. She had to do something. Fast! Something to fix this egregious mistake of hers before it completely destroyed Nevan's event. If only she'd had her forgetfulness powder with her, she could make them all forget they'd ever seen her wings open and watched her levitate more than six feet off the floor.

As a swarm of impatient reporters pushed and elbowed to get closer, a single, superb idea lodged itself in Aladee's brain, boldly making itself known to her. She'd clearly heard the suggestion from the calming voice of Rebekka Eriksen, Grandma Bekka, as the gentle spirit whispered in her ear. Aladee was grateful for the idea, hoping it would work well enough to save the night.

Swallowing hard, Aladee spread her arms and hands wide, broadcasting the best show performer smile she could, while shouting a tuneful, "*Ta-da*! Welcome one and all to the spectacular grand reopening celebration of Nevan Malone's Half Potato Pub! We hope you're enjoying your evening, your delectable food, and delicious libations, and, of course, Nevan's special, one of a kind show!" She gestured to herself from top to bottom, presenting her most engaging smile as she slowly twirled in a circle so everyone could get a better look.

With that, her wings fluttered gently and Aladee floated back down to the floor, only to be quickly inundated with reporters, customers, and the entire Malone cadre, with everyone scrambling to find out how she did it. Before saying a word or doing anything else, she retracted her wings and they disappeared into her back.

The crowd erupted with shouts, cheers, whistles, and applause.

"Hey, where are the wires?"

"Malone, how did you rig this up?"

"What the hell did I just see?"

Questions shot like rapid fire. People were gobsmacked.

Praying her unplanned stunt, her stupid mistake turned performance, had the positive effect she hoped it would, Aladee watched as Nevan walked toward her.

The look he gave her was part chastisement, part jubilation. Taking Aladee's hand, he raised it high, as if they were a magician and his assistant at the end of a successful performance.

"As you can see, Half Potato Pub is unique," Nevan told the crowd. "Sure we could have entertained you with a beautiful woman," he gestured to Aladee, "jumping out of a cake, but here at my pub we don't do mundane. Our goal is to bring the absolute best, the freshest, the newest to all of you to enjoy."

"Come on, Malone," one of the local reporters asked, sticking out his microphone. "The Glassfloat Bay Gazette has always done right by you, haven't we?" Nevan gave a confirming nod. "So level with us. How did you manage an impressive stunt like this? It doesn't seem possible."

The reporter's scrutinizing gaze hunted for whatever mechanism had been used to hoist Aladee into the air and back down again. His final question was, "And where the heck did her wings go?"

"They used video projection," someone yelled out.

Aladee found it difficult to hear what the reporter was saying because of the din, with everyone shouting out how fabulous Nevan's amazing trick was, how phenomenal her performance was, and their theories about how it had been pulled off. No doubt about it, dear Bekka's idea had worked even better than Aladee hoped.

Still holding Aladee's hand, Nevan shifted his gaze to her, giving her a full-blown, white-toothed smile this time.

"How did we do it?" he responded to the Gazette's reporter, while addressing everyone in attendance. "Why, magic, of course. Pure and simple. Well," he gazed down at his shoes with a purposeful shrug, "either that, or..." he looked up again, "or this lovely young lady is a winged nymph who's come to celebrate with us all the way from her home up on Mount Olympus." He pointed skyward.

Aladee caught Nevan shooting a glance to his family and nodding at them a single time. She knew it was his way of telling them that Aladee was, indeed, a nymph, while leaving the crowd to wonder how they'd performed the extraordinary feat of *magic*.

Chapter Eleven

~<>~

"I THOUGHT MY eyeballs were going to pop right out of my head when I saw your wings expand and watched you rise toward the ceiling." Nevan unlocked the front door to Bekka House, ushering Aladee inside. "Thanks to your brilliant bit of marketing, Half Potato Pub will be all over the news and probably go viral on social media."

"Viral?" Aladee's eyebrows pinched in confusion. "As in an infection, like a cold, or chickenpox? Oh no..."

Nevan laughed. It was a sound she'd come to thoroughly enjoy.

"No, when something goes viral, it means..." He paused, giving a dismissive wave. "Nah, way too much to try to explain. I'll tell you another time. Right now I just want to focus on my beautiful, brainy nymph." He kissed her forehead and she felt the tingle clear to her toes. "How did you ever come up with such a promotional gem, Aladee? Was it on your own, or did you have help from Red, or my mom and sister?"

"I didn't have any help from them." Aladee debated how best to answer Nevan's question. It was the third time he'd asked her since they left his pub, and she'd been deflecting until she could figure out what to say. She'd love for Nevan to be proud of her, to be favorably impressed with her abilities. She wanted more than anything to pretend she was a marketing genius, rather than a scatterbrained idiot who happened to get lucky after creating a gigantic blunder.

"Well that's even more reason to be proud of yourself, Aladee."

She had to tell him the truth. Nevan deserved that. Inhaling a deep breath, she let it out slowly. "Nevan, I—"

"Have I told you," his gaze traversed her body, "you look like a million bucks in that dress? Really beautiful."

Though she was full of anxiety, Nevan's compliment had her smiling. She'd never forget the surprised look of wonder on his face when he first spotted her tonight. That solitary, appreciative expression of his had made her feel utterly desirable and attractive.

"Thank you. I'm glad you like the dress."

"It's not just the dress. It's *you* in it that makes it so special."

An unexpected sigh passed her lips. She'd be daydreaming about this moment since meeting Nevan.

"I know it's late but I thought we'd relax over a glass of wine. This is a malbec, from Argentina." He presented the bottle of deep red wine. "A nice balance between dry and sweet. Kady suggested it."

"That sounds nice but I've already had three mojitos tonight. My inhibitions become fairly loose if I imbibe too much." She watched as Nevan's eyes darkened and his expression intensified at her words. "Since I must be up and out early tomorrow to search for Cupid, I want to avoid the terrible achy head and upset stomach from too much alcohol."

"Hangover," Nevan said. He must have sensed her confusion because he added, "A hangover is what you get after drinking too much—the headache and upset stomach."

"Oh!" Aladee laughed along with him. "More Earth vernacular I haven't yet mastered."

"We'll just have one glass." Leading Aladee into the family room, Nevan turned on the silver tree's rotating light wheel and the room glowed with changing colors. The atmosphere it created, especially at night, was enchanting.

"Have a seat," he motioned to the couch, "while I pour us a glass." He set the bottle on the coffee table in front of them, drawing a corkscrew from his pocket and showing it to her. "I like to come prepared."

He did the same eyebrow jiggle Kady had done earlier. Aladee assumed it must be a Malone trait. Uncorking the bottle, he filled the stemmed glasses half full.

"Your pub's celebration was wonderful, but I saw how hard you were working the entire time. You must be exhausted, Nevan. You don't have to sit here to keep me company."

"Don't you like my company?" he said in such a way that was suggestive rather than wounded.

"I do, it's just...Nevan I need to tell you—"

"I've never known a nymph before," he gazed straight into her eyes, "and I'm betting I'll never meet one again. I want to spend as much time with you as possible before you leave. Let's toast." He held his glass aloft and she did the same. "To new friends, successful searches, safe journeys, and, of course, to my favorite nymph."

"I can't be your favorite because—" The look of mild exasperation Nevan gave her told Aladee she'd misunderstood. This wouldn't do at all. The last thing she wanted was to come across as silly or senseless. She longed for Nevan to take her seriously. She wanted to fill their short time together with passionate, magical memories so she could draw upon them whenever she needed to feel comforted. She never wanted to forget this wonderful, handsome mortal.

It was all so tragic she nearly cried. She wholeheartedly believed she and Nevan were a love match. How cruel that it was impossible for nymph and mortal to make a life together. They'd soon part forever. While Aladee would remember him always, Nevan and his family would have no memory of her after the required memory-loss treatment.

"Yes," she raised her glass, "a toast to all you said, and to one of my favorite male mortals."

Before they sipped, Nevan chuckled and clapped his chest. "I'm not your favorite?"

"You are...along with Red." She gave him her best smile. "Of course, I'm aware that only one of you has a carnal interest in me." She mimicked Kady's eyebrow jiggling, hoping she used it correctly. It seemed like the right time. She must have succeeded because, as he drank, Nevan's eyes bugged and he nearly spit out his wine.

She murmured her satisfaction with the first sip as the liquid traveled in a warm stream down her insides, settling near the spot where she felt powerful Nevan-related cravings.

"Damn, Aladee." Nevan closed his eyes for a long moment. "And here I was planning on being a complete gentleman tonight. Fair warning, my little nymph, if you talk like that, you'll make me crazy and I won't be able to keep my hands off you."

She took another sip of wine, regarding Nevan over the rim of her glass. "I'm not opposed to a little craziness." She tried not to smile as she watched his eyes grow darker at her provocative teasing. Setting her wineglass on the table next to the bottle, she scooted closer to Nevan, who placed his glass next to hers.

Aladee didn't have to wait long for the anticipated kiss. Clasping her shoulders, he tugged her close, whispering her name before covering her mouth with his.

By gods, this mortal knew how to kiss, instilling her with passion and powerful sensations. His chest muscles pressed into her soft skin, sending spikes of desire coursing through her faster than a rapid team of horses surging across the sky. Their kiss was textbook perfect, sparking lively, spirited vibrations in her secret places.

As their tongues danced to the timeless rhythm of lovers, every nerve ending in her body hummed, confirming Nevan was *the one*. Her perfect love match. She could imagine remaining in his arms like this for all eternity.

"Mmm..." Her eyes still closed, Aladee licked her lips. "Perfect," she said once their lips parted and she opened her eyes. "I selfishly wanted to have one ideal kiss before I share the truth with you."

"The truth?" His head tilted to the left. "Please don't tell me you really are a lesbian."

Aladee giggled at that. "No, nothing like that." With a deep, fortifying breath, she confessed, "I'm not the brilliant marketing person you think I am. I'm nothing but a forgetful, walking *and* flying disaster who creates complications wherever she goes." Her gaze shifted to the rotating color wheel, hoping it might help calm her.

"I don't know where you get these screwy ideas, Aladee, but that's not true. I think—"

"Nevan," she clasped his arm, "please let me finish, or I'll never be able to get it out. What I did at your pub tonight, with my wings opening and me flying toward the ceiling, wasn't planned. It was an accident. I'd been thoroughly coached by Red, Astrid, and Kady, and still, even knowing the vast importance of your celebration being a success, I forgot myself and caused a scene." A single fat tear rolled down her cheek.

Nevan cupped her face, wiping her tear with his thumb and looking at her far more kindly than she deserved.

"Who cares?" The kindness in his voice mirrored his smile. "You took a potentially bad situation and turned it into gold, Aladee. You made tonight more successful and memorable than it ever could have been without your flying stunt. So stop tormenting yourself over a mistake anyone could have made." One eyebrow lifted as he chuckled. "Well, anyone with wings."

Nevan wiped beneath her eyes with a napkin. "You took your mistake and turned it around, all by yourself."

"No," she shook her head, "I didn't. Your grandmother, Bekka, whispered the idea to me. If she hadn't—"

"If she hadn't, you would have come up with it yourself." Nevan tipped her chin up with his finger, bringing her gaze to his. "You know what makes you truly special, really unique?"

"No," she answered in a tiny voice.

"The fact that you told me the truth when you didn't have to. I never would have guessed this wasn't some genius master plan of yours if you hadn't told me about Bekka. After your wings popped open and you flew toward the ceiling, what did you do? Cry and whine about it? No. Make excuses for yourself? No. You thought fast and created one of the best damn marketing ploys anyone in Glassfloat Bay, or the Pacific Northwest coast, has ever seen."

"I appreciate that, Nevan, but—"

"Shhh." Nevan put his finger to her lips. "You were afraid I'd be angry after I found out what really happened, but you still told me the truth anyway, because honesty was more important to you than what I might think of you. That makes you one very special person in my book."

"Really? Which book?"

Laughing, Nevan drew Aladee into an embrace, rocking her from side to side.

The thump of his heartbeat made her feel better, safe and secure.

Cupping her face again, he kissed her nose, cheeks and forehead before kissing her lips. "Now just sit for a while and watch the color wheel while sipping from your wine. It'll help you relax."

"For someone so strong, masculine and occasionally obstinate, you certainly can be soft, sweet and caring. You're a good man, Nevan. Kind and considerate, like your cousin, Red." She caressed his cheek, brushing her fingers over the dark whiskers sprouting at his jawline.

His smile made Aladee feel more relaxed than the wine or the rotating colors.

"Hey, I'm not a hearts and flowers kind of guy. I'm hard as nails. I was just trying to make you feel better so you wouldn't cry. As for me and Red? We couldn't be more different."

"You're more alike than you realize."

Nevan rolled his eyes and groaned. "How about we just keep that to ourselves. I don't want Red starting all that crap about me having an inner woman again. I wouldn't want to harm my macho image, you know?"

"No," her eyebrows knitted in confusion, "I don't know. What's a macho image?"

Laughing again, Nevan said, "You crack me up, Aladee." His hand shot up before she could speak. "Figuratively, not literally."

"That's a relief." She smiled at him. "But you do have an inner woman, Nevan. All men do."

"Aladee."

"Yes?" Gazing into the depths of Nevan's eyes, she thought of the pools of rich, dark hot fudge she'd enjoyed with her ice cream earlier.

"Just shut up and kiss me."

Happy to comply, she slanted her head and his lips were on hers.

Being held close in his arms was the answer to her innermost dreams. She felt the full extent of her nymph powers coursing through her veins, through her entire being.

Her wings opened, flapping mightily. In the blink of an eye she'd lifted them both from the family room couch and into the air.

"Holy jumpin' Jehoshaphat!" Nevan clutched Aladee harder. "I'm...I'm up in the air. I didn't know you could fly with me, Aladee."

"I didn't either," she admitted dreamily. "I'd heard stories that it was possible under certain conditions, but assumed they were just boastful tales. It's wonderful, isn't it, Nevan?"

Sucking in a deep breath and expelling it, Nevan finally smiled. "Yeah...I've got to admit it's pretty cool." He captured her lips in another kiss. "You're just one little bundle of surprises, aren't you?"

Lifting them toward the high ceiling, she twirled them in slow circles above the ornamental tree. Dancing on air, literally, they deepened their kiss. Allowing himself to relax, Nevan cupped Aladee's bottom, drawing her closer to him, making her fully aware of his desire.

"I wonder if we could make love together," Nevan said, his voice thick with passion. "Right here. Right now." He kissed her neck, her ears, her shoulders. "You think that's possible, Aladee?"

"I'm not sure but I'd love to try." She stilled Nevan's hand as he lifted the skirt to her dress. "There's just one problem."

"Hmm?" His voice was wistful as he gazed at her in question.

"Kady and your mom were about to leave the pub just after we did. Astrid should be dropping Kady off here any minute. It probably wouldn't be a good idea for her to see—"

"Whoa!" Instantly, Nevan was fully alert and squirming. "Time for us to get our feet back on the floor."

Less than two minutes after they'd landed and Aladee retracted her wings, they heard Kady's key in the door. Exchanging relieved glances, Nevan and Aladee succumbed to laughter.

"Now *that* would have been a true *ta-da!* performance for sure!" Nevan said, making Aladee laugh harder.

"Hello? Nevan? Aladee? It's me!" Kady called loudly upon entering, keeping her head down, looking at the floor. "Hope I'm not interrupting anything."

Returning to the sofa, Nevan ran his hand through his hair, straightening it. "We're in here, Kady. And we're decent." Relieved, they held each other's hand. "I was just about to leave," he finished.

Kady sauntered into the family room, setting her purse on the coffee table. "That was one dynamite performance, Aladee. People will be talking about it for years."

"I'm glad it worked out well," Aladee said, with Nevan giving her a conspirator's smile.

"Red and I will pick you up at eight tomorrow morning," Nevan told Aladee. "We'll grab breakfast at Griffin's Café and plan our search before heading out to find Cupid. We should be done by the time the family arrives."

"That's when we tell them about my identity, right?" Nevan nodded. "I'll be ready at eight, but I worry about you and Red taking more time away from your businesses because of me."

"Tomorrow's Sunday," Nevan said. "The pub will be well-staffed, and Red said Edwina's feeling better, so she and Alfred can manage the flower shop while we're out searching."

Aladee was thankful. After what transpired on her walk from Lonan's chariot to the flower shop, she didn't relish searching for Cupid alone.

Chapter Twelve

Sunday

~<>~

"YOU'LL LOVE the Dutch baby pancake." Annalise jotted on her order pad. "All the Malone women do. It's big, puffy, and oven baked, served with fresh lemon wedges, real butter and powdered sugar." She licked her lips and Aladee automatically did the same.

"So tell me," Red addressed Aladee as Annalise left the large table reserved for the Malones, "how do we find Cupid? I don't suppose you have a map or a two-way radio or something like that."

Aladee trilled a sigh. "There *was* a map, but I left it behind. And one of my satchels was equipped with a pair of communication devices. They're like a technologically more advanced version of your handheld phones. However..." She dropped her gaze, sighing again.

"You lost them," Red surmised and Aladee nodded.

"As hard as I try, I just don't seem to fit in with the other students. They're so organized, studious and well-prepared...while I keep making foolish mistakes. I don't know why I'm so absentminded."

Nevan hated seeing Aladee so dejected.

"I'll do my best to follow your directions today so I don't cause any blunders. I'd hate to leave you with unpleasant memories of me after I've gone."

Nevan stilled at her words. He didn't want to think about her leaving. No more wings, no more flying. He gazed into her eyes, experiencing an inexplicable connection he'd never felt before. As if he'd known Aladee forever.

Sipping from his coffee, he shook the ridiculous notion from his head. Hell, it was just his over eager libido talking. How could he help feeling lustful after nearly having sex while floating just beneath the ceiling last night?

"There, there," Red soothed, patting Aladee's hand. "You're only human...well, sort of. Don't be so hard on yourself. Nevan and I love you just the way you are." Turning to Nevan, he gave a shrewd smile. "Don't we, Nevan?"

Nope. Nevan didn't toss the L-word around like empty peanut shells at a pub. There was no way his buttinski cousin was going to drag an undying pledge of love from his lips, especially after he'd known Aladee for only a day.

Taking the cue from Red, he patted Aladee's hand. "Aladee's a real doll."

Piercing a slice of the eggy pancake and putting it in her mouth, her eyelids drifted closed as tiny moans of satisfaction hummed in her throat. "Now I see why these are a Malone family favorite. Mmm, sublime." While sprinkling more powdered sugar on her pancake, a sign posted on the café's wall snagged Aladee's attention.

"Interesting." She pointed to it. "*You have two ears and one mouth so that you can listen twice as much as you speak.* My parents often reminded me of that when I was a young nymphet. It's a quote from Epictetus."

Digging into his spinach and cheddar omelet, Red looked up. "I don't recognize his name but I'm certainly familiar with his sentiment."

"Was this Epicure guy somebody on..." Nevan lowered his voice to a whisper, "Mount Olympus?"

"No, Epictetus lived in the first century," Aladee said. "I learned about him in my Stoicism philosophy class. He was born a Greek and later became a Roman slave. Eventually he was known as one of the Stoic philosophers. It was a school of philosophy founded in three-hundred-eight BC, based upon the teachings of Zeno of Citium."

"That's all Greek to me," Nevan joked before biting into a crispy strip of bacon.

Obviously his attempt at humor went right over Aladee's head because she replied, "No, I was speaking Americanized English. If I'd been speaking Greek, I would have said—" And, with a bright smile, the brainy nymph proceeded to repeat it all in both modern and ancient Greek.

Red and Nevan exchanged stupefied expressions. "Methinks we're in the midst of a true academic intellectual," Red told Nevan.

"Methinks youthinks right," Nevan agreeably teased.

"You may be absentminded," Red said, "but I'll bet you're every bit as sharp as your fellow classmates. Probably even smarter."

"Red's right," Nevan said. "That's some brainy stuff, Aladee. It's way over my head."

"Not really." She studied both the sign and Nevan. "It's only approximately forty-five-point-seventy-two centimeters, which translates to eighteen inches, above your current line of vision."

Chuckling, Nevan lifted his hands in surrender.

Hiking one shoulder in an elegant shrug, Aladee answered Red's observation. "It's true, Red, I'm exceptionally bright. Unfortunately, my lamentable daydreaming and easy distraction often overshadow my intelligence."

"Your Exodus quote—" Nevan began.

"Epictetus," Red corrected.

"Whatever." Nevan rolled his eyes. "Anyway, it reminds me that I've got a personal intellectual favorite quote. *You only go around once in life, so you've got to grab all the gusto you can.* Schlitz, 1970s." Folding his arms across his chest, Nevan sat back, snickering.

"Wise words." Aladee looked thoughtful. "I'm not familiar with that quotation or this Schlitz. Was he a philosopher?"

"Definitely," Nevan said with a playful smile.

"Hardly. It's from a decades-old beer commercial," Red said with distaste. "Beer trivia is about the extent of my cousin's cultural aptitude."

Aladee gazed at Nevan, a sweet smile lighting her features. "There's nothing wrong with beer. I like it. It's long been a favorite of the gods too."

She'd just added another gold star to her growing list of attributes as far as Nevan was concerned.

"May I have some of your money?" she asked.

"Sure." Nevan reached into his back pocket for his wallet. "How much do you need?"

"Enough to purchase a sizeable bag of the crusty bread rolls in that glass case," she pointed toward the café's entrance, "and enough of these to go along with them." She fingered the gold foil-wrapped butter pats on the small plate at the center of the table.

"Are you sure that'll be enough to tide you over until dinner?" Nevan kidded.

"Oh, they're not for me." Aladee missed his humor again, while confirming to Nevan he made a wise choice to forfeit his childhood dream of being a standup comic.

"Are you taking them to Cupid?" Nevan asked.

"No, Cupid might presume I was attempting to curry favor through devious means."

"She doesn't want him to think she's a suck-up," Red clarified, as if Nevan was a dimwit.

"Thanks, Einstein, I know what she meant. You want to take the bread rolls back to Olympus with you?"

"No, I want to give them to the people sitting on the streets here in Glassfloat Bay. They look so lost and forlorn. I saw many of them when I was looking for Cupid after Lonan dropped me off. It makes my heart sad to see them. And I feel guilty enjoying a sumptuous feast like this," she spread her hands over their table, "while I suspect they're hungry."

"You're talking about the homeless," Nevan said. "That's very thoughtful, Aladee. We'll buy as many rolls and pats of butter as you like. Keep in mind you'll still need to be cautious, okay? Just because somebody is homeless doesn't necessarily mean they're a nice or safe person."

"Nevan's right, Aladee," Red agreed.

"No need to worry." She nodded confidently. "I read the chapter entitled Street Smarts in my textbook."

"Good." Nevan forked a hunk of golden hash browns, remembering Aladee's reported encounter with the scumbag she'd kneed in the groin before she found Red's shop. "So how do we find Cupid?"

"Lonan said Cupid's headquarters was within walking distance from the park, so it can't be very far. I thought we'd traverse the surrounding area, asking if anyone knows of Cupid's whereabouts."

"Not a good idea." Nevan winced. "People will think we're nuts."

"These are Portland environs, Nevan," Red pointed out. "Kooks abound."

"True." Nevan shrugged. "Guess we don't have much choice. Without a map or address, we're pretty much in the dark. Damn, I hate asking for directions."

"This will be a perfect chance for you to get in touch with your inner—" Red cringed when he glimpsed Nevan's warning glare. "Sorry. Habit, I guess."

Nevan pulled up a walking map of the city on his phone. "We'll start here," he indicated their current location, "and work our way north a few blocks. Then we'll scour the area around the park, street by street, until we return to our starting point."

"Let's separate to save time," Red suggested. "I'll go this way," he pointed, "and you and Aladee can go that way."

"Okay, I just sent you the link to the map," Nevan told him.

"If we split up three ways we'll save even more time," Aladee offered. "I'll go down this street by myself, while you—"

"No!" the cousins chorused.

"It's better that you stick with one of us," Red said. "There's a big cycling event going on today, which means there'll be throngs of people. Too easy to get lost."

"Red's right. You'll stick with me." Nevan looked up to see his family entering the café. He waved, showing them where they were seated. Checking the time before pocketing his phone, he said, "We'll talk to them for half an hour, then head out. Red, let's text every thirty minutes to monitor our progress."

"Sounds good," Red agreed, "except once we tell them about Aladee I doubt the family will be finished grilling us in just half an hour." He and Nevan laughed together because Red was spot on. "If you find Cupid first, call me right away so I can give Aladee a big goodbye hug before she leaves."

"Yeah...sure..." Nevan realized at that moment he hoped Aladee would never find Cupid or her classmates.

~<>~

"I think Drake had the most questions," Aladee said as she and Nevan walked down the street.

"He always does." Nevan laughed. "The professor loves nothing more than doing endless research and learning new facts. Ask him anything, other than something sports related, and he'll have the answer. The guy's like a walking Google."

"Google?"

"Yeah, it's like...like a huge online information center."

"Ah," Aladee nodded, "so Drake is like a sage."

Nevan thought of the stuff in that bundle of tiny twigs Kady lit on fire, waving Thanksgiving-scented smoke around his pub and

Red's shop. Smudging, she'd called it. Somehow he didn't think Aladee was talking about that kind of sage.

"If you say so," he said. Unlike Drake, Nevan was content to avoid listening to explanations about stuff he had zero interest in. His mind was already littered enough with useless information.

"It's interesting that none of them seemed shocked when you told them about me," Aladee noted.

"They took it all in stride." Nevan wasn't surprised at his family's reaction—not after all the weird stuff they'd experienced over the past few years. "That's what happens when your family is surrounded with all sorts of woo-woo."

"Yes, I remember your description of *woo-woo*. Your family is wonderful, Nevan. Your mother said I can be an honorary Malone. Isn't that nice? I've missed being part of a family."

While walking for hours, they'd heard accounts of one possible Cupid sighting after another, as well as several guys claiming to be Cupid himself. It was hard keeping Aladee from being overly sympathetic and trusting when faced with a sea of crafty, or crazy, imposters.

"I saw Cupid a couple minutes ago," a spacey-looking guy with pink-tipped purple hair said. "He was buzzing around my head with his bow and arrow. *Zip, zap, boing.*"

The man of indeterminate age gestured dramatically as he spoke, the row of silver studs along his forearm catching Nevan's attention as they glinted in the early evening sunlight. They weren't part of a jacket...they were just embedded in his skin. Nevan couldn't help shuddering.

"Cupid was just zooming around, you know?"

"Yes, he often does that." Aladee nodded. "Did he share the location of his headquarters with you?" she asked eagerly, obviously taking the guy seriously.

"Yeah, he did." He bent down, giving Nevan a bird's-eye view as the guy's skin-tight leggings crept low enough to highlight his butt crack.

Pointing to a spot where the building's brick met the sidewalk, the guy said, "There. He's in a mousehole with tiny furniture. Whoa—he just flew by again." He grabbed at the air around his head. "See him?"

"Oh..." Realization finally setting in, Aladee's shoulders sagged and Nevan ached at her disappointed expression. "Thank you." Reaching into the paper bag, she dug out the last bread roll and butter pat. "This is for you. Please take care of yourself."

"Cool. Thanks." He unwrapped the butter, popped it in his mouth and swallowed. Then he clamped his teeth on the roll, devouring it as if he hadn't eaten in a week.

"What a nice young man," Aladee said as they headed down the street. "Perhaps a wee bit addled," she tapped her temple, "but quite personable."

"Addled, yeah, that's appropriate," Nevan said as his phone rang. "Nope, no luck, Red. You neither, huh?" He felt guilty for being relieved Aladee hadn't found Cupid yet. "We may as well knock off for dinner. We've been on our feet for hours. I'm starving and poor Aladee's got to be exhausted and hungry. Thai? Just a minute." He turned to her. "Is Thai food okay with you?"

"It will be a new experience," she answered with an affirmative nod. "I have yet to find a cuisine I don't enjoy."

"Meet you at Bangkok Crossing in about five minutes, Red." Nevan pocketed his phone. "I'm sorry you didn't have any luck finding Cupid today, Aladee," he lied. "Maybe you'll have better luck tomorrow."

"I hope so. I'm missing all the valuable lessons Cupid is teaching. I'll never be able to catch up with the class."

"Sure you will. You're a real smart cookie." When her mouth popped open, he winked. "Not literally." Draping his arm around her shoulder, he gave Aladee a buddy hug, when what he longed to do was pull her into an embrace and kiss her senseless.

"Will you be accompanying me tomorrow again?"

An image of the wide-eyed innocent, who thought she had street smarts, scampering about town and asking strange men if they knew where to find Cupid sent a jolt through Nevan.

"Yes." His mind raced as he mentally sorted out his appointments, responsibilities, and staff over the next couple of days. Damn, he owned the pub, didn't he? What better time for him to learn to let go and delegate? He had a good, dedicated, dependable crew, each capable of handling a variety of tasks. All it would take is a few calls.

"What's made you laugh?" Aladee smiled up at him.

"I was thinking about the reaction of my crew when I tell them I'm taking a few days off. They'll never believe it."

"Why not?"

"I'm sort of a workaholic," Nevan explained with a shrug. "No days off, no vacations."

"You must really enjoy your work."

"I do." Nevan knew how fortunate he was to work at a job he loved. "Until now, there's never really been any reason to take time off."

"Until me, you mean," Aladee noted, worrying her bottom lip.

Nevan watched her nibble, then drag the pouty lip between her teeth—a simple innocuous act. Even the most routine things about her were a turn-on.

"I feel bad taking you away from your pub work, Nevan. I don't want to keep Red from his flower shop either. You've both been so kind. I don't want to disrupt your lives any more than I already have."

"Too late. You've already turned my life upside down," Nevan admitted while tipping her chin with his knuckle. "But only in the best possible way." He bent to give her a quick kiss. "There's nothing I'd rather do than spend the day with you tomorrow and the day after."

"What about the nights?" She leaned against him. "We haven't tried our special flying feat yet." The anticipation in her eyes was crystal clear. "We could stay with each other for the next two nights in your apartment so we don't disturb Kady." Aladee rested her head on his chest, smoothing her fingers over his T-shirt.

Red flag. The nymph was getting attached.

Sure, he was up for some out of this world experimentation, but staying with a woman all night? Two nights in a row? That crossed the line for him—a definite rule breaker.

What if Aladee never found Cupid and was stuck here forever? He couldn't have her thinking they were a permanent item—that he had any intention of getting a ring stuck through his nose. No, after the newness wore off, he'd be on his way, ready for someone new. After a quick roll in the hay, or in the air, he'd bring Aladee back to Bekka House and he'd go back to his place. Alone.

Looking down at her, the same instant she gazed up into his eyes and smiled, he heard himself say, "Okay," astounded he hadn't choked on the word. "We'll spend the next two nights together at my place."

"That makes me so happy, Nevan," she cooed.

He'd lost it. No doubt about it. His brain had taken a hike, leaving *Little Nevan* to do all the thinking and talking for him.

"I'm sorry, what was that?" Aladee said, inclining her head toward the curb.

"I didn't say anything." Nevan hoped reading minds wasn't among her skills.

"Not you," Aladee told him, patting his arm. "I was talking to the flowers."

"To the..." Stuffing his hands in his jeans pockets, Nevan said, "Oh, sure. Of course. I do it all the time."

"Really? Oh, that's lovely, Nevan."

He watched Aladee squat, addressing the colorful array of flowers planted in the grassy area between the sidewalk and curb.

"Is that so?" she said to the apparently chatty blossoms. "You poor dears. Don't worry, I'll get you some right now." Rising to her feet, she was all pink-cheeked and clearly incensed. When she looked at Nevan, he realized it was the first time he'd seen that particular look in her eyes.

Planting her fists against her hips, she cocked her head to read the sign on the building. "What's a sports bar?"

"It's like a pub where they serve lots of beer and show sports on big TV screens. Something tells me you're not asking because you're in the mood for a beer or a ballgame."

"No, but they should have what's needed." Aladee moved past Nevan, opening the bar's door and entering the establishment with a purposeful strut that announced she was ready to rumble.

Belting out a resigned sigh, Nevan followed her, only to hear the interior erupt in wolf whistles and animated conversation as the curvaceous blonde approached the bar.

"Well, well, well," the bartender mused in a singsong voice, giving Aladee a onceover and slick smile. His eyes glued to her breasts, he asked, "What can I get for you, honey?" Nevan wasn't too happy with the way the guy ogled his nymph.

"Water, please," Aladee said. "Enough for thorough saturation."

"Spring or sparkling?" The bartender plucked two clear plastic bottles from a refrigerated area, plopping them on the counter in front of her.

Aladee touched each bottle and frowned. "Spring. But it must be room temperature. Cold water shocks the system."

"Lemme see what I got." He squatted, looking through his behind-the-bar inventory and coming up with two bottles of room temperature water. "One for each of you?" he said, acknowledging Nevan's presence for the first time.

"This isn't enough. They'll need much more. At least a full pail. They're terribly thirsty. Some of them are close to death."

"Death? What? Who?" The bartender glanced around to see if he'd missed someone who came in with them. "What are you talking about?"

"The flowers."

He shifted his skewed glance to Nevan who threw up his hands in a don't-ask-me gesture.

"What flowers?" the guy asked, totally perplexed.

Chin elevated, Aladee asked, "Are you the owner of this sports bar?"

"Yeah, but—"

One fist balled against her hip while she pointed outside with her other hand, she went on, "And are those sweet, beautiful flowers out there not in your care?"

"Well yeah, but—"

"Can't you see they're in desperate need of water?" she asked, all righteous and fuming. "They said it's been unseasonably dry this summer and you never take care of them."

By this time, most eyes in the place were on the bartender, who looked none too happy about it. "*They told you?*" He slanted her a look that telegraphed he thought she was nuts. "Hey," he asked Nevan, while making a swirly motion at his temple, "has your girlfriend got a few screws loose?"

"All of my screws are firmly attached." Aladee bristled. "Also, since I am the one addressing you, I would appreciate it if you responded directly to me, rather than the man accompanying me."

Her diatribe brought a smile to Nevan's face. So his nymph was a feisty feminist too. Good for her!

Standing shoulders back and ramrod straight, Aladee drew the attention of every damn guy in the place. "I'm well versed in botany, sir. I was schooled at the academy on Olympus and count many flowers among my friends."

Nevan knew damn well Aladee sounded nutty, but he found himself caught up in an unfamiliar protective mode. He didn't like the fact that this guy was insulting his nymph.

"If I may?" Nevan asked Aladee with a curt bow. With an affirmative nod, she extended her hand toward the bartender. Turning to him, Nevan warned, "I wouldn't mess with her if I were you," just as the guy opened his mouth, no doubt to remark about Aladee having flowers as part of her social circle. "She's Glassfloat Bay's OFC."

The bartender scowled at him. "O...F...what"

"OFC. Official Flower Caretaker," Nevan explained, without a clue as to where the hell that had come from. "She's been issuing citations all day. At three hundred bucks a pop."

"For not watering flowers?" the burly bartender practically squeaked.

"Yup."

"No shit." He glanced from Nevan to Aladee. "Hey, ma'am, I was just about to go out and water them before you came in," He filled a large pitcher with tap water.

"Is the water in the bottles of a better quality?" Aladee asked. "If it is, I want you to use that instead. It's the least you can do after neglecting and mistreating those blooms and their fragile root systems."

His hands held up in surrender, the bartender assured, "No problem." He called to one of his crew, telling him to watch the bar while he watered the flowers. The assistant snickered and the bartender shot him a narrow-eyed glare that squelched the snicker in midstream.

"See that you keep it up," Nevan said, holding the door open for the guy whose arms were full of bottled water. "The OFC will be making regular rounds."

"Will do, buddy."

"You're very welcome," Aladee said to the flowers after they'd been watered. "He promised to be more attentive from now on."

As they headed down the street, she looped her arm through Nevan's. "Thank you. I'm so impressed with the way you put that flower abuser in his place. Does Glassfloat Bay actually have an Official Flower Caretaker? Or did you make it up, the same way I made up my performance last night?" Her lip quirked into a smile.

"Guilty as charged," he answered.

"It's okay, you can tell me," Aladee said. "Did Bekka whisper the idea in your ear?"

Laughing, Nevan told her, "Nope, I pulled that idea right out of my a— Um, I mean out of thin air."

"Brilliant. Perhaps you should suggest the development of such an important position to the city of Glassfloat Bay's officials."

"I'll look into it," he told Aladee, who gave him a gratified smile. He could imagine the reception he'd get with that suggestion. On the other hand, in green-friendly Glassfloat Bay, it just might fly. "So you can really communicate with flowers?"

"I'm a nymph, Nevan," she said, as if that explained it all. And Nevan guessed that it did.

He liked that she was bighearted, brainy, and bold enough to stand up for her beliefs. With her environmentalist tree-hugger spirit, she'd fit right in with Oregon's ecologically concerned population.

"How do they feel about being picked?" he asked, imagining flowers with expressive horror-stricken cartoon-like faces screaming *Help me, help meeeee!* in itty-bitty voices as eager, plucking fingers approached.

"They consider it an honor," Aladee explained, surprising him. "Providing pleasure and happiness through their beauty, fragrance and delicate taste is their primary purpose, their life's mission. Unlike a withering death from lack of water or sunlight, being picked and admired at their peak brings flowers infinite joy and fulfillment."

"I'll never think of picking daisies the same way again." Nevan snaked his arm around her waist, slipping his hand into the back pocket of her jeans. She let out a delighted hum at the familiarity.

He'd never thought he'd be turned on by a flower activist. She sure as hell didn't resemble any Earth Mother types he'd encountered. Aladee was a fascinating anomaly, unlike any other woman he'd known.

A moment later, he yanked open the door of Bangkok Crossing, stepping aside for Aladee to enter. She gave an enthusiastic wave when she spotted Red sitting at one of the tables. Nevan decided he needed to incinerate all those cloying commitment-related thoughts about Aladee from his brain with some spicy hot Thai food.

"That was an awfully long five minutes," Red complained. "Where were you—or shouldn't I ask?" He snickered.

"Get your mind out of the gutter," Nevan said. "We got involved in a serious case of flower abuse."

Red's eyebrows shot up with interest.

"Your heart would break if you saw those poor, neglected little posies," Aladee told Red, her expression full of compassion.

"Aladee gave the owner of Packy's Sports Bar what for."

"I did." Aladee nodded. "Thanks to Nevan's quick thinking, the situation has been rectified."

"Nevan's quick thinking? Well, I *am* impressed. You're clearly a good influence on my cousin, Aladee."

Halfway through the meal, with alarming notions of relationship commitment coloring his thoughts, Nevan blotted blinding sweat from his face. He'd asked for the *Gaeng Ped Dang* hot and he sure as hell got it that way. The inferno in his mouth prevented him from distinguishing between sweet basil leaves, eggplant, bamboo shoots, bell peppers, or pork swimming in the red curry sauce.

Water made it worse, rice appeased the burn somewhat, and the Thai beer felt like liquid fire baptizing his gullet.

"Since when did you become such an aficionado of hot and spicy?" Red swallowed a mouthful of *Pad Thai* noodles. Nevan's glance slid to Aladee for the briefest instant, which was long enough for Red to decipher what was going on. He held up his hand. "I withdraw the question." Snickering, he plainly enjoyed Nevan's torment.

Aladee murmured her pleasure at the peanutty sweetness of her *Panang* curry with chicken. "Mmm, exquisite cuisine." She helped herself to a forkful of Red's noodles at his urging. "Both strong and delicate with floral undertones, a fine nuance of herbs and spices. I wish I could stay long enough to sample more of Earth's cuisine."

"You have an educated palate," Red observed.

"I just love good food." Aladee shrugged. "It's one of life's greatest enjoyments, along with carnal pleasures."

"Indeed," Red agreed, as Nevan blotted his forehead like a wild man.

"Do you have someone special in your life, Red? A lover, perhaps?" Aladee asked matter-of-factly.

"No. I'm still waiting for Mr. Right to come along."

"With all you have to offer, I'm surprised you haven't found someone."

"Thank you. Maybe you could arrange a love match for me with your bow and arrow," Red playfully suggested.

"I believe Lonan would find you most appealing." Aladee scooped some curry into her mouth and licked her lips. "Without the need of my bow and arrow."

Red's eyebrow lifted. "Lonan's gay?"

"Yes. He reminds me of you and Nevan, except Lonan is blond with blue eyes. He's very handsome with a muscular body."

Struggling to take in a full breath because of the spicy food, Nevan's eyes bugged at her nonchalant comparison of him to two gay men.

"You and Lonan share a flair for design, an interest in the arts, and excellent fashion sense. It is a pity you and Lonan are from different worlds. I can visualize the two of you walking arm in arm, then sitting beneath a golden apple tree, with one of you reading poetry aloud as the other strums soft music on a lyre."

"Heaven," Red said, closing his eyes. "Maybe I'll stow away on the chariot." He deposited a forkful of noodles and shrimp on his tongue.

"I doubt that would be possible," Aladee answered, unaware Red was joking.

"How old is Lonan? Older than me, I hope. It's getting harder to attract the young ones now that I'm practically over the hill." Red leaned in close, cupping his hand at his mouth. "I'm thirty-seven...closing in on forty fast," he whispered.

"My goodness, Red," Aladee dabbed her mouth with the napkin as she chuckled, "you're just a boy. Lonan turned nine-hundred-seventy on his last birthday."

Red and Nevan looked aghast.

"You're not serious," Nevan said. "Nobody lives that long."

"Quite serious. Unlike me, Lonan is immortal."

"What do you mean, unlike you? Didn't you say you were three-hundred something?" Nevan asked.

"Three hundred fifty," she readily offered, unlike the average age-phobic Earth woman.

"That sounds pretty immortal to me," Nevan noted. It also sounded insane.

"Nymphs have a long lifespan. At least a few thousand years."

Nevan struggled to mentally sort all this. It sounded preposterous, but then, so did the notion of wings sprouting out of a woman's back. "So Lonan isn't a nymph?"

Aladee giggled at his question. "No, he's a god."

"A god! That's it, Nevan. I'm packing my bags." Red's expression lit with a smile. "I'll send you a postcard from Olympus."

"If I were a man," Aladee covered Red's hand with hers, gifting him with a tender smile, "or a god, I would surely court you. Aside from your physical beauty, you are most endearing, with a good heart."

"Well, thank you, Aladee. If you were a man, I'd welcome the attention from someone as refreshing and forthright as you."

"You two are making me gag," Nevan offered with a huff.

"If anything's making you gag, it's that glut of peppers in your food. There's no need for the envy monster to surface. My only interest in your delightful nymph is camaraderie."

"I'm not envious, and she's not *my* nymph," Nevan spat, immediately regretting it when he caught the look of pained surprise in Aladee's eyes. He was a bona fide jackass. "I didn't mean to sound so harsh, Aladee. I just meant you're only here with us temporarily."

"It's all right, Nevan. I understand." Her smile was wistful. "Regardless of what you may think, I am indeed *your* nymph. Your Aladee. However, I haven't been here long enough yet for you to realize that I'm your perfect love match. Perhaps you'll come to the realization before I depart Tuesday morning."

Nevan cocked his head, a prickly feeling that had nothing to do with the hot peppers jogging up his spine. "I don't understand. What do you mean, love match?"

"Us, Nevan. Being fated lovers," Aladee explained. "Fate can be cruel. Just because soul mates find each other doesn't necessarily mean the lovers are destined to spend their lives together. There are often extenuating circumstances, like ours. Through a twist of fate we've found each other, only to lose each other in a fleeting moment of time."

She was talking about leaving again, bringing up all the stuff Nevan didn't want to think about, like love and spending lifetimes together. Why did women always feel the need to attach all their hopes and dreams to what should simply be a mutually satisfying romp between the sheets?

She thought they were soul mates. What the hell could he possibly say to her now that wouldn't make him come across like a selfish, coldhearted bastard?

"Aladee, you're a special woman. Nymph," Nevan corrected when she opened her mouth to speak. "We've shared some special times. The key to making the most of our remaining time together is to forget about goodbyes and enjoy each other fully while we can."

"I agree," Aladee said. "Creating memories to last a lifetime." Lifting Nevan's hand to her cheek, she held it there a moment. "While leave-taking will be sad, we'll always carry a part of each other in a special corner of our hearts."

Nodding, Nevan hoped the subject wouldn't come up again while she was still here. It's not that he was eager to see her go...there just wasn't room in his life for a winged nymph with a fierce passion for botany, no matter how sweet and sexy she was.

Nevan and Aladee turned toward Red in surprise when they heard him blow his nose with a honk.

"My apologies." He wiped his nose and eyes with a tissue. "It's just so tragic. Like Tristan and Isolde, without the king or the love triangle, and without the terrible deaths at the end, and without—"

"Red."

He looked up at Nevan. "Hmm?"

"We get the idea. Look, there's nothing tragic about me and Aladee. We're having fun together, right, Aladee?"

"We are," she answered, quickly mopping a tear from her cheek and putting on a brave smile.

Groaning a sigh, Nevan was happy he hadn't added, *but all good things must come to an end.*

"Sorry," Aladee sniffed, "I was just thinking about the opera Red mentioned."

"It sounds like a real downer," Nevan said.

"The beautiful but tragic legend of Tristan and Isolde takes place during the Earth's Middle Ages," Aladee explained, "when knighthood and the chivalric code prevailed. It made me weepy because I can so easily imagine you as a chivalrous knight, Nevan."

"Hardly," Nevan and Red chorused, and Nevan gave his cousin a narrow-eyed glare.

"Let's change the subject," Nevan suggested, "and talk about happy stuff like football, baseball, or video games."

Aladee brightened. "Can we talk about hot fudge sundaes?"

"Good idea!" Nevan was happy to dive in to any subject other than soul mates and tragic love affairs. "Ice cream it is."

"Love it," Red said. "As long as it's premium. I don't like the cheap stuff with all the air pumped into it."

"As long as it's cold and sweet, I don't care," Nevan said. "I like the ice cream cones from the grocery store that are dipped in chocolate and nuts."

"They'll do in an emergency," Red agreed. "Ice cream is comfort food here on Earth," he explained to Aladee. "Scientific studies have proven eating ice cream releases positive chemicals in the brain that create feelings of calm and happiness, even euphoria."

"That makes it both medicine and a health food." Nevan grinned.

"It definitely makes me euphoric," Aladee agreed. "Especially with the fudge sauce and whipped cream. I'd love to have another before I go home so I can study the components and write everything down. Perhaps I could make them for myself."

"I'm sure Aunt Astrid or one of Nevan's sisters has a recipe," Red said.

"Perfect! Each time I eat a hot fudge sundae," Aladee's voice caught and her eyes grew glassy with unshed tears, "I'll think of you both, along with the wonderful Malone family, and the amazing time I had with you dear people here on Earth."

A muffled snort sounded in Red's throat. Nevan looked over to see his cousin's chin tremble as he started sniffling again.

Damn.

Heaving a resigned sigh, Nevan rose from his seat. "Come on, let's go get some ice cream and stir up a little euphoria."

Chapter Thirteen

~<>~

"IT'S TOO BAD Red wasn't able to join us for ice cream." Aladee glanced around with wonder. She'd never been in a supermarket before. So many foods readily available to the masses all in one location. It was extraordinary.

"I tease and gripe about Red but he's a good guy," Nevan said. "I think he made himself scarce to give us time alone."

"You're both good guys." Aladee gave Nevan a warm smile. Never had she spent so much time with one being before and felt so content.

With the abrupt rush of icy air as someone opened a glass door, her eyes widened and her mouth morphed into a big O. "What's that sudden coldness?" she gasped, confused yet delighted.

Nevan chuckled. She noticed he engaged in that sort of light partial laughter often, and Aladee liked it. The creases at the outside corners of his eyes told her he's a man who laughs easily. That was an important component in finding her love match. The thought made her sigh. Not one to usually question the wisdom of the gods, she found it terribly sad and unfair to finally connect with her soul mate, only to lose him so soon.

"It's the freezer section," Nevan explained, returning her thoughts to the moment. "This is where they keep the ice cream and other frozen foods."

"May I open a door?"

"Knock yourself out." Nevan gestured to a freezer.

Studying his expression, and becoming more familiar with his way of speaking, she decided he wasn't being literal—it was just another odd scrap of Earth vernacular. Extending an arm inside the freezer compartment, she watched as goose bumps arose. Rubbing her arms briskly, she marveled at the immense variety of cartons labeled *ice cream.*

"What a big assortment." The flavor names were interesting and unfamiliar.

"Pick out whatever sounds good and we'll make our own sundaes," Nevan told her. "We'll get a jar of chocolate fudge, some whipped cream, chopped nuts, and maraschino cherries."

"We can make sundaes ourselves? Tonight?" Aladee asked, delighted at the thought.

"In my apartment."

"Ah yes, the skeleton apartment." When he looked baffled, she thought for a moment, trying to recall his words. "Bare bones!" She laughed.

"It may be bare bones but there's plenty of space to fly around, and a big bed for after we exhaust ourselves from all that sexy air dancing we're going to do."

With a mischievous smile, she asked, "Will we make love first, or create our sundaes and eat them before we're intimate?"

"We're going to kill two birds with one stone," Nevan informed Aladee, to her horror.

She clasped his forearm, squeezing it. "Oh no, Nevan. I could never throw stones at a bird. Please, we mustn't do such a terrible thing. There must be another form of foreplay we can indulge in instead."

"Relax, sweetheart. It's just a saying. It means we're going to do both things at the same time."

"But...won't that be very messy?" Aladee tried to imagine balancing her bowl of ice cream as they commenced with sexual activity.

"Very," Nevan said with a wicked gleam in his eye. Grabbing a package from the freezer, he said, "This one's for Buster. It's healthier and safer for dogs than regular ice cream. He loves it. And," his eyebrows danced, "it'll keep him busy while we're...occupied."

"You really love Buster, don't you?"

"Yeah," his dark eyes brightened, "I don't know what I'd do without him. He's my best buddy. My pal. When I come home after being out, even for a short while, he greets me like he hasn't seen me in months. I never thought I was a dog person until Buster came into my life."

"Do you know anything about his previous owners, or Buster's past?"

Nevan plucked one item after another from shelves and cold cases, adding them to the shopping cart.

"Nothing, other than he was badly mistreated. The vet estimates Buster was about two years old when I found him. He's a mutt. The vet said probably part golden retriever and part German shepherd."

"He's part collie too."

Nevan whipped his head toward her in surprise. "What makes you say that?"

"Buster told me."

"Wow...that's crazy that you can communicate with him like that. I always suspected he might be part collie, but the vet didn't think so."

Aladee enjoyed seeing how animated Nevan became when talking about his rescue dog. "Buster said the time he's spent with you has been the best and happiest in his life. You're his entire world, Nevan. He'd give up his life for you."

Nevan opened his mouth and closed it. With his eyes glistening, he turned away, giving his eyes a quick wipe with his fingers. Pushing the cart along again, a few feet in front of Aladee now, he focused on selecting more foodstuffs. She could tell he was trying to conceal his emotions, his soul-deep affection and devotion for this dear animal he'd saved, nurtured, and loved.

By the time they stood in the checkout line, Nevan was in full control of his emotions again, back to making the silly, habitually unfunny jokes he enjoyed telling. His teasing and trite humor were quite endearing—rather like a mischievous little boy. Although, Aladee noticed it was no little boy eyeing her now. Nevan's alpha side looked at her as if he were a starving man and she were a banquet.

~<>~

Aladee and Nevan held each other close as they slowly descended after learning firsthand exactly what was and wasn't physically possible during airborne sexual union.

As far as Aladee was concerned, she and Nevan hadn't merely had sex, they'd made love. There was a distinct difference. She'd imagined joining with this mortal would be textbook perfect lovemaking but it went beyond anything she'd read in a book. Her body, her entire being, reacted in ways she'd never dreamed possible. While her textbooks were detailed and well-written, they failed to accurately convey the magic of lovemaking.

The bliss and beauty, the symmetry, the profound sensual connection, and soul-deep satisfaction were...they were... She had no words. What she'd experienced with Nevan was inexplicable.

Turning her gaze on him as he stood before her now, completely unclothed, Aladee's wings retracted and she took time to appraise his body. She'd been too eager and impatient before they'd made love to give her investigation of his physicality much time.

"By gods, Nevan, you have the fine-honed physique of an Olympian athlete."

"Thanks. I work out a lot." Puffing out his chest with pride, he added, "I guess all those tedious hours of pumping iron paid off." Bending both arms, he made his biceps jump. "It helps reduce stress."

"Never have I joined with a being as handsomely put together as you." Aladee's voice was so soft it was almost a whisper. "What a remarkable experience."

"Well that just might be the best damned thing anyone's ever said to me."

She watched a shaft of lamplight illuminating one side of his handsome face as he spoke, diffusing as it traveled down his neck, shoulder and chest, imparting a soft glow down the length of his body.

"And you, Aladee, are perfection. You may be a nymph but you look like an angel sent from Heaven...with the power to turn my nice clean thoughts dirty and devilish, just by looking at you." Nevan cupped her face, holding her in place for a long moment, looking into her eyes in such a way that Aladee felt a mighty twinge at the seat of her soul.

She'd studied that look, knew it well, though she'd never seen it directed at her before. It was the look of love. Seeing it on Nevan's face when he gazed at her brought tears to her eyes.

Wrapping her arms around his waist, Aladee allowed her wings to open again. An instant later they were floating once more in an effortless lift from the floor of his bedroom.

"I still can't believe all we're able to do while in the air," he said as they rotated slowly. "I figured it would be amazing, but it's way beyond that." Nevan captured her lips in a kiss so soft, sweet and tender, it spoke further of love without the need for mere words.

"Aladee, I-I—"

Gazing deep into his eyes, she knew Nevan couldn't yet bring himself to voice the words...couldn't say *I love you*. His heart and soul knew, but his conscious mind fought against the knowledge. Aladee understood, not only because she'd studied the chapters on the male psyche, but because she'd come to know and understand Nevan well during their brief time together. It wasn't in his nature to commit to one woman. Yet.

Perhaps before she left she might hear those words spill from his lips. She knew he felt the sensations deep inside. That would have to be enough for her.

"I think you're wonderful," Nevan said instead of telling her he loved her.

Aladee shifted, taking them in a different direction around the room. It wasn't necessary to say she loved him because he already knew it deep inside. The words would only hang in the air as an awkward admission for someone who wasn't ready to hear them or utter them in return.

"After what we just shared," she said instead, "I've decided you're a perfect love machine."

"Love machine?" She nodded and he grinned. "Good...I like that."

"It's from a story I read, or maybe a film I watched. Lonan teaches us to be creative about things of a sexual nature. So in preparation for our first lovemaking session, I've been trying to remember as many imaginative synonyms for your manroot as possible."

"My *what*?" Nevan erupted with startled laughter.

"Your big salami."

"Oh, jeez. You're killing me." Still laughing, he wiped his eyes.

"If sausage references aren't to your liking there's also schlong, dipstick, joystick, wiener...oops sorry, that's another meat reference." She shrugged and continued, "Rocket, pecker, jutting spear, and hot throbbing organ." She counted the terms off on her fingers. "Are any of those more preferable than big salami?"

Looking down at himself as they continued floating in the air, Nevan noted, "By all rights, I should be shrunk down to the size of a peanut after laughing so hard but, damn if you and your silly synonyms don't have my throbbing joystick jutting." His laughter ceased when he felt her fingers smoothing over his manroot. The last vestiges of his chuckle morphed into a long low groan.

"When I think of you in the future, Aladee," he hugged her to his chest, cradling her in his arms as they twirled slowly, "this is what I'll picture. You, gloriously naked, with your silky, iridescent wings spread wide." His fingers gently fluttered across her wings. "Each time the light hits them I see a whole new range of colors. Every part of you is so beautiful, Aladee."

"You will remember my nakedness, Nevan, but not the wings," she murmured against his ear.

"Are you kidding? How could I ever forget them, and all the fun we've had flying around this room, enjoying sex right side up, upside down, and even sideways. Nope, not forgetting that anytime soon. I guarantee it."

She felt the deep rumble of his laughter vibrate through her body. "Once I find Cupid, when I rendezvous with the chariot that takes me home, your memory of me will be altered. You'll recall that you met a woman and we enjoyed each other's company, including having sex, but you'll have no memory of my wings, or me being a nymph. You won't remember our conversations about Cupid, chariots, Olympus, or anything related."

Nevan clasped her arms just beneath her shoulders, his gaze narrowing as he looked deep into her eyes. "I don't understand. What are you talking about?"

"It's one of the first rules we're taught." She brought them to the floor and retracted her wings, aware that the more often she used her wings, the more control she had over them. "While many mortals have known otherworldly beings, all recollection of what you refer

"It's okay...well, not *okay*, but I'm glad you told me about the memory zapping. It's not your fault." His eyes locked on hers. "It's just that I never want to forget you, or what's happened since you arrived. Because I..." Again, he paused at the moment most awkward and uncomfortable for him. "Because you're the most special woman I've ever known...or probably ever will know."

The way he looked at her, the soul-deep expression in his eyes, the sadness combined with the love he couldn't admit to himself nearly had Aladee giving in to the avalanche of tears threatening to spill. She had no idea where her self-control came from at that moment, but she somehow held her flood of emotions in check.

An instant later, she knew, and silently thanked dear Bekka for once again coming to her aid—and Nevan's. As added confirmation, Buster stared at a spot on the ceiling, tilting his head and looking for all the world like he was smiling.

Chapter Fourteen

Monday

~<>~

"WHY IS ALFRED crying?" Aladee whispered to Red as she cuddled his cat in her arms. Nevan had brought Buster with them today and Aladee had to laugh at the growling, hissing behavior of the pets. They seemed to have a love-hate relationship...similar to Nevan and Red. It was clear that Buster and Cupid cared for each other, but they were as different as night from day, which had them getting annoyed with each other easily.

"Alfred's always crying about something or other." Nevan sneered. "The sky is blue, Alfred. *Boo-hoo.* The grass is green, Alfred. *Boo-hoo.*" He gave a dismissive wave.

"Bad breakup," Red replied, ignoring his cousin's snide remark. "Alfred and Leonard were together for two years. Last night, Alfred got home to find Leonard gone. No note, nothing. I'm sorry to let you down, Aladee, but I need to stay here at the shop until Alfred can compose himself enough to interact with customers."

"I understand." Aladee smoothed her hand over Red's shoulder. "Nevan will contact you if we find Cupid so you can come say goodbye." She held the cat out to Red who took it in his arms, whispering babytalk as he brought Cupid to his pink-fenced castle area.

"Yeah, and get your brain freeze," Nevan added with a roll of the eyes. Aladee shot him a wounded, surprised look. Damn. Nevan promised her he wouldn't tell Red about the memory zapping thing. He shrugged an apology.

"You've been in a shitty mood all morning, Nev," Red said. "And now you're jabbering nonsense. If I didn't know better, I'd say you had PMS."

"Ha-ha, very funny."

Arms crossed over his chest, Red eyed him with that *I-can-see-right-through-you* look of his. Nevan hated that look. It meant Red was getting ready to probe with a list of touchy-feely questions.

"You're suffering from pre-separation anxiety, aren't you?"

"Pre what?" Nevan coughed a laugh. "Red, that is such bullshit."

"You may as well admit it, Nevan. It's written all over you." Buster offered a soft bark that seemed to indicate his agreement with Red.

"Mind your own beeswax, Red," Nevan warned. "You too, Buster. I don't have time to play twenty questions with you. I've got to help Aladee find Cu—" Nevan hesitated, glancing first at Alfred who, although still sobbing, clearly had his ears perked, and then at the couple of customers in the shop. "To find her *teacher*," he finished. "Come on, Aladee." Nevan clasped her arm while giving Buster's leash a tug.

"He doesn't mean to be so harsh, Red," Aladee said, stroking Nevan's arm. "He's having a difficult time."

Nevan hissed an exasperated sigh. "I am *not* having a difficult time with anything," he protested, well aware it was a lie. "I'm just tired. Can't a guy just be tired?"

"It's no wonder after the amazing intimacy we shared last night," Aladee said, only to have Nevan shush her.

"Ahhh, I see." There was a twinkle in Red's eye. "Get yourself a strong cup of coffee, Nev, so you're not a bear to poor Aladee on her last day here with us."

Last day here... The words grated across Nevan's mind like fingernails on a chalkboard. Why was the idea of her leaving so difficult? After all, he was the one who usually initiated the end of an affair, thoroughly enjoying the return of his freedom when the woman was out of the picture. But Aladee was different. Special. She was—

Steeling his expression, he stiffened, shoving all sappy thoughts of Aladee from his mind as he hauled her and Buster to the door of Red's shop. Dammit, he'd never been a fool over a woman before, and he wasn't about to start now.

"I thought we'd never get out of there," he said as soon as they exited Cupid's Headquarters, heading in the opposite direction they'd taken yesterday.

"It's okay, Nevan. I understand."

"Understand what?" He set a brisk pace pulling Buster along as the dog paused to sniff everything along the way.

Yanking on his shirt sleeve, Aladee pulled him to a stop. Caressing his jaw and giving him an angelic smile he didn't deserve, she said, "I understand you're upset because I'm leaving soon."

Shit. Was there some neon sign flashing *I'm a sap* over his head or something? "Look, I'm not upset, Aladee. It's too bad our time together is ending but—" Buster chose that moment to sit on the sidewalk, look up at Nevan and whimper. "Knock it off, Buster." Rolling his eyes skyward, Nevan let out a half-growl, half-sigh. "As I was saying, we had fun, right? And some really hot sex. What more could we ask for?"

Winking, he chucked her chin with his knuckle and resumed walking. "Besides, we'll probably see each other again in the future." Keeping pace at his side, Buster whimpered again. What the hell? Since when did his mutt turn into *Buster the Amazing Psychic Dog*?

"No." Nearly running to keep up with his long strides, Aladee said, "Once I leave Earth, I won't be permitted to interact with you again on future visits. It would be too painful for both of us. I must allow you to get on with your life and find someone else."

Nevan was half tempted to slap his hands over his ears singing *la-la-la* the way kids do when they don't want to listen.

Last night's sex was amazing. After Buster enjoyed his special ice cream treat, Aladee gave him the new bone and toy they'd bought for him. Bringing a tray containing their ingredients, she and Nevan headed for the bedroom, closing the door behind them. Buster never let out a peep.

Getting on the bed naked, as Nevan suggested, Aladee propped up on her elbows, watching his preparations.

"You forgot the bowls and spoons," she said helpfully.

Nevan gave her a sly smile. "We don't need any bowls or spoons." His eyebrows jiggled playfully as he picked up a can of whipped cream and shook it.

And that's when Aladee finally understood.

"Oh, Nevan, you're brilliant! A genius. You mean for us to—" he quieted her by spraying ringlets of whipped cream all over her, centering a maraschino cherry in each ring.

"But what about the—" Aladee started, only to suck in a gasp as Nevan plopped a spoonful of ice cream onto her warm belly and a dab of fudge sauce on top. "Oh!" He enjoyed watching her delightful expression shift as the icy sensation mixed with the heat of his tongue as he licked it all up.

She had fun painstakingly creating mini hot fudge sundaes on Nevan's belly, then swooping her tongue, licking and nibbling her way to his bare skin. The two of them may have indulged in additional licking and nibbling that wasn't ice cream related. The experience couldn't have been tastier or sexier. The night was capped off with a final, perfect round of in-flight lovemaking.

And now, this morning, she had to go spoil everything with talk about them never seeing each other again...and Nevan finding somebody else.

"Hey, cheer up." He heard the forced bravado in his voice. "We've got all night tonight. You, me, those wings of yours, plus more ice cream sundae fixings. We'll have a great time, Aladee."

"Not if I find Cupid and my classmates today," Aladee reminded him. "Once I locate them, we must say goodbye, Nevan. Forever."

Nevan saw her chin tremble, making him want to grab her tight, whispering in her ear that everything would be all right and they'd be together forever. *Forever?* Aw, man...he was losing it. Stuffing his hands in his pockets, he kept walking.

A sideways glance revealed a fat tear coursing down her cheek.

"Leaving you will be the hardest thing I've ever had to do. I've come to care deeply for you, Nevan."

Her words felt like a stomach punch where the aftereffects just kept on churning deep inside. Maybe it hurt so much because she was voicing the same feelings he had.

Feelings?

Damn, there was that word again. Red's favorite word. Nevan suddenly found himself crossing into new territory. He didn't like it in Touchy-Feely Land one single bit.

Slowing his pace, he smoothed his thumb across Aladee's cheek, wiping away her tear. Touching her was a big mistake, opening the floodgates of his emotions. He might never see her again. Never hold her close. Never experience that firestorm of ecstasy in her eyes at the moment he brought her to the peak—at the moment her wings spread and she sang out in joy with those strangely beautiful notes of hers.

The realization struck deep in his gut, like a hot knife twisting away at wax.

Words escaped him as Aladee took a deep breath, swiping the tears from her eyes. Whimpering again, Buster licked her shin before looking up at her adoringly.

"Sorry. I'm better now." She offered a bright smile—a counterfeit smile that didn't reach her eyes. "I didn't mean to get overemotional. I must be overtired."

Nevan knew he should say something back to her, telling her he cared for her too, but he didn't speak. He just kept walking alongside her like a big dumb cluck, because if he opened his mouth, he knew he'd say something stupid. Something he'd regret later, like telling Aladee he wanted her to stay with him. Always.

That was just plain insane. He'd arranged his bachelor life perfectly. No ties, no sticky relationships. Just plenty of casual fun with lots of different women—none of whom he'd ever slept with all night, besides Aladee...who looked amazingly enticing first thing in the morning.

He had a rule about sleepovers. No waking up in the morning with some babe at his side, no matter how hot she might be. It made things too messy. They'd start getting needy and clingy—getting ideas about love, marriage, babies, houses with white picket fences, and all that happily ever after crap.

Free and clear, that's the life Nevan wanted. Hell, he wasn't even forty yet. Maybe he'd settle down when he was sixty. But now? Uh-uh. No way. No messy romantic entanglements for him. He was perfectly satisfied with his best buddy, Buster, at his side. That's all he needed.

So why did his insides feel like they were being jabbed with a red-hot poker?

He'd only known Aladee a couple of amazing days and spectacular nights, but there was something special, something unfathomable about her. He glanced at her, walking alongside him with a bounce to her step as she scouted the area, hoping to find Cupid. Buster dutifully strode along, presumably doing his best to sniff out Cupid—the Valentine guy, not the cat.

Catching him gazing at her, she held out her hand. Extracting his hand from his pocket, he took her hand. Her smile was immediate. Gently swinging their arms as they walked, she hummed a buoyant tune, looking at ease.

Why that simple act of togetherness made him feel so satisfied he had no idea, but it did.

"The weather's perfect for our search today." Taking in a deep sniff, she said, "I love the smell of the breeze coming in from the ocean, don't you? The sky is blue with fluffy white clouds, the sun is smiling on us, the flowers are blooming, and it seems everyone is outdoors enjoying life. What an ideal day in Glassfloat Bay."

"Yeah, it's a nice day." Nevan hadn't even noticed. His only interest was Aladee.

She was all in blue today, wearing an outfit Red selected for her. The silky blouse matched the deep blue of her eyes, while her cropped jeans hugged her curves to perfection. It was a casual outfit, nothing particularly sexy or provocative about it—except on Aladee. She looked sexier in that getup than most women did wearing something purposely seductive.

It was like Aladee had become a part of him somehow. If she disappeared from his life, he feared a portion of his soul would be ripped out and the gaping hole might never heal. Scowling at the thought, he told himself that was just more of Red's touchy-feely talk rubbing off on him.

It wasn't possible to fall in love with someone you'd known just a couple of days. He'd heard his sisters complain, saying exactly that after reading some romance novel, or watching a romance movie. They insisted love at first sight never happened in real life. It was too farfetched. Preposterous. Ridiculous. Although...now that he thought about it, his sisters had changed their minds after they, themselves, fell in love almost instantly.

Love? Did that word really just flit across his mind—several times—as if it was a word he tossed around every day? He had to get a grip. A few rounds of in-flight sex and he was thinking like a guy ready to make a commitment.

The sooner they could locate Cupid and Aladee's classmates, the better. A quick hug, a chaste so long peck on the lips, a smiley *adios* and he'd be outta there, on his way back to the perfect bachelor's existence he'd created for himself. The more he thought about it, Nevan decided zapping his memories was for the best.

"Oh dear gods, did you see that?"

Aladee's voice snapped Nevan out of his reverie. "What?" He looked around, not seeing anything out of the ordinary. "Did you see Cupid or one of your classmates?"

"No..." she said absently. "Excuse me for a moment, Nevan."

Before he had a chance to say anything, Aladee disengaged her hand from his and hurried to the bus stop. She spoke to a guy in a suit who was too damned good looking for Nevan's comfort. *What the hell?* was the first thing crossing Nevan's mind. And the second.

Buster looked up at him, huffing a soft bark. "Yeah, Buster, I want to know what's going on too." Reaching Aladee, Nevan slipped a territorial arm around her waist, asking what was happening. As she spoke to the stranger, she raised her hand like a crossing guard in answer to Nevan's question. That, along with a shushing sound, was all she offered.

"Well, *that* was real reassuring," Nevan grumbled to Buster, who offered a look of agreement.

"Yes, right there," Aladee said to the thirty-ish man. "She's the one dressed in red and black." Both Nevan and the other guy followed her gesture until Nevan spotted an attractive woman across the street waiting for the bus going in the opposite direction. "Trust me," she told the guy. "That woman is your intended. Your soul mate."

"Come on, that's ridiculous," the guy said, eyeing the shapely brunette across the street. "How could you possibly know something like that? Is this some sort of scam?"

"No, I know because I'm a nym...um...because I'm psychic. Yes, that's it. I'm extremely psychic," Aladee said and Nevan groaned. Poor little thing was a lousy liar. "Now hurry, before her bus comes. You must prevent her from getting on."

"What?" Still watching the woman, the guy scrunched his face. "I can't just walk up to a stranger and tell her not to get on the bus. She'll think I'm an idiot—or worse. Is this a joke? Like one of those hidden camera things?" He gazed around him.

"Please believe me." Aladee gripped the man's arms, shaking him. "I'm telling you the truth. If you don't intervene, you'll miss your chance. She'll meet another man on her bus and end up marrying him."

"But—"

Aladee sucked in a gasp. "The bus approaches! Go, quickly!"

To Nevan's astonishment, the guy didn't hesitate. He ran across the street, catching the brunette by the elbow just before she stepped aboard the bus.

Aladee dragged Nevan a few feet to the side to get a better look. The woman looked annoyed at first, whipping her elbow from the man's grasp, but as he spoke, her expression became relaxed, then pleasant, and she finally smiled. The bus rolled by as he led her into the coffee shop at the corner.

"Well I'll be damned," Nevan said.

"Another perfect love match." Breathing a sigh of relief, Aladee beamed a gratified smile at Nevan. "It would have been so much easier if I'd had my bow and arrows with me."

"We're not going back to get them so don't even think about it," Nevan told her.

"I won't. I made a pledge to Lonan that I'd refrain from using them until I found Cupid. Also, it would be difficult shooting invisible arrows at people without being cloaked in my invisibility garment, or using the invisibility serum. People might stare at my strange actions and try to interfere with my mission."

"Most likely." Nevan had visions of the Glassfloat Bay police cuffing Aladee and hauling her away for psychiatric observation.

'I feel a sense of pride for a job well done." She straightened her shoulders, indulging in a mile-wide grin. Buster offered her a companionable bark.

"Are those two really soul mates...or did you make it up, just putting two attractive people together, betting they'd eventually fall in love?"

Aladee's hand flew to her chest and she gasped. "Oh, Nevan, I could never, *ever*, do that to anyone. Why, that would be tampering with the sacred laws of love matching."

"But how can you possibly know sure? What if you made a mistake?"

"They're absolutely meant for each other. I'm certain," she said with conviction. "Remember, I've been trained, Nevan. Schooled in the fine art of detecting and promoting perfect love matches." She spoke the way a lawyer or doctor might talk about their schooling. Of course, they wouldn't have received their diplomas from some invisible academy in the clouds.

"Also, as a nymph I'm able to detect certain pheromones." Nevan gave her a clueless look. "Chemicals secreted externally to send information to members of the same species," Aladee clarified in the brainy professor-like tone he'd heard her use before. Thumbing toward the coffee shop, she smiled. "Rest assured they're a perfect match."

"So you can sniff out soul mates."

"In a sense, yes." Aladee chuckled. "Once I have the couple in sight, I'm able to tune in to capture brief glimpses of their futures. That's how I knew she was about to meet another man who'd become her husband if I didn't intervene."

"So you really are psychic, then?" Nevan asked, praying she couldn't read the jumbled touchy-feely thoughts swimming inside his head all morning.

"Only somewhat." Aladee held her thumb and forefinger an inch apart. "When I'm directly involved in a love match situation. In this case, I saw flashes of a dull, unhappy life for the woman if she married the other man. The relationship would be devoid of true love, friendship, or satisfaction."

Nevan was impressed. "That's pretty cool."

"More warm than cool, actually," Aladee said, interpreting his statement literally. Nevan stifled a rising chuckle as she went on. "Thought waves emanating from people are akin to a warm, gentle summer breeze with a touch of electrical current."

"That's amazing. In fact, *you're* amazing." He drew her close, planting a brief kiss on her lips.

"You are too." She returned the kiss. "I haven't encountered many mortal men as adaptable and tolerant as you, Nevan."

"Me?" His voice came out almost in a squeak as he slapped a hand against his chest. "I think Red might have a thing or two to say about that." He laughed.

"Perhaps, but only in jest. He enjoys ribcaging you as much as you ribcage him." She'd obviously caught Nevan's *about to bust out laughing* expression. "Not ribcaging?"

"Ribbing," Nevan corrected gently.

"Ah...thank you. Earth vernacular and slang are difficult to master. Anyway, Red loves you very much, and it's evident he respects you."

Nevan tugged her close, nuzzling his chin in the sun-warmed curls atop her head. "Yeah, Red's okay."

Aladee stopped. "Cupid's Love Shack," she read aloud from a bright pink sign splashed with black and silver lettering. She turned a hopeful smile on Nevan. "This must be the place!" she said, all bouncy and excited. "What do you think, Buster?"

Buster growled in response, mirroring Nevan's exact reaction. Before he could tell her it was just a seedy dive where women danced topless on the bar, Aladee raced into the place.

"Aw, shit," Nevan mumbled, following her inside.

He arrived just in time to hear the brawny tattooed bruiser's deep baritone. "Lookin' for some lovin', sweet cheeks?" Nevan stiffened as the guy ran a finger up Aladee's arm. Double shit. The last thing he wanted was to get tangled with some horny meathead twice his size.

"Come on, Aladee. This isn't the right place," Nevan said loud enough for her to hear over the booming base reverberating through the darkened room. Locking onto her arm, he tugged. She stood firm. Buster got into the act, nosing and pushing against her leg.

"No thank you," she answered the greasy-haired bruiser as if he were an upstanding member of society. "I have plenty of loving from Nevan." She smiled up at Nevan, patting his chest. "I'm looking for Cupid and his headquarters. Am I in the right establishment?"

"Like the sign outside says, this is Cupid's Love Shack. If you're lookin' for work," he gave Aladee an appreciative once-over, "talk to the man himself."

"The man? Cupid?" Aladee asked, expectation dancing in her eyes.

"Yup. Over there." He motioned toward a guy in a shiny blue suit with slicked back hair and plenty of gold around his neck, wrist and fingers. His stark blue-black hair was an obvious dye job because he looked sixty-ish.

"Thank you," Aladee said. "By the way, I think your flesh artwork is lovely." Reaching up on her tiptoes, she ran her fingers along the tattoo of a bleeding skull at the top of his shaved head. "Very imaginative."

"Thanks." Bruiser cracked a gap-toothed smile. "If you like that, I got me some other even more imaginative tattoos I can show you," he oozed with a snicker and devilish eyebrow jiggle.

"She's not interested." Nevan swallowed hard when the bruiser looked down at him as if he relished the idea of squashing Nevan like a cockroach. He could probably do it too.

"Perhaps another time," Aladee said, with a kind smile before turning back to Nevan. "That was very rude, Nevan," she whispered as Nevan dragged her back toward the entrance. "You may have hurt his feelings."

"There's no room under all that beef for feelings," Nevan said at her ear, tugging her harder. "I already told you, Aladee, this isn't the right place. Now let's get out of here before you get us in trouble."

"I must be sure, Nevan." Aladee shook off Nevan's hand, hurrying toward Mr. Slick and Shiny, aka *Cupid*.

"Damn hardheaded, impulsive nymph," Nevan muttered beneath his breath. "I'm telling you, Buster, whoever ends up marrying her is going to have his hands full." He went after Aladee.

"Hi, sugar," a female voice oozed. "How about a lap dance? Aw, what a cute pooch."

Nevan looked up to see a redhead pole-dancing on the bar. Wearing a G-string and silver star-shaped pasties with tassels, her breasts were the size of a pair of cantaloupes. Though she couldn't hold a candle to Aladee's fresh, natural beauty or sensuousness, the independent-minded *Little Nevan* gave a hearty *Well, helloooo there!* salute in response.

"Hey there, handsome," another dancer said. "Like what you see?"

This one had bright pink hair, a matching G-string, and pink-daisy pasties. One glance had *Little Nevan* ready to do the horizontal mambo. Damn, stupid, traitorous appendage. Didn't he already have more than enough to handle with his stubborn nymph?

"I'm sorry," he heard Aladee say a few yards away, "but my book's chapter on street smarts advised that disrobing in public here on Earth was strongly discouraged and could lead to unwieldy situations. Those are your own rules, are they not, Cupid?"

Aw hell. "Thanks, ladies, but Buster and I have to take a pass." He offered a polite nod before double-timing it over to Aladee and the guy she thought was Cupid.

"No problem. We've got a back room," the guy coaxed. "*Very* private."

"I still don't understand why you need to see..." She angled her head in confusion. "What was it you called them, Cupid?"

"Your titties and ass," he helpfully elucidated with an oily smile.

"Yes," Aladee nodded, her eyebrows knitting. "Well I can assure you my titties and ass are in good condition after my journey from Olympus."

"Jesus, Aladee, what the hell's wrong with you!" Grabbing her, Nevan turned her toward him, shaking her. If he hadn't taken today off, there's no telling what dangerous fixes she'd wind up in. "Are you so lamebrained you can't tell this scumbag isn't Cupid?"

"Hey, I take exception to that," the scumbag said, lifting his forefinger. "You can't expect me to hire exotic dancers without eyeing the goods, can you?" His lip curled into a half-smile.

"He assured me he's Cupid, Nevan. He showed me his official chariot license to prove it."

Nevan screwed his features. "His what?!"

Flipping out his wallet, he gave Nevan a gander at his driver's license. It read *Cupid Batagglia.* "See? I'm on the up and up, pal," he said, as if expecting Nevan to give him a seal of approval.

"Listen to me, Aladee. He's not—"

"Cupid's supposed to be incognito, remember?" she cut in, her voice nearly a whisper. "He's playacting, pretending to be an uncouth individual." Her chin trembled as she looked up at Nevan with a wide, innocent, trusting gaze and he felt like a goddamned bully.

"Aladee, honey, do you honestly think Cupid's going to run around Earth disguised as a pervert?"

"I take exception to that," Batagglia argued again.

"You got a problem here, Mr. Batagglia?" the bald, tattooed bruiser piped up, edging toward them. When he flexed his muscles in a show of strength, his biceps looked bigger than the dancer's cantaloupes.

"I was conducting an employment interview with this lovely young thing when this sleazeball insulted me," he accused.

"*I'm* a sleazeball?" Nevan squeaked out in surprise, clapping a hand against his chest. "Oh, that's rich. Look, you oily son of a bitch—"

"I take exception to that." Battaglia gave a nod to the bruiser who stepped in, grabbing Nevan by the seat of the pants and shirt collar as if he weighed no more than a sack of flour. That had Buster barking his head off, before attaching his teeth to the guy's pantleg, shaking his head back and forth with ferocity.

"Hey. *Hey!* Put me down, you meathead."

The bruiser complied once he'd carted Nevan to the entrance, kicked open the door and tossed him onto the sidewalk like yesterday's garbage. Buster let go of the guy's pantleg to see how Nevan was doing.

Soundly deposited on his ass in the midst of curious passersby, Nevan scrambled to his feet to give the brute what for. But before he could act, he watched in astonishment as Aladee's balled fist connected with the bruiser's nose with a resounding crunch.

"How dare you manhandle the man I love!" Wincing, she waved her hand. Nevan wouldn't be surprised if she'd sprained it punching the oaf.

"What the hell! What the hell! What the hell!" The bruiser bellowed, his hand cupping his nose and blood seeping through his fingers. "You stupid broad, you broke my nose!" His expression turned murderous as he stepped toward Aladee.

Buster was going crazy, barking like Nevan had never heard before.

"Unless you cease and desist," Aladee cautioned, bravely standing her ground, "I shall be forced to inflict further bodily harm. It is not my desire to mete out damage to any mortal being, so I beseech you to retreat now while you still have the opportunity."

Just as the guy pulled back his fist to sock Aladee, Nevan captured it in one hand while connecting his other fist with the guy's nose, resulting in another sickening crunch.

"Don't even think about messing with the woman I love," Nevan growled. "Now go back to the hole you crawled out of, you worthless piece of shit."

Aladee gasped. "Oh, Nevan!" she shouted as she jumped up on him, wrapping her arms around his neck, and her legs around his waist, planting kisses all over his face. "You love me! I knew it. I *knew* it!"

In all the commotion, including Buster's continuing harangue, Nevan hadn't even realized he'd said the L word, but bursting out with it that way sort of felt good.

"I admit it. You've addlepated my brain, Aladee." He laughed as she continued sprinkling him with kisses. "Hell, yeah, I love you," he confessed, locking his lips with hers. "It's impossible not to," he added once their kiss ended.

"Dammit! *Dammit!*" the bruiser yelled.

At the sound of his roar, Nevan dropped Aladee, pushing her aside. She stumbled and fell on her butt, giving an *Oooph!* as she landed.

The brute was livid. His face a mask of rage with a fusion of tears and blood smearing his cheeks.

"You fucking assholes! I'm gonna kill the both of ya."

As Nevan prepared to defend himself, Aladee jumped up and hopped on the guy's back, beating on him with her fists and biting his ears. Damn, his nymph was a firecracker!

In the meantime, Buster attached himself higher on the guy's leg, growling and tearing until he practically ripped the guy's pants to shreds.

The brief moment Nevan took to admire Aladee's foolish bravado cost him dearly. Before he knew what was happening Nevan spotted the guy's ham hock fist an instant before it made contact with his nose. This time, the sickening crunch came from Nevan. He clutched his nose in an attempt to stop the flow of blood.

Belting out a deafening cry, Aladee jumped off the guy's back, to be replaced by Buster, who the brute was doing his best to shrug off as the dog tore at his shirt. Aladee came around to the front of the guy, waving a chastising finger as she gave him a verbal what for.

"I warned you!" she shouted. "But you didn't listen." The jerk responded by swatting her in the face with the back of his hand. Tears sprouted, but she stood her ground while Buster let out a howl like a werewolf.

"Aladee, sweetheart, get back!" Nevan yelled.

Seeing the bloodthirsty look in his dog's eyes as Buster's body stiffened and he bared his teeth, Nevan sensed he was about to attack. "Buster, no! Stop!" He didn't know if the big galoot was carrying a gun or knife. The mere thought that he could be armed made Nevan's blood run cold. He could lose both Aladee and Buster in an instant. And if Buster attacked and survived, he'd be sent to the pound.

"Buster, look at me," Aladee called, clearly sensing Nevan's agitation. Oddly enough, the big tattooed oaf stopped, looking at Aladee as she spoke to the dog. Gazing at Buster with a look of intensity, Aladee remained silent for a long moment. When she'd finished, Buster licked his chops and dropped to the sidewalk, panting like mad but staying in place as he'd been instructed.

"Good boy." Glancing at Nevan, Aladee saw the look of incredulity on his face. "I told him there's never been a more important time that he listen to you. And that if he attacked, he might never see you again."

"Thanks. Good boy, Buster! Stay!" It was hard to comprehend how she'd managed that but Nevan didn't have time to analyze Aladee's incredible abilities right now. Before he could move in to push her aside and beat the living shit out of the asshole who'd struck her, she grabbed the guy's shirt, fisting it in a bunch before thrusting her knee up, swift and hard, between his legs, obviously connecting with his groin by the sick wail the guy made. Then she kicked him on one knee, using some sort of sideways judo move. It all happened so fast, Nevan almost missed it.

The big guy collapsed to the sidewalk, squealing like a baby pig as he supported his groin with one hand, and clutched his twice-cracked nose with the other. Damn, he looked like he was in agony, but with the image of him swatting Aladee across her face, Nevan gave in to his baser instincts and kicked the guy in the gut, just for the hell of it.

"Nevan! Are you all right?" Aladee cried, wrapping her arms around him, and being joined by a concerned Buster amidst whooping shouts, applause and whistles from the crowd that had gathered. It had all happened so fast, Nevan hadn't a clue that anyone else was even there.

Scratching his head, Nevan teased, "I think this is the part where I'm supposed to say *my hero* and give you a big kiss, Aladee." Unfortunately, laughter only increasing the blinding pain at the center of his face.

"No, you're the hero," she said adoringly. Nevan liked the way it sounded, even though she was the one who basically beat the crap out of the guy.

"I'm okay," he told her. "Just a broken nose. What about you?" He winced as he spotted the pink imprint of the guy's paw across Aladee's pale cheek. "Son of a bitch." He smoothed his fingers over her hot cheek. "You're going to have a black eye from that."

"I'll be fine," Aladee said. "Buster, sweetie, you were such a good boy!" She hugged the dog, cooing in his ear as he licked her face.

Nevan lifted Aladee's fierce punching hand to examine it. "Can you move your fingers?" Aladee wiggled them and nodded.

"It hurts, but there aren't any broken bones," she said.

His arm secured around Aladee's waist, Nevan kissed her cheek. "Let's get out of here."

"Not so fast, buddy," a man's voice rang out as the sound of sirens drew close.

Nevan looked up at the uniformed guy whose hand rested on his holstered gun. Damn. The cops.

"Up against the wall," the cop said. "Both of you. Feet spread. Turning to his partner, he said, Connor, get hold of the dog and call animal control."

Damn. "It's okay, Buster," Nevan called. "Be a good boy."

A squad car pulled up, lights flashing, siren winding down, and two more cops got out, inspecting the scene, talking among themselves and handling the crybaby bruiser.

"This one's got two knives and a handgun," one of the cops told another.

"My God..." Nevan shuddered at thought of what might have happened.

Following Nevan's lead, Aladee positioned her hands high on the brick. "What's happening, Nevan? I'm frightened."

"Oh, so *now* you're frightened," Nevan answered with ironic laughter as the first cop read them their rights. "It appears we're being arrested. For disorderly conduct. Don't worry, everything's going to be okay once we get down to the station and explain."

"We've been busted?" Aladee sucked in a gasp. "Oh no. I've read about this and watched many films on the subject. What will Lonan and Cupid say when they return to Earth and discover I've become part of a chain gang, a convict in shackles? Oh, Nevan, I don't look good in horizontal stripes, or the color orange...or with a shaved head."

Nevan chuckled. Like everything else since he'd met her, Aladee was going to ensure his first arrest experience was exceptionally memorable. He was just about to say something reassuring when Aladee raised her voice.

"Police Brutality! We want a lawyer! Attica! Attica!"

Nevan's jaw dropped. "*Holy shit!* Aladee, what the hell do you think you're doing?"

"Demanding our rights," she explained with conviction. "The legal chapter of my textbook covered the topic of prisoner rights, inhumane conditions, and—"

"Aladee."

"Yes?"

"Just shut up...please."

"But—"

"Ma'am, if I were you, I'd listen to your boyfriend," the cop advised.

"Remember the part where the nice police officer said we have the right to remain silent?" Nevan asked Aladee.

"Yes."

"This might be a good time to do that."

"Okay." Aladee's voice was small and quiet now.

"Hey, is that you, Nevan?" one of the cops asked.

Turning his head to get a glimpse, Nevan breathed easier. "Hi, Officer Hartinger, yeah, it's me." Fortunately—or not—he and the Malones had known the cop for years. His kids had been tutored by Professor Tore Thorkelson, Astrid's husband.

"It's okay, you two can turn around now," Hartinger told them. "Hey, Grossman," he addressed his partner, "this is Nevan Malone, the guy I was telling you about—the owner of Half Potato Pub who put on that great show last night where the woman was flying up in—" He stopped short. "Hey, it was you." He pointed to Aladee. "Wasn't it?"

"Ta-da!" she replied with outstretched arms, giving such an endearing smile only an ogre wouldn't have been enchanted.

"How'd you manage that flying bit?" he asked her. "The wife and I loved it."

"Magicians should never reveal their secrets," she told him. "It spoils the suspense and surprise."

"Oh yeah...sure. Say, was all this," his hand circled the area, "another promotional performance for your pub, Nev?"

"Take a look at my face...and hers. Does this look like part of a show?" Nevan asked.

"I thought maybe it was stage makeup," Hartinger noted.

"Nope."

"Aw, too bad." Hartinger frowned. "We'll get that looked at for you in a few minutes."

"The tough guy writhing around down there attacked us," Nevan told him.

"For what?" Hartinger glanced back at the injured oaf, now tended to by an EMT. "What was the provocation?"

"I'm so glad you asked, Officer Hartinger," Aladee said. "After this—"

"Aladee, shush!" Nevan warned, wincing when the act of scowling sent a jolt of pain across his nose and face.

"It's all right, Nevan." Smiling, Aladee lifted her hand toward him in what he assumed was meant to be a comforting, pausing gesture. "Please allow me to handle this. I've studied the art of crucial communication vernacular between law enforcement and the accused. We, of course," she pointed to herself and Nevan, "being the wrongfully accused."

"Aw, jeez, we're doomed." Nevan shook his head back and forth.

"Anyway, Officer," Aladee forged ahead, "after this behemoth gangster ruffian willfully, and with malice aforethought, hurled the man I love, alias Mr. Nevan Malone, to the ground as if he weighed no more than a handheld phone device," in demonstration, Aladee whipped her hand to the side, "I struck the sadistic assailant's nose with a non-lethal fisted jab," she demonstrated her punch, "after which he continued relentlessly with an onslaught of violent and hostile acts of aggression, administrating vicious blows to both myself and Mr. Malone."

Hartinger and his partner, Grossman, just stood there and stared.

"Of course," Aladee continued, "that left me with no choice but to defend our very lives," all righteous, she pointed up like the Statue of Liberty, "by deftly and forcibly thrusting my knee to the attacker's vulnerable nether regions, and my foot to his left knee, using a martial arts technique." She demonstrated her sideways kick.

Still staring at Aladee, Hartinger said, "Uh-huh."

Apparently not satisfied with the depth of the hole she was digging, Aladee said, "This antagonist is clearly a menace to society. Officers...arrest this man," she pointed at the battered bruiser, "and throw him in shackles!"

Shifting his attention to Nevan, Officer Hartinger elbowed him and grinned. "She's pretty funny."

"A regular riot," Nevan haplessly agreed.

"So," Hartinger addressed Aladee, "you readily admit to causing this man bodily harm and throwing the first punch?"

"Aladee..." Nevan warned, arching an eyebrow at her.

"Well, I..." Glancing from Nevan who did his best to give her a cautionary glare, to the cop, and back again, a wide-eyed Aladee nervously licked her lips. "Officer?" Hartinger inclined his head, nodding. "I believe it would be in our best interest if we had an attorney present before we answer any more questions."

"Our and we?" Nevan asked, huffing a laugh. "Thanks for including me in your blanket self-incrimination, Aladee."

"We've got to take you to the station, Nev," Hartinger said. "Sorry, but it's protocol."

"I understand. Hey, is it okay if I take Buster along? You know my dog, he's a harmless little guy."

"Sure, no problem." Hartinger had Connor bring Buster to Nevan. The dog was so happy he practically wagged himself right out of his skin. Nevan understood, because he felt the same way.

"You know," Hartinger shook his head and laughed, "your family has given me and the guys more to talk about than probably anything else here in town."

Sighing, Nevan said, "I don't doubt it for a minute."

"I'll never forget," Hartinger continued, "the first time I met Zak when he was brought in with your sister, Laila, for driving without a license and crashing into that mailbox. Remember that, Grossman?" He elbowed his partner, who nodded, laughing at the memory. "Zak tried to tell us he was a five thousand year old genie," Hartinger said. "We thought the guy was a nut case or on drugs. I seem to recall he was on some new prescribed medication that made him wonky."

"Yeah, that was it," Nevan confirmed.

"But I thought Zak really was a gen—" With one narrow-eyed, warning glare from Nevan, Aladee stopped.

Finished patching up the oaf, the EMTs checked out Nevan and Aladee, bandaging Nevan's nose.

"Nevan?"

He let out noisy sigh of exasperation. "Yeah?"

"I-I'm truly sorry I got us into trouble because I refused to listen to you about Mr. Battaglia not being the real Cupid."

Closing his eyes as the pain from his broken nose throbbed like a drumbeat in his head, Nevan mumbled, "Forget about it."

"Nevan?"

"What."

"I love you," she whispered.

"Yeah," he sighed. "Me too."

Chapter Fifteen

~<>~

"IT'S NOT THAT funny, Red."

"I beg to differ. You look like a thug, Nevan." Wiping tears of laughter from his eyes, Red caught Nevan in the viewfinder of his phone's camera and took a picture as his cousin fumed. "My mother always warned me about the rowdy, low-class Malone side of the family. Imagine her sense of righteous triumph if she could see you now, here at the police station."

"Aunt Colleen can go...suck an egg," Nevan said, avoiding the curse he wanted to spew. "Where's that compassionate inner woman of yours when I need it?" he complained, fingering the thick gauze bandage over his nose. "I've got a broken nose, for chrissakes."

Red patted his cousin on the shoulder. "The crooked line will give your face additional character. Women love that sort of thing" Turning to glance at Aladee, Red's expression softened. "Aw, sweetie, your cheek looks nasty. Didn't they put any ice on it?"

"Aladee told the nurse that nymphs don't like ice," Nevan said with a resigned roll of his eyes. "That's after she answered all of Officer's Hartinger's questions. You know, like her full name being Aladee, daughter of Arrius and Venuvia, her age being three hundred fifty, her address being Mount Olympus and her race being nymph, part Dryad and part Limoniad. When Hartinger asked for identification, she told him she failed the chariot test twice and doesn't have a license yet."

"Oh my God..." Red laughed. "I'm surprised they didn't keep her for psychiatric evaluation."

"Hartinger just kept laughing...until he took her to get tested her for drugs," Nevan said.

Aladee nodded. "They made me urinate into a plastic cup."

"She obviously passed the pee test," Red noted.

"I did indeed." Aladee beamed a smile. "I was so relieved when they didn't make me drink it." She creased her features.

"It seems you two had quite an interesting experience," Red said.

"You could say that. With all of Aladee's *help*," clearing his throat, Nevan hung invisible quotes around the word, "it's a miracle they didn't lock us up and throw away the key. Fortunately, Hartinger was at the scene, and several witnesses, people who'd been at the pub last night and saw the flying show, came down to the station and corroborated our story."

"Can we leave now?" Aladee whispered. "I'm not particularly fond of this place. It makes me feel itchy all over." She shook her body, wiggling everything as she shuddered. In that instant, every male eye in the vicinity was on her.

"Of course." Wrapping an arm around Aladee's shoulder, Red led her to the Glassfloat Bay Police Station exit, leaving Nevan to follow. "I hope you're not planning on resuming your search for Cupid at this late hour. I think you and my cousin, *the thug*, have probably been through enough excitement for one day."

"Gee, Red, you're a real comedian," Nevan said. "Have you thought about taking your show on the road?" Red offered a saccharine smile in response.

Breathing a sigh, Aladee shrugged. "No...no more searching. I'd just like to rest for a while. If I haven't found Cupid by now, I doubt I will. His headquarters are well hidden indeed. Besides," she reached for Nevan's hand, clasped it and smiling up at him when he squeezed back, "I'd like to spend the rest of my time with Nevan before I have to leave for Olympus in the morning."

Hearing her say the words again stabbed at Nevan's gut.

"That's a wise idea. Our building's just a few blocks from here," Red said as they left the station. "Feel like walking or should we take the bus?"

"I prefer walking, if that's okay." Both men nodded in agreement. "Is Alfred feeling better?"

"Much," Red responded. "We shared some good conversation over shortbread cookies and chamomile tea this morning. He realizes Leonard was a user, an opportunist. I think Alfred finally accepts the idea that he deserves better."

"Of course he does," Aladee agreed. "I only wish I could be here long enough to help him find his soul mate."

Red kissed her forehead. "You're very sweet and caring."

"Thank you, Red. So are you." She planted a kiss on his jaw. "Well, at least one positive thing came out of the trouble I caused today." When Red lifted an eyebrow in interest, Aladee smiled. "Nevan admitted that he loves me." The way she bounced and bubbled with excitement as she said it warmed Nevan's insides like a shot of single malt scotch.

"It's about time." Red grinned at Nevan, giving him a hearty pat on the back. "I've known it from the start. From the moment I walked into Cupid's Headquarters and saw you two together."

"Me too." Aladee trilled a voluminous sigh. "If only Nevan and I could have had more time together, but the fates don't have that in store for us."

"You're not going anywhere. You're staying here with me," Nevan announced and both Aladee and Red shot him startled looks as they halted in their tracks.

"Oh but, Nevan, my love, I can't do that." Stroking Nevan's jaw Aladee gazed up at him with an expression so tender and loving it nearly shattered him. "It's not permitted. I must return to Olympus. How I wish it could be different, but, alas, it cannot."

"No." Nevan shook his head back and forth as he grabbed Aladee's upper arms and held tight. "I won't let you go. I'll...I'll tie you up and hide you in a closet or something until they leave."

Aladee uttered a pained, forlorn kind of laugh. "They would find me, Nevan. Their tracking methods are quite advanced. If there was any way I could stay here with you, I would. Leaving you will be the most difficult thing I've ever had to do."

"But—"

"Remember," she kissed her fingertip and touched his broken nose, "unlike your broken nose, our parting will only be painful for a short while. Once your memory is cleansed, you'll be left with only a slight, almost imperceptible, sensation of melancholy."

"I don't want to forget! I want to remember everything about you." Nevan felt the sting of tears prick his eyes. Blinking them back, he yanked Aladee hard against him, holding her as if his life depended on it. In a way, it did.

He gazed at her, totally at a loss for words as he contemplated the bleakness of life without the infectious sound of her laughter, her sweet naiveté, the warm soft feel of her luscious curves, their incredible sex adventures, and, yes, even her penchant for inadvertently creating all manner of havoc.

Still bracing Aladee's head against his chest, Nevan looked at his cousin with pleading eyes. "Red...help me. I can't lose her."

Quickly flicking the tears from his eyes, Red straightened, his chin elevated with an air of confidence. "I refuse to allow this to develop into another Tristan and Isolde tragedy," he announced. "Trust me, Nevan, we'll find a way to keep you and Aladee together."

~<>~

"Mmm-hmm, here it is." Red tapped his finger against the page of one of the thick books he'd drawn from the shelves holding his extensive mythology collection. He sat cross-legged on an oversized, tasseled magenta pillow on the floor of his apartment while Nevan sat on the futon and Aladee curled up in a swinging chair, suspended from the ceiling. Each of them had several books.

"I know there's Google," Red said with a flit of his hand, "but it would be too difficult locating the depth of information we need. It's all here, indexed in these books."

"You found the story of Cupid and Psyche?" Aladee asked animatedly, clapping her book closed.

Red nodded, his features evidencing faraway thoughts. "She was a mortal so beautiful that Venus, the goddess of love, grew jealous," he read aloud. "She instructed her son, Cupid, to make Psyche fall in love with a hideous monster." Red look up from the page and smiled. "Ah, but *au contraire*—instead, Cupid fell in love with Psyche himself."

"I love that part," Aladee said, dreamy-eyed. "It's so romantic."

"Cupid's a god, right?" Nevan asked, suddenly finding mythology, a topic that once made him snore, intensely interesting.

"Yes." Red nodded.

"The god of love, sex and eroticism," Aladee added.

"His mother was the goddess of love. Who was Cupid's father?" Nevan asked.

"Mars," Red answered. "The god of war. One of Venus's many lovers. It seems there's a lot of promiscuity and inter-family relations weaving through the gods."

"Interesting. That makes Cupid a byproduct of love and war," Nevan mused. "So Cupid's daddy was named after the planet?"

Aladee laughed. "The celestial planet Mars was named after the god of war because it shines with a red color resembling blood."

Shrugging a shoulder, Nevan made an acknowledging expression. "Makes sense."

Skimming his finger along the page, Red said, "This says Cupid took Psyche as his wife, but as a mortal she was forbidden to look at him."

"How was that supposed to work?" Nevan said.

Holding up a finger, Red read on. "Psyche was happy until her sisters persuaded her to look at Cupid. As soon as she did, Cupid punished her by leaving."

Nevan screwed his features. "Talk about harsh."

Aladee sighed. "The gods are known for being quick to temper and meting out harsh punishment."

"As Psyche wandered, trying to find her love," Red continued, "she came upon the temple of Venus. Intent on destroying Psyche, Venus gave her a series of difficult tasks." Red's eyebrows knitted. "Ouch...some were downright nasty."

A celebratory grin split Red's face. "Here it is!" He tapped the page. "The clincher. Cupid could no longer bear to witness Psyche's suffering or to be apart from her, so he pleaded their case to the gods and, *voila*! Psyche becomes an immortal—a minor goddess—and the lovers are united forever!"

"Children on Olympus learn their story even before beginning school," Aladee told them.

"Red, I apologize." Nevan gave his cousin a solid pat on the back.

"You what?!" Red's hand flew to his chest and he gasped. "Are you trying to give me a heart attack?"

"I mean it. I take back every mean, rotten thing I ever said about your obsession with Greek and Roman mythology. In the last two hours, we've come up with several different instances where residents of Olympus and Earth have managed to remain together, either up there or down here. Hell, if Cupid himself went through this with a mortal, then he's *got* to be sympathetic."

He glanced across the room at Aladee. "We can do this, Aladee. I know we can."

A wary look crossed her features. "I'm not important enough for the gods to consider. It's not like I've accomplished an incredible feat or have any real stature. I'm not a goddess, I'm just a—"

"A nymph who fell in love with a mortal man," Red interrupted. "These books are filled with stories of love matches like yours and Nevan's. And you know all the hubbub you keep making about being nothing but a lowly nymph?" Aladee gave a tentative nod and Red wagged a chastising finger. "It seems you've been telling little white lies."

Nevan frowned. "What are you talking about?"

"According to what I've read," Red explained, "nymphs are classified as minor female deities. That would make our Aladee a minor goddess. Just like Psyche."

Nevan looked agape at Aladee. "But you said—"

"It's an age-old controversy," Aladee broke in. "Some believe nymphs are minor deities, while others believe we're merely spirits of nature with extended lifespans. I choose to think of myself as the latter." She huffed a sigh. "I'm too absentminded to be a minor deity. Besides, I'm of mixed heritage, which might make me ineligible to be a goddess."

Nevan and Red exchanged glances. "Well, don't leave us hanging," Red said.

"It happened generations ago. You see," she paused, running her fingers through her hair, "I'm part Dryad and part Limoniad," she finished, as if it made perfect sense.

"Meaning...?" Nevan asked.

"Each nymph subtype presides over a certain aspect of nature," Aladee explained. "The habitat of Dryads is the forest while the habitat of Limoniads is meadows. I'm happiest and most productive in either. That's why I'm partial to flowers and foliage. It's also why I enjoy your Earthly city of Glassfloat Bay, Oregon so much, with its lush mix of forest, meadow and ocean."

"That settles it." Red slammed his thick hardcover book shut with a loud thud, capturing Nevan and Aladee's full attention. "Dryad or Limoniad, Aladee, there's no damn reason why you, a minor goddess, and my mortal cousin can't plead your case before the gods. Period."

Aladee sucked in a small gasp and nibbled her bottom lip. "The Council of Deities..." she said with reverence, and what Nevan construed as considerable dread.

"How do we do that?" Nevan asked. "The council is on Olympus, right?"

Aladee nodded silently.

"If you truly love Aladee," Red said, "I'm sure you'll find a way. Of course," he polished his nails against his shirt, inspecting them, "perhaps you don't have the stamina that a mortal woman like Psyche had." He indulged in a shrewd smile.

"This is crazy." Nevan stared at nothing, trying to piece all the bizarre information together. "We're talking about me, Nevan Malone," he thumbed his chest, "flying into the clouds," his hands darted skyward, "in an airborne chariot." He dropped his head in his hands, massaging his temples and groaning. "It's insane."

"Would you really be willing to do that for me?" Aladee asked hopefully. "Plead before the Council of Deities?"

Gazing at his beautiful, brainy, absentminded nymph, Nevan wanted to hold her close and never let her go. Slapping his hands against his thighs, he said, "Bring it on," and got to his feet. "I'll do whatever it takes for us to stay together."

Aladee bolted upright in her chair, which made it spin. "Even if it means battling dragons or braving the fiery domain of Pluto?" Dragging her foot on the floor, she stalled the movement.

Bug-eyed, Nevan swallowed hard. "The former planet?" he asked, fairly certain that wasn't what Aladee meant.

"I believe she's referring to what we call Hell," Red offered, his complexion taking on a sickly pallor that failed to instill Nevan with confidence.

Aladee nodded slowly. "In Greek mythology, it's known as the domain of Hades."

"You're kidding, right?" Nevan looked from Aladee to Red and back again. "Fire-breathing dragons and the pits of Hell..." His laugh sounded like a wounded hyena. "Tell me you're not serious."

Aladee lowered her eyes, picking at invisible bits of dust.

"You're not kidding." Nevan took in a sharp breath, letting it out with a whoosh. His head pounded with the mind-boggling madness of it all, along with the pain of his broken nose, reminding him he should have taken his pain medication almost an hour ago. How did he suddenly get stuck in the middle of a fairytale, or was it a myth? He could lose his life. Damn, if he got barbequed by a dragon he'd be dead before he was forty.

But then, he glanced at Aladee, what kind of life would he have if he played it safe and lived to ninety, without ever seeing or holding her again? Was he willing to go through life like a walking zombie without Aladee at his side?

"See? This is why I never wanted to fall in love." He wagged an accusatory finger toward the wide-eyed Aladee. "As soon as I do, look what happens. Dragons and Hell and..." He watched her chin tremble.

"Aladee..." Her name was like a vow on his lips. Plucking her from her twirling chair, he hugged her close, nestling his broken nose in her hair and breathing in the fragrance of sunshine, spring flowers, and the sweet scent of the woman he loved.

"Bring on the dragons, Pluto, and whatever else." He kissed her with meaning. "Nevan Malone, master purveyor of beer, wine and whiskey, will tackle them all!"

Chapter Sixteen

Tuesday Morning

~<>~

LAST NIGHT had been the most wonderful, yet the saddest, in Aladee's life. They'd gathered together at Bekka House for a farewell dinner with Nevan's family and the few close friends, like Annalise, who knew her story. At first, the biggest topic of conversation was Nevan's two black eyes and bandaged nose, as well as the swollen red handprint across Aladee's cheek, accompanied by a black eye on that side of her face. They made quite a pair.

Nevan, Aladee, and Red filled them in on what happened, with Red dramatizing one segment after another and Aladee embellishing the rest. While listening to the three of them, the family shifted back and forth from wide-eyed and shocked, to teary-eyed laughter.

Initially, Aladee, Nevan, and Red decided it would be best not to let on that Nevan would try to accompany Aladee to Mount Olympus to make his plea to the Council of Deities. It would only cause Astrid and the others to worry.

As dinner plates were being cleared for dessert, Kady confronted the trio privately, asking them to follow her to the library where they wouldn't be overheard.

"I know something more is going on." Kady closed the double doors to the room. "Please don't keep us in the dark. It's not fair to all of us who love you, Nevan."

"Nothing else is going on," Nevan lied, his gaze dropping to his shoes as he shuffled his foot back and forth.

Kady offered a considerate smile, stroking her brother's bruised cheek before pulling him into a hug. "You know I can always tell when you're lying, Nev." She held him at arm's length. "Please...tell me whatever it is."

Nevan's eyes closed. "Damn."

Aladee was touched by the obvious love between brother and sister.

"You're going to try to go with Aladee, aren't you?"

Nevan gaped at Kady in amazement. "How could you possibly know that?"

"I didn't, exactly," her smile stretched wide, "but now I know for sure."

"I didn't say that," Nevan protested.

Turning her attention to Red, Kady took his hand. "I'm right about Nevan going with Aladee, aren't I, Redmond?"

"Oh, well, I—that is, we—um..." Aladee watched the color drain from Red's face as he hemmed and hawed, seemingly unable to outright lie, yet not wanting to give away their secret.

"You're amazingly perceptive," Aladee told her. "I have some psychic ability but not like yours."

"It's something I've had all my life," Kady said. "I get feelings...knowings. Not like I know everything that's going to happen. I can't pick winning lottery numbers or anything like that." She laughed. "But when I do *see* something," she added air quotes to the word, "I'm spot on most of the time."

Folding her arms across her chest, Kady smiled at the trio standing before her. "Which is how I know I'm right about this feeling. Nevan's going to try getting on that chariot to Mount Olympus because he—" Stopping abruptly, Kady stood there with a surprised grin on her face.

"What's wrong?" Nevan asked.

"Oh my God...because you *love* her!" Kady finished. "Nevan Malone, you've fallen in love with Aladee."

Taking Aladee by the hand, Nevan returned his sister's smile. "Guilty as charged. It was almost," he snapped his fingers, "instantaneous."

"That's the way true love is," Kady said. "Am I right, Aladee?"

"Definitely."

"I believe love is ever present," Kady continued. "It's there all the time, waiting for us to recognize or discover it. It takes some people longer than others, and, sadly, some people never do find their intended others. For some, like you and Aladee, it happens instantly. Love at first sight is as real as a love that's been cultivated over many years."

"What a perfect explanation," Aladee said. "It's almost as if you'd read my textbooks."

"We may as well tell her," Red said. "Kady can help us decide if we should tell the rest of the family."

After much discussion, the four of them knew they couldn't keep something this important from everyone. Nevan's loved ones were always supportive and encouraging. They didn't deserve being lied to. If something happened and he didn't return from Olympus, they had a right to know why.

The four of them returned to the dining area, where the family was enjoying fresh plum cobbler with vanilla bean ice cream, and confessed about everything.

Astrid, understandably, worried about the fate of her *little boy*, afraid she might never see Nevan again. He assured her he'd be fine and would return soon, if they even allowed him to go at all. Aladee assured Astrid and the others that she'd do her utmost to ensure Nevan's safety. Red and Kady chimed in, saying they supported the idea of Nevan pleading his case to the gods.

"I have to be honest," Nevan's sister, Laila, said. "The idea of facing the gods makes me nervous. I remember when Zak and I had to deal with Inanna." She shuddered.

"Queen of Heaven, goddess of love and war," Zak said, nodding. "She's the powerful goddess who imprisoned me in a bottle."

"I'm familiar with Inanna, also known as Ishtar," Aladee said, forcing herself not to shudder at the name of the often cruel, forbidding goddess. "She's an ancient Mesopotamian goddess, known to be impulsive, and power hungry. I recall, a century ago, when she visited the gods on Olympus. Inanna was...memorable. You say she confined you to a bottle?" she asked Zak, who replied with a confirming nod.

"Trying to free Zak was a chilling experience," Drake added. "Reen and I tried to help. We met Inanna and got a taste of her authority."

"As well as her whims," Reen said.

"Will she be there?" a wide-eyed Astrid asked.

With a reassuring smile, Aladee said, "No, she doesn't reside on Mount Olympus."

"Good." Astrid breathed a sigh of relief.

Aladee wasn't about to tell them that the gods on Olympus could be an ornery bunch, and that Nevan had little hope of winning his case...or coming out of it unharmed.

Some of them asked if they could come to the park, where Aladee would rendezvous with the chariot, so they could see Aladee and Nevan off. Aladee told them it was forbidden and might cause Nevan to lose his chance to go. The real reason she didn't want any of them there was because they'd have to have their memories wiped clean. If that happened, none of them would have any idea what happened to Nevan if he didn't return.

Regardless of the rules Aladee had pledged to follow, she couldn't in all good conscience do that to these wonderful people who'd been so kind to her, treating her as one of their own. Since they were already familiar with gods, genies, angels, and spirits, she decided it was safe leaving them with their memories of her as a nymph and all that had transpired.

If it was discovered she'd directly disobeyed one of Cupid Academy's most important rules, Aladee knew she'd be expelled. She cared so deeply for the Malones, it was a risk she was willing to take.

Throughout the night, the lovemaking they shared was deeply passionate, intense and full of intention. This strong alpha male whispered sweet, tender words of love at her ear as he gently held her in his arms, caressing her as if she were a fragile porcelain doll he feared might break.

The man she loved made her feel so loved and cherished, she'd wept with joy. As they made love for the final time, he kissed away her tears. They created a soul connection that had them ascending to astounding new heights, without the need for any wings.

And now it was the morning of her scheduled departure.

"I'm glad I got a chance to wear my LBD." Aladee fondly fingered the black wraparound dress before laying it out neatly on Nevan's bed. Her gaze rose to meet his solemn expression.

"The moment I saw you in that, you took my breath away," he said.

With a sigh, she smoothed the creases in the fabric. "The tags are still on the dress as well as most of the other outfits from the mall. Kady said you should have no trouble returning them for a refund."

"The clothes are staying right here," Nevan announced, avoiding eye contact with Aladee as he grabbed his keys from the dresser and shoved them into his jeans pocket. "You'll need them," he added with a quick glance, "after everything is settled and we come back here."

Aladee's heart ached for Nevan, her darling soul mate, her perfect love match... Such a worthy mortal, blessed with a bold spirit, and a strong fusion of positive qualities. She feared losing him forever, whether to a proclamation of the gods, or to a fearsome test to which he might be assigned.

"If the Council of Deities grants our request, we might have to live on Olympus," Aladee pointed out. "I wouldn't need any of these clothes then."

Nevan gave her a curious look. "Funny, I never thought of that—me living up there in some mythical place in the clouds. Wearing a toga." His lip hiking into a smirk, he shook his head briskly. "Somehow I doubt I'd fit in."

"I think you're right," Aladee agreed. "You'd stick out like a sick thumb."

"Sore thumb," Nevan corrected with a laugh.

Looking down at his dog, he chuckled. "Would Buster have to wear a toga too? He doesn't even like wearing his harness, much less some girly dress."

"I don't think so...although he'd look pretty cute in one."

Buster growled, making his sentiments known.

Aladee was glad for the sound of Nevan's laughter. He'd seemed so tense and gloomy since they woke up. "I'd rather remain here on Earth," she said. "I've always felt comfortable and at home here."

Taking her in his arms, Nevan kissed the handprint across her cheek. "I don't care if they send us to the moon. As long as we're together, everything's going to be okay."

"I believe that with all my heart. I'm so glad you're bringing Buster. I can't imagine the two of you being apart."

Squatting to Buster's level, Nevan mussed his fur. "Not going to happen. My best buddy and I stick together, here, on Olympus, or on the moon. Right pal?" He put his head next to Buster's and got a likeminded lick in return.

In the event Nevan was allowed to travel with her, Aladee had no idea if Buster would be permitted to accompany them. She prayed

Cupid, Lonan and her classmates would find the dog too darling to leave behind. She'd already had a telepathic talk with Buster, explaining the importance of being on his best behavior today.

There was a knock at the door. Glancing at his phone, Nevan blew out a gust of breath when he saw the time. The muscle in his jaw clenching, he said, "That must be Red."

"Aladee, you look radiant," Red said once Nevan opened the door. He held Cupid in his arms. The dog and cat snarled, greeting each other in the usual way. Taking one of Aladee's hands and stepping back, Red did a smiling appraisal.

He'd suggested she wear the silky champagne-colored dress this morning, saying she looked especially sweet and innocent in it. That sold Aladee on Red's idea. She needed all the help she could to make her look as engaging and guiltless as possible when she faced Cupid. She was also partial to the dress because Nevan said it was almost the same color as her wings and reminded him of their airborne lovemaking escapades.

"Thank you, Red. You selected the perfect garment for me. See how it matches my gold-tipped sandals?" Looking down at her feet, she wiggled her toes. It was the first time she'd worn her sandals since she went to the mall.

"Hello you adorable ball of fluff." Aladee nuzzled her face in Cupid's snow white fur, getting a round of gentle purring in return.

"Got the, um, you know?" Nevan asked Red in a half-whisper.

Red nodded as he set Cupid on the floor. "Be nice now, boys," he told Cupid and Buster, who ignored each other. Red extracted a small hinged box from the back waistband of his jeans, handing it to Aladee.

"This is a small token of our affection," he said softly. "Just in case..." He glanced at Nevan, whose expression was somber. Clearing his throat, Red continued, "In case something unforeseen happens and our memories get wiped and you have to leave." He and Nevan heaved weighty sighs once Red finished.

Aladee had forgotten about the possibility that their memories could be erased. What an awful situation that would be if they had no memory of her but their entire family still did. It would mean yet another gargantuan blunder on her part.

While her thoughts buzzed, Aladee stared at the closed black velvet-covered box until Nevan urged, "Go ahead, open it."

Doing so, she glimpsed a gold heart-shaped locket with a small diamond chip at the center. Her eyes filled with tears. Tracing her fingers over the heart and its fine chain, she smiled.

"What a lovely, delicate gift. This is so precious. Beautiful." She looked up at the cousins, each doing his best to smile through their vexed expressions. "Thank you so much."

"Take a look inside," Red said. "And on the back."

She opened the tiny clasp on the locket, made a little gasp and immediately began weeping. On the left was a tiny photo of Red with his cat, and on the right a photo of Nevan and Buster. "This is wonderful. So perfect." Swiping at her tears, Aladee turned the locket over and read the inscription aloud. "*Forever in our hearts. Love, Nevan and Red.*"

"That way you'll..." Nevan's voice caught and he paused. "You'll never forget us...even if we're not able to remember you."

Clasping the locket to her breast, Aladee gathered the cousins into a hug. "I'll always wear this next to my heart and treasure it forever. It's the finest, most valuable possession I've ever owned." Handing the locket to Nevan, she turned her back to him, lifting the curls at her neck to give him access.

Nevan fumbled with the clasp on the tiny chain until, with a frustrated sigh, he turned it over to Red who managed the clasp and locked the chain around her neck.

She turned back to them, giving each a kiss on the cheek. "I want you to know I love you both with all my heart."

"The feeling's mutual," Red said. "You've been a breath of fresh air in our lives, Aladee." He glanced at the clock, then at his cousin. "Time to go," he advised softly. "We don't want to irritate Cupid by Aladee being late." Red scooped Cupid up from the floor.

Nodding, Aladee took in a deep breath. "Cupid's quick to anger. He's also notorious for being mischievous and arrogant," she cautioned. "Take care not to rile him."

"She means don't piss Cupid off." Red elbowed his cousin.

"I know what she means." Nevan whapped Red's arm.

Cupid leapt from Red's arms into Aladee's, cuddling against her. "He knows," Aladee said. "He's saying goodbye and telling me he loves me. I love you two, you sweet thing." She kissed the top of his head and he leapt back into Red's waiting arms.

Buster's whimpering caught their attention. Standing on his hind legs, he reached up to her.

"Careful, Buster's heavy," Nevan said. "Let me pick him up for you."

"No need. Let's do it this way instead." Sitting on the edge of the bed, she patted the space next to her. Buster easily leapt up, getting onto her lap. She hugged him as he made earnest vocal sounds that almost mimicked speech. Their thoughts connecting, she and Buster exchanged their love and their goodbyes.

"Cupid and Buster love you very much," Nevan said.

"They adore you as much as we do." Red put the little red leather cat harness and leash on Cupid. "He hates this but I can't afford losing him in the excitement this morning. Holding Cupid up high, Red looked up at the frowning cat. "You don't mind just for today, do you, precious?"

"He says he understands this is an important occasion," Aladee said, "plus he knows he looks good in that particular shade of red." She laughed.

Cradling him again, Red looked at Aladee. "Seriously? He really said that?"

"You have my word. Whoa!" Aladee held her head. "I've got dueling incoming from the cat and dog. Buster says he looks handsome in his blue denim harness. You do, sweetie. You both look perfect for your meeting with Cupid."

Aladee gathered her *Welcome to Glassfloat Bay, Oregon!* canvas tote bag containing her uniform, a few personal items, and a cookbook filled with recipes for Bekka's pepperkaker, Laila's scones, a Dutch baby pancake, and some ice cream creations. With an intake of breath, she announced, "I'm ready. Let's go."

Red opened the door, ushering Aladee into the hall. "Alfred's already in the shop this morning, so we don't have to worry about me getting back for a few hours."

"Aladee." Drawing her into his arms, Nevan crushed her against his chest. There was a sense of desperation in his voice that nearly broke her heart. "Aladee," he whispered again as he kissed her with such love and concentration it made her knees go weak.

The waterfront park was only a few blocks away, a walk made even shorter as they sped up their gait. Both Buster and Cupid behaved perfectly.

Aladee gasped, murmuring, "Oh gods," as they crossed the grass, nearing the spot where Lonan's chariot had landed three days earlier. "There he is. There's Cupid."

"The guy with the brown hair in the jeans and white shirt?" Nevan asked, clearly surprised.

"Mmm-hmm. To blend in, he usually adopts the local garb when traveling. Togas tend to attract too much attention."

As they neared the spot, the three clasped hands. Aladee didn't have the heart to tell Nevan his grasp was crushing her fingers.

"Good timing," Nevan noted. "Looks like you're the first one here. No other classmates yet."

"I'm the last. They're just wearing their invisibility traveling garments," she explained, groaning as she remembered she'd have to confess losing hers to Lonan sooner or later. "If you listen carefully, you can hear their chatter in the distance."

"Of course. How silly of me." Nevan's usual levity sounded forced.

Cupid, dashing and handsome as always, planted his fists at his hips, glowering at Aladee as she approached. "There you are, my errant little nymph. Where have you been? Lonan said he deposited you here three days ago." He took her chin, turning her face left and right. "What the Hades happened to your face?"

Swallowing hard, Aladee said, "I am sincerely sorry, Cupid." She lowered her gaze. "I...um, encountered a few tiny problems, including a minor scuffle," she touched her swollen cheek, "and I—" She stopped abruptly when she heard laughter coming from her left. Aladee looked up to see a nearby cluster of trees and bushes rustle.

"What did I tell you, Cupid? Jupiter only knows what sort of mayhem Aladee's wreaked this time."

Aladee immediately recognized the jovial voice.

"Who's talking?" Nevan whispered to Aladee out of the side of his mouth.

"My teacher, Lonan," she whispered. "He's invisible right now."

"This is too much." Nevan swallowed hard. Detecting a slight shudder coming from him, she squeezed his hand for support. "Hey," Nevan cocked his ear, "I hear horses." He glanced around, sniffing the air. "Smell them too." Before Aladee could say anything, he raised his hand. "I know. They're invisible, right?"

"As is the chariot," Aladee confirmed.

Nevan sighed. "That's just dandy." Both Buster and Cupid the cat were actively sniffing the air.

"Who are these lowly, mangy mortals you've brought to our rendezvous?" Cupid stormed, flicking a hand toward Red and Nevan.

"Mangy?" Red gasped. "Why, I'll have you know this is silk shantung." He fingered his pink shirt.

Dismissing Red with a surly scowl, Cupid addressed Aladee again. "Why haven't you administered the forgetfulness powder to them yet? The more they see, the more memories we have to deal with."

"There's an excellent reason," Aladee began. "Oh no! Cupid, wait!" she pleaded, as he opened a small leather pouch hanging from his waistband. "Please don't use the powder yet. I have," she swallowed hard, "a favor to ask of you."

"Favor?" Narrowing his gaze, Cupid grumbled. "We're on a schedule, Aladee. What's going on?"

"I'm Lonan," her teacher broke in before Aladee could answer. She looked up to see that her handsome blond, blue-eyed teacher had shed his invisibility garment. Standing directly in front of Red, he extended his hand. "And you are?"

As soon as Red caught sight of Lonan in his short, gold-embellished off-white toga, his jaw dropped. "Red," he breathed, taking Lonan's hand in both of his and clasping it. "Redmond Devington. Lowly, mangy mortal," he added. Lonan laughed at his quip.

"Just as I thought," Aladee said proudly. At least she could do *something* right. "I told Red I believed you would find each other most compatible, Lonan. Even without the need for intervention from Cupid's arrows." She noticed Cupid frowned at that.

"Quite perceptive, Aladee," Lonan answered her, never taking his gaze from Red, their hands still clasped.

"I've never doubted anything Aladee's told me," Red said. "This only proves her spot-on acumen."

"Nice shirt," Lonan said with a devilish smile, sampling the pink silk fabric against Red's biceps with his fingers. "That shade of pink complements your onyx hair and dark eyes. Cerise, isn't it?"

Red arched an eyebrow, clearly impressed. "It is. I see you're a man who knows his colors." Red smoothed his hand along the fabric covering Lonan's chest. "Nice toga. That particular shade of ecru complements your well-defined muscle groups."

As Red and Lonan exchanged banter, Cupid engaged in a gargantuan yawn. "This is terribly sweet and charming, fellas, but I'm getting bored. Let's go. Psyche will have my head if I'm late for dinner again."

"Aladee and I want to stay together," Nevan blurted at the same moment Aladee cried, "I want to stay with Nevan."

"Uh-oh." Lonan gave a low whistle. A muffled din arose from the cloaked chariot. "Aladee's classmates," Lonan said in explanation to Red and Nevan's inquisitive looks. "Mind your own business back there," Lonan called to them. "Start reading chapter fifteen on Earthly etiquette and proper decorum. There's going to be a test." The sound of grousing was followed by the sound of pages being flipped.

"Nevan and Aladee truly are a perfect love match," Red chimed in. "Go ahead, Cupid, test it for yourself."

Cupid gawked at Red as if he had three eyes. "I'm not in the habit of taking orders from mortals," he huffed. Arms folded across his chest, he shifted his stormy gaze from Aladee to Nevan and back again.

Aladee felt a twinge of hope, because, with that brief glimpse, she noted the recognition of true love in Cupid's eyes. He *was* the god of love, after all. How could he deny it?

"All right. It appears you're correct in your assessment," Cupid admitted. "Such unfortunate mistakes do sometimes occur. I'm sorry, Aladee, but you know the rules. No extended hanky-panky allowed between nymphs of Olympus and Earthly mortals. Now, will you use your forgetfulness powder on them or should I use mine?" Cupid's hand rested at his small leather pouch again.

"Cupid, please!" Aladee pleaded, clutching his arm and holding it in place. "Allow us to plead our case. It's not merely hanky-panky. While Nevan is highly skilled in carnal pleasures and the sexual unions we shared were indeed spectacular..." she paused as Nevan groaned, "it's true love that prompts my plea."

"You wish to plead before the Council of Deities?" Cupid spat. "Impossible. Preposterous." He shook off Aladee's hands. "Now stop all this lovesick nonsense and be a good little nymph. Find yourself a nice satyr to settle down with and make baby nymphs. There's one in your class, Vibius. He's got a major crush on you." Cupid gave a conspiratorial wink.

"Vibius? Ugh!" Aladee ground out. "I barely escaped intact from that one dreadful date we had. He wouldn't take no for an answer. Really, Cupid, how can you think to pair me with a hard-drinking, wild, carousing satyr when the mortal I love is a fine, decent, upstanding example of manhood?" She gestured toward Nevan, splaying her hand on his chest.

Buster backed up Aladee's plea with a soft bark.

"What is *that*?" Cupid pointed at Buster as if the dog were something putrid.

"Nevan's beloved dog. He's a rescue dog. Nevan saved him from a life of abuse and neglect, nurturing him to good health. Buster's good and kind and—"

"All right, enough." Cupid rolled his eyes.

"What's a satyr," Nevan asked Aladee.

"The male equivalent of a nymph," she explained with a monumental sigh. "Half human, half beast. The upper part of the body is that of a human, except for the horns of a goat on their head." She illustrated her point by wiggling two fingers atop her curls. "They usually have a goat's tail, flanks and hooves."

Looking at her like she was crazy, Nevan turned the same expression on Cupid. "You can't be serious. You want Aladee getting hitched to a goat-man? That's really disgusting."

"You're being both insolent and insulting, mortal," Cupid warned.

"Insulting?" Bristling, Nevan's chin elevated a notch and he stood toe-to toe with Cupid. "I don't think so. I never implied *you* looked like a goat, did I?"

"I think I understand how you came to have two black eyes and a battered nose, mouthy mortal."

Aladee shushed Nevan, pulling him back, feeling the tenseness in his muscles. "Don't forget, you're addressing a powerful god," she whispered. "Remember when I told you about the Feast of Lupercalia? I explained how it celebrates spring and Faunus, the god of nature and agriculture."

"Yeah, so?"

"You may know Faunus better as Pan," she clarified.

"The demonic-looking goat-guy with the flute?"

Aladee nodded. "He closely resembles a satyr. He and Cupid are good friends and chair the planning committee for the feast each year."

"Oh." Glancing back at Cupid, Nevan shrugged. "Sorry, didn't mean to insult your buddy. I'm sure he's a fine looking...uh..."

"God," Cupid said with a smug air. "Is that the word you're looking for, mortal?"

"Yes, absolutely," Nevan answered.

"You said it was an unfortunate mistake that Nevan and Aladee are in love," Red braved. "Is that how you felt when you and Psyche fell in love?" Cupid pinned Red with a furious glare as a chorus of hushed *oooohs* emanated from the students in the chariot. "Is that what you thought when you, yourself, appealed to the Council of Deities, asking them to allow you and Psyche, a mortal woman, to marry?"

"Why you-you impudent son of a belching boar," Cupid sputtered, his face reddening.

Cupid the cat let out a powerful hiss as he leapt into Red's arms, glaring at Cupid, the god.

"Ugh, you mortals and your ever-present pets," Cupid said. "Do you realize that with a mere snap of my fingers I could have you and your cat—"

"Red's my cousin," Nevan cut in, wedging himself between them to shield Red from Cupid's hair-trigger wrath. "He's so fond of mythology that he named his most prized possession, his cat," Nevan patted the top of the cat's head, "after you."

"A cat with me as its namesake?" Cupid shuddered. "Good grief, what's this planet coming to? If only you had a third eye," Cupid nearly growled at Nevan, "I could blacken that one too."

"Cupid, listen, please...Red's only trying to help me," Nevan went on, "so please don't obliterate him or his cat. I'm the one you want to deal with. I love Aladee, Cupid. With everything I've got inside me, I love her. And she feels the same about me."

He tugged Aladee close to his side. "I read about you and Psyche and the challenges you went through to be together, so I know somewhere deep inside you have to understand. You *must* still remember what it feels like to love someone so much it hurts. To care about a woman so deeply it's like a part of your soul is missing when you're not together. I'm just asking for a chance, that's all. A chance to have our case heard before you zap the memories from our minds."

"Oh, Nevan." Aladee buried her head in the crook of his arm. "That was wonderful."

"Granted, the mortal sounds sincere, and made a few good points," Cupid admitted grudgingly, and Aladee noted his expression had softened, "but that still doesn't mean—"

"Cupid," Lonan said gently, resting his hand on Cupid's arm. "When's the last time we had a request like this from a student?"

Cupid rubbed his jaw. "Not that long ago. Maybe fifty years." He studied Lonan. "Oh, cousin," he groaned. "How well I know that look. You're going to ask me to take them, aren't you? Dammit, Lonan." Hands on hips, Cupid lowered his head, shaking it slowly from left to right. When he looked up again, he was grinning, much to Aladee's astonishment.

"You old dog," he chuckled, giving Lonan a playful punch. "You've always been the levelheaded one. Besides," he shot a glance at Red, "it looks like you may have your own reasons for my being soft on these mortals, hmm?"

"Indeed." Lonan clasped Red's hand, gazing at him with a warm smile. "I've waited centuries for an opportunity like this." He waved a chastising finger at Cupid. "And you owe me, Cupid. Remember the time we—"

Cupid bellowed an exasperated groan. "Oh, all right, don't hound me to death just because I've lost a few bets with you."

"Good. Fortunately, we have room for two more in the chariot," Lonan announced.

"Two?" Cupid barked. His glower softened as he gazed at Lonan, looking fondly toward Red. Throwing his hands up in the air and letting his arms fall, slapping his sides, Cupid laughed. "Okay, you win. We'll take them both."

Red sucked in a gasp and blinked. "Well, this is something I never expected."

"That makes two of us." Lonan patted his hand, then stroked the cat's fur. "We owe it to ourselves to know each other better."

Red sucked in a deep breath. "As much as I long to come with you, Lonan—and God knows I do—I have responsibilities here. I own a flower shop and—"

"Really? I'm passionate about flowers. Wait until you glimpse my vibrant, colorful gardens, Red. Floral splendor at its finest. And you needn't worry, even if we're gone for days, we can arrange to return you here to Earth only a moment later than we left. It will be as if you'd never been gone."

Red arched an eyebrow. "Time travel?"

Lonan shrugged. "Of course."

Exchanging glances, Red and Nevan shrugged and chorused, "Of course."

"You may as well come along for the journey," Cupid said to Red with a yawn. "After all, as Aladee suspected, you and Lonan are a perfect love match. It's all but glowing out of your pores."

"Oh, Cupid," Aladee gushed, taking his hand and kissing it several times. "You're every bit as wonderful and magnificent and superb and brilliant and wonderful as all the legends claim."

"You said wonderful twice," Cupid noted. "Is she always such a suck up?" he asked Lonan.

"Not usually. I think she's just blinded by your glorious radiance, oh magnificent one," Lonan teased.

Roaring laughter, Cupid led them to the invisible chariot. As the dog and cat came along, Cupid halted. "We can't bring the animals too."

"They're like beloved family members," Aladee said. "Nevan and Red feel about them like parents feel about their children. My classmates will enjoy playing with them during the trip. Buster and Cupid the cat are quite endearing."

"If I give permission," Cupid asked her, "will you cease all your incessant chatter and stop talking my ears off?"

"Oh yes, Cupid, I will. Absolutely. I promise."

"Very well then. You may bring them aboard."

"Oh thank you, Cupid, thank you! I know how much this means to Nevan and Red and—"

Cupid held up one hand, arched an eyebrow, and placed his forefinger against her lips, shushing her. "You promised," he chastised.

"You have all your school materials, don't you, Aladee?" Lonan asked as they neared the vehicle.

Her heart thumping madly, Aladee swallowed hard. Flashing her most engaging grin, she patted her canvas tote. "Of course, Lonan," she lied.

Turning back, Cupid gazed at Aladee. "You've used your forgetfulness powder on all who know any particulars about you, right?"

"Absolutely, Cupid," she lied again, afraid to chance a glance at Nevan or Red.

By the gods, she was a marked nymph for sure.

Chapter Seventeen

~<>~

"WHAT DO YOU mean, *Step on up*?" Nevan groused. "How can I step on something I can't see?" The distinct sound of giggling distracted him. "They're all watching me, aren't they?" he whispered to Aladee.

"Yes, Nevan." She patted his butt. "Now show my classmates what a brave, wonderful mortal I've chosen by lifting your foot and locating the chariot's platform. Don't worry about the dog and cat, I've got them. Do you want me to give you a push?" She pressed her hands against his butt.

"Certainly not." Nevan noticed Aladee couldn't help laughing. Oh, yeah, easy for her, she was in her own element now. Trying not to make any more of an ass of himself than necessary, Nevan sucked in a breath, grasped the invisible rail Aladee guided him to, and planted his foot on a solid surface, hiking himself up onto the floor of the chariot—the invisible chariot, tethered to a team of invisible whinnying horses, loaded with a bunch of invisible nymphs and goat-men, and God only knew what else.

"Damn." He looked down at the ground a good thirty-some inches beneath his feet as Aladee's invisible classmates applauded. It was hard to look cool when your gut was flipping somersaults.

He stuck out his hand for Red who, looking as eager and gleeful as a kid at a carnival, hopped on board with little effort.

"Isn't this marvelous, Nevan? Wondrous!"

"Yeah. Yippee." Nevan wholly disagreed with his cousin's assessment. There's nothing he hated more than not feeling in control. This was definitely one of those times.

222

"Now call Buster and Cupid to follow you," Aladee instructed. Nevan and Red did just that. Without any hesitation, both animals hopped onboard. Aladee was next to climb up.

"Nevan and Red," Lonan said as he and Cupid boarded, "we'll be lifting into the air shortly. Sit on the floor toward the center of the chariot, clutching a leather loop for safety. Aladee, why don't you slip your invisibility garment on while I hide the cousins beneath the invisibility shield for take-off."

"Oh...I'll just huddle under the shield with Nevan, Red, and their pets to maintain calm until we get in the air," Aladee said, hunching down beside the cousins and flashing them a guilty smile.

Giving her a reassuring wink, Nevan hoped Lonan didn't find out about her missing class materials until after they pleaded their case to the Council.

"Do your best, mortals, not to shriek like frightened, shivering puppies when we leave the terra firma," Cupid said, walking to what Nevan supposed was the head of the chariot. The next instant he was invisible too, just like Lonan a moment later.

"Can you see me, Red?" Nevan asked. Under cover of the shield, all he saw was the park and people milling around as usual. He couldn't even see his own feet or hands. It was like he was suddenly a ghost. It's not a sensation he'd ever wanted to experience until he was, well, a ghost.

"No," Red gushed. "Isn't this thrilling?"

"I can barely contain my excitement." Nevan clamped down on the inside of his cheeks with his teeth to keep from shrieking like a frightened, shivering puppy when the chariot soared into the air. He'd never been particularly afraid of heights but when he glanced down and saw miles of nothingness between him and the ground, he squeezed his eyes shut, trying to still his racing heart by petting Buster.

The next time he took a peek, he breathed a sigh of relief seeing the wooden floorboards of the chariot beneath him.

"We're clear now." Lonan lifted the invisibility shield from the cousins and Aladee. "You won't need this anymore until we return you to Earth." He smoothed Red's dark hair. "Doing all right?"

"This is the most incredible experience I've ever had." Red glanced around at the now visible means of transportation. "I had no idea chariots could be so immense."

"Having just two wheels, personal vehicles are smaller," Lonan explained. "The more generous, four-wheel models like this one are used for transporting groups, such as students from the academy."

"Fascinating." Red looked like a kid at Christmas.

"Would you like to come to the front with me and watch as I govern the horses and pilot the craft?"

"Very much. Can I bring Cupid?"

"Of course. I'll take him while you hold onto me for support." Lonan presented his forearm, hand fisted.

"*O Captain! My Captain!*" Red breathed, clasping Lonan's arm and rising to his feet.

"Walt Whitman," Lonan noted. "A favorite of mine. Arguably one of America's most influential and innovative poets."

"An admirer of Earth's poets?" Red arched an eyebrow. "I'm surprised...and impressed."

"I'm well versed in Earth's culture and literary heritage," Lonan said. "A favorite passage from Shakespeare comes to mind. *Shall I compare thee to a summer's day?*" he spoke softly as he leaned close to Red's ear, covering his hand. "*Thou art more lovely and more temperate.*"

"A striking man who pilots a chariot and quotes Shakespeare too." Red sighed, looping his arm through Lonan's.

"He's got it bad," Nevan whispered, watching his cousin gaze adoringly at Aladee's teacher.

"Which one?" Aladee asked, snuggling close to Nevan.

Studying Red and Lonan as they headed, arm in arm, to the front of the chariot, Nevan smiled. "Both of them."

Nevan's eyes widened and he gulped air as the other occupants of the chariot became visible. As his gaze swept from one creature to another, he felt like he was in the middle of a fantastical Tolkien tale.

"Who...or *what* are all those?" he whispered to Aladee, observing a quirky mix of beings with wings, scales, blue flesh, green flesh, horns, and more than one head.

"My classmates." Aladee gave a nonchalant shrug. "A pixie, two nixies, one banshee—"

"As is screaming, wild?" Nevan interrupted, taking in the thin, ashen female dressed in yards of drab gray veiling.

"Yes, but Kreshti's only a wailing harbinger of death when absolutely necessary," Aladee explained. "Otherwise, she's great fun to be with." Smiling, Aladee greeted the banshee with a finger wave, which the banshee returned.

"I can just imagine," Nevan offered, not meaning a word.

She nodded toward the rest of the creatures. "Liliphant is a sprite, sweet but mischievous. And then—" Aladee frowned. "Don't even think about it, Seraletta," she called.

Nevan followed Aladee's wagging finger to a sexy, pale blue woman with snow-white hair, startling sea-blue eyes and one generous breast bared. Whatever the creature was, she was giving Nevan an unmistakable come-hither look.

"Oh but, Aladee, he's mouthwatering," Seraletta protested, licking her full lips as she gazed at Nevan. "He looks so meaty and delicious. Perhaps you'll consider a trade."

"She wants to eat me?" Nevan asked, incredulous.

"Don't be silly," Aladee whispered before addressing the blue female again. "Sorry, Seraletta. This human is mine," she warned, looping her arm through Nevan's in a possessive gesture. Leaning close, she whispered in his ear. "Steer clear of her. Seraletta's an undine, a type of water sprite. The only way undines can acquire a soul is by marrying a human being."

"Huh." Nevan was fascinated by the absurdity of it all.

"Next to Seraletta," Aladee pointed out, "there's a brownie, a fairy, a sylph, and a dwarf. And that's Vibius, the satyr who wants to mate with me. Ugh." She shuddered.

Nevan gaze flew to the horned half man, half animal with the evil grin, playing some weird tune on his flute. Well-muscled, with dark curly hair, bronzed skin and green eyes, he wasn't bad looking. For a goat.

Vibius eyeballed Aladee as if she was a juicy, rare steak he couldn't wait to sink his teeth—and other parts—into. Narrowing his gaze at goat boy, Nevan wrapped his arm around Aladee, tugging her close. Goat boy sneered.

"Don't bruise her, Neanderthal," Vibius said. "Aladee's mine."

A gasp of outrage flew out of Aladee's lips. "In your dreams, Vibius."

"You're always in my dreams, Aladee." Vibius grinned. "On your knees with your plump, ripe ass in the air, begging me to f—"

"Hey, pal, watch your mouth," Nevan warned. "There are ladies present. And Aladee's my woman, got it? Hands off." Buster offered a soft bark of concord.

A muffled din rolled through the chariot as all eyes were on Nevan and Vibius.

Vibius narrowed his gaze. "You may have wormed your way into her heart, interloper, but the nymph is mine."

"Look, goat boy—" Nevan began.

"The mortal and I are soul mates, Vibius. I love him," Aladee cut in, her cheeks pink with indignation. As she clung to Nevan, he could feel her trembling with fury, or was it fear? He held her closer, soothing her arm with his hand.

"Don't be selfish, Aladee," Seraletta the undine said. "Why don't you take Vibius and let me have the mortal?" she offered, blowing a kiss to Nevan.

Vibius rose from his seat, a fierce scowl across his face. He stood a good seven feet tall and looked ready to rumble. "What absurd folderol you speak, nymph. We are of the same kind, Aladee. We are destined to mate. The gods will never agree to—"

"Enough, Vibius!" Cupid's voice bellowed. He strode toward Vibius from the front of the chariot and stood before him, hands fisted on hips. "Since when do you dare presume to speak for the gods?"

Vibius straightened, chin elevated as he looked Cupid in the eye. "But, Cupid, I—"

"Would you truly chance quarrelling with me, satyr?" Cupid spat. "Knowing full well I could turn you into a horned toad with the snap of my fingers?" Cupid held up his hand, fingers poised to snap.

Eyes flashing with alarm, Vibius immediately took his seat. "My humble apologies, Cupid. I meant no disrespect."

With a glance toward Nevan and Aladee, Cupid returned to the front of the chariot where Lonan tended the reins.

Heaving a shuddering sigh, Aladee said, "Thank Jupiter for Cupid's interference. I don't know what would have happened if he hadn't stepped in to put Vibius in his place."

"I would have punched his lights out if he laid a hand on you," Nevan assured as he and Vibius exchanged sneering glances.

"I would fear for you greatly, my love. Satyrs are far stronger than mortal men."

Nevan studied goat boy, the horns, the hoofs, the powerful looking goat flanks. "I could take him," he lied with false bravado. "Why don't you finish telling me about all the other people...uh, creatures, here in the chariot."

Aladee nodded, taking a deep breath and expelling it. "On the other side of the chariot, starting closest to us, there are two elves, a gnome, a troll, a goblin and a kobold."

"What, no ogres or leprechauns?" Nevan teased, thoroughly awestruck by the curious beings, most of whom were at least partially nude.

"Cupid Academy teachers have had countless problems trying to tame and educate ogres over the centuries. Last year during the Feast of Lupercalia, Bubbadoofik was expelled for conduct unbecoming a student."

"Bubba who?"

"Bubbadoofik. The ogre."

"Uh-huh." Nevan nodded, as if this was normal, everyday conversation. "So what did old Bubba do, swipe a leg of lamb or something?" He chuckled as he formed a mental image.

"No, he tried to eat Liliphant." Aladee gestured toward the pretty, youthful looking sprite.

Nevan's mouth gaped open. "You're kidding?" He didn't know why he bothered to ask because, of course, she wasn't.

"Lonan had such high hopes for Bubbadoofik too. As for leprechauns, Clarence is the only one in our class, but he's on holiday right now. He's a master shoemaker and a really nice guy. He made these sandals for me." Aladee shifted her position to display a gold-tipped shoe. "He's visiting his kinfolk in Ireland for their family reunion."

"So...uh..." Nevan gave a surreptitious glance to the chariot's occupants. "Besides Seraletta, who's in search of a soul, and Vibius, who's itching to buck my ass with those goat hooves, is there anyone else here I need to be wary of? I mean, human flesh isn't considered a delicacy is it?"

He couldn't help wondering, the way some of Aladee's classmates sniffed the air, eyeing him as if picturing him trussed on a platter, nestled between a mound of mashed potatoes and buttered ears of corn,.

"Bubbadoofik would have been in ecstasy, had he been here," Aladee said. "As for the others, most are just impish. Except for Edgar the goblin. Don't get on his bad side. He can be downright mean."

She tapped her chin while scanning the other students. "That's Ofradurn, the troll." She nodded in the direction of a burly, ugly-as-sin, wild-haired little creature. "Trolls have an aversion to loud noises, so keep that in mind. I felt so sorry for poor Kreshti the last time she let out an earsplitting wail. Ofradurn actually taped the poor banshee's mouth shut. Can you imagine?"

Nevan was silent a moment. "Give me a minute...I'm trying."

"I almost forgot about Dunniger," Aladee said thoughtfully. "He's the charming, dashing one there in the corner. The one who looks like a finely honed Greek god. While he claims to have given up the consumption of human flesh over a century ago, one can never be too sure, so keep your distance."

"What is he?" Nevan thought he looked like an ordinary, attractive guy until he caught sight of the way his skin shone faintly with iridescent green scales that were almost imperceptible unless caught by the sun's rays. He bore an air of sophistication and confidence.

"A dragon," Aladee answered, and you could have knocked Nevan over with a feather.

"Get the hell out of here," he said.

"While we're in midair?" Aladee gasped. "What if my wings don't open?"

Nevan laughed. "It's just an expression meaning I found what you said hard to believe. I thought dragons were huge reptilian creatures with claws who breathed fire. This guy looks suave, like a male model. Well, except for the greenish scales."

"Dunniger is able to change his form just like that." Aladee snapped her fingers. "The brownies and sprites find his natural size and appearance too menacing, so he usually maintains a human shape when they're around. He's quite the ladies' man and has many female admirers."

"But he's an actual dragon...like the ones in medieval stories?"

"A fierce, mighty one." Aladee nodded. "Who could roast and consume you before you've even blinked an eye. So try not to do anything to rile him."

Nevan stared at the debonair dragon a moment before shifting his gaze back to Aladee. "Right," he said. Really, what else *could* he say?

"As for Mookie," Aladee motioned to a cute, pudgy little guy who looked harmless, "as long as he doesn't sense you're after his treasure, you'll be fine."

"What is he?"

"Mookie's a gnome. To be on the safe side, avoid the topic of finances with him. He looks sweet and innocent enough, but if he feels threatened he bares his sharpened teeth. It's a fairly daunting sight."

"The little guy's rich, huh?"

"He probably has more gold than your government's treasury," Aladee answered. "His hoard is hidden away near his permanent home underground."

"On Olympus?"

"I don't know." Aladee shrugged. "Mookie's very secretive. No one knows exactly where he lives." Aladee squeezed Nevan's hand. "Would you like to move to the side of the chariot so you can take a look down?" She smiled when he hesitated. "It's quite a splendid panorama, I assure you."

Nevan looked into Aladee's eyes. Usually a deep blue, they were lighter now—clear and bright as they soared through the clouds.

Her pouty pink lips were curved into a smile and her gold curls glinted in the sunlight.

"Sure, why not?" He got to his feet and helped Aladee up. A quick glance at the back of the chariot had him swallowing hard. "You'd think they'd put backs on these things. Does anyone ever fall out?" As he asked the question, the chariot dipped, jostling everyone and Nevan yelped as he fought to keep his balance.

"Quiet!" Ofradurn the troll warned, and Nevan noticed the guy patting a roll of what looked like duct tape looped at the belt of his grungy tan suede tunic.

"Yes, on occasion, passengers have fallen out, but they're usually rescued by one of the flying patrols before plummeting to their deaths," Aladee said.

"Flying patrols...you mean like air police?"

"I'd liken them more to coast guards who monitor your beaches and keep swimmers safe," she answered. "The patrols are dispatched from Olympus to keep passengers of the skies safe. Winged horses, lesser gods and even some of the stronger nymphs and fairies are employed. But I'd recommend that you try to avoid spilling out of the chariot if possible, Nevan. It's a terrible, ghastly fright before you get scooped up and carried back to safety."

Nevan eyed her, smiling as he caught Aladee nibbling her bottom lip. "It sounds like you're speaking from firsthand experience."

"I'm afraid so," Aladee said just above a whisper. "Twice so far."

"Well, that just makes me feel so much safer standing here in the middle of a backless flying chariot with you, sweetheart," Nevan said, tongue firmly planted in cheek.

"Why, thank you, Nevan." Aladee beamed a smile at him. "That's nice of you to say."

Chuckling, Nevan wrapped his arm around Aladee's waist, ready to guide her to the side rail.

"Sorry, Buster," he scratched behind the dog's ears, "but I've got to keep the harness on you during our trip. I don't want you falling out." With thoughts of Vibius, the goat boy, in mind, he muttered, "Or thrown out."

"Don't fret, Nevan, I've already prepared both Buster and Cupid for the flight. They understand the dangers of jumping out."

That made Nevan feel better. Aladee certainly did have a way with Buster, and Red's cat.

Standing at the chariot's rail together, they gazed at the passing vistas. Damn. She was right. The view was magnificent. Breathtaking. Mountains, canyons, and winding bodies of water. Clouds and mystical winged creatures soaring by. Every so often, he witnessed a strange hazy flash. Like an image trying to come into focus, but just missing.

"What are those weird cloudy flashes?"

"Brief glimpses into different time periods," Aladee said. "Due to the speed, location and magical properties of the chariot."

Nevan was getting used to hearing bizarre answers to his questions, so he took her explanation in stride. If there were ogres, leprechauns, dragons, and screaming wild banshees, why not time travel too?

"What's that in the distance?" Nevan asked, eyeing something that resembled a city, glinting like gold, high atop a mountain beneath the cover of fluffy white clouds.

"Olympus." Taking his hands in hers, Aladee turned to face him. "Wait until you see it, Nevan. It's the most wondrous, magical place. Quite unlike Earth. We'll have such fun together there."

At the mention of Olympus, thoughts of meeting with the ominous Council of Deities surged through Nevan's mind. Fun? He wondered for a split second if he might be better off just diving off the chariot now.

Chapter Eighteen

~<>~

"I FEEL LIKE I'm in a museum." Roaming around Lonan's vast residence, Nevan had a new understanding of feeling like a fish out of water.

"Habitats here do differ greatly from those on Earth," Aladee said. "But why a museum?"

Stuffing his hands in his pockets, Nevan gave an uneasy shrug. "I'm surrounded by huge marble columns, big, ornate paintings unlike any I've ever seen in anybody's house, carved stone statues and busts of famous people throughout history, and—"

"Watch this, Nevan," Aladee interrupted, boasting an impish smile as she waved her hand over a few of the chiseled busts, astounding Nevan as the heads came to life, made eye contact, smiled, and spoke of their deeds, accomplishments and history.

"Whoa! That's incredible. See what I mean? Definitely museum-worthy, just like all the rest of the expensive-looking stuff everywhere I look. Everything's marble, silver, gold...tons of glass and fragile things. I'm afraid to breathe too hard because I might break something. Look at Buster, he's afraid too."

Bending to pet the dog's back, Aladee laughed. "Neither of you have to worry. I'm the clumsy one, not you."

Forgetting his discomfort with the posh surroundings, Nevan drew her into a hug, scraping his chin through the curls atop her head. "You're not clumsy. A little absentminded, a tad impulsive, and a smidgen reckless." He chuckled as Aladee's mouth gaped. "But never clumsy." He captured her lips in a soft kiss.

"You think I'm reckless?" Aladee gazed up at him, all wide-eyed and innocent.

"Definitely. But," he added when she opened her pretty mouth to protest, "I wouldn't want you any other way. I love you for who you are, Aladee. All of it. The whole tamale."

"Tamale..." Aladee frowned. "It will take a lifetime for me to learn the curious meanings of all your favorite expressions, Nevan."

"If everything works out the way we hope, we'll have that lifetime, sweetheart."

"From your lips to Jupiter's ears," Aladee said, clapping her hands against her abdomen when her stomach growled. "Apparently, I'm famished." She laughed. "Lonan said there would be a palatable repast awaiting us in the garden. Would you like to partake?"

Scratching his head, Nevan grinned. "Looks like you're not the only one who's got to learn about foreign expressions. If you're asking me if I'm hungry and want to eat, the answer is yes. Hopefully Lonan's got something I can feed Buster too."

"I'm sure he does. He has pets of his own."

"He's got a dog too?"

"Mmm..." she tapped her chin, "not exactly."

When she didn't elucidate, Nevan asked, "A cat?" Aladee remained silent, simply smiling at him. "A turtle? Goldfish? Hamster? What?"

"You'll see," she said in a singsong voice, clearly relishing keeping Nevan in suspense.

"Okay, now you're scaring me. It's not like a giant cyclops or something, is it?"

"Don't be silly, Nevan. A cyclops would be a friend, not a pet. Don't worry, my big, brave he-man. Lonan doesn't own any mortal-eating monsters."

Admittedly relieved, Nevan followed as Aladee led him through Lonan's gargantuan house. "This place is so big, you could get lost getting to the bathroom and back."

"It's immense," Aladee agreed. "And this is only the east wing. There are three others. Lonan and Red are at the other end of the house in the west wing. I'm somewhat familiar with the design plan because Lonan has hosted brunches and dinners here for his students. He loves to entertain and he's a marvelous cook."

"Looks like he can afford to hire a five-star restaurant staff to do his cooking for him," Nevan said with a low whistle as they walked through the elaborate, state-of-the-art kitchen. He paused, studying the hardware on the kitchen cabinets and drawers, which was weird because he couldn't remember finding *anything* in a kitchen the least bit interesting before, except for the food that came out of it.

The ornate hinges, door pulls and knobs were brass, or maybe they were gold. Each was carved into the shape of a different mythical creature. Even for non-art lovers like Nevan, it was impossible not to be awestruck.

"Lonan has a full staff, but still enjoys preparing meals on his own," Aladee said. "It's one of his hobbies. He also enjoys working in the garden, and painting, like the mural on the opposite wall." Aladee gestured to a striking, museum-quality painting of a picnic under a bank of lush trees that spanned one entire wall.

"Whoa..." Nevan was incredulous. "Lonan painted that?"

"Half of it. He likes to provide visuals for his students, believing that a picture is worth a thousand words. The portion from the left to the center of the wall is solely by Lonan's hand. His art students painted the portion from the center to the right. Lonan taught them so well, it's a seamless meeting of paint and styles."

Filled with new respect for Aladee's teacher, Nevan walked closer to the mural. "I'm not an art lover. I don't even claim to understand it, but even I can tell a work of artistic genius when I see it. It looks like da Vinci or Michelangelo could have painted this."

"A portion of it. Look close, there in the middle of the right portion, you can make out their signatures."

"You can't be serious." Leaning close enough to spot the signatures, Nevan gasped, staggered by Aladee's incredible revelation. "I can't believe it. You're talking about the guy who painted the Mona Lisa, and the guy who did the Sistine Chapel, right?"

"They were Lonan's students during the Renaissance. Oh, the tales Lonan has told of those days!" Aladee laughed. "Apparently, Leonardo and his younger rival, Michelangelo, didn't get along very well. One was always trying to sabotage the other."

Nevan plowed a hand through his hair, cursing beneath his breath. "Lonan taught them how to paint?"

"And how to sculpt, and cast, and understand perspective, and, well, basically everything else necessary for the success of an artist and craftsperson." Her stomach growled again. Taking Nevan's hand, she tugged. "We'll look at it again later. Let's eat."

She led him toward a colossal wall of glass, showcasing the magnificent garden beyond. It was so clean and clear it was barely visible. While Nevan watched, Aladee made a waving motion with her hand, then proceeded to walk smack dab into the glass with a loud thud.

"Oh!"

"Aladee!" Buster barked along with Nevan's exclamation.

She reeled back, rubbing her forehead with the heel of her hand as Nevan put his arm around her. "I wasn't expecting that." Buster got up on his hind legs, pawing Aladee with concern.

"Glass will do that," Nevan offered, determined not to laugh out loud at the ridiculous sight of Aladee meeting the huge panel of glass head on. "Mind telling me what the heck you were doing?"

"Walking through the glass partition to the garden," she explained, massaging her nose with her fingers. "I'm okay, Buster. Good boy." She mussed his fur.

"Um..." Nevan was quickly losing the battle not to laugh. "Maybe if we opened the patio door instead..." he suggested through his inevitable laughter.

Shooting him a distinct frown at first, Aladee soon joined him in laughter. "I suppose that did look rather curious. Lonan has glass panels throughout the house set up to dissolve with a particular hand command. And I, well, I..." She nibbled her bottom lip.

"Let me take a wild guess. You forgot the special abracadabra hand signal, right?"

"Let me try another," Aladee said with determination, clearly concentrating as she made another grand flourish. This time she reached out for the glass instead of walking into it. "Ouch," she complained, nursing her hand after banging it on the solid partition. This time, Buster stood looking at her, turning his head left and right in puzzlement.

"Maybe Lonan has some leftovers in the fridge," Nevan said, looking around. "Where is it?"

"Behind the unicorn," Aladee said absently as she fluttered, waved, and brandished her hand to no avail.

Nevan rummaged around the kitchen, coming up empty handed. "What unicorn?"

Turning, Aladee pointed to the small stone unicorn perched atop a waist-high marble column. "Tug on its horn."

Nevan did and the wall opened, revealing a huge, walk-in refrigerator. "Son of a bitch," he breathed as he spied a roasted hog's head, two deep shelves of what appeared to be prime fillets of beef, three separate cases containing wines and cheese, four full suckling pigs, trussed and ready for roasting, and endless other edibles.

"And a partridge in a pear tree," Nevan muttered. Noticing Buster's rapt attention as he licked his muzzle, Nevan told him, "Nope, sorry, boy, nothing here for you." He signaled for Buster to get out of the gargantuan fridge. Eventually he obeyed.

A sheet of paper taped to one of the shelves caught Nevan's eye. As soon as he read it, he laughed. Whisking it from the shelf, he brought it to Aladee.

"Master Lonan asked me to place this here for you, Aladee," she read aloud. "Regards, Hercules." Beneath the note was a sketched diagram outlining the proper hand gesture to dissolve the glass panels. Aladee gave a small, embarrassed laugh. "Lonan knows me too well."

"So, Hercules..." Nevan began. "Is he..."

"No," Aladee smiled, patting Nevan's arm, "he's not *that* Hercules. This one is Lonan's manservant. He's a lovely, very efficient older man who's been with Lonan for years."

"Centuries, probably," Nevan mused, surprised at how quickly he'd come to accept all this mystical, magical fairytale stuff. It was woo-woo to the max!

"Most likely," Aladee agreed, studying the paper and practicing. "Okay, Nevan. I've got it now. Take my hand and we'll walk through the glass together." She beamed a smile up at him, only to pout when Nevan hesitated. "Don't you trust me?"

She looked so determined, Nevan figured it was worth a good bang on the noggin to show her he believed in her. "Sure I do. Let's go."

Bracing himself for a clunk while Aladee gestured, Nevan mumbled, "Well, I'll be damned," as they walked right through the glass. Or the dissolved glass. Or whatever the hell just happened.

Once outside, a gentle floral fragrance surrounded them. "Reminds me of Red's flower shop," Nevan noted. "Hey, look," he pointed as they turned the corner, "there's a swimming pool too."

"And a hidden waterfall just over there." Aladee pointed a short distance away.

"I can think of lots of squeaky-clean fun we can have in there."

"Me too," Aladee said, a blush coloring her cheeks. "But that comes after we eat." She headed to a table and chairs positioned on the stone patio near one vine-covered wall. Sniffing the air, she closed her eyes. "Mmmm! I smell coda alla vaccinara!"

"Coda whoda?" Whatever it was, it smelled mighty good.

"Roman oxtail stew," Aladee clarified and Nevan couldn't help sneering. "Oh, it's delicious, Nevan. It's made from true oxen meat, not beef. The tails are combined with pine nuts, cinnamon, cloves, nutmeg, raisins and other ingredients, simmered together for hours in red wine with plum tomatoes. Lonan is so sweet. He remembered this is one of my favorite dishes. I wonder what he made for himself and Red."

"Whatever it is, I'm pretty damn sure Red will love it down to the last crumb." Nevan lifted the linen napkin from a basket and licked his lips. "Crusty bread. Excellent!"

"Perfect for dipping into the stew." Aladee sat in a chair, placing a napkin in her lap.

Nevan's smile grew wider when he spied a small plate stacked with pale yellow pats. "And butter! Lonan didn't let me down, either." He took a seat, realizing he was hungrier than he'd thought.

"Wait until you taste the wine." Aladee held up her glass, tilting it this way and that as she admired the deep red liquid. "It's from Lonan's own vineyards. Shall we make a toast?"

Aladee's expectant look told him it would mean a lot to her if he said something romantic. He wasn't eloquent, or a romantic, but he'd try his best.

"To the only woman who's ever heard me use the L word directed at her. My darling Aladee, the most beautiful nymph on

Earth, Olympus, or anywhere else." Nevan figured it wouldn't hurt to add, "May we live long and prosper."

"Oh, Nevan," Aladee trilled the words out on a sigh. Since she was all dreamy-eyed, Nevan knew he'd scored. "That was so romantic. How did you know Spock is one of my favorite fictional characters?"

Clueless about that fact, Nevan offered a confident smile. "I made it my business to find out," he lied. If a little white lie made her so happy, what was the harm? "I'll bet you thought Red was the only one in the family who could spout great poetic lines."

"You're truly an amazing man, Nevan." She held up one hand in a Vulcan salute, which Nevan met with his own, as they clinked glasses and drank.

Surprised by the wine's delicious taste, Nevan looked into its red depths. "I've never tasted anything like this." He studied her silently for a moment before asking, "So, how do you know about Spock and Vulcans, but not something simple like hot fudge sundaes?"

"Because we finished studying the history of Earth media but haven't gotten to the chapter on Earthly culinary habits yet." She ladled some of the rich stew into Nevan's bowl. "Oxtails are said to increase a man's stamina," she noted. "So be sure you eat a hearty portion...maybe two." She snuck a glance at him and giggled.

Hesitant to take the first bite, Nevan ended up scarfing down three bowls of the delicious concoction, plus plenty of good bread, butter, and wine. The chariot ride must have given him an appetite. He should have been bursting at the seams, but instead of being stuffed, he felt perfect, well fed and ready to do the horizontal mambo. Of course, with his amazing winged nymph, it didn't necessarily have to be horizontal.

"Let's see what Lonan had his cook prepare for our dessert." Aladee lifted the dome cover from one of the chilled servers. "Mmm, another of my favorites." She set one goblet in front of Nevan, and the other at her place.

Looking at the white and brown stuff in his dish, Nevan wrinkled his nose. "What is it?"

"Greek yogurt with raw honey, rose water, almonds, roasted pecans, and a dash of cinnamon."

Nevan pushed it away. "Sorry. I don't like yogurt."

"Do you like ice cream?"

His smile turned devilish. "You know I do...especially when I get to lick it off your delicious little body."

"How about cheesecake?" Aladee went on, clearly doing her best to ignore Nevan's comment, but the pink spots in her cheeks gave her away.

"Love it," Nevan said. "And I bet it tastes even better spread all over your—"

"Good, then you'll like this," she cut in. "It's made from full-fat milk and cream, so there's less tang. It's drained until it's nearly as thick as cheese." She scooped a dollop onto Nevan's spoon and leaned toward him, pressing the tip of the cool metal to his lips. "Try it," she urged.

Taking the spoon into his mouth, Nevan was surprised the yogurt was as tasty as Aladee promised. The raw honey was so thick it was almost fudgy. As her hand started to retreat, Nevan held it firm, locking gazes with her as he licked the spoon, then trailed his tongue across her fingers and thumb. He couldn't wait to finish their first dessert...so he could start in on his second. He kissed the inside of her wrist and she sighed.

The nearby sound of three short muffled gongs captured his attention. "Doorbell?" He sat straight up in his chair.

"Three gongs means there's a message for us. It must be important, about our plea to the Council of Deities, otherwise

Lonan wouldn't have had us disturbed," Aladee noted. Scooting her chair back, she rose to her feet. "I'll be right back."

It seemed like a small eternity before Aladee returned, which wasn't surprising considering how gigantic Lonan's house was. Returning to the table, she carried what looked like a parchment scroll. Aladee looked a little green.

"Bad news?" Nevan asked.

"I don't know." Sucking in a deep breath, she expelled it with a whoosh. "I haven't read it yet, but it's from the council." She dragged her chair next to Nevan's, pushed the dessert away and set the scroll on the table between them. "You open it," she said. "I'm too nervous."

Nevan unrolled the document, skimming until he got past all the mumbo-jumbo. "Looks like even the gods use attorneys," he quipped before going on. He got to the part that had to do with him and Aladee and read carefully. Looking up at Aladee, who was busy wringing her hands, Nevan smiled.

"The good news is that we're getting this all over with tomorrow. The even better news is that Lonan and Red are pleading before the council too." He smoothed the scroll out in front of her. "See?"

Aladee mumbled the passage aloud. After corkscrewing her features, she covered her face with her hands and burst into tears.

"What's wrong, sweetheart?" Nevan pulled her into a hug, caressing her back. "This is good news, isn't it?" Damn, he hated seeing a woman cry. He never knew what to do or say to make it better. "Don't cry, Aladee, don't cry," is all he managed to come up with.

"I-I'm crying because I'm so happy," she wailed through a hiccupping sob. "Because the council has agreed to hear our plea and...and because the second and third most favorite men in my life are so much in love they want to be together forever."

"Well I'm glad those are happy tears." Nevan kissed her cheek.

"Oh Nevan, it made my heart so glad to see how perfect Lonan and Red are for each other. They have so much in common. Did you see the way they looked at each other during the chariot ride, and afterwards when the four of us gathered together for coffee and pastries on Lonan's patio? It was like they had stars in their eyes."

"Yeah," he nodded, "I saw it too. They got along as if they'd known each other for years rather than hours. It seems Red has adapted to his surroundings to the point where he might even be mistaken for a resident of Olympus." Laughing quietly, Nevan added, "Who knew Red's lifelong fascination with mythology would come in so handy for him one day."

"Indeed." Aladee gave him a watery-eyed smile. "I'm so glad you can see the love there too."

"While I don't necessarily consider myself observant when it comes to romance," Nevan admitted, "I've never seen Red so..." he fought to come up with the right word to describe it, "*happy*." He shrugged. "*Happy* might not be a fancy ten-dollar word, but there's nothing more prized. True happiness is hard to find, and easily lost once it's found. What I saw with Red and Lonan was powerful—pure, unadulterated happiness."

"It's probably the same thing your cousin and Lonan see when they look at us," Aladee noted. "All the money in the world can't buy the amazing feeling that comes with the happiness love creates."

"No matter what happens from this point forward," Nevan took Aladee's hands, holding them against his heart, "I will always be grateful you and I, as well as Red and Lonan, were able to discover and experience love—happiness in its truest form." Leaning close, he kissed her.

"That was so utterly, entirely beautiful, Nevan." Tears streamed down Aladee's cheeks. After dabbing her eyes with her napkin she sniveled. "Can you find a pink rose and bring it to me please?"

Stopping himself before closing in for another kiss, Nevan said, "What? You mean now?"

She nodded. "Please." She started bawling again.

Deciding this was no time to start asking questions, he got up, scouting around the vast garden looking for a pink rose. He'd never paid attention to whether roses grew on trees or out of the ground like dandelions, so he just inspected everything that looked pink, had petals and smelled like a rose.

It wasn't long before he found what looked like a rosebush, but the blooms were all red. Another one next to it had all white roses. "Does it have to be pink?" he called to Aladee.

"Yes. A true pink, not peach."

"Who the hell does she think I am, Red?" Nevan groused under his breath. "What the hell could she possibly need a pink rose for now, right this very minute when things were getting nice and— Ouch! Damn thorns."

He'd never understood women. It looked like he wasn't having any better luck with nymphs. "This is nuts," he muttered, digging through the section where he'd spotted the other roses and swearing every time he got stuck by a thorn, which was often. Finally, he found an entire shitload of pink roses.

"How many do you want?" he asked. "A dozen?"

"Just one large perfect bloom," Aladee answered.

"Like I'm really gonna know the difference," Nevan mumbled to himself. Braving thorns, spiders and other creepy-crawly things for the woman he loved, Nevan plucked the pink rose that looked the best to him and hightailed it back to the table where she sat.

"Should I put it in a vase or something?"

Tears still streaming down her face, Aladee shook her head back and forth, snatched the rose from Nevan's fingers and promptly began devouring the petals.

"Aladee?" Maybe she was having some sort of nymph breakdown. Maybe everything was suddenly caving in on her. "Aladee...?"

"Pink roses have a tranquilizing effect on nymphs," she explained, plucking another petal and popping it into her mouth. Damned if Nevan couldn't see her features relax with each petal she ate. By the time she finished the flower, her eyes were dry and her nose and eyes weren't blotchy anymore.

She cradled the thorny stem in her hands and kissed it. "Thank you for your kind sustenance," she said to the naked stem before setting it on the table and smiling at it.

Nevan leaned his ear close, listening.

"What are you doing, Nevan?"

"Waiting to hear—" Suddenly feeling like a jackass, he said, "Damn. It's not going to answer you, is it, Aladee?"

Chuckling, she smoothed her fingers along his jaw. "Of course not. It's a flower, Nevan. Flowers don't have any vocal chords."

"I just thought that maybe up here on Olympus..."

Aladee shook her head. "Nope." She frowned as she glanced at his arms. "Oh, my poor Nevan, look at you. You're bleeding! Your neck and chest too."

Flaunting a hero's smile and chivalrous shrug, Nevan said, "I'd brave anything to make you happy." He kissed the tip of her nose, silently hoping a few scratches from thorns would be the worst of his injuries after tomorrow.

"Let's go to that waterfall you were telling me about." Holding Aladee close as they romped around in the water together would be just the tranquilizer he needed.

Chapter Nineteen

~<>~

NEVAN FLUNG his jeans across a sculpted hedge at the same time Aladee struggled to get out of her dress.

"I'm not used to these sliding tracks," she complained, her arms twisted at her back. She grumbled, acting as if she were snagged in a spider's web as she scraped and tugged.

"It's called a zipper. Here, let me help." Nevan glided the zipper down her back.

Shrugging out of the dress, Aladee breathed a sigh of relief. "I love many things I've discovered on Earth, but can't understand why they make clothing so restrictive and fumblesome. I'll miss easy, comfortable garments when I leave Olympus."

The reminder of what loomed ahead for them tomorrow at the hands of the council stung. Nevan didn't like his life being toyed with, no matter how omnipotent the players might be. Being at the mercy of a group of beings he'd always considered to be mythical was disconcerting at best.

The sight of Aladee's dress flying through the air toward the hedge snagged his attention back to the present.

Off came her bra and panties, tossed on the bushes to join her dress and Nevan's clothes.

An hour later, exhausted and depleted from making love to his insatiable winged nymph beneath the waterfall, Nevan yawned. He was satisfied, sated and entirely content. Aladee took time kissing each of his scratches...in fact, seeing him bloodied seemed to turn her on.

"Nevan?" Sitting on a deep, flat stone, Aladee swished her feet in the water as she worked on a chain of flowers.

"Hmm?" he asked lazily, resting his head against one smooth rock as he reclined against another.

"Are you worried about our meeting with the council tomorrow?"

"Let's just say I'll be glad when it's all over."

"I hope you don't have to fight any dragons or battle any other fierce beasts."

Heaving a sigh, Nevan pulled himself up on his elbows, slanting Aladee a skeptical look. "Aladee."

"Mmm-hmm." She joined the ends of the flower chain, positioning the ring of blooms on her head. A true flower child, complete with butterfly wings, it looked perfectly natural on her.

"Can you maybe keep your fascination with bloodied heroes limited to wrestling thorny rose bushes and not getting barbecued by dragons or skewered by one-eyed monsters twice a man's size?"

She turned, looking at him in surprise. "Oh, Nevan, I never meant—"

"Uh-uh." Wagging a finger at her, he shook his head. "I'm not buying it. I've watched plenty of movies with dragons and fiendish monsters. I've seen how the female is always breathing heavy and getting that certain look in her eyes when her hero returns home bleeding and battered.

"It's a rather romantic notion when a man is wounded after fighting for his love," she said sheepishly.

"Well, forget about it, okay?" Nevan sat up fully, scooting next to Aladee and swinging his feet in the water. "This isn't a romance novel, this is real life."

"Perhaps you'll only have to battle a small troll," she offered helpfully.

"And perhaps we'll go to this council thing," Nevan countered, "and discover everything's handled in a sane, sensible, responsible adult manner. Without any bloody skirmishes."

Aladee patted his thigh. "Keep practicing your positive thinking, Nevan. I'm sure it can't hurt."

"So if they let us remain together, and you haven't managed to get me eviscerated by some gargoyle or something, I guess that means I'll grow to be old and pruny while you still look young, bouncy and perky, huh?"

"Yes," Aladee said with a wistful sigh. "The notion makes me very sad."

"Yeah, well I'm not all that crazy about getting old either. Although it would be cool to be a wrinkled old geezer with a hot babe on his arm. There's always Viagra."

"Who is she?"

"No one." Nevan chuckled. "It's a medication that helps men perform...sexually."

"Ah, I see. It's not your youthful looks or ability to perform sexually that I fear losing, Nevan. It's you." She poked his chest just above his heart and gazed into his eyes. "I love you—the you that's inside." Leaning her head against his chest, she sighed. "Oh Nevan, whatever will I do once your short lifespan has ended? I can't even imagine enduring that pain."

Draping his arm around her shoulder, Nevan drew Aladee close. "Don't worry about that now, sweetheart. We've got a good forty-some years together before I check out."

"Check out?" She gave him that wide-eyed clueless look.

"Kick the bucket. Keel over. Bite the dust." He couldn't help grinning as he saw her perplexed expression. "You know, when I've cashed in my chips, bought the farm, and I'm pushing up daisies."

Aladee nodded thoughtfully. "Those must be euphemisms for death, right?"

"You're not the only creative one around here." Nevan winked as he tapped his finger against her temple.

"That's sweet of you to avoid using the word *die* when referring to your imminent death so as not to upset me."

"Imminent? Hey, you're not fixating on dragons again, are you?"

"Of course not. I'm simply thinking about the forty-some years you mentioned. It will pass in the mere blink of an eye, Nevan. We will have such a short time together before you...bite the bucket." Her chin trembled.

"Whoa, time to change the subject before you start crying again and send me out searching for more pink roses. It's getting dark out and I might not find my way back," Nevan teased.

"You could get mightily scratched up," Aladee said with a bit too much enthusiasm.

"Forget about it, sweet lips."

Lowering her head, Aladee glanced up at him through her lashes and smiled. "I was just making levity."

"Uh-huh." He studied her for a moment before resting his chin atop her head. Her hair smelled faintly of the flowers ringing her curls. "Funny. We've known each other less than a week and I feel like I've known you all my life."

"That's because we're true soul mates."

"Look at Red and Lonan," Nevan noted. "They've only known each other a day and they're ready to commit for life."

"Lonan has waited a long time to meet his soul mate."

"Red too. He's a good guy. The best. Always putting everyone else's needs before his own. I know we tease each other mercilessly but I," Nevan sucked in a deep breath, "well, I love the guy. Red deserves to find someone who really cares about him—especially after all the crap his family put him through. When he and Lonan first saw each other..." Nevan shook his head back and forth, "honestly, Aladee, I can't ever remember seeing my cousin look so happy."

"I felt the same for Lonan," Aladee said. "His expression turned to pure love and contentment when he met Red. I pray the council grants their wish to be together. Perhaps because Lonan is a god, it will be easier for him to get a positive ruling from his peers. I hope so."

"I know my cousin. If they stay together, I'm sure he'd rather live on Olympus than back on Earth." The sudden realization that he and Red might not get to see each other again after tomorrow clawed at Nevan's gut. "What happens if we're down there and Red and Lonan are up here? I mean, do we get visitation rights?"

"I have no idea, Nevan. Our futures will be determined tomorrow by the whim of the gods." She kissed his shoulder. "All I know is that I want to make this night we have together unforgettable. It may be our last. Let's go back to the house." She shivered, pressing herself harder against him. "It's getting chilly out here."

A potent combination of love and lust churned deep in Nevan's gut as he caressed Aladee, never wanting to let her go. "I hope we don't need a map to the bedroom."

"I remember where it is."

"Famous last words." Nevan gave a husky chuckle.

"The kitchen is at the center core of the house, used by all the wings, so it's easy to find." An instant after she placed her hand over Nevan's, a blue light shone between her fingers, growing until it surrounded them.

With a surprised gasp, she said, "By gods, what is that, Nevan?" Snatching her hand back, the light dissolved.

"That?" Nevan waved his hand in dismissal. "Oh, that's nothing. It's just my—" Still sitting on the rock, Nevan bolted to his feet, spreading his hand before him. "Holy shit!"

"I don't understand." Angling her head to the side, Aladee looked at him strangely. "How odd to speak of excrement as being sacred. Really, Nevan, your Earth vernacular is quite—"

"It's my ring, Aladee!" Nevan wiggled his fingers. "The heartwish ring!" He'd completely forgotten he had it until Aladee's touch generated the glow. "Come on, sweetheart, let's dry off and get back to the house. I'll tell you everything."

Once they'd returned to their wing of Lonan's house, Nevan sat Aladee down, telling her all he knew about the heartwish rings. Having missed them, Buster sat at rapt attention, listening to his master's tale.

"I never believed any of this before but I've heard about it all my life," Nevan told Aladee as he ruffled Buster's fur. "This ring's been passed down through my mother's family, the Norwegian side of my family, for generations. Legend says it was given to the matriarch of a Viking king by Odin, the most powerful of Norse gods. Odin broke the enchanted stone in half, dividing it between two deserving families. Aside from this ring," Nevan held his hand aloft and the stone glowed with soft blue light, "there's another matching half. My family possesses both of the rings at this time."

Entranced by the pale blue glow emanating from the ring, Buster shifted his head left and right, his gaze glued to the stone.

"How fortunate you are." Aladee watched the gentle glow come and go from the stone. "There's nothing to be worried about," she told Buster, petting him. "My paternal grandfather, Quintus, knew Odin. He rode into battle with him during the Aesir-Vanir war, also known as the war of the gods."

"Wow, that must have been hundreds of years ago."

Placing her hand over Nevan's ring again, Aladee nodded. "It was. My family knew Odin as Woden, which was one of many names he used. Your modern weekday name, Wednesday, comes from the Old English Wodnesdaeg, meaning day of Woden." The ring glowed brighter this time, causing Buster to give a soft bark. He appeared more curious than frightened.

"Maybe that's why the ring is glowing," Nevan said, finally letting go of his science-driven phosphorus theory. "Because of the family connection. If Odin liked your grandfather, then maybe we've got an even better chance of the ring working for us."

"They were indeed allies. So you think you can make a wish for us to remain together by using this ring? Even if the council rules against us?"

"I hope so." Shrugging, Nevan frowned, his attention still focused on the heartwish ring. "I honestly have no idea. The ring apparently worked wonders for other members of my family. Hopefully it'll do the same for me. The thing is," Nevan breathed a sigh of frustration, "I guess there's a right and wrong way to use the ring."

His fingers raked through his hair. "I must have heard the rules hundreds of times but...I never really paid much attention because I didn't believe in all the woo-woo stuff. So I'm not sure what I'm supposed to say or how to say it when I make a wish. The one thing I remember for sure is that the wish is supposed to come from the heart."

He looked away from the ring and into Aladee's eyes, clasping her hand. "Oh, God, Aladee, I don't want to screw this up. What if I say the wrong thing and we lose our chance—all because I was too much of a dumbass to pay attention when my grandmother or my mom talked about the ring?" This time Buster whimpered. It was amazing how in tune he was to Nevan's emotions at times.

Giving Nevan a kiss on the cheek, Aladee hugged him close. "You won't screw up, Nevan. You'll speak from your heart. Mighty Odin will hear your plea and grant your wish. I truly believe that." That earned a confirming bark from Buster, along with an expression that made him look like he was smiling.

"I suppose I should wait until the council gives us their verdict before I make the wish," Nevan said. "If the council gives us the go ahead, but rules against Red and Lonan, then I can use the wish for them."

"That sounds fair and wise, Nevan." Aladee gave him a warm smile. "And most definitely from the heart."

Scooping Aladee into his arms, Nevan carried her to their bed chamber. She wrapped her arms around his neck, cooing words of love while resting her head at his shoulder.

At that moment, Nevan knew without a doubt he'd willingly battle dragons, beasts, trolls or anything else they threw at him if it meant being able to hold Aladee in his arms like this for even one more day.

Chapter Twenty

~<>~

"I'M NOT GOING there dressed like a girl," Nevan complained.

"Trust me, Nevan, you don't look like a girl." Red heaved a monumental sigh. "You look sophisticated. Like an Olympian."

"It's a skirt, Red."

"It's a toga," Red corrected. "You look very masculine in it. Look at me, don't I look masculine in my toga?"

Nevan gave his cousin a quick appraisal. "I'm putting my jeans back on," he announced, snatching them from the chest of drawers.

"Listen, this is important, Nevan. You can't show up at the council wearing a torn bloody shirt and jeans. Your clothes look like you were in a barroom brawl, for heaven's sake." Grabbing the jeans from his cousin, Red studied them before letting them drop to the floor of the dressing room in a wrinkled heap. The shirt followed.

"What in the world were you and Aladee up to last night? Were there whips and chains involved?" Red snickered.

"Hardly. But don't give her any ideas, okay?" Nevan laughed. "She's bloodthirsty enough already."

"I can see where you might have gotten all those scratches from her fingernails in the heat of passion, but that doesn't explain the ripped clothes."

"It's from the damn rose bushes." Nevan sighed. "I got caught in the thorns."

"Hmmm, and little Aladee got turned on when she glimpsed her big strong he-man all torn up. Is that it?"

"Something like that." Nevan fidgeted, flipping the skirt of his mid-thigh length toga and wiggling his toes. "What's with these girly sandals with all the crisscross laces up to my knees? I feel ridiculous—like a ballerina, for chrissakes. What if I walk in there and they all start laughing?"

"Will you *puhleeze* stop bellyaching! You look just like Marc Antony. Like a brave Roman soldier."

"Maybe I'd feel better if I had some armor."

Red tsked. "Guess what I did last night."

Nevan narrowed one eye. "I have a good idea, cuz. No details necessary."

"I played with Lonan's unicorn."

"Aw, jeez, Red, I *really* don't want to hear—"

"Get your mind out of the gutter." Red laughed. "I mean I literally played with a unicorn. Lonan has a miniature one. His name is Sabellius. Sabby for short. My Cupid already adores him. They slept side by side all night."

"That's great." Grumbling, Nevan fiddled with his girly outfit.

"Nevan."

"What."

"I love you."

Nevan stopped his fiddling and looked up at his cousin with surprise. Red's expression was serious, solemn.

"There's a chance we may never see each other again after today." Red clapped a hand on Nevan's shoulder. "I'm not sure I could bear losing you, Nevan."

"We're not going to lose each other." Nevan grabbed his cousin into a buddy hug, giving him a hearty pat on the back. "I've got the heartwish ring, remember?" He wiggled his fingers. "Everything's going to be just fine. You'll see." He backed out of the embrace. "Hey, Red?"

"Yes?"

"I love you too."

Red sniffed, then busied himself in front of the full length three-way mirror, primping. "What do you think of my hair like this?" he asked, fingering the dark curls flattened at his forehead. "I thought I'd go for a classic Roman look."

"It's all right, I guess." Nevan shrugged. "If you like curlicues. So, you really love this guy, right? I mean, you and Lonan have only known each other for a day and—"

"And one spectacular night," Red breathed.

"I don't want to hear about it."

Something nudged Nevan's bare leg and he glanced down. With his eye on the small unicorn, Nevan jumped back. "What the hell is that?"

"I already told you." Getting to his knees, Red patted the unicorn. "Say hello to Sabellius." Red smoothed the little creature's mane.

Dropping his head into his hand, Nevan groaned. "I dunno, Red. This is all too much. Unicorns, gods, chariots, flying nymphs, and... How did we get ourselves mixed up in all this?"

Red arched an eyebrow. "Are you saying you're sorry you met Aladee?"

"No. *Hell* no." His shoulders sagging, Nevan sucked in a deep breath, letting it out with a whoosh. "I love her more than I ever thought I could love a woman. It's like she's a part of me." He extended his hand and the unicorn licked it. Then it nuzzled up to Nevan's leg. The little guy was a lot like a dog—with a big corkscrew horn coming out of its head. He patted Sabby's flanks.

"There's my sweetie pie," Red said, bending with his hands resting on his knees as he greeted Cupid who'd come to play with Sabby. "It looks like you two have become fast friends. That's good." Giving the cat and the unicorn pats on the head, he returned his attention to Nevan. "The way you feel about Aladee is the same way I feel about Lonan—which means we have nothing to regret or complain about, right?"

"Right, but it's all happened so fast," Nevan said. "How can you be sure you want to spend the rest of your life with Lonan after knowing the guy for just a day—and one spectacular night," he added quickly before Red could.

"Lonan's been waiting for me for centuries." Red had a faraway look in his eyes. "And I've been looking for him all my life. It doesn't matter if falling in love takes a lifetime or happens instantly. All that matters is that we find our soul mates and recognize them as such before we do something foolish enough to lose them forever. We've been given a rare and precious gift, you and I."

"Yeah, you're right," Nevan agreed. "It's been fast and weird, and it'll probably get a lot weirder before the day is over, but if it means I can stay with Aladee and you can stay with Lonan, then it's all been worth it." He clasped his cousin's arm. "I'm glad you found someone, Red, especially after everything you've gone through with your family, disowning you like that and treating you like a piece of—" Nevan stopped, taking a deep breath. Thinking about what happened to Red made his blood boil. "You, more than anyone, deserve to be happy...to be with the person you love and who loves you back. Lonan seems like a great guy."

"He's unlike anyone I've ever known, Nevan. Lonan reminds me of the mythical gods I've always read about." Red smiled. "Which makes me feel like I've stepped into one of the myths I've studied for decades."

"I've got to admit," Nevan nodded, "spending the rest of your days with a god on Mount Olympus is a perfect fairytale happily ever after ending for you." Reminded of Lonan's amazing painting skills, he asked, "Did you see his kitchen yet?"

"No, we woke up late and had brunch served in bed. Why?"

"It's magnificent, Red. One particular wall is most astounding thing I've ever seen. Lonan is an extraordinarily talented man."

Clearly taken aback, Red said, "My cousin...waxing poetic over a kitchen?" He rested the back of his hand against his cousin's forehead. "Are you all right? That doesn't sound a bit like my macho cousin. You sure you haven't been taken over by aliens? I understand those are real too."

Nevan laughed. "I guess it might sound that way. You'll see what I mean when you see the kitchen. Which reminds me..." Patting his hips, he rolled his eyes and growled. Grabbing his phone from the jeans he'd tossed aside, Nevan checked the time.

"That's another thing about these damn togas," he complained. "Where the hell am I supposed to put my phone?" He waved his phone in the air before returning it to his jeans. "We should head to the kitchen now. Aladee and Lonan are meeting us there. I just hope we don't get lost along the way. It took us thirty minutes to find the damn bedroom last night."

"This place really is magnificent, isn't it?" Red asked as they left the dressing room and walked down the art-lined hall, with Cupid strolling and Sabby trotting by their side. "I've never felt so at home anyplace before."

"I told Aladee you'd feel that way. Me?" Nevan gazed around him. "I feel like I'm in a museum. Too big, too marbly, too artsy."

Red laughed. "I'm not surprised. This isn't your style. Lonan told me about the waterfall cave on your side of the garden. How did you like that?"

"Now *that* I liked." They rounded a corner, entering a long gallery of huge framed paintings and sculptures. "It was like something right out of a romantic chick flick, with all the flowers, candles, and chanty music. All the stuff women eat up."

Red stopped in front of a pedestal holding a four-foot tall stone sculpture. "I'll bet you any amount of money you can't guess the name of the artist who created this statue of Lonan."

Nevan studied the statue. It reminded him of something he'd seen in history books. Then he remembered the kitchen. "Michelangelo," he said, laughing as Red's jaw dropped in astonishment.

His hand flying to his chest, Red gasped. "How in the world did you come up with that? I didn't even know you knew who Michelangelo was."

"He was a contemporary of Leonardo da Vinci." Red gasped again. "Hey, I'm not completely lacking in artistic knowledge, you know. Mom took us kids to museums and made us read books about the art we saw there. Besides," Nevan grinned, "I saw Lonan's kitchen."

The sound of Lonan's voice and Aladee's laughter caught their attention. Nevan pointed. "Follow that sound." A moment later, they entered the kitchen and Buster came to his side, greeting Nevan. Soon, Buster, along with the mini unicorn, and Red's cat, took off together, huddling in a corner of the kitchen. It was strange to see three animals that wouldn't be expected to like each other bond so well. Most surprising of all was the camaraderie Buster and Cupid had developed after all their skirmishes.

"Oh, my goodness, Nevan, how handsome you look," Aladee said. "You too, Red."

When Red reached Aladee, he lifted her hand and kissed it. "And you look like a goddess."

"Wow..." Nevan stared at Aladee a moment. "Red's right. You take my breath away." He eyed her white floor-length gown, draping in soft folds as it meandered down Aladee's curves. Her gold curls were piled high atop her head, crowned with a woven ring of laurel leaves. A gold coil wound around one arm above her elbow. Afraid to mess her up, with a hug and kiss, Nevan followed Red's lead by kissing Aladee's hand.

"You look just like one of those sexy chicks in a Hercules movie," he told her.

Aladee cocked her head. "Oh, is he making movies now?"

"She does look magnificent," Lonan said. "All eyes will be on her when we enter the auditorium."

Aladee blushed peppermint pink. "Thank you. I must admit I do feel quite pretty today." She patted the back of her sophisticated hairdo. "Psyche came to offer words of encouragement, and she did my hair too."

Lonan turned his attention to Nevan. "How is your nose feeling? It doesn't look quite as angry today."

Chuckling, Nevan said, "It feels just like I thought a broken nose would feel. All in all, it's not too bad."

"Good. You certainly clean up well," Lonan noted. "It's a far better look than those raggedy clothes you had on earlier."

Glancing down at his toga and sandals, Nevan said, "So you don't think I look silly—like a girl?"

The toga-clad Lonan rose from his seat, hands fisted at his hips and a mighty scowl across his features. "Does anything about my appearance strike you as girlish?" he nearly roared.

"No. Absolutely not." Nevan held up his hands in surrender. "No way. I didn't mean to imply you look girly in those dresses you wear, I—"

"Togas," Lonan corrected.

"Right, yes, togas," Nevan amended. "It's just that I'm used to wearing men's clothes." Lonan's frown deepened. "Uh...pants, I mean. I'm used to wearing slacks. Jeans."

"The toga is a time-honored tradition, Nevan. Strong, brave, intelligent men have worn them centuries longer than denim jeans."

"That's true." Nevan nodded thoughtfully, nervously licking his lips. "Good point." Shit, the last thing he wanted to do was piss off the one god he could depend on.

Suddenly, Lonan broke into laughter. "Relax, Nevan," he came to give him a hearty clap on the back, "I'm teasing you. We wear a wide variety of garments here on Olympus, including jeans. Togas are worn for special occasions and celebrations, or official matters concerning the council."

"Whew," Nevan wiped his forehead, "you had me going for a minute there."

"I find a bit of levity cuts through the tension," Lonan told him with a warm smile.

"Aladee showed me your artwork yesterday," Nevan said, quickly changing the subject. "She told me all about it, and your art students. It's amazing. Some of the finest painting I've ever seen."

"I appreciate that. Thank you." Lonan nodded and smiled.

Nevan nudged his cousin and gestured to the wall at the far end of the kitchen. "See, Red? That's what I was talking about."

His gaze following Nevan's outstretched finger, Red was clearly astounded. "No!" Reaching for Lonan's arm, he clasped it. "*You* painted that? Lonan, it's exquisite."

"There's an interesting story behind it." Lonan covered Red's hand with his and they strolled to the other side of the kitchen.

"That was a close one." Nevan wiped the sweat from his brow. "So, how are you feeling, Aladee? Ready to face the gods?"

"As ready as I can be." Aladee sighed. "And you, Nevan? Are you prepared to stand before the council?"

Nodding, Nevan leaned close to whisper, "I'd feel a whole lot better if I wasn't all dolled up in this bed sheet."

Aladee giggled. "Have no fear. You look magnificent and very mannish. Just pretend you're attending a masquerade party."

A gong sounded, similar to the one Nevan had heard the night before.

"Another message?"

Aladee shook her head. "A single gong signifies someone is at Lonan's door."

A big, burly, handsome guy, about fifty-ish, entered the kitchen. "Your chariot awaits, Master Lonan."

"Thank you, Hercules," Lonan said. "We'll be there momentarily." His manservant nodded and left the room. As they walked across the length of the massive kitchen, Lonan and Red exchanged loving looks, speaking to each other in hushed tones.

Nevan swallowed hard and looked at Aladee. She had the distinct look of a deer caught in headlights. "It's going to be okay, sweetheart," he assured, drawing her near. "Before the day is over, the four of us will be celebrating. Trust me." Nevan just wished he could believe his own words. He was practically shaking in his sandals worrying about what might happen, but if he let Aladee suspect that, she'd be a basket case.

"We must make haste." Lonan led them from the house to his chariot. "The council's center of operations is a goodly distance from here."

The long walk through the house and the front garden to the chariot reminded Nevan of a death march. All that was missing was the sound of a death knell—or maybe the wail of a screaming banshee.

"What a stunning vehicle," Red said.

Nevan studied the ultra-fancy white chariot, complete with extensive raised gold scrollwork, fine black detailing and rows of what appeared to be inlaid turquoise. The horses were big, black and shiny—proud looking animals with jeweled harnesses.

The best part, as far as Nevan was concerned, was that the chariot was outfitted with black leather upholstered seats. One up front for the driver and a passenger, and another seat big enough for two in back. While the back of the vehicle was open, at least this chariot had two large side doors, one on each side, allowing easy step-up access.

"Great looking chariot," Nevan agreed. "I like the horses."

"Thank you both." Lonan ushered them into the vehicle. "It's one of my formal chariots. I felt it was befitting the occasion." He patted Red's hand as Red stood next to him. "The horses are my finest obsidian-black stallions."

They all sat still for a long moment, exchanging glances.

Filling his lungs with air and expelling a loud breath, Lonan, reins in hand, signaled his horses and they were off.

"Interlopers. I simply can't abide by interlopers," Venus growled. Pacing back and forth, the stunning woman perfumed the air with the delicate scent of lilacs.

"Remember, there was a time you thought of me as an interloper too," Psyche said, hurrying along to keep up with her mother-in-law.

Venus stopped her pacing long enough to hike an eyebrow at Psyche. "And when did that time stop?"

Psyche laughed. "At least I'm an interloper who can put up with your mischievous, naughty son, and keep him out of too much trouble."

"True." A smile curved Venus's lips. "I'll give you that."

"My ears are ringing." Cupid strode into the large auditorium, stretching and bellowing a lion-like yawn. "What are my two favorite girls saying about me, hmm?" He draped his arms around their shoulders, giving each woman a kiss on the cheek.

"We were discussing the pleas of Lonan, Aladee and the mortals, darling," Psyche said, snaking her hand around her husband's arm.

"They're expected soon. And, of course, we were also extolling your countless virtues. Isn't that right, Venus?"

"Indubitably." Venus offered Psyche a conspiratorial wink. "What are you doing here, Cupid? You're not on the council."

"I'm here to support Lonan, and Psyche is here in support of Aladee. Believe me, mother, if it weren't for the fact that Lonan was involved in this, I'd waste no time in giving that flighty nymph and her mortal boyfriend a thumbs down. But since Lonan is an old friend, and since he's smitten to the point of distraction with the mortal boyfriend's cousin, I've agreed to act in his favor."

"All these years and I still can't understand how you ended up being the god of love and eroticism," Psyche said. "You should be elated that Aladee and Lonan have found love matches, Cupid."

"I'm thrilled," he said with another yawn.

"Mmm-hmm. You don't fool me for a minute," Psyche chastised. "I know how fond you are of Aladee. She's an excellent, devoted student of your academy."

"I—" Cupid started.

"And I saw that sparkle of admiration in your eye," Psyche cut him off, "as you told me how the brave mortal defended Aladee and stood up to Vibius's repulsive antics. You *should* have turned that vile satyr into a horned toad."

Cupid shrugged, a smile teasing his lips. "Perhaps Aladee and the mortals aren't so bad. Seriously, how long do you think this will take? I've got a new shipment of gold plated arrows coming in that I want to inspect."

"I'm the only one of the twelve here so far," Venus said. "But then I'm always the most punctual. If the other eleven don't get their lazy asses here soon, this hearing could drag on well into the night."

"My lazy ass is here, madam," Mars boomed, strutting across the floor to the bank of thrones, slumping into his velvet-lined seat.

"What's all this nonsense about Lonan being enamored of a mortal? He's always been so levelheaded. What's gotten into him?"

"He's a good guy, Dad," Cupid said. "The best teacher I've got. Give him a break."

"He's taking up valuable time that could otherwise be spent making war," Mars grumbled, reaching for a cluster of grapes from one of the platters on the table and plucking the fruit off with his teeth.

"My, aren't we grumpy this afternoon?" Apollo skipped into the room in time to the lively melody he played on his golden lyre. "I'm simply dying to set eyes on the mortal that's finally turned Lonan's head after all these centuries. He must be absolutely delicious."

"I agree. It all sounds positively sweet to me," Diana said, as she came toward the group, motioning for Egeria, the water nymph who was her servant and assistant midwife, to take a seat in the auditorium. The seats were filling quickly. "Hello, cousin dear." Diana exchanged air kisses with Apollo. "I say Lonan deserves to find himself a hot little stud muffin."

"Puhleeze." Venus rolled her eyes. "This coming from the virgin goddess."

"Oh, mee-ow, Venus," Diana countered. "You know very well I'm a goddess *to* virgins—it doesn't mean I'm one myself. You're just jealous because I can shoot arrows twice the distance you can." She raised her empty bow, aimed it at Venus and plucked.

"Well, duh, you're a huntress." Venus moved Diana's bow to the side and crossed her arms over her breasts. "Must you always carry that thing around?"

"Are you two at it again?" Ceres said as she crossed the room, depositing a large basket of fruits and flowers on the table in front of the thrones. She carefully adjusted the garland of wheat ears circling her head.

"Aren't they always?" Psyche chuckled, looped her arm through Cupid's and led him to the reserved seating section at the front of the auditorium.

"It's been eons since we've had two Earthly mortals making a plea," Ceres noted. "It's the first time in quite a while that they've been cousins. Fascinating. Cupid tells me they're both quite attractive."

"I knew it." Apollo gave an impish grin while strumming his lyre. Heading to his throne, he took a seat. "He'd have to be a hunk to snag Lonan."

"Ceres, we all know where your loyalties lie," Venus accused. "After all, you *are* the goddess of the Earth and all that warm fuzzy maternal stuff that goes along with it." She gave a dismissive wave.

"Well, the way *some* of you have a habit of ganging up on mortals," Ceres countered, "it's a good thing they've got someone like me in their corner."

"How are the thrones holding up?" Vulcan asked, seemingly oblivious to the conversation as he strode past the others and headed for the bank of thrones.

"Sturdy and solid as always, cousin," Mars said. "Not a creak to be heard."

"Nice and comfy," Apollo offered as Vulcan tested each chair, making sure it didn't rock or squeak. "You clearly made them to last forever."

"Don't bother saying hello, Vulcan, dear," Venus quipped.

Vulcan looked up, clearly distracted. "Oh, hello, Venus. You're looking lovely as usual," he said in such a way that meant he hadn't really noticed.

"Of course I am." She patted her golden upswept locks. "It's what I do best."

A stern looking woman garbed in a long dress, and with her head covered, moved past them without uttering a word.

"There goes Vesta," Diana whispered. "I swear to Jupiter the woman never even cracks a smile."

"She's been hanging around her adoring Vestal Virgins too long." Venus snickered.

"I heard that." Vesta deposited her scepter on the table in front of her throne chair, then took a seat after Vulcan finished examining it. "As far as I'm concerned, this is a serious and solemn occasion. One not to be taken lightly."

"So says the goddess of hearth and home," Ceres said, applauding Vesta before taking her seat next to her.

"Miserable mortals and nymphs be damned for ruining my holiday," Neptune groused, striking the tip of his trident hard against the marble floor with each step he took toward the front of the room. "There had better not be any lengthy grandstanding." Scowling, he plunked down into the seat of his throne. "I want this over fast so I can to get back to my vacation."

"Where are you vacationing?" Apollo asked, absently plucking the strings of his lyre.

"Inland." Neptune grinned, grabbing a skewer of shish kabob from a platter and pulling a handful of the roast meat from the blade. "A marvelous little place on Earth called Arizona where there's barely a speck of water to be found. Nice break from the daily deluge." His expression quickly soured. "Until I got dragged back here for this lovey-dovey nonsense." He popped the meat into his mouth, chewing vigorously.

"Look," Venus said to Diana as she clasped the woman's arm. "There's Lonan and the other three." She narrowed her eyes and frowned. "I don't like the looks of Aladee. She's too attractive for her own good."

"For *your* own good, you mean." Diana laughed. "It's a miracle your skin doesn't turn green from all that envy coursing through your veins. Oh dear, poor Lonan looks tense, doesn't he?"

"As well he should," Venus huffed. "He knows damn well we don't take kindly to the pairing of gods and mortals. Look at the others with him." Venus chortled. "They look about to faint. And what's with those black eyes on the one mortal and Aladee?"

"Mmm, but the two mortals *are* indeed scrumptious, aren't they?" Diana observed. "I can tell, even with the one's bandaged nose and bruised eyes. Come on," she tugged Venus's arm, "let's take our seats before the head honchos make their grand entrance."

"All rise, all rise!" Mercury announced a moment later, holding his caduceus aloft as his winged helmet and sandals allowed him to glide through the air two feet off the floor. Everyone in the auditorium got to their feet. "The great ones arrive!" When Mercury reached the front of the room, he took his place standing before one of the four vacant thrones.

Trumpeting music swelled as Minerva entered. Wearing a coat of mail and a helmet, she carried a spear in one hand and braced an owl on the other.

She was followed by her father, Jupiter, and his wife, Juno. In one hand Jupiter clutched a cluster of thunderbolts and on the other an eagle rested. The majestic Juno wore a diadem on her head while clutching a pomegranate in one hand and leading a peacock on a fine, slender gold chain with her other.

Once the trio was seated, the music ended and all the gods but Mercury took their seats. Unrolling a ceremonial scroll, Mercury read aloud, introducing the *Dii Consentes*, the twelve major gods of the Roman pantheon, to all in attendance.

"Here sits before you Jupiter, supreme god. Ruler of the gods." Jupiter raised his hand and the auditorium cheered.

"At his side sits Juno, queen of the gods. Goddess of women and fertility." She nodded and again the room erupted in cheers.

Mercury gestured to the next throne. "Minerva, daughter of Jupiter and Metis. Goddess of wisdom, art crafts and industry." Minerva gave a queenly wave and the audience applauded.

"From this point forward," Mercury said, "I ask you to hold your cheers and applause until I've introduced all the gods." Once the gathering stilled, he proceeded.

"Here sits Vesta, goddess of hearth and home. In her temple the sacred flame burns eternal, maintained by the Vestal Virgins. To her side is Ceres, goddess of the earth. Next is Diana, goddess of the hunt."

Each goddess nodded as she was mentioned.

"Venus, goddess of love and beauty, daughter of Jupiter and mother of Cupid sits here." Mercury gestured.

"And here sits Mars, god of war, anger, revenge, and courage. Next to him is Neptune, god of the sea. Supreme dweller of the ocean floor. To my left," he continued, "sits Vulcan, god of blacksmiths, fire and volcanoes. And to my right sits Apollo, god of music and athletics."

As Apollo made grand, sweeping gestures while Mercury exalted his attributes, the crowd ignored Mercury's edict and cheered.

Arrowing a cautionary eyebrow at Apollo, Mercury rerolled the scroll, taking a seat himself. "And I am Mercury, messenger of the gods. God of travelers, tradesmen, and merchants."

With the last of the twelve gods introduced, the room erupted in cheers, whistles and applause.

Mercury struck the table three times with his caduceus. "Let the pleaders come forward so we may sit in judgment and put forth our rulings."

Chapter Twenty-One

~<>~

"THIS IS IT," Nevan whispered to Aladee, Red and Lonan as the three stood up.

With Lonan in the lead, they marched to the front of the room, standing before the council side by side. Nevan fought the urge to fidget as Mercury read the pleas aloud. The damned recitation went on forever. The council apparently felt the same way because the mighty yawn Neptune roared was infectious. Soon each of them was yawning. It was nearly impossible for Nevan not to give in to one himself.

"What say you, Lonan," Jupiter boomed in a deep, formidable voice that echoed off the marble walls of the auditorium, "god of teaching, god of intellectual achievement and education, god of literature and the fine arts—" Jupiter glanced down at the document in his hand. "Etcetera, etcetera." He gave a dismissive wave.

"Make it short, teacher," warned Mars. "I'm not in the mood for lengthy dialogue."

"Hear, hear," Neptune chimed in.

"Esteemed council members," Lonan began with a courtly bow. "I stand before you for the first time in all my days to plead for myself. You all know me. I've taught you as well as your children and your children's children. My life has been full, rich, satisfying and complete with the exception of one key element—a soul mate with whom to share my existence.

"In the educated, cultured, witty, caring mortal florist, Redmond Devington, known as Red, I've found my true love at last. I entreat each of you to grant my request to keep my beloved Red," Lonan clasped Red's hand, "at my side here on Olympus evermore."

"Mortal," Venus addressed Red, "what makes you think you would integrate well with Olympians?"

Standing proud, shoulders back and chin elevated, Red said with assurance, "I was born to live on Olympus." A collective gasp was heard throughout the auditorium.

"Uh-oh," Nevan muttered under his breath.

"Self-important human," Vulcan groused quietly as Neptune nodded his concurrence.

"Is that so, mortal?" Minerva didn't look pleased. "On what, pray tell, do you base this high and mighty assumption?"

"I state this not to be arrogant," Red said, "but, rather, to honestly express my heartfelt belief. I've spent my entire life studying your history and customs. I believe with all my heart, mind and soul that spending the rest of my life here with Lonan is my intended fate. My destiny."

"No wonder you fell for him, Lonan," Apollo said with a broad smile.

"He has balls," Mars added with a toothy grin. "I like that in a mortal."

The gods whispered among themselves for a few moments. It looked to Nevan that Red and Lonan had won most of them over, but there were a few holdouts.

"What if we decreed you could stay together," Diana asked, "but you would have to live on Earth. Lonan? Red?"

Red and Lonan looked at each other and smiled. "While I strongly desire to remain here and continue teaching the residents of Olympus," Lonan said, "I will go anywhere the council deems, as long as it means we can be together."

"Thank you." Red squeezed Lonan's hand. "My love for Lonan is so great," he told the council, "that I would give him up and remain on Earth alone for the rest of my life rather than to pluck him from this life he loves so dearly."

"Well said," Vesta noted.

"Beautiful." Ceres wiped a tear from her eye.

"What of his status as a short-lived mortal, Lonan?" Juno asked. "How will the two of you cope when your mortal's body descends into inevitable decay?"

"I care not that Red will lose his youthful appearance, but I confess it will break my heart to lose him when the time comes for him to journey to the afterlife. It is with this in mind that I humbly request the council consider bestowing the gift of immortality on Red."

"The audacity!" Venus gasped.

"What, besides your obvious affection for him," Minerva asked, "makes you believe this mortal is worthy of becoming a minor god?"

"Aside from what I included in my written plea," several of the gods scanned their documents, "Red brings exceptional botanical skills and talents to share with our residents. He is a florist of incomparable skill, even to the point of understanding the fine art of communication with flora. With his talents, each of your gardens would be as lush and abundant as mine, perhaps even more."

"If we grant your plea, Redmond," Jupiter bellowed, "what will you do if it is under the condition that you and your cousin may never see each other again?"

Red turned toward Nevan, reaching out for his cousin's hand and clasping it hard. It was all Nevan could do at that moment not to tell the bastards sitting up there all righteous-looking in their fancy thrones to go to hell.

"I honestly don't know how to answer that," Red said softly, his gaze still locked with Nevan's. "It would be like asking me to tear my heart and soul in half."

"Is it okay if I say something here?" Nevan asked.

"No," Venus snapped. "It's not your turn."

"You may speak," Jupiter overruled the snarky goddess.

"I love my cousin," Nevan said. "Red's the best, kindest, most deserving, selfless guy I've ever known. He has more positive qualities than I could ever list. Nobody deserves to be with their soul mate more than he does. Yeah, it would kill me if I could never see Red again, the worst hurt I can imagine. But it's more important to me that he and Lonan are able to be together than any pain I might go through if I lost Red."

Nevan went to stuff his hands into his pockets only to remember he was wearing a damn bed sheet. "Anyway, I wanted you all to know that before you make your decision."

"Nevan," Red said, yanking his cousin into a fierce hug. "I love you so much." And then he let out a sob.

"Dammit, Red." Nevan squeezed his cousin hard and took a deep breath. "Don't you go and make me cry in front of Aladee and all these gods while I'm standing here in a skirt."

Red chuckled at that. "Okay." He wiped his eyes quickly as he and Nevan ended their embrace.

"Your cousinly love is very touching," Juno said with a smile. "Does anyone in attendance have anything to add in support of this plea?"

Cupid stood in the front row. "I do. I doubt any of you council members has ever heard a single complaint about Lonan. He's well liked, respected, a damn fine teacher, and an even better friend. I trust his judgment implicitly. That includes his choice in a life mate. I recommend the council approve his request and grant Red status as a minor god."

Lonan turned and nodded at his friend. "Thank you." Cupid winked and took his seat again.

"What in the world is that menagerie at your side, Cupid?" Jupiter boomed.

Glancing down at Buster, Cupid the cat, and Sabby, Cupid said, "These worthy animals are their pets. I'm caring for them during the proceedings."

"We have something to add in support of this plea," came a chorus of voices from further back in the auditorium. Nevan looked behind him to see Aladee's classmates from the chariot sitting together with their hands raised.

"Speak," Juno said.

Kreshti the banshee stood. "I speak for the entire class," she boomed.

"Fine, fine, just keep it down and don't break into one of your wails, banshee," Vulcan warned.

"I'll do my best, sir. We all believe that our teacher, Lonan, is greatly deserving of having his plea request settled in his favor. Let him and Red live together for all eternity!" She and the rest of the students erupted with cheers, whistles and applause.

"Silence!" Jupiter scolded, holding one of his thunderbolts aloft. The eagle at his side squawked. "Is there anyone who can show just cause why Lonan and..." he looked down at his document, "Redmond Devington, should not have their plea granted?"

The room was silent. "Very well. I believe we have enough evidence with which to make a ruling. Agreed?" he asked the other eleven gods. With their concurrence, he said, "We will hear the plea of the nymph and the other mortal before retiring to chambers to discuss the matters and reach our rulings.

"What say you, Aladee?" Jupiter boomed before glancing at his paperwork again. "Dryad and Limoniad nymph, Daughter of Arrius and Venuvia, granddaughter of Quintus who rode with Woden in the Aesir-Vanir war."

Nevan and Aladee exchanged glances. He smiled, imparting as much support and love as possible in that single gesture.

"Thank you, Your Graciousness, for..." She paused when she heard giggles around her. She cleared her throat and continued. "For honoring me, a mere lowly, humble, insignificant, inconsequential, undeserving, unworthy—"

She stopped when Lonan nudged her and shook his head. "Um...thank you for hearing my plea," she finished with a curtsy. As she lowered her head, a cluster of curls popped loose. "Oh dear." She tried tucking them back in place, only to loosen more ringlets. "I did so want to look sophisticated today."

More muffled giggles were heard.

If Nevan wasn't so damned nervous and concerned for poor Aladee, he would have been laughing himself. "That's okay, honey." Taking Aladee's hand, he offered a reassuring smile. "You're doing just fine."

"Oh, goodness, I'm so nervous I've completely forgotten what I wanted to say. Please excuse me for just a moment, oh Great Mighty Ones."

Nevan wondered what in the hell Aladee was doing when she let go of his hand and snaked her hand inside the top of her gown, fishing around. She pulled out a folded paper, opening it.

"Whew!" Beaming a smile, she waved the paper. "I'm glad I remembered to take this." She cleared her throat again, loudly. "Thank you, Your Graciousness, for honoring me," she read aloud, "a mere—"

"We've already heard that part," Neptune grumbled, giving a dismissive wave. "Get on with it."

"I'm sorry. Yes." Aladee scanned her paper, mumbling aloud as she found her place. "While Nevan Malone may be nothing but a lowly, mangy mortal, as Cupid called him upon their first meeting," she began and Nevan groaned. "I would like the council to know that he is also a fine, good-hearted, and extremely handsome man with exceptional carnal skills."

"Well, I'm sold," Diana quipped.

Aladee frowned when she heard giggles behind her. "Nevan is a brilliant master bartender," she continued reading, "who, in his Irish-style pub, personally provides customers with enough intoxicating beer, wine and whiskey to keep them happily mind-altered for hours."

"He's sounding better all the time," Mars quipped.

"Of course, Nevan isn't perfect," Aladee continued. "Being a mortal, he has good and bad points. One glaring fault is his inability to," as she looked down at her paper, Nevan started to sweat, "tell jokes that are actually funny."

"Ouch," Nevan muttered.

"But a good point is that Nevan isn't a quitter. Determined, he continues making cringeworthy jokes, regardless of how many people groan, which makes Nevan tenacious. While it's true he could never fulfill his boyhood dream of being a successful standup comic, he chose to be a pub owner instead, who excels at keeping his patrons inebriated while they listen to his jokes."

She paused to look up at Nevan, Red and Lonan, who were pinching the spot between their noses and foreheads, chuckling. Aladee smiled at them and continued. "Nevan is a man who—"

"Good grief, there's more?" Venus grumbled.

"It's all vital information," Aladee insisted. "I'll be brief." She cleared her throat. "Nevan is a man who is brave and fearless enough to battle fire-breathing dragons, and ten-foot-tall one-eyed monsters if that is the only way we can remain together."

"Whoa...Aladee...sweetheart..." Nevan clasped her arm.

"Yes, Nevan?" She looked up at him, all bright-eyed and pink-cheeked.

"Can I see that paper of yours?"

"Certainly." She handed it to Nevan.

He skimmed the paper and grinned. While it would generate ample laughs, if Aladee kept going, he'd most likely be thrown to the lions, and she'd be demoted to the rank of fruit fly. He tore the paper two ways and tucked the pieces back between her breasts, kissing the tip of her nose when she gave him that wide-eyed clueless look she did so well.

"Oh, that's a shame," Apollo said. "That was the most entertainment I've had in a week."

"We're not here for your entertainment," Diana scolded.

"Aw, sis..." Apollo grumbled.

"I'm Nevan Malone," Nevan addressed the council. "The lowly, mangy, painfully unfunny mortal Aladee was describing. The reason we're here is simple. We love each other and want to spend the rest of our lives together. Period. I'm just an average Earth guy, but I make a good living as a pub owner. I can provide Aladee with a nice little house with a picket fence, a bunch of kids, pets, like our dog, Buster, and everything else that goes along with the American dream. The whole enchilada."

"That sounds just like marriage," Aladee said, an adoring look of expectancy on her face.

"It should, because it is," Nevan said. "What do you think I've been talking about all this time?"

"Oh, Nevan!" Getting on her tiptoes, Aladee wrapped her arms around his neck. "You want to marry me and provide me with the entire enchilada!"

The audience resounded with *awwws,* sighs and applause.

"Yeah, but first I'd like for us to get out of this place alive." He winked at her.

Focusing on the council members again, Nevan said, "That's about it. End of story. According to the rules you guys set up, we're here to ask you to have a heart and let us stay together."

"How did your nose get broken and your eyes blackened?" Mars asked. "Were you and Aladee brawling?"

"No sir, I would never hit a woman. Ever. This happened when we were searching for Cupid and I—"

"Oh Nevan was *so* brave," Aladee cut in. "He valiantly attempted to protect me from the attack of a vicious brute. His darling dog, Buster, helped too." Turning, she finger waved at Buster, who gave a soft bark of acknowledgement. "I punched the attacker in the nose," she swung her arm in demonstration, "as he pummeled Nevan, then I kicked him hard," she made the motion, "in his nether regions, causing him to fall and whimper like a crybaby—the brute, not Nevan."

Shrugging in surrender, Nevan confessed, "Yup, Aladee's my hero." He shrugged again.

Mars and Vulcan roared with laughter.

"You can't possibly imagine yourself becoming a resident of Olympus, Nevan," Venus said, looking down her nose at him. "What could you possibly have in common with Olympians."

"Not much," Nevan readily admitted. "I don't imagine myself becoming a resident here, so you don't have to worry about that. Aladee and I want to settle down in Glassfloat Bay, Oregon, where the rest of my family lives, back on Earth. We'd both feel more comfortable there."

"What would Aladee do there?" Ceres asked. "She has no real skills other than what she's learned in Lonan's classes."

"I beg to differ," Nevan countered. "Aladee is remarkably intelligent, plus she has a close personal relationship with plants and flowers, which would make her a first-rate florist. Red agreed if everything works out, he'll put her in charge of his flower shop. The shop, along with my pub located in the same historic building, would be a perfect permanent meeting place for Cupid Academy students when they travel to Earth on assignments. Since Cupid's

Headquarters is the name of Red's shop, it would lessen confusion, and the chance of students getting lost trying to find the right location."

"I don't know," Diana said. "I understand Aladee's rather scatterbrained and absentminded."

"No kidding," Venus interjected.

"What guarantee would we have," Diana continued, "that she wouldn't cause embarrassing situations acting as an official representative of the academy?"

"I'd be exceedingly careful not to disgrace the fine reputation of the academy," Aladee assured, reaching for the crown of laurel leaves that slipped to the floor when she nodded. She parked it back on her head, askew. Nevan reached over, nudging it in place.

"May I?" Cupid asked from the audience, rising to his feet.

"Of course, son," Venus said with a warm smile.

"Lonan and I discussed the prospect of Aladee maintaining an Earth outpost and contact station for Cupid Academy travelers. We believe it's an excellent idea. While Aladee may be forgetful every so often, she's bright, diligent and wholly devoted to the academy. With her mortal partner being more of a linear thinker, Lonan and I believe Nevan will be a positive influence on her as far as organization and structure goes."

"And you would accept the responsibility of managing Aladee's duties as an Earthly contact?" Vesta asked Nevan.

"Absolutely. No problem. Organization's my middle name."

"How curious," Minerva mused.

"I don't believe he means it literally," Mars said.

"Ah," Minerva nodded, "so this is one of the unfunny attempts at humor Aladee told us about."

"Can you adequately protect your nymph from the dark forces?" Mars asked.

"Uh..." Clueless, Nevan looked at Aladee and Lonan, then back to Mars. "Can you give me an example?"

"Malevolent interlopers attempting to steal the academy's materials and secrets," Mars clarified with a frown. "There are many who would fight to the death for an opportunity to possess Cupid's secrets."

"Definitely." Nevan figured no thieving interloper could be as bad as dragons or monsters.

"Some of them may be dragons or monsters," Mars added.

Nevan laughed to himself. "I vow to do my best to protect Aladee and all of Cupid's secrets."

"You've got balls, just like your cousin, kid," Mars announced with a resolute nod.

Nevan looked down at his mid-thigh skirt and scratched his head. "I usually prefer to keep them covered in a pair of jeans."

Mars, along with several of the other gods, goddesses and audience members roared with laughter.

"It appears he has the ability to be humorous when he needs to be," Neptune said.

"Does anyone in attendance have anything to add in support of this plea?" Juno asked.

"I do." Red raised his hand. "I just want to add that if I'm granted immortality and minor god status, then I hope Nevan is too."

"You can say that again," Nevan said. "The last thing I want to be reminded of by my cousin is that he's a god and I'm not." Muffled laughter followed his statement.

"Happily, it appears the gods disagree with my assertion regarding your inability to be humorous," Aladee whispered to Nevan.

"A word, if I may," Psyche said from the front row where she sat next to Cupid. "My beloved husband and I are a prime example of what can come of a mixed marriage. While most believed our relationship was ill-fated, I think you'd all agree that the strength of our love, devotion and commitment to each other is proof that the success of such unions can surpass all expectations. I know Aladee personally and am proud to call this fine, honorable nymph my friend. It's evident that she and Nevan are deeply in love, as are Lonan and Red. Please grant their pleas."

She took her seat again, with an adoring Cupid planting a kiss on her cheek.

"I'd like to add something."

Nevan turned to see a big, buff, beefed up, really handsome guy he hadn't seen before.

"Speak, Hercules," Juno said.

Nevan looked at Aladee and she nodded. "Yes, he's the one you've read about," she whispered.

"As you all know, I was a mortal who became a god and—"

"Oh but, darling," Venus cut in. "Look at you and look at them. They're positively puny compared to your muscled magnificence." As Venus spoke, Nevan caught Diana making a *call me* gesture to Hercules at the same time Apollo was doing the same.

"Size doesn't matter," Hercules said, and this time the women roared with laughter. "I don't know these mortals personally," Hercules continued when it quieted down, "but it's clear to me they're deeply in love, intelligent, valiant and more than willing to protect the secrets and traditions of Olympus. Isn't that what being a god is all about?"

"Hey, thanks, buddy," Nevan said. Hercules smiled and waved as he sat down.

"May we speak?" It was the group of Aladee's classmates. Juno nodded, extending her hand. Dunniger the dragon was the spokesperson this time. Nevan eyed him cautiously.

"First of all," Dunniger said, "I take exception to all the negative dialogue about dragons. We're like honey bees. Gentle unless provoked." He offered a pleasant, soothing smile. "We had a chance to meet the mortal, Nevan Malone, on the chariot ride and found him to be charming and likeable, as well as noble when faced with...a particularly negative influence." Dunniger shot a heated glance at Vibius.

"And who doesn't adore Aladee?" he continued. "She's sweet, generous, and fully deserving to be with the man of her dreams. We hereby request that their plea be granted." Most of the students chimed in with cheers of agreement.

"Silence!" Jupiter warned, reaching for a thunderbolt. "Is there anyone who can show just cause why Aladee and Eleven—"

"It's Nevan, sir," Nevan said.

Jupiter looked down at his document. "Whatever. Any objections to this plea?"

"I object," came a familiar voice from the crowd.

"Aw, shit," Nevan muttered as he spotted goat boy standing and walking toward the front of the auditorium.

"State your objection," Jupiter instructed.

"Aladee and I were to be mated until this Neanderthal interfered," Vibius said.

Aladee gasped. "Vibius, that's a lie!"

"Vibius speaks the truth," Seraletta the undine said, rising to stand with Vibius. "Aladee is flighty and self-centered. Here one of her own kind, a fine, strapping satyr, desires to make her his mate and what does the nymph do? She leads him on only to break his heart when her juices run for this mortal. I will agree to take the mortal off her hands so Aladee can return to Vibius, her true intended, and make amends."

"Sorry, Seraletta," Nevan said. "You'll have to do your soul searching elsewhere. I'm sticking with Aladee."

Aladee fisted her hands against her hips, telegraphing a narrow-eyed glare the undine's way. "Everyone in attendance knows you just want to steal my mortal for your own selfish reasons, Seraletta."

"The protesters have the floor," Minerva warned. "Aladee...Nevan, refrain from speaking until their objections have been heard."

"I'm curious," Seraletta cooed in all innocence. "Is it the custom of the council to place physically flawed beings in positions of great importance?"

"You know it's not," Venus said.

Seraletta shrugged. "Then perhaps the council should be made aware that the nymph is defective."

'Defective?!" Aladee nearly screeched. "I beg your pardon."

"How so, Seraletta?" Juno urged.

Seraletta's expression grew gleefully malevolent as she glared at Aladee. "Why not command her to spread her wings for you and see for yourself? An easy enough task for a nymph of the winged variety, is it not?"

"Oh, Seraletta..." Aladee shook her head. "I told you about that in strictest confidence. I truly believed you were my friend." Nevan longed to take Aladee in his arms and soothe her when he saw how stricken she looked.

Minerva tsked, gesturing toward Aladee with a wave of her hand. "Go ahead and demonstrate for us, Aladee."

Aladee hung her head. "I-I'm unable to comply at the moment."

Nevan remembered Aladee saying she was only able to open her wings when she was extremely happy. Trial by the gods obviously was not one of those occasions.

"Aha!" Venus slapped the tabletop. "I knew the nymph seemed too perfect to be true," she said, clearly brimming with joy.

"Even though Aladee is physically deficient," Vibius said, "I'll agree to take the deformed nymph as my mate—as long as all her sexual parts work." His quip was met with silence.

"Forget about it," Nevan said.

"Silence, Neanderthal! I have the floor. It's my belief," Vibius addressed the council, "that this scrawny, unctuous mortal wove some heinous black magic, or perhaps drugged Aladee to win her affections. Look at him." Sneering, Vibius pointed at Nevan. "How else could she possibly choose this diminutive human with the battered eyes and nose over me?" He elevated his chin.

"The only magic going on is the magic of love," Nevan said. "But I doubt that's something you'd understand. And for your information, just because I'm not a colossal, ruthless goat doesn't mean I'm scrawny...goat boy."

In an instant, Vibius was at Nevan's side, grabbing his arm and twirling Nevan to face him. Nevan had to look up, *way up*, to lock gazes with the seven-footer. The pronounced smell of alcohol on the satyr's breath was unmistakable.

"You insult me," Vibius sneered, digging his long nails into Nevan's arm and drawing blood. "Is this acceptable behavior for one who seeks to become a minor god?" he asked the council.

Nevan shrugged free of Vibius's grip. "If you want to talk about acceptable behavior," he countered, "how about those lewd remarks you made to my woman on the chariot? You know, when Cupid threatened to turn you into a frog unless you shut up."

"She is *not* your woman." Vibius shoved Nevan's shoulder with enough force to knock him off balance and to the floor. "You don't belong with Aladee," he growled as Nevan shot back up to his feet, adopting a fighting stance. "You are not of her kind."

"You leave Nevan alone," Aladee shouted, getting on her toes to pummel Vibius's hairy chest with her fists.

"Aladee," Nevan cried, "stay away from him, he's drunk."

"Mind your place, nymph!" Vibius warned, swatting Aladee aside. A swat from him was akin to a full blow from a human male. She careened backward, falling on her bottom.

Buster growled and barked. "Buster, it's okay, stay!" Nevan called. If Cupid hadn't been restraining him, the dog would have pounced on Vibius, who probably would have killed him.

"You son of a bitch," Nevan shouted, swinging a fist at Vibius and connecting with his chin while aiming for the tall guy's nose. "Instead of picking on defenseless women, how about taking on someone your own size?" As soon as the words left his lips, Nevan realized how ludicrous they were. "Don't you ever touch Aladee again!" Glancing at Aladee, he asked, "Are you okay?" She nodded as Red helped her to her feet and then they both gasped. Before Nevan had a chance to realize why, Vibius gored his upper arm with one of his horns.

"Nevan!" Aladee screamed, struggling to rush to Nevan's side as Red and Lonan held her back.

"Enough!" Jupiter bellowed. "Return to your seat at once, Vibius."

Nevan looked down at his bleeding arm in disbelief. "God damn," he muttered, "that hurt like a motherfucker." Buster was barking his fool head off now, baring his teeth and growling.

Nevan pulled back his fist, but Vibius was too fast. Goat boy ducked, then kicked Nevan in the thigh with one of his hooves, again with enough force to send Nevan hurtling to the floor. Blood gushed from the wound, but Nevan was on his feet in the blink of an eye, dizzy from the pain but determined not to keel over. This time when he punched, his fist made direct contact with Vibius's nose.

Nevan waited for blood to pour from the wound, but Vibius just stood there with a big shit-eating grin on his face.

"Puny, pathetic human," he snorted, raising his arm to backhand Nevan. He connected with Nevan's already broken nose, providing a sickening crack. The pain was blinding.

"Enough, I said!" Jupiter roared.

"Let them at it," Mars bellowed, a bloodthirsty gleam in his eye as he swung his fists in the air, grinning like a hyena. "There's nothing to spice up a plea hearing like a good bloody fight."

Ignoring Jupiter's command, Vibius rammed Nevan's chest with his horns, knocking the wind out of Nevan and sending him sailing through the air. Vibius galloped to where Nevan had fallen, standing over him with one hoof raised, ready to stomp."

"Oh dear God, Nevan!" Red yelled, racing toward his cousin. With Vibius poised to clomp, Red let out a tribal yell, tackling goat boy just like an ace football player.

"The mortals are impressive," Diana noted, her voice husky.

Unfortunately, Red's full body tackle had little effect on the powerful satyr, who smacked the well-built Red clear across the floor as if he were nothing more than a bug.

"Holy shit," Nevan managed to eke out as he rolled and struggled to his feet. "Red!"

"Red, my love!" Lonan called out as he rushed to Red's aid. "Vibius, have you gone mad?" Lonan shouted, helping Red to his feet and holding him close. "I demand you desist in this idiocy at once!"

"Or what, teacher?" Vibius scoffed. "You'll put a red check next to my name in class?" He roared with laughter.

"Oh, Nevan," Aladee cried, hurrying to Nevan's side. "Are you all right?" Her eyes filled with tears. "Look how you're bleeding."

Through blazing pain, Nevan did his best to offer a chuckle. "Don't get any funny ideas." He winked. "I'm not up to it just now, honey."

Lonan helped a limping Red to where Nevan and Aladee stood. An instant later, Vibius's ferocious naying baaah shocked the hell out of them as they looked up to see the satyr hunching his shoulders, snorting and swiping his hooves on the floor, much the same way a bull does a moment before it attacks.

"Oh, shit," Nevan and Red chorused.

As Vibius galloped toward the foursome, the auditorium filled with an earsplitting, bloodcurdling wail so piercing Nevan and the others covered their ears.

Turning, Nevan saw Kreshti, bless her wild screaming banshee heart, standing at her chair, mouth open wide, clearly in an attempt to divert Vibius. Screaming in agony, poor little Ofradurn the troll clapped his hands over his ears and rushed from Kreshti's side toward Vibius, nipping at the satyr's ankles to distract him. He got a swift kick for his efforts.

"Oh, Ofie!" Kreshti cried out, her howl increasing as she ran to him.

"Damn, that banshee can hold a note," Apollo said with admiration, playing along with her wail on his lyre.

"Cease your incessant shrieking, banshee, or I'll crush you along with the others," Vibius spewed, raising his hand to swat Kreshti. Nevan, Red and Lonan ran at him, tackling the satyr together. They could have been characters in a cartoon the way they slammed into goat boy, then bounced off, falling to the floor without so much as throwing him off balance.

In the blink of an eye, Vibius stomped on the legs of Nevan, Red and Lonan, leaving the trio writhing in agony and unable to get to their feet. Poised to stomp on Nevan's head, Vibius was distracted by Cupid calling out, "Vibius, cease!" While Nevan managed to roll, Vibius still stomped, crushing Nevan's shoulder, before stomping again on his pelvis. The pain was beyond excruciating.

~ ~ ~

"Nevan!" Both Aladee and Red cried, drawing the attention of the snarling satyr who rushed to Red, delivering the same treatment he'd just given Nevan. As Lonan cried out to Red, Vibius kicked Lonan's knee.

Aladee was beside herself and didn't know what to do. The din throughout the large hall was deafening, with the gods and audience crying out, begging for Vibius to stop, and shouting threats at him. It seemed to Aladee the satyr had gone completely berserk.

Due to their determined struggling, trying to get free to protect their owners, Cupid lost control of all three animals. Aladee watched as Buster ran full speed toward Vibius, looking for all the world like a fearsome devil-dog. She tried communicating with him telepathically but Buster was solely focused on saving his beloved master.

"Buster, no!" Nevan shouted, obviously angry and frustrated that he couldn't get up to intervene and save his dog. "Buster! I can't lose you, boy. Stop!" His entreaty fell on deaf ears as the medium-sized dog tackled Vibius's left side, doing his best to tear into the violent satyr, who shook the dog off as if he were an annoying bug, and stomped on all four of his legs with his hooves, two at a time, preventing Buster from getting to his feet. The dog's whimper was heartbreaking.

"Please!" Aladee cried, getting to her knees at Buster's side and doing her best to comfort the suffering animal. "Won't somebody do something to stop this maniac!"

"Aladee, get out of his way," Nevan called to her, his voice weak and wobbly. Get to safety." Fighting not to lose consciousness, Nevan turned to his dog who lay lifeless now. "Buster...my poor Buster..."

"Oh Nevan, my dearest Nevan." Aladee cradled his head, wincing at the severity of his wounds. His cheeks were wet with a mixture of tears and blood as she watched him fight to stay awake. Nevan's voice became so soft she could barely hear it.

"Can't lose you, Buster...can't lose my good boy. Aladee...Aladee...love you...love you...love..." Nevan's eyes closed and his jaw went slack.

"Nevan!" Red cried. "Dear God, please don't be dead. Nevan!" Red struggled to move but couldn't. He was in terrible shape as well. Aladee feared she would lose them both.

Red's cat, Cupid, turned into a raging hellcat, while Lonan's mini-unicorn, Sabby, became a diabolic fighting machine. Fearless, they followed Buster's lead, out for Vibius's blood. The cat offered the mightiest, fiercest growl possible from a small ball of fluff on four legs as he leapt at Vibius's right side while, horn lowered and positioned to stab, the usually gentle, mild-mannered Sabby snorted before galloping head on toward Vibius's center.

Little Cupid the cat's fate was similar to Buster's. Vibius's stomp landed on the cat's hind quarter, crushing his pelvis with an audible crack.

"My precious baby," Red called to his cat. "Dear God...no...no..." His cheeks wet with tears, Red, too, soon lost consciousness.

Before meeting an appalling fate, comparable to the dog and cat, Sabby stabbed Vibius in the thigh, causing him to howl. The brave little animal paid the price when Vibius exacted revenge.

Aladee had never been so terrified. There was blood all around her...senseless carnage. Along with her teacher, Lonan, her two beloved mortals, and their beloved pets lay nearly lifeless.

She ran to Nevan's side, trying to wake him to no avail. "Oh Nevan, please don't leave me. I've only just found you, my love, don't die...oh please, Nevan, wake up." She kissed his cheek and gently moved his arm. It was difficult finding a place on his body that wasn't severely injured. Resting her head on his chest, she listened, prayed, for a heartbeat, hopeful when she detected a faint beat.

Heartbeat...the word reminded her of *heartwish*. Looking up she saw Vibius coming for her, grinning as drool dripped from his mouth while he eyed her like she was a raw steak he yearned to sink his teeth into. She had just one chance to make a wish to save them all. And she had to act *fast*! Aladee tried pulling the heartwish ring from

Nevan's hand. It wouldn't budge. A glance to her side told her she was too late to escape the satyr.

Petrified as she glimpsed the ferocious, yet lustful look in Vibius's eyes as he grabbed her forearms, Aladee kicked, punched and butted him with her head, all of which merely had him laughing. His long tongue swooped over Aladee's face, causing him to utter a pleasured *mmmm*. Gathering her inner strength, the helpless Aladee closed her eyes, preparing herself for the end.

As Vibius's hand snaked beneath the flowing skirt of her long gown, headed for her nether regions, Aladee's thoughts traveled to a happier time and place. *I will love you forever, my dearest Nevan. Always and always.*

Dunniger the dragon rushed forth, his eyes blazing red. "Desist, satyr, and unhand the nymph, lest I convert you into a smoking platter of crisp roast goat as an offering to the gods." Smoke curled up from his nostrils.

"Dunniger, don't!" Cupid called as the dragon filled his lungs, ready to spew fire.

"Let the dragon roast him," Neptune called out. "Grilled goat would be a nice change from all that fish and seafood."

"Hear, hear!" Mars shouted in accord.

"The honey bee has been provoked," Dunniger snarled. "Allow me this one simple pleasure, Cupid."

"No, you've come so far, Dunniger," Cupid told him. "I don't want you backsliding. Vibius isn't worth it." With Hercules at his side, Cupid hopped over the rail that separated the audience from the main floor of the court.

"Cupid, no!" Psyche shouted, rising from her chair. "Vibius will kill you!"

"Best heed the wife, love god," Vibius taunted. "I shall enjoy picking my teeth with your bones, after I've sampled Aladee's juicy lady-parts."

Hercules bounded toward the satyr, who planted his hooves firmly and growled at Hercules with a *come-and-get-me* challenge. With no more effort than plucking a doll from a toy chest, Hercules snatched the heavily inebriated Vibius off his feet with one hand, elevating his arm and holding the snarling creature high over his head. At some point the satyr released Aladee, who fell into Cupid's waiting arms.

"He's all yours, Cupid," Hercules said.

"What? No!" Vibius howled, eyes wide with trepidation as Cupid set Aladee down, then raised his hand, fingers poised to snap. "You're supposed to be the god of love. You can't do this to me. It's not an act of love!"

"Love?" Cupid's features skewed. "Thou art a boil," he spat, "a plague sore, an embossed carbuncle."

Aladee was never happier when she heard Red's soft voice say in response, "Shakespeare, King Lear." Happy tears sprouted with confirmation that Red was still alive.

"This, Vibius, is for my dear, longtime friend, Lonan." With a snap of Cupid's fingers, Vibius instantly morphed into a horned toad.

"Lonan warned you countless times, Vibius." Cupid took the small green creature from Hercules's hand, holding it between his thumb and forefinger. "As did I." He sniffed the air and cringed.

"By gods, you smell like a distillery, toad." Cupid motioned to one of his aides, instructing, "Take him to detox." Returning his attention to Vibius before the aide left, he said, "Shame on you, satyr. You'll remain a toad in detox pondering your dishonorable deeds until it's time for you to go on trial."

Cupid returned his attention to Aladee. "Are you all right?"

Nodding, she said, "I'll be fine. Tend to the others."

"All rise," Mercury cried out and all eyes were on the twelve gods as they filed out of the auditorium. "The council retires to chambers to resolve the fates of the pleaders."

Chapter Twenty-Two

~<>~

HEALING PRACTITIONERS tended to Aladee's considerable bruises and worked on the extensive wounds of Nevan, Red, Lonan, and Ofradurn the troll. Unfortunately, immortality didn't ease the pain of injuries, which meant Lonan suffered greatly as his wounds healed. Aladee was thankful Lonan was up and around, caring for Red within half an hour. Nevan's wounds were the most grave. They'd nearly lost him. He was still unconscious while Aladee went to the animal treatment area to check on the three injured pets.

Her heart broke when she saw the brave, wounded little pets, struggling to stay alive. While the immortal Sabby's wounds would heal, the outlook for Buster and Cupid was grim. Both the dog and cat would have to be euthanized. Even with the advanced medicinal techniques of Olympus, their injuries were too severe to save them. They suffered not only from broken bones, but from massive internal injuries. Both animals were heavily sedated until Nevan and Red could say their final goodbyes.

"Poor, sweet, brave, foolish darlings," Aladee said to them, ever so gently petting them. She couldn't conceive of the pain both Nevan and Red would endure when they learned they'd be losing Buster and Cupid. After kissing the pets, Aladee returned to see how Nevan was doing.

The time she sat, waiting before learning anything certain, seemed interminable. It took more than an hour before the physicians were able to bring both Red and Nevan back from Death's threshold. They'd both had non-invasive surgery to repair multiple damaged organs, and had their broken bones mended with progressive curative treatment. With medical care on Olympus being considerably more advanced than Earth's, injuries that would be deadly on Earth were usually less consequential.

Before Aladee was allowed to see Nevan or Red, Lonan and Cupid came to her, conveying solemn expressions. "We need to speak privately," Cupid said, leading them to a private room.

Once seated, Cupid studied Aladee's face. "I'm so sorry you were injured, but I'm glad the physicians were able to heal your lovely face."

Her hands touching her cheeks, Aladee admitted, "I didn't even realize. There's been too much going on for me to worry about myself or check a mirror."

"They healed Nevan's nose and black eyes as well," Cupid said. "The rest of his injuries, of course, are far more serious and will take considerable time to heal."

"I'm so relieved to hear Nevan will survive. I worried that I'd lost him. The pain he endured," Aladee shook her head and tears flowed, "must have been agonizing."

Drawing in a deep breath, Cupid expelled it, telling her and Lonan. "I didn't actually bring you here to give you a medical update."

"I thought not," Lonan said.

"I spoke with members of the council," Cupid said. "In light of the life-threatening injuries from this morning's debacle, and the mental stress both of you are no doubt experiencing as you wait to hear about the condition of Nevan and Redmond, they've allowed me to prepare you in advance of their public ruling. They prefer that I do this to help avoid histrionics when you're called back to appear before them when the official verdict is announced."

Lowering his gaze, Cupid brushed at invisible crumbs on the table, rather than look directly at Aladee or Lonan. "As you can surmise, the council didn't take kindly to the spectacle with Vibius.

They likened it to the uncouth brawling customary on Earth." Lifting his head, Cupid looked at Lonan. "Lonan, they'll be ruling in yours and Red's favor, permitting Red to remain here on Olympus with you and granting him the status of minor god."

Relief and happiness were evident on Lonan's face.

The room was silent for what seemed like a small eternity to Aladee.

Cupid turned to her. "Aladee..." His eyebrows pinched, sorrow apparent in his eyes as he looked at her...and she knew. Aladee knew.

Clasping one of her hands, he continued, "I so deeply regret..." the words hammered throughout her head, "that the council will rule against you and Nevan."

With a quick intake of breath, Aladee sat motionless, blinking her eyes to keep from sobbing.

"It's partly because of the outrageous fiasco with Vibius, partly because you're unable to control your wings, and because you've been careless with important class materials too often for the council's comfort."

A single fat tear coursed down Aladee's cheek. "I understand." Her bottom lip trembled as Lonan took her other hand in his, giving it a supportive squeeze. "I feared as much. Because of my physical defect, my carelessness, and the satyr's obsession with me, Nevan and I have lost our one chance to remain together." She shook her head back and forth slowly. "I accept full responsibility."

"You're not defective, Aladee—or at fault." Lonan lifted her chin, offering a comforting smile as he gazed into her eyes. "You're simply wired somewhat different than most. My dear, if you can generate a wingspan during a moment of elation, I fully believe you have the capability of producing the same effect at other times. But it's not I who must believe, Aladee...it's you." He kissed her forehead.

"Thank you, Lonan, and my thanks to you, Cupid, for preparing me in advance of the public ruling."

Gazing down at his Roman sandals, Cupid said, "I'm afraid the unwelcome news doesn't stop there."

"No..." Lonan pressed against his temples, clearly dreading Cupid's next words.

Slowly lifting his gaze, Cupid said, "All memory of Aladee, and anything related to her, will be expunged from Nevan's memory."

Part of Aladee's heart and soul died.

"Regarding Red," Cupid continued, "Nevan will only know that his cousin has disappeared. Family and friends who know the truth will also have their memories erased. Nevan and Red are not permitted to be in contact with each other in the future. Red will permanently relinquish all connection to his family and friends on Earth. If he makes any attempt at contact, he will immediately be returned to Earth, with memories of Lonan and Olympus obliterated."

"Such a merciless outcome." No longer able to maintain her composure, Aladee wept. "Nevan and Red love each other so much, and Red is so close to all the Malones."

"This will be inconceivably difficult for Red," Lonan said. "Losing his cousin, his beloved cat, and all the people he cares about on Earth..." Lonan's voice caught. "This ruling couldn't be more cruel and forbidding."

"I wish the news was better," Cupid said. "I know it's exceptionally bleak."

"Being the bearer of such bad news couldn't have been easy," Lonan said. "Thank you, Cupid, you're a true friend." Standing, Lonan shook his hand.

Aladee knew exactly what she needed to do next. "I'm going to check on Nevan's progress."

"I'll want to check on Redmond too," Lonan said.

Pulling the door open, Cupid went in one direction while Aladee and Lonan went in another.

A moment later, Aladee stopped walking.

"Aladee? Are you all right?" Lonan asked.

"I need you to know what's in my heart," she said, attempting a smile. "I've been so fortunate to have you as my instructor, Lonan. You're a good man, truly deserving of love and happiness. Regardless of what's happened for me, I'm sincerely glad you and Red will be able to remain together. Your love for each other is so evident." Leaning close, she gave him a kiss on the cheek.

Touching the spot she kissed, Lonan smiled. "Thank you. Your words touch my heart. Know that you're deserving of happiness too, Aladee." His expression was pained. "I'm heartily sorry about you and Nevan." He drew her into a quick embrace while Aladee struggled not to weep.

"With our greatly advanced medical skills," she said as they started walking again, "I can't understand why they can't save Buster and Cupid."

"If the satyr's hooves nearly killed Red and Nevan," Lonan noted, "imagine what the same intensity did to those small bodies. Poor little things. They were so brave."

"As was Sabby,"Aladee said. "I'm so glad he'll survive."

Lonan covered his face before running his hands through his hair. "I fear for Red when he hears the news."

Aladee knew Red and Nevan would be devastated. Crushed. The pain they'd experience would dwarf the agony caused by Vibius.

Again, she fought to keep from crying, telling herself that after the council reconvened, publicly announcing their decision, she could break down and sob for hours...days. Maybe months. Imagining life without Nevan was unbearable.

Her mind spoke the words *Smile, Aladee* with each step. She couldn't let Nevan see her upset, suspecting the worst now when he needed all his strength and resolve to heal. *Smile, Aladee...*

Entering the healing area, Aladee saw the technicians assisting Red from his bed into a wheelchair. It did her heart glad to see him on the mend.

"Redmond, my love." Lonan came from behind Aladee, taking Red's hands ever so gently. "I was afraid I'd lost you. You were incredibly brave and fearless in coming to Nevan's defense."

"How about that rebel yell?" Red asked through anemic laughter. "I didn't know I had anything like that inside me. I just saw red, no pun intended, when that hairy, overgrown beast attacked my cousin."

"You were the epitome of Prince Charming," Lonan said. "Are you in a great deal of pain?"

Following a long blink, Red admitted, "It was utterly blinding at first, but they gave me some excellent pain medication. They said it significantly reduces pain without the addictive qualities of opiates. As for my Prince Charming-esque performance, I was quite the dashing gay blade, wasn't I?" Red quipped, the sparkle returning to his eyes.

"I wish you could have seen the look of awe and respect in Nevan's eyes after your brave intervention," Aladee told him. "I know Nevan will never forget how you put your life in jeopardy for him." She held back a sob then, because, of course, Nevan *would* forget. He'd remember nothing.

"Nevan would have done the same for me," Red assured. "We're best friends as well as cousins. Always..." She spotted the anguished uncertainty in Red's eyes. "If, that is, the council rules in our favor." His eyebrows knitted. "Any word yet...about our ruling, or how my precious little Cupid and Nevan's Buster are doing?"

"Not yet," Lonan said, giving Aladee a fleeting glance. As they'd walked from their meeting with Cupid, he and Aladee agreed it was best to remain silent about the verdict and the heartbreaking fate of the pets for now. They'd wait until the time was right. Aladee swallowed hard. As if there could ever possibly be a right time for such tragic news.

"Aladee." Lonan nodded ahead.

She looked up, watching Dunniger the dragon wheel a bandaged Nevan toward them on a mobile hospital bed. Cupid was right about his nose and eyes being healed. His face looked remarkably better, although he was nearly as white as the sheet half covering him. It was understandable with the severity of his injuries.

Damning, un-nymph-like thoughts raced across her mind. She hoped Vibius would never be allowed to live as a satyr again. Even life as a horned toad was too kind a fate for him after the pain he'd caused.

"The physicians estimate it will be about thirty minutes before he regains consciousness," Dunniger said. "But your mortal is going to be okay, Aladee." He offered a sincere smile.

Her mortal. Aladee offered a weak smile. *Not for long.* But, gods, she was so heartily thankful to hear Nevan would survive and thrive.

"I've known many mortals in my time," Dunniger said, "but yours really impressed me. Nevan's a good man with a brave heart. He's a fine mate for you, Aladee."

"The finest," she agreed, almost afraid to touch Nevan. His body was a patchwork of wounds. Gingerly, she rested her hand against his chest, feeling his heartbeat.

"Let's leave them alone for a while," Lonan said to Dunniger. "We'll pester Red for a bit instead."

"My poor, sweet, brave Nevan," Aladee whispered to him once they'd left. "How I adore you." Carefully lifting his hand to her chest, she smiled when the heartwish ring's stone shone a small circle of blue light. "You'll forever live here in my heart, along with my precious memories of each and every moment we've spent together, my dearest love." She could no longer keep her tears from spilling.

Surreptitiously looking around her, Aladee kept hold of his hand, trying to take the ring from his finger. She was still unable to dislodge it. It was almost as if it had fused with him.

Satisfied no one was within close hearing range, Aladee whispered, "Oh great Odin, hear my plea. I am Aladee, granddaughter of Quintus, who rode into battle with you during the Aesir-Vanir war. You told Quintus to call upon you if he ever needed your help. Grandfather is long gone now and never asked you for anything. In his place, I now call on you in Quintus's name, imploring you, mighty Odin, to transfer Nevan Malone's ring and his heartwish to me now. I vow my heartwish will be fitting and honorable. Please, I beg you, heed my heartfelt request."

Instantly, Aladee was able to slip the ring from Nevan's finger and onto her own. It fit as if custom made for her, which was curious because Nevan's fingers were much larger than hers. She hated being away from Nevan for even a moment. Each second she had left with him was golden—but she had a mission to accomplish before Nevan regained consciousness and before their hearing was reconvened.

Kissing each of his fingers, she placed his hand gently at his side and walked away, heading for the animal care room where Buster and Cupid were being kept comfortable.

Aladee explained to the healing staff that she wanted to spend some time alone with the pets to say goodbye. They assured her she wouldn't be disturbed.

The room was quiet, except for the calming sound of water streaming from a small tabletop fountain. Buster and Cupid were in little beds on wheels that resembled hospital nursery bassinets. Containers of fresh flowers and lush greenery were positioned on ledges, bookcases, and the few small café-style tables with chairs. The purposeful design imparted peace, comfort, and tranquility. Melodic instrumental music was piped in, adding to the serene atmosphere.

Through her tears, Aladee smiled. It was the perfect setting to make her heartwish.

~<>~

Mercury's announcement was heard throughout the complex, stating the council would reconvene to give their ruling in thirty minutes, and calling for all parties to be in place.

Aladee returned to Nevan's bed, heartened to see he was sitting up, but bitterly saddened to see Red sitting on the edge of the bed, the two of them with their heads together and arms around each other. They were in tears.

Taking Aladee by the elbow, Lonan said, "The staff told them about Buster and Cupid moments ago. They're having great difficulty processing the tragic news."

Aladee sent up a silent plea to Odin asking that her wish be granted in its entirety. It was frustrating not knowing if she'd succeeded or not, and she had no idea when she'd find out. She was weary of failing at everything and prayed she'd done this one very important thing right.

"Nevan...Red, I heard the heartbreaking news," Aladee said, gently clasping their hands. "I'm devastated. I loved Buster and Cupid—and I love you both, as well."

"Buster was my best pal, my buddy. We did everything together. He started his short life being abused and..." Nevan's voice caught, "it ended for him the same way because of that coldblooded son of a bitch, Vibius. Buster didn't deserve that. Neither did little Cupid." Nevan closed his eyes tight, trying to maintain his composure. "I could kill Vibius." Nevan's face was a mask of pain, and his eyes red with tears.

"I'm a proponent of non-violence," Red said, "but I'm not ashamed to say I feel the same way." He grabbed a fresh tissue, wiping his eyes and nose before handing another tissue to Nevan. "My sweet, precious baby lost his life trying to protect me." Red paused before trying to speak again. His voice cracking, he continued, "The pain from those heavy goat hooves was intense, for me...a grown man. When I think of what it must have been like for my little Cupid..." Covering his face with his hands, Red wept openly. "Damn Vibius," he managed to get out.

"I completely understand the way you both feel," Aladee said.

"I could smell the alcohol on him from quite a distance," Red noted.

"He was stinking drunk." Nevan said, grabbing another tissue from the box and wiping his eyes.

"I don't know what got into him." Aladee shook her head. "He's always been contrary and belligerent, but his behavior today was contemptable."

"Because he couldn't bear the thought of losing you." Nevan squeezed her hand. "*That*, I can understand." He brought Aladee's fingers to his lips, kissing them, as her heart broke into a thousand tiny fragments.

"At least he'll never hurt anyone again," Red said.

"Unless he finds toads smaller than him." Nevan huffed a humorless laugh. "He's a ruthless bully, regardless of his size."

"Fifteen minutes," Mercury's voice sounded overhead.

"We need to go," Aladee said. "We can't be late."

"Have you heard anything," Nevan asked.

Evading the question, Aladee said, "We'll find out soon enough," and signaled for aides to assist Nevan and Red into wheelchairs.

"Hell no. I'm walking in there on my own two feet," Nevan insisted.

"Same here," Red said.

"You can't," Aladee said as Nevan sat up, trying to get off the bed. "You're both still too weak. You nearly lost your lives, for heaven's sake."

"Ah, but we have fabulous pain meds." Red smiled. "We'll help each other. We cousins stick together, right, Nevan?"

"Right." Nevan threw his arm over Red's shoulder, while Red mirrored Nevan's position. "Nothing's ever going to tear us apart. You're stuck with me and vice versa, Red."

Together, with Lonan and the aides nervously lending a hand while cautioning against Nevan and Red getting on their feet, they managed to get both men up from the bed. Their legs wobbled and the cousins held each other tight until they got their bearings. In another few minutes they were standing and taking small steps together.

Preparing for their walk to the auditorium, Nevan smiled at Red. "Little did I know that there was an inner he-man living next door to your inner woman. Damn, Red, you were awesome out there. Like a linebacker, for chrissakes. If it weren't for you, Redmond, there'd be a big hoof indentation where my heart's supposed to be." He gave Red a hearty pat on the back, making both of them wobble.

Wincing, Red said, "I honestly can't think about what happened too much, Nev. Honestly, being reminded of the fear I had, worrying that I'd lost you forever, is too much for me to handle."

"You're both heroes as far as I'm concerned," Lonan said.

"Unfortunately, the three of you look like holy excrement," Aladee said, "with your togas dirty, torn, and stained with blood." Looking down at her own garment, Aladee shrugged. "It appears I fall into the same category."

"Holy excrement?" Red asked. Lonan was clearly waiting for an answer too.

Nevan laughed. "She means *holy shit*. Obviously I didn't do a good enough job explaining the saying."

"Well she's partly right," Red said. "We do look like excrement, minus the holy prefix."

"We do indeed." Lonan laughed along with them.

Aladee understood the reason for their banter and attempts at humor. Her three favorite men were doing their best to put up a good front to keep themselves from sinking too deep into apprehension...or depression.

"Sooo...ready to face the council?" Lonan asked, also giving Aladee a furtive glance.

"Let's do this," Nevan said, as they walked to the auditorium, "so we can all go home and start living our happily-ever-afters."

"Wait until you meet Aunt Astrid, Nevan's mother," Red said to Lonan. "She's amazing. A real doll. She helped me so much when my family disowned me. You'll like her husband, Tore, Nevan's stepdad, too. And Nevan's five siblings? Not a bad apple in the bunch."

This was almost too painful for Aladee to hear.

"My brother-in-law, Drake Slattery," Nevan told Lonan, "is a professor, with umpteen degrees in several subjects, basically everything except for sports." He laughed. "He'll love talking to you. You two will really hit it off."

"I'm sure we will," Lonan said. "I-I look forward to meeting them all."

Nevan and Red exchanged wide-eyed, worried glances when a fleeting sob escaped Lonan's throat.

Chapter Twenty-Three

~<>~

"ALL RISE!" Mercury announced, floating through the air as the other eleven gods followed him into the auditorium.

Aladee sucked in a sharp breath as the deities took their seats. She still had no sign whether or not her wish had worked but Lonan's inadvertent snivel had alerted Nevan and Red to possible trouble.

"It's been a most interesting occasion," Jupiter boomed. "A long while since the council has witnessed such a melee."

"More like a circus," Venus huffed, sitting back with her arms crossed over her breasts as Jupiter held his hand aloft, signaling for her silence.

"This doesn't sound good," Nevan whispered out the side of his mouth. Aladee squeezed his hand in response. She scanned the gods' faces. All looked quite somber, except for Venus, whose beautiful face was marred by a sneer.

"We've been dismayed and left aghast by some appalling behavior," Jupiter said. "We've also been pleasantly surprised and amused by other actions. Mercury will now proclaim the council's findings."

"In the matter of Lonan and Redmond," Mercury read aloud from a scroll and Aladee heard Red's intake of breath. "The council finds no cause for denying this plea. After centuries of excellent service, Lonan has earned the right to live alongside his soul mate."

Aladee heard Red release the breath he'd been holding with a whoosh. "Thank God," he whispered.

"The council was duly impressed by the well-versed mortal, Redmond Devington," Mercury continued, "and has agreed he is destined to dwell on Olympus. The rank of minor god is to be bestowed upon Red, carrying with it all due responsibilities and the rare and precious gift of immortality."

"Yes!" Nevan yanked his cousin into a hug. He and Red winced in physical discomfort, but Aladee knew their joy eclipsed their bodily pain.

"In the matter of Aladee and Nevan," Mercury went on, seizing their attention, "the council regrets..."

Regrets... Although Aladee knew what was coming, her knees went weak, while Nevan stiffened. He squeezed her hand so tightly it felt as if their flesh had fused.

"The council regrets they must deny this plea."

Nevan muttered a string of words beneath his breath, none of which Aladee had heard before. But she didn't need precise translation to understand the sentiment.

"We were duly impressed with the mortal's fortitude, bravery and sense of honor. While he is unpolished, the council believes Nevan shows great promise and willingness. The gods have confidence in his skills and ability to manage an Earthly outpost for Cupid Academy. However, the nymph, Aladee, cannot be elevated to the position of Earthly contact due to her physical deficiency."

"Can I ask a question?" Nevan said and Jupiter nodded. "What does it matter if she has a physical deficiency as you call it? Aladee's smart and devoted. You'd never find anyone who'd do a better job. Please..." Nevan's voice caught. "Please..."

"We have nothing against Aladee personally," Juno said kindly. "She's endearing and charming. But she must be lawfully recognized as a minor goddess to be promoted to such an important position. To bestow the official rank of minor goddess on her, Aladee must be without any noteworthy imperfections. As a winged nymph, the inability to spread her wings upon demand is considered a significant deficiency."

"Excuse me," Red asked. Juno nodded. "Is this the only reason the council is denying their plea?"

"No," Juno said. "The council also believes Aladee bears partial responsibility for the horrific scene with Vibius, and—"

"What?!" Nevan called out. "That's ridiculous!"

"Silence, mortal!" Jupiter commanded. "Proceed, Juno"

"In addition," Juno continued, "Aladee has carelessly left important class materials behind on Earth too often. I'm sorry. We wish it could be different."

Mercury read from his scroll, "The council sincerely regrets that the nymph, Aladee, must remain on Olympus, while the mortal, Nevan, is returned to Earth.

"Oh my God," Red said while Nevan stood ramrod straight and expressionless.

"Furthermore," Mercury continued, "all memories of Aladee and Olympus will be expunged from Nevan, as well as anyone else he knows who's been told about Aladee."

"What will Nevan think each time he and I meet in the future?" Red asked. "Where will he think I live?"

"Unfortunately, you and Nevan will have no future contact. Nevan will believe you've disappeared. You will never be permitted to see or speak to each other again."

"No...no..." Red muttered, shaking his head as his knees buckled and Lonan supported him. "Dear God...no..."

Dead silence filled the auditorium. Aladee looked up at Nevan, who remained stoic except for a single tear trickling down one cheek as he looked straight ahead.

Aladee's heart splintered into a thousand shards at the sickening reality that her heartwish clearly hadn't worked.

During the prolonged silence, Aladee spotted one of the animal-care staff members coming forward. With permission granted to approach, he handed Jupiter a rectangular piece of glass or plastic, the size of the credit card she'd seen Nevan use. Huddled together, the gods conferred in a soft whisper. Jupiter handed the card to Mercury who inserted it into a device atop the long table where the gods sat.

"We've received additional information regarding this case," Jupiter said. "The healing rooms are equipped with audiovisual equipment so the sick and injured can be monitored. The card holds a recording from earlier today when Aladee was in the room alone with the dog and cat."

Jupiter nodded at Mercury, who pressed a button. An instant later, a three-dimensional image bloomed to life in the center of the auditorium, allowing all present to see it from every angle.

The image showed Aladee in the room with the two injured pets. The entire auditorium watched with rapt attention as the image of Aladee, positioned on bended knees between the bassinets holding Buster and Cupid, lifted her hand, caressing the ring on her finger. A soft blue light glowed around her, eliciting awed murmurs from the spectators.

Nevan lifted his hand, realizing his heartwish ring was no longer there. "What the...what happened? You...you made the wish without me knowing about it?" He looked more puzzled than angry.

"I took it while you were unconscious," Aladee explained. "My apologies, Nevan. After I learned about the council's verdict earlier, it was the only way to try to make a positive difference."

She smiled at the perplexed Nevan while tears silently streamed down her cheeks, her heart and mind overflowing with emotion as she recalled the wish she'd made, still not aware of the outcome. She hadn't intended for anyone else, much less all the gods of Olympus, to see or hear her very personal, very private heartwish.

~ ~ ~

In the projected image, Aladee spoke:

"Mighty Odin, this heartwish ring belonging to Nevan Malone holds half of the stone you broke in two eons ago. My wish comes from the depths of my heart and soul. Having been advised of the ominous prognosis for Buster and Cupid, as well as the council's upcoming verdict, I make this wish accordingly. The ring has made it clear that my wish must be benevolent and unselfish. I shall do my best to make it so.

"Nevan is a fine, praiseworthy man. I am grateful for the brief, wonderful time we shared. I wish for my darling Nevan to find true love and never lose it. While he'll have no trouble finding a satisfying love match, Nevan will never have another Red, or another Buster. Likewise, the good, kind Redmond Devington will never have another Nevan, or another cat like his beloved Cupid.

"I ask for lasting robust life to be restored to Nevan's dog and Red's cat, so they may live alongside their beloved masters until Nevan and Red breathe their last. I ask that my beloved Nevan and dearest Red be allowed to remain in close contact for the rest of their lives."

The image of Aladee closed her eyes in a long blink as tears coursed down her cheeks and she swiped them away with the back of her hand.

"I make no wish for myself. I'm imperfect and undeserving. My wings only seem to open when I'm euphoric, as it was when I spent time with Nevan and his loving family. My level of joy was breathtaking and my wings bloomed often.

"I accept full responsibility for Vibius's acts of violence. If I had agreed to mate with the abusive satyr as he insisted, perhaps no injuries would have occurred. My lack of bravery created an atmosphere ripe for the satyr's sadistic rampage and the pain it caused those I love.

"While I've been honored to be in Cupid's classes, and would lay down my life for him, Lonan, and my classmates, my good intentions are meaningless. Rather, my inept, absentminded actions will become my eternal legacy. I am clearly not suitable to oversee the operations of Red's flower shop, much less an Earthly Cupid Academy outpost.

"I greatly respect the gods of Olympus and hold no bitterness in my heart due to their decision. However, with sincere apologies to the Council of Deities, I make this heartwish altering their ruling, because I believe with every fiber of my being that those I love should not be punished for my mistakes.

"Oh my beloved Nevan, my dearest heart, how I shall miss your kisses and the taste of your lips; the kind, loving, generous heart you strive so hard to conceal; your engaging, awkward attempts at humor; as well as our wondrous nocturnal flights together."

Holding her hand with the heartwish ring against her heart, Aladee's image finished with:

"While you won't remember me, Nevan, I shall never forget you or the joy we shared. A part of you will reside in a corner of my heart forever. I love you, my cherished mortal, more than life itself. Goodbye my dearest love, my sweet, darling Nevan. Be happy in your life.

"My humble thanks, great Odin, for hearing my multilayered wish and granting it."

In the image, the room filled with a calming blue glow just as Mercury's announcement came over the system, declaring the council would reconvene soon. The final moment of the image showed Aladee rising to her feet, kissing Buster and Cupid, and leaving the room.

~ ~ ~

Aladee was tugged hard against Nevan's chest. He held her so tight she had trouble catching a breath. His lips were upon her and he kissed her profoundly while whispering words of love.

"I can't lose you, Aladee...I-I can't. Take your wish back."

Gazing into his eyes, Aladee caressed Nevan's cheek with the palm of her hand as tears ran down her own cheeks. "Wishing for my own happiness would be selfish, which is contrary to the ring's purpose. If my wish is granted, you'll find love again someday, and you and your cousin will always have each other. Our separation will cause you only brief pain. Once they've erased me from your memory, you'll be fine. It will be like we never met."

"No! I don't want to forget you...ever! And I don't want any other woman, Aladee. I just want you." Nevan pulled her into another embrace, this time with Red joining them in a three-way hug.

"That was the most beautiful, unselfish gesture I've ever witnessed," Red told Aladee, kissing her forehead. "For someone who's never at a loss for words, I'm truly speechless at your gracious and selfless act. You have my eternal love and thanks, Aladee." Taking her hands in his, he kissed them.

The auditorium erupted in cheers and applause from the gods as well as audience members. Women, including goddesses, openly cried. A good many of the males had tears in their eyes as well.

Aladee was astonished by their reaction. She'd feared reprisal from the gods, rather than approval.

Turning his attention to the panel, Cupid cried out to them, "Council of gods, I beseech you. You can't possibly tell me Aladee's incredibly giving gesture, her exquisite spirit of generosity, hasn't touched your hearts. Won't you reconsider your austere ruling and allow this worthy couple to remain together?"

Cupid's sincere entreaty touched Aladee's heart. She'd come to know an entirely different side of the god of love through this ordeal.

Before any of the gods responded, another animal-care staff member entered the great hall, leading the harnessed Buster and Cupid on leashes as the happy, cavorting pets scrambled to reach their owners. Nevan and Red, on bended knee and with open arms, gleefully shouted out their names as they approached.

Before they reached Nevan and Red though, the pets surprised Aladee by jumping and climbing on her. She squatted to get down to their level. With all their eagerness she was soon fully on the floor where they climbed all over her, licking and kissing her, making her laugh while crying tears of joy. What a fabulous greeting!

Through the commotion, she realized they were communicating with her telepathically, thanking her for saving their lives and bringing them back to Nevan and Red. Giving them each her love and a hug, she released them so they could give their beloved owners the same elated treatment. The exuberance at watching the now vigorous pets reuniting with their *parents* was the essence of delight. Nevan and Red laughed and cried happy tears while hugging their pets. Their shared happiness was phenomenal.

"It worked," Aladee said excitedly. "My heartwish worked...well, at least this portion of it."

Her gaze shifted to the gods as they huddled together. A few minutes later, Jupiter's commanding voice called Aladee's name. The crowd hushed as the jubilant pandemonium subsided throughout the auditorium. Even Buster and Cupid sat silently at their masters' sides.

Standing stock-still, an alarmed Aladee ceased her merrymaking. "Yes great Jupiter?"

"There are only two of Odin's famed heartwish rings in existence. How is it that you, a simple nymph of no particular ranking, came to possess one of these esteemed rings?"

"I stole it," she said, to everyone's shock. "The ring belongs to Nevan. It's been handed down through his family for generations. When I learned of the council's ruling, I took it from Nevan's finger while he was unconscious. Odin had promised to aid my grandfather, Quintus, if he ever needed his help. Quintus never had reason to call upon Odin...but I did. Happily, Odin followed through with his pledge to my grandfather, through me, allowing me to make my wish."

"Why didn't you let Nevan make the wish when he awoke?"

Aladee's gazed swung from Jupiter to Nevan. Taking Nevan's hand, she smiled. "The choice would have been near impossible for Nevan to make. He may have lost the opportunity to remain in contact with his cousin. I couldn't let that happen because of me. How could I live with myself?"

Jupiter surprised Aladee by doing something rarely seen—he grinned. "Well done, Aladee. The aftermath of your daring wish has automatically altered the official documents of this trial," he waved a stack of papers at her, "to reflect your wishes in their entirety. What's more, after watching your purely earnest heartwish, there's not a single council member who objects to the revisions your heartwish has made." He looked down the dais. "Tell them, Venus," he said, nodding to Cupid's mother.

"From this day forward," Venus said with a rare, genuine smile, "Nevan and Red will be allowed to remain in contact for the rest of their lives. Further, we will not erase Nevan Malone's memories of this place, or of Aladee. And now, Aladee, the council has a request to make of you."

Happiest tears streaming down her face, Aladee nodded. "Anything!" The heartbreak of losing Nevan was offset by the joy of knowing he and Red wouldn't lose each other.

Standing before his throne, Jupiter gazed solemnly at Aladee. "Aladee, daughter of Arrius and Venuvia, granddaughter of Quintus who rode with Odin in the Aesir-Vanir war—SPREAD YOUR WINGS AND FLY!"

That wasn't at all what Aladee expected. She looked again at Jupiter's grave countenance and it scared the Hades right out of her.

"Ha! She can't!" Seraletta the undine jeered form the audience section. "The heartwish can't change the fact that the nymph is defective. Broken. Damaged!"

Aladee was glad for Seraletta's spiteful taunting. It gave her the courage to overcome her fear. Primary in her thoughts were Lonan's frequent words of support, encouraging Aladee to believe in herself. Lifting her eyes to the heavens, the sky's azure beauty displayed through the clear glass ceiling, Aladee raised her arms high, whispering, "I believe I can, I believe I can...I have enough love in my heart for Nevan to overcome all obstacles. I can do this!"

As tears of hope and anticipation streamed down her cheeks, Aladee sang out a faultless note as her wings fluttered open wide in all their glory and majesty.

"No!" Seraletta screamed. "No!"

Aladee lifted from the floor and rose, chanting and singing as Apollo accompanied her on his lyre. Halfway to the ceiling, she flew around the entire auditorium, soaring above her classmates as they gasped in awe, floating above the council as they gazed up at her, then bringing herself to a graceful touchdown next to Nevan. As soon as she'd landed, he grabbed her, hugging her hard and muttering sweet nothings as he kissed her eyes, nose, cheeks and lips.

"It's a fluke," Seraletta shouted, "an accident. This proves nothing."

"Aladee," Minerva said, "retract your wings and spread them again. Immediately."

With a deep, shuddering, hopeful breath, Aladee closed her wings, waited a moment, then flapped them open wide, smiling as she lifted from the floor and floated in place, this time carrying Nevan with her, to the sound of the audience's ovations.

"Again," Ceres said.

After returning Nevan to the floor, Aladee repeated the process with ease and grace. She duplicated it several more times at the request of others on the council.

"Well damn." Venus sat forward, propping her elbows on the table and supporting her chin on her fisted hands. "It appears the nymph isn't defective after all." Raising her hand high, Venus added, "I hereby rescind my objection to making Aladee a minor goddess."

"Seconded," Diana concurred, her hand shooting up. One by one, the rest of the council chorused their agreement.

"I've always loved a happy ending," Mars roared. "Especially following a big, bold, bloody battle."

"Does this mean what I think it does?" Nevan said to Aladee, Red and Lonan.

"It certainly appears so." Lonan beamed a hopeful smile. "But let's not get ahead of ourselves. We need to pay close attention." He nodded toward the dais, where the gods were clustered together.

"In light of the fact that we may have made a rare error in judgment," Jupiter said in a softer voice than he'd used during the rest of the proceedings, "the council hereby grants the plea of Aladee and Nevan to remain together on Earth." Hurling one of his lightning bolts high toward the ceiling, both lightning and thunder cracked overhead. "So be it!" Jupiter decreed in a sturdier voice.

The auditorium erupted with wild cheers and applause.

"Aladee!" Nevan shouted to be heard about the roar, squeezing her so tight she had trouble catching a breath. "Oh my darling Aladee! You did it! Sweetheart, you did it! But how did you manage to open your wings on command like that?"

"By believing I could," Aladee yelled back. "Because, my beloved soul mate, I love you and my life would be meaningless if I lost you." She reached over and took Lonan's hand. "Thank you, dear, dear Lonan. Your frequent words of encouragement came to me when I needed them most." When she glanced back at the council, they were all laughing and cheering.

"Silence!" Jupiter bellowed, clearly trying to hide a jovial smile. "We still have one important issue to address. Juno, my dear." He gestured to his wife.

"It is with great satisfaction," Juno said, "the council decrees that the rank of minor goddess is bestowed upon Aladee, and the rank of minor god is bestowed upon Nevan, carrying with them all due responsibilities and the rare and precious gift of immortality."

The healing power of immense joy allowed Nevan and Red to jump in place, regardless of their wounds, as they shouted and cheered. Seeing their gladness had Aladee's wings popping open again.

"Nevan and Red?" Juno continued.

"Yes ma'am?" the cousins chorused, boasting grins so wide Aladee thought it was a miracle their faces didn't split open.

"The rank of minor god is highly venerated. It means vast changes for both your lives. All gods are expected to act and conduct themselves honorably in accordance with our rules and bylaws. The gift of immortality is not given or to be taken lightly. We expect your dedication, devotion and loyalty so the mystic secrets of Olympus will remain preserved and protected for eternity. Are you in agreement?"

"Absolutely," they again said in unison.

Juno smiled. "Thanks to Aladee's heartwish, this means Buster and Cupid the cat will be with you always. In addition, special dispensation will be granted to allow you both extended travel privileges to and from Olympus."

"Unbelievable. That's fantastic!" Nevan shrieked. Grabbing his cousin, he planted kisses all over Red's face as he hopped around doing a happy dance.

"Why, Nevan! Your inner woman has finally emerged!" Red said, laughing and crying at the same time while grasping his cousin close.

"I guess it has." Nevan winked.

"Details of your new rank and responsibilities," Juno added, "will be outlined in a briefing session. Lonan, you're the instructor who tutors new gods and goddesses, correct?"

"I am." Lonan nodded. "And may I say I've never been happier in all my nine hundred seventy years. Thank you, one and all."

Tears of happiness spilling down her cheeks, Aladee retracted her wings and spread them again, giving silent thanks to Odin for coming to her aid and granting her wish. Clutching Nevan in her arms, she lifted them from the floor a few feet, gently twirling as she captured his lips in a deep, soul-reaching kiss.

Chapter Twenty-Four

~<>~

GLIDING PAST flickering white stars dotting the deep cobalt blue sky as they sat in Lonan's chariot, heading for Earth, Nevan recalled the pleasant evening he and Aladee spent the night before. Along with Red and Lonan, they'd been invited to Cupid and Psyche's home for dinner. Sampling the variety of unusual fare was much more enjoyable than the night before their plea was heard, when Nevan had been a bundle of nerves.

He and Red learned a great deal about their new status as immortal minor gods during a fascinating discussion. Being a minor god wasn't an empty title bestowed on just anyone. It was akin to a badge of honor and came with real responsibilities as well as a significant list of tasks to perform.

Nevan and Red likened it to being in the Boy Scouts, or like the extra-special super-private club Nevan, Gard, Red and a few of their friends created when they were kids, still living in the Chicago area. They'd designed their boys-only, girls-not-allowed club complete with secret decoder rings, special badges, and a list of solemn oaths they'd pledged to protect and follow forever.

Over their feast at Cupid's table, with a different wine for each course, they all got to know each other better, swapping stories of their youth, and talking about customs on Mount Olympus as well as Earth. After dinner, Psyche set out a platter of her homemade pastries, including custard tartlets, and slightly sweet cookie rolls, which she suggested would go perfectly with glasses of Quilted Heart Nectar, Cupid's private label liqueur. The herbaceous spirits were unlike anything Nevan or Red had tasted before.

They'd learned creating aromatic liqueurs was a hobby of Cupid's. He'd had a private distillery set up in a small building adjoining his house. He'd instilled this particular liqueur with honey infused with organic rose petals from the rose bushes lining his home. The addition of aromatic herbs and botanicals, combined with sweet spices including cinnamon bark, cardamom, nutmeg, and clove resulted in an elegant mixture.

They all toasted to Buster, and Red's cat, Cupid, and the new long-living status of the pets as well. Since their miraculous healing, the former furry adversaries had become inseparable best buddies. Red's cat used to bat the heck out of Buster's head with his paws before, for no apparent reason, other than Buster's mere presence annoyed him. Now? Cupid gently stroked Buster's fur, giving him massages instead. Damnedest thing they'd ever seen.

By the end of the evening, Nevan and Red had developed what Nevan hoped would be long-lasting friendships with Cupid and Lonan, just as Aladee and Psyche had become fast friends. To Nevan's wonder, he decided Cupid was really an okay guy, with tremendous knowledge and a surprisingly good sense of humor. At least Nevan thought so, Psyche groaned at Cupid's jokes...much the way Aladee did at Nevan's. Cupid, Psyche, and Lonan agreed to visit the Malones on Earth to get to know them.

Astrid would be in seventh heaven. And so would Drake...and Kady...and—well, the entire Malone clan would love it. Nevan had no trouble imagining the sizeable feast they'd make and set up at Bekka House in their honor—with Nevan's own Irish pork pie at the center.

Rather than return to Lonan's home after dinner, Aladee brought Nevan to her own home, where they spent the night together. The charming fairytale-like cottage was tucked away in the middle of a dense Olympian forest. It had a rounded thatched roof, reminding Nevan of the cottages he'd seen on his trip to Ireland. The exterior was painted a delicate shade of pink.

The walls and ceiling were swathed with understated floral wallpaper. Paintings of forest scenes and winged creatures dotted the walls. While Aladee had created most of the impressive artwork herself, the rest had been painted by her late mother. Furniture was covered with calico and chintz, in pastel colors. And Aladee's fourposter bed was surrounded by draped pale pink netting and what Nevan assumed must be silk, pooling at the floor in all four corners.

Nevan wasn't into interior design, but this place was so attractive and well put together it could be on the cover of Architectural Digest. It was the girliest place he'd ever been in, and so perfectly, utterly Aladee. Originally owned by her parents, it was the only home she'd ever known.

The most striking, and by far the sexiest, feature in this storybook space was Aladee herself as she stood before him wearing nothing but her wings, a ruffled apron that looped over her head and tied behind her back, a pair of crotchless lacy-pink panties—worn as they should be instead of as headgear—and the pair of high heels she'd brought with her from her trip to the shopping mall in Glassfloat Bay.

She set a platter of tiny fresh-baked herbed biscuits and butter on the bed, and the bottle of champagne Cupid had given them next to the champagne flutes on the night stand. Even after their filling dinner and dessert an hour before, the aroma of the biscuits Aladee baked made his mouth water.

"I love the smell of fresh herbs," she told him with a sweet smile. "I grow them in a little patch outside in my garden in back of the house." She looked so much more relaxed and at ease than she had during the lengthy ordeal with the council earlier.

"Come on," Aladee patted the bed, "make yourself comfortable."

"I'm afraid I'll wreck your bedspread...or whatever this is." Nevan carefully smoothed his hand across the fragrant, living blanket of soft roses—of the thornless variety.

"It's meant to be enjoyed. I make a new one every few days." She got onto the bed, tapping the space next to her. Once he joined her, Nevan noticed Aladee was mindful not to do anything that might irritate his multiple wounds from Vibius's hooves.

"Your wounds are mending nicely," Aladee noted and Nevan agreed. He couldn't get over how quickly the substantial injuries were healing. Lonan explained it was one of the benefits of being immortal. He could still be injured, but he healed quickly.

Immortal. He still couldn't believe it. Nevan Seamus Malone, and Redmond Bartholomew Devington—immortal minor gods. He chuckled at the implausible notion.

Drawing circles over his chest with her fingertip, Aladee asked, "What makes you half-laugh, husband-to-be?"

He got a kick out the new *husband-to-be* title she'd given him. She seemed to prefer that to fiancé. "I was just thinking that it's going to take one hell of a long time for me to come to grips with my new existence." His smile grew broad. "Wait until my family and friends find out about it!" He was sure he'd get plenty of razzing but, man, what a conversation!

"Remember," Aladee reminded him, "the knowledge of your status must be given only to those you trust implicitly. And, for their own protection, once they know your story, they'll be prohibited from speaking of it to anyone who didn't get the knowledge from you directly."

"Gotcha." Nevan nodded. "I suppose it's all in the rule book Lonan gave us."

"It is." Her face even with his chest, Aladee kissed it while lightly rimming one of the bandages on his thigh with her fingers. "Do your injuries still hurt terribly?" She deposited tiny kisses from his neck to his belly.

"When you have that pretty mouth of yours on me, I can honestly say I feel no pain."

Aladee's eyebrow arched high. "Do you speak the truth or are you just trying to be brave?"

"Maybe a little of both." He laughed. "I'm feeling much better, which is amazing, considering the impact of goat boy's hooves. What a maniac...a real psycho."

"Vibius is a deeply troubled creature to be sure." Aladee added more pillows for Nevan to prop up on. Folding his hands behind his head, he leaned back against them and smiled, thinking he was the luckiest guy on the planet...if Mount Olympus was still considered to be on the planet, that is.

"The doctor said you could remove the bandages this evening if you want to." Aladee gently swept her fingers across his arms and chest. "May I remove them so I can check your wounds for myself? As a nymph, I've been thoroughly trained in the healing arts. I can put healing salve on any of the injuries that still bother you. I'll be very careful. If I cause you any pain, let me know."

"Sure, go ahead. Don't worry, I'm not going to break." He gave her a smile, reminded again of how fortunate he was to have Aladee in his life. Sometimes he worried he'd open his eyes and it would all be a weird, fantastical dream.

"Just lie there, relax, and think of pleasant things." She worked slowly, unwrapping him like a fragile birthday present.

"You mean pleasant things like you and me making passionate love together for all eternity?" Nevan asked.

Aladee's cheeks pinked as she tittered a laugh. "Your minor god status has turned you into a romantic."

"I hope you're not disappointed," he quipped.

"In you?" Aladee looked at him with pure love. "That could never happen." Leaning over him, she kissed his lips. Once more of the bandages were removed, she studied his numerous wounds.

"Everything looks much better. I still need to unwrap your chest and belly." She pecked a ring of kisses around each visible wound. "The bleeding has stopped and the swelling is subsiding. Oh, Nevan, you were so brave." She traced the circumference of a hoof print. "But incredibly foolhardy. Vibius could have easily slain you." She trailed kisses along the discolored flesh where the crazed satyr rammed Nevan with his horns.

"No argument from me there," Nevan assured. "Goat boy was like fighting something out of a nightmare."

"My poor Nevan." Aladee uncovered his bandaged arm, running her finger next to the tear along his biceps. "My gallant, courageous hero." She gently cradled his wounded arm between her hands. "It must have hurt mightily when Vibius gored you."

"Mightily," Nevan agreed, ignoring his base urge to tell Aladee it hurt like a motherfucker when that psycho monster ripped open his flesh.

She continued removing wide strips of gauze. "Nevan?"

"Hmm?" He played with her hair, coiling ringlets of blonde around his fingers.

"Did you mean it when you told the council you planned to provide me with the whole tortilla?"

"The what?" He gave her a curious look.

"You said a little house with a picket fence, a dog, babies, and everything else that goes along with the American dream."

"Oh!" He tugged her face down to his, kissing her. "The whole *enchilada*. Of course I meant it." He tapped the tip of her nose with his finger. "Whatever your little heart desires, sweetheart, as long as you're happy."

"Our future together sounds lovely." Her smile was ear to ear.

Remembering watching Aladee make her incredibly selfless heartwish squeezed his heart. "I don't deserve you."

Her expression crumpled as her eyes grew wide. "You're right. I'm sorry."

"What are you talking about?" he asked, clueless.

"About you not deserving the hell I put you through."

"Come here you little idiot." Nevan wrapped his arms around her. "I love you, Aladee. I meant you're too good for me, not the other way around. Now turn that frown upside down, okay?" He used his fingers to move her lips into a smile, the same way his mother had when he was a kid.

"Oh...I misunderstood." She gave him a quick kiss on the lips. "Do you even love me enough to help keep me organized and focused on my Cupid Academy responsibilities, as well as my new duties operating Red's flower shop while you continue to work at your pub?"

"Yes, I even love you that much." He laughed. "Just promise you'll do your best not to misplace things."

"I promise."

"By the way...when are you going to fess up and tell Lonan about those class items that flew off the chariot?"

"Oh...that..."

Nibbling her bottom lip was a dead giveaway that Aladee was nervous.

"Yes, that." Nevan kissed her forehead.

"I will...eventually."

He had to strain to hear that last word.

"I just hope..." she went on, nibbling again.

"You hope what, sweetheart?"

"That my bow and arrows are still where I left them in the flower shop. In all the commotion, I forgot to fetch them and bring them back to Olympus."

Nevan had forgotten about her archery set until she mentioned it. "Nobody's going to see them because they're invisible. So there's no problem...right?"

"I hope not. If a mortal gets his hands on them, the effect can be intoxicating enough to make the mortal quite..." She twirled her finger at her temple to indicate craziness.

"Addlepated," Nevan finished for her and Aladee nodded,

Once she finished removing the rest of his bandages, she snuggled close to him on the bed. "Let me know if I'm hurting you."

With one swift move, Nevan lifted Aladee, setting her over him.

"Oh my goodness!" Her mouth formed a surprised O. "Be careful, Nevan, you'll worsen your wounds."

"I'll be fine. The best medicine is having you right here, exactly where you belong."

"You're being romantic again." Aladee smiled at him.

"Apparently that comes with the territory. I think it's time for this minor god and goddess to see whether our brand new shiny titles make a difference in, um, more ways than one." His eyebrows danced with mischief.

"What do you mean, Nevan?" she asked in all innocence.

Minor god, Nevan Malone, had no trouble at all showing his goddess exactly what he meant.

~ ~ ~

Red's voice broke Nevan's reverie about the amazing night he and Aladee had spent together.

"Sorry, Red, what was that?" Nevan asked, bringing his thoughts back to the present as they flew through the air.

"I asked about the set of keys I gave you for the shop and my apartment," Red said as Lonan's chariot began the descent toward Earth. "You have them all, right?"

It was unusual to see him without Cupid in his lap, but the little cat and Buster cuddled together, tucked close and napping in a corner of the chariot.

"*The* set of keys...as in singular?" Smirking, Nevan recalled the trio of key sets Red had made for him, *just to be on the safe side.* "Well," clapping his hand against his back pocket, checking for the keys he already knew were there, he said, "I've got one set here, one in my apartment in my sock drawer, and another in the safe in my office at the pub. Just as you suggested. All safe and sound. So quit worrying." He gave his cousin a supportive smile.

"Good...good..." Now Red was the one nibbling his bottom lip. "If you have any questions, just call me. Oh!" His fingers flew to his lips. "I guess we can't do that, can we? Good God, Nevan, this is all so new. It's wonderful and amazing but a bit daunting too. I'm a nervous wreck. Do I look like a wreck?" Red patted his hair. "Please say no."

"You look fine, Red. Just like one of those marble busts of an immortal minor god." Nevan grinned.

"Nevan's right," Lonan told Red. "You do indeed, my love."

Red's face lit up with a smile so radiant his eyes twinkled. It had been years since Nevan saw him looking so happy. Nobody deserved it more than him.

Red's eyebrows knitted as he studied Lonan. "You're really here, aren't you, Lonan?" Clasping Lonan's forearm, Red gazed at him with a tender look of love. "The two of us are together, aren't we? It's not all just a glorious dream, right?"

"It's a dream come true, Redmond." Lonan clasped Red's hand, giving it a squeeze as he gazed into Red's eyes.

Nevan couldn't help smiling. Even someone as unobservant as him could see how deeply these two cared for each other.

"Now, I don't want you two to worry a bit," Lonan said. "Communication, including telepathic, is covered in your Minor

God 101 instruction manual." As he spoke, Lonan guided the horses toward their destination. "Red, you and I will return to Glassfloat Bay in a few months along with Cupid and Aladee's former classmates, to see how Nevan and Aladee are adjusting, and to check on the design of Cupid's Headquarters."

"Who would have thought that Glassfloat Bay's branch of Olympian Contractors was exactly that?" Nevan huffed a laugh. "Construction workers from Mount Olympus."

"We have branches in key locations around the world," Lonan said. "We actually use plenty of Earth workers, like your sister-in-law Sabrina's brother, Hudson Griffin, with his Griffin of all Trades contractor business. He's done contract work for us several times, without knowing our Olympus roots, of course." Lonan winked.

Nevan caught Aladee winking back, as she always seemed to do whenever anyone winked. Deciding she didn't quite understand the meaning of the gesture, Nevan added it to his mental list of things she needed coaching about.

"Griffin's a good man with an eye for detail," Lonan continued. "He'll be in charge of the work crew for the Cupid's Headquarters project. They'll know exactly what to do to transform Red's shop into an official contact location."

"I hope they'll maintain the feel of the place," Red said. "I'd hate to lose the sensation of romance and elegance, along with the mythological feeling I worked hard to instill."

"All the particulars you gave me will implemented exactly as you specified," Lonan assured him. "Aladee, you'll find all the documentation necessary to show you're a certified florist, in case anyone asks. With your extensive knowledge of flora, and floral design, you're more than qualified to work as a florist."

"I can attest to that," Red agreed. "Aladee's work is stunning. It rivals mine. Believe me, that's not a compliment to be taken lightly."

"Thank you. I can't believe all this is happening," Aladee said, mirroring Nevan's thoughts. "I can't wait to begin my life with Nevan on Earth. But I'll miss you and Red so much," she told Lonan.

"I have a feeling the next few months will go by in a whirling blur," Red offered with a snap of his fingers. "Just like that."

Chuckling, Lonan stilled Red's fingers. "The three of you must read the chapter in the manual about snapping your fingers. Now that you're minor gods, there can be dire consequences."

"No problem," Nevan said. "I want to learn everything I can about my ultra-cool new status and everything that comes along with it."

"Aladee," Lonan wagged a finger under her nose, "do not, under any circumstances, misplace your new manual."

Nevan saw Aladee gulp. "Never, Lonan. I promise."

"We're almost ready to land," Lonan added a moment later. "I've veiled the chariot so it's invisible, and we're each wearing our invisibility traveling gear so there won't be any problem. Nevan, keep Buster tucked beneath your invisibility garment until it's safe. You and Aladee have appropriate Earth clothing on beneath your gear, so you're set to blend in."

"I like having the ability to see invisible stuff now." Nevan looked down at himself. "I'll finally be able to see that bow and arrow set of yours," he said to Aladee.

She winced and made a shushing motion as the chariot came to a smooth stop.

Lonan turned to her, his expression serious. "Exactly where *are* your bow and arrows, Aladee? Come to think of it, I don't remember seeing them since I last dropped you off on Earth. You haven't lost them, have you?"

"Of course not, Lonan. I know exactly where they are. They're safe and protected. But...um..."

"But?" Lonan arched an inquisitive eyebrow.

"Well, Lonan, the funniest thing happened on my last trip to Earth with you." Aladee erupted in nervous giggles. "It's so funny it will make you laugh too. Isn't that right, Nevan?"

Nevan just gazed at her silently, feeling sorry as hell for Aladee, but figuring it was best if he kept his mouth shut.

"Red?" Aladee tried with a pleading look. Chewing his fingernails, Red looked away. "Oh dear," Aladee muttered before giggling again.

"Why don't you tell me all about it so I may join you in laughter, Aladee." Lonan folded his arms across his chest, looking none too amused.

"Right." Aladee cleared her throat. "Remember how bumpy that chariot ride was? There was a lot of turbulence. Remember?"

"I recall it was a somewhat bumpy flight."

"Well, you see..." After clearing her throat again, Aladee was gripped by another round of nervous giggles. "During the midst of some powerful jolts and thuds, all of a sudden, *zap*!" She slid her hands together, making a flying motion.

"Zap?"

"Yes! Out flew a few of my belongings before I could catch them."

"Such as?" The muscle in Lonan's jaw clenched and unclenched.

"Oh..." she gave a dismissive wave, "just a miniscule amount of insignificant items." More throat clearing.

"How insignificant?" Lonan gave her a warning look.

"Um, well," she counted on her fingers, "there was the forgetfulness powder and," again she cleared her throat—if there was a frog in it, it would be dead by now, Nevan thought, "the invisibility serum. Then there was my Perfect Love Matches 101 textbook, and my notebook and, um, my invisibility traveling garment. That's all."

The poor thing did her best to give Lonan a carefree smile, making Nevan wince.

"*That's all?!*" Lonan boomed. "Aladee, that was nearly everything you had with you."

"At least my bow and arrows are safe," she offered, making Nevan wonder if that was still true.

"You call this loss insignificant? Oh, Aladee, Aladee, Aladee." He shook his head slowly. "It's a good thing I didn't know of this before your council plea because..." He paused, looking into her fear-widened eyes and at her trembling chin and heaved a sigh. "Nevan, do you have any idea what a serious and monumental responsibility you're undertaking in watching over Aladee?"

"Yes, I do." *No, he didn't.* "I'll make sure Aladee is extremely cautious from now on."

Lonan's shoulders slumped and he breathed another sigh. "I'll have to dispatch a team of investigators to search out and retrieve the items. They could be anywhere, lost in any time period, past or future."

Another time? That staggering bit of news surprised Nevan.

"I just wish you had told me earlier, Aladee, so I could have sent out a team by now."

"I'm truly sorry, Lonan. I know how profoundly I've disappointed you. Please, please forgive me." Aladee rested her hand on Lonan's arm. "You're so very dear to me. If you hated me for the rest of my life, especially seeing as how I'm immortal now and that will be an *extremely* long time indeed, I don't know what I'd do."

"I'm sure we'll succeed in recovering the items." Lonan patted Aladee's hand, giving her a tired smile. "And of course I don't hate you, Aladee. How could I hate my favorite student?" He smoothed one knuckle along her cheek.

Clapping her hand against her chest, Aladee gasped. "Me?"

"I'm only telling you that now because you're no longer officially a member of my class. So make sure you keep the information to yourself."

"Oh, you can *always* trust me, Lonan," Aladee assured, and Lonan just groaned.

The foursome made their final goodbyes, complete with hugs, kisses, words of affection and a few tears. Oddly enough, the most difficult parting was the separation of Buster and little Cupid. The dog and cat clung to each other, whimpering and mewing until Nevan and Red coaxed them apart. Aladee said she'd communicated with them, letting them know they'd see each other again soon.

Then Lonan and Red were off again, leaving Nevan, Aladee, and Buster in the waterfront park, scurrying behind a cluster of bushes to remove their invisibility garments.

"Do *not* drop that anywhere." Nevan poked the garment in her hands.

"Have no fear, Nevan." Aladee clutched it tight to her chest. "You can count on me. I've definitely learned my lesson...several times."

While he loved Aladee with all his heart, Nevan didn't yet have the confidence in her to be as careful as she needed to be. Unable to keep from narrowing one eye at her, he said, "Here, give it to me, sweetheart. I'll carry it for you until we can put it in a safe place."

Glancing down at his Minor God 101 instruction manual, Nevan rapped his knuckles on the book's leather cover and smiled. Then he glanced at the manual Aladee held in the arm she swung lackadaisically at her side. Plucking it from her hand, he carried it with his own.

With some remarkable feat of magic, Lonan had arranged the return trip to Earth so that Aladee and Nevan arrived back in Glassfloat Bay a mere hour after they left when, in reality, they'd been gone for nearly a week. Just thinking about how it was even remotely possible, made his head spin.

"Let's go see my family before we head for the flower shop or my pub," Nevan said. "I know they're waiting to hear we made it back safely."

"I agree. I can't wait to see my future mother and siblings of the law."

Nevan loved how she kept cracking him up unintentionally, then looked up at him with those big, questioning baby blues when he couldn't keep himself from laughing at what she'd said.

"Mother-in-law, sister-in-law, brother-in-law," he clarified.

"Ahh, I see. Will Annalise be my friend-in-law?"

"No, she—" Nevan stopped short. Once he started explaining, it would open the door to a flood of new questions that would take hours to answer because each of his responses would lead to another squirrelly question. He took his phone from his pocket. "I'll call my mom and have her tell everyone to meet us at Bekka House in an hour. That gives us a little time to freshen up after our chariot ride."

Chapter Twenty-Five

Still Tuesday Morning on Earth

~<>~

AS THEY WALKED toward Bekka House, Nevan marveled at everything that had transpired in a week's time. Too bad he couldn't add Immortal Minor God just below Master Purveyor of Beer, Wine, and Spirits on his business card.

Who would have thought that one day Nevan and his cousin would be minor gods?

Or immortal?

He still had trouble wrapping his mind around it. And then it hit him.

His good boy, Buster, was basically immortal too, since he'd live as long as his master. He looked down at the tongue-lolling dog and stopped in place, bending to give his best pal, the one he'd almost lost forever, a hug. He received an ample face-lick in return.

~<>~

Family and friends gathered around the long dining table, with all the table leaves in place, for an impromptu brunch. After Nevan's call, Astrid let everyone know food and drink were needed at Bekka House, pronto. It never ceased to amaze Nevan how fast an appetizing spread could be produced on very short notice.

Everyone listened with rapt attention as Nevan and Aladee relayed all that had happened.

"We're delighted that you're here with us, Aladee," Astrid said, camera in hand. "And that you're going to be a part of our family. Smile!" *click...click...*

"So, Your Highness," Gard said to Nevan, "does this mean we have to bow down when you enter a room?"

"Of course it does." Nevan gave a lofty smile. "And you'll need to ask permission before you can sit in my royal presence."

"You're not royalty, you big dodo," Drake said. "You're on a whole different level. You're divine."

"Why thank you, darling." Nevan fluttered his eyelashes. "You're not so bad yourself."

"I don't think Nevan's a dodo, Drake," Varik said. "He and Red have risen above the dodo bird category. Being minor gods puts them even above ostriches in the pecking order."

"Like a majestic eagle!" Nevan spread his arms wide.

"I think he means more like a waddling little penguin in a tux," Gard quipped.

"Ha-ha," Nevan said, "very funny, guys. Better behave or I won't let you kiss my ring." He held out his hand, turning it back and forth. Immediately after Aladee's heartwish had been revealed at the council, the ring disappeared from her hand and returned to Nevan's.

"As a minor god, Nevan could be the king of MiLB," Zak said, tongue firmly in cheek.

"MiLB?" Drake's eyebrows arrowed down in confusion.

"Baseball, Professor," Gard said. "Whoosh," he added, making the motion of a joke going over Drake's head.

"They're talking about the minor leagues," Tore explained to Drake. When Drake still looked clueless, he clarified, "Minor league baseball."

"Ohhhh, yeah...yeah." Drake's sports-empty head bobbed too quickly. "Sure, I get it."

Leaning toward Astrid and the other women, Aladee confessed, "Even with the chapter in my book on Earth vernacular, I doubt I'd be able to follow any of this discussion."

"Don't worry," Astrid assured, "the rest of us Earthlings at the table don't get it either." She winked and Aladee winked back. "The boys are just pulling Nevan's leg." *click...click* She'd busied herself taking one photo after another since everyone arrived.

"Why would they do that?" Aladee bent, looking under the table, causing the women to bite back a round of laughter so she wouldn't feel foolish. Like Nevan, they realized Aladee wasn't purposely trying to be funny.

Across the table from Aladee, Kady said, "I'm so happy we'll be sisters-in-law...or maybe it's nymphs-in-law." She and the others chuckled.

"Me too." Aladee offered a genuinely happy smile. "And Annalise is my official friend-in-law."

"Yes I am." Annalise nodded with conviction. "Nevan mentioned you can communicate with animals. Can you really?"

"Yes, through a sort of telepathic connection. It works well as long as the animal is willing and open to the idea. Let me show you..." Focusing on Buster, who was happily visiting everyone at the table in hopes of getting some food scraps, Aladee placed her fingers at her temples and closed her eyes. In a short while, Buster came directly to her and sat. Without her saying a word, he twirled once in place, and then rolled over. Back on his feet at her side again, he looked up at her adoringly, wagging his tail.

"What a good boy you are, Buster." Aladee ruffled his fur. "I have a treat for you." Tearing a slice of cheese into small pieces, she offered them to the dog who immediately ate them up. "He prefers cheddar over Swiss," she said, "but he'll gladly take what's offered."

"Amazing," Reen said. "So you silently gave him the commands to sit, twirl in place, and roll over?"

"Well, I asked rather than commanded." Aladee chuckled. "Buster is so eager to please, especially after he was so badly injured and the heartwish brought him back from the brink. He was happy to perform for you all and knows you all love him."

"Nevan told us about your heartwish, Aladee," Reen said. "It was so beautiful and unselfish. It actually made me cry." She glanced at her dog, Hazelnut, who'd been following Buster's fairly successful food-scrap scavenging trip around the table. "I'd love it so much if you could try communicating with Hazelnut sometime."

"I already have. Buster introduced me to Hazel earlier," Aladee told Reen, whose mouth opened in an O as her eyes popped wide with surprise.

"No!"

"Yes!" Aladee's face lit with delighted laughter. "She loves you so much, Reen, and remembers the day you came to the pound to rescue her. Hazelnut told me there was just her and four other dogs there that day. As soon as you saw her, she felt a soul to soul connection was made. She also said she's happy you called her Hazelnut rather than Filbert or Nutella."

"What!?" Reen slapped the tabletop. "Oh my God, Aladee, I can't believe it!" Reen laughed and the others joined in. "I only told those alternate names to Hazel. No one else knew! Well, except for Drake, but being a typical guy, he probably forgot about five seconds after I told him." She chuckled. "Wow, this is so awesome."

Aladee looked around the table and smiled. "In case any of you are wondering, the answer is no, I can't read minds, so don't worry. But I can sense those of you with pets would like to have me communicate with them too. I'd be happy to try. There's no rush because I'll be here in Glassfloat Bay with you all for a long time."

"Think about it." Reen gazed around the table. "We could be famous." Moving her hand as if across a movie marquee, she said,

"Presenting, the Amazing Aladee, Glassfloat Bay's very own Pet Psychic!"

"Careful, Aladee," Drake said, "or my very persuasive wife will talk you into taking your amazing dog-whispering act on the road."

"What a great idea, Drake." Reen clasped his forearm. "I could make cute little knitted dog scarves with the name of your show on it, Aladee. We'd sell them, giving half to pet charities and keep the other half. We'd make a fortune! You'd be on YouTube, all over social media, all the early morning and late night TV shows." She bounced in her seat like an animated kid. "Can you talk to cats, rabbits, and squirrels too?"

As Aladee nodded, Nevan caught the clueless smile he'd come to recognize while Aladee tried to make heads or tails out of Drake and Reen's banter.

"I have absolutely no idea what any of that means," Aladee confessed, offering an exaggerated shrug. "But I appreciate the warning. I promise to be careful about taking my Amazing Aladee act on the road."

"What's your last name, dear?" Astrid asked.

"I don't have one as such. Most of us don't have surnames on Mount Olympus as you do here on Earth. Depending on who is being addressed, we're sometimes known by our lineage, such as Aladee, daughter of Arrius and Venuvia, granddaughter of Quintus who rode with Odin in the Aesir-Vanir war. Other times we're known by our skillset, such as Aladee, Dryad nymph of forest and woods, and Limoniad nymph of the meadows."

"Wow," Laila said. "Those are quite a mouthful."

"Indeed. I can't wait until I am known simply as," she looked at them all, beaming an enthusiastic smile, "Aladee Malone!"

click...click...

"Then you won't be just an honorary Malone, you'll be the real deal," Nevan said.

"Real deal..." With a sigh, Aladee said, "I really must get busy studying Earth lingo now that Earth is my home."

"I guess that would make me Annalise, maker of hot fudge sundaes and Dutch baby pancakes." She laughed.

"Not just maker," Aladee offered, "Queen!"

"I like the way Aladee thinks," Annalise said.

"Have you and Nevan talked about your wedding plans yet?" Astrid asked.

"Jeez, Mom," Nevan said, "first of all, we just got engaged. Second, we just returned from a harrowing trial by a jury of some really intimidating gods, not to mention a knock-down-drag-out with a psychotic satyr. We haven't had time to talk about a wedding yet."

Nevan watched his mother morph into her ecstatic mother-of-the-groom mode.

"Well," beaming a smile, Astrid tapped the table a few times, "there's no time like the present, right? Aladee, dear, we can have your wedding right here in Bekka House if you like. I know you lost your family, but now you have all of us as your new family. We'll all be here for you and help you every step of the way. That means with your wedding...and always."

Blinking back tears, Aladee fluttered her hand at her throat. "That means so much to me. Thank you."

"The wedding can be in the family room, right in front of our wonderful, magical, silver Christmas tree," Delaney suggested.

"That's what Drake and I did," Reen said with a melodic sigh. "Oh, Aladee, it was *so* romantic."

"Yeah," Drake agreed, "especially the part where everyone in town was standing elbow to elbow in one room gawking at us. *Sooo* romantic." He rolled his eyes and Reen gave him a playful whap.

"I'm happy to do whatever the wonderful Malones think is best," Aladee said. "Nevan and I will discuss it after we've had a good night's sleep and give the topic the attention it deserves. It's been a fitful week for us."

"So weird how it's been a week for you two," Delaney said, "but on our end, you were only gone an hour or two. Oh, Aladee, you and I have lots of talking to do. There's so much I want to learn!"

"Caution alert, Aladee," Laila warned with a wink, and Aladee winked back. "Delaney writes a syndicated humor and human interest column that appears in the newspaper and online. She loves to blab all our secrets."

"Anything you tell Delaney might end up in one of her columns or books," Reen agreed.

"Delaney's made us all famous...or, rather *infamous*," Kady said with a good-natured roll of her eyes.

"Oh goodness." Her fingers flying to her lips, Aladee was wide-eyed. "Then I must be cautious, lest I accidentally reveal something I shouldn't. I don't want to rile Cupid or any of the gods by overstepping my bounds."

"Hey, come on," Nevan said. "You're scaring her. Remember, Aladee's not used to joking around the way we all do, okay?"

"Nevan's right, girls," Astrid said. "Don't worry, Aladee. My oldest daughter is wise enough not to embarrass her future sister-in-law by telling tales out of school." She gave Delaney a pointed look. "Isn't that right, Delaney?"

"Yes, ma'am." Delaney gave an impish smile. "So, do you think Cupid might read my column?"

"I'll make certain he and his wife, Psyche, receive it," Aladee promised. "I look forward to reading your past columns so I can learn all the secrets of my new family. I'm not afraid of finding out about all the bones in the Malone closet." Pausing, she offered an expectant smile. "I learned about the bones phrase from the Earth vernacular chapter. Did I use it correctly?"

"Great attempt, sweetheart," Nevan told her. "The phrase is actually *skeletons in the closet*, but you were really close."

"I never imagined Mount Olympus was a real place." Tore shook his head. "Cupid, nymphs, satyrs, banshees...and flying chariots? It makes my head spin."

"Oh...that doesn't sound good," Aladee noted. "I hope you speak figuratively and not literally." Getting a kick out of that, Tore laughed and nodded.

"How can you be surprised after having a bona fide genie in the family, Tore?" Laila asked, chuckling at her stepdad's comment.

"Or getting to know our friendly family ghosts?" his wife, Astrid, reminded him.

"Not to mention the amazing feats we've witnessed due to the heartwish rings," Reen said.

"Aladee, what did you mean about us not being able to tell anyone else about any of this hocus-pocus?" Gard's wife, Sabrina asked. "I mean, the Olympus gods wouldn't do something to harm any of us, would they?"

"No, but there would be consequences. Maintaining secrecy is one of the most stringent rules set forth by the gods. If you attempt to tell someone outside the circle of knowing people, the words will..." Aladee thought for a moment. "I believe the correct phrase is...the words will get stuck in your throat. Same with attempting to communicate secrets by any other means. If someone ignores the rules for a third time, their memory of any discussion of Olympus or its residents will be erased. They'll only know that Nevan and I met when I visited Red's flower shop."

"Wow," Annalise said. "That's a bit harsh...but I guess I can understand it. There'd be mayhem down here if people knew about invisible flying chariots, carrying gods and invisible mystical passengers, landing right here in Glassfloat Bay."

Aladee nodded. "While the rules may seem severe, they're ultimately for the protection of all concerned."

"I wish Red could have been here with us," Delaney said, "I'm tickled pink that our cousin has finally found the happiness he deserves." Everyone agreed. "I hope we'll get to meet Lonan one day. He sounds like a terrific guy."

"Aladee told me he and Red will be at the wedding," Astrid said. "Maybe Cupid too. Speaking of the wedding, have you decided what you'd like to wear, dear?" she asked Aladee.

"Well, I—"

"Looks like you can forget about Mom letting go of the wedding talk, Nev." Gard laughed.

"You should spread your wings and fly into the family room, meeting Nevan at the altar!" Zak said to Aladee.

"She can't do that," Laila said, "unless we're the only people in attendance. How would we ever explain Aladee flying around to anyone else?"

"We could explain it like we did for the Half Potato Pub's celebration," Varik said. "You know, wires and mechanisms and such."

"With your coloring you'd look stunning in pale petal pink mixed with the white, Aladee," Reen said.

"Maybe you can knit her a veil," Drake joked.

"Ooh...she could crochet the most beautiful bouquet of flowers," Sabrina suggested. "That way she can keep them forever."

Raising her hand, Annalise said, "I've got dibs on catering. I can do everything except for Laila's delicious scones and the groom's fabulous Irish pork pie."

"How about having the wedding at Bekka House and the reception at Half Potato Pub?" Drake suggested.

"Perfect," Gard said.

"As my first declaration as a minor goddess," Aladee said with an ear-to-ear grin, "I hereby decree that we must have Annalise Griffin's superb hot fudge sundaes at the wedding reception!" She giggled and the women applauded her perfectly sound decree.

As Nevan listened to everyone's joy-and-laughter-filled communal exchange, he felt his heart swell with love and gratitude. A week ago he could never have imagined a regular guy like him being lucky enough to meet and fall in love with an amazing nymph who would change his life forever.

The magnitude of love he felt for Aladee sometimes left him gobsmacked. While all this newness must be exciting for her, it was probably fairly intimidating too. Since she'd had to completely transform her life for the man she loved, then Nevan was damn glad she'd have the unconditional love and support of the Malone family and their good friends behind her.

Chapter Twenty-Six

Late Tuesday Afternoon

~<>~

AFTER BRUNCH, Nevan and Aladee spent some time alone in his apartment before heading to Red's shop in the same building. He really liked his apartment. It was clean, minimalistic, and functional. He'd gone with an open, industrial vibe with exposed brick walls, reclaimed wood plank flooring left over from his pub's renovation, and a few visible pipes edging the ceiling.

The location couldn't be more convenient, since it was only a short walk to his pub and Red's shop...well, it was basically Aladee's shop now. Aladee claimed she liked Nevan's sparse apartment—she loved using the *bare bones* expression—although he could definitely imagine her being pleased with the addition of some fancy, frilly, girly touches like the ones filling her cottage on Olympus.

Since Nevan owned the building, and the apartment next to him was empty, he asked Aladee her thoughts about expanding the living space to give them more room, including space for a nursery when they had children. She loved it. Hud Griffin's crew could knock out the adjoining wall.

The décor of the new half of their larger apartment would be entirely up to Aladee to design however she liked. Nevan would be fine with her bringing the feeling of the home she'd always known right here to make her feel more comfortable and, hopefully, keep her from missing Olympus too much. She'd told him that as much as she loved the cottage, it was just a space inside four walls. That didn't make it a home—love accomplished that.

The two of them made excellent use of their time before heading for the flower shop to see how Alfred and Edwina were doing. The intimate time Nevan and Aladee shared was nothing short of magical. It wasn't the airborne sex that made it that way, it was the purest expression of soul-deep love that made their joining feel enchanted.

It still amazed Nevan how he'd transformed from a commitment-phobe who steadfastly avoided all-night sleepovers, to a guy who was profoundly in love with a woman he'd known for just a week. Before Aladee, he'd never believed any woman could make him look forward to waking up with her at his side each morning.

Though he was head over heels in love with her, it wasn't just burning emotion that he felt coursing through his veins. It was so much more. He liked Aladee. Respected her. Admired her. Cherished and appreciated her. She was the other half of his soul.

As they walked hand-in-hand to Cupid's Headquarters, Nevan wasn't too concerned about any screw-ups happening. He'd taken the warnings Lonan and Cupid gave him to heart. He'd do his utmost to protect Aladee and help her avoid getting into trouble. He'd enjoy keeping a watchful eye on his flighty nymph, helping her to become more trustworthy and, hopefully, less absentminded.

Yes indeed, Lonan, Cupid, Red and all Aladee's old classmates would find everything running smooth when they came back. Just like clockwork.

Nevan and Aladee entered Cupid's Headquarters, gazing into each other's eyes and talking about the future. As soon as the little bell over the door jingled, Red's fulltime employee, Edwina, rushed to greet them, wringing her hands.

"Oh, Nevan" the middle-aged woman said, "I've been trying to reach your cousin for the last few hours. Something strange has happened. Where is Red?"

"He decided to take an extended vacation with a friend," Nevan said smoothly, just as he and Red had coordinated. "My fiancée, Aladee, is a certified florist. Red asked her to take care of the shop during his absence. What's up, Edwina?"

"Oh, it's Alfred. I-I think he's gone bananas." She twirled her finger at her temple.

Nevan wasn't too surprised. Alfred was always in the midst of one crisis or another. "I remember he had some sort of predicament the other day," Nevan said. "He was crying buckets over..." his hand swooped through the air, "something or other."

"His boyfriend, Leonard, broke his heart," Aladee reminded him.

"Yeah, that's it. So what's wrong, Edwina? Has Alfred been blubbering all over the place, or did he call in sick, or what?"

Whipping her head back and forth, Edwina's eyes grew saucer-like. "No. It's really bizarre. The two of us were putting away a new shipment of supplies when, all of a sudden, Alfred swore a blue streak." Gazing left and right, she added in a whisper, "Including the F-word. Alfred never uses harsh language. When I came to see what was wrong, I found him hunched down behind the front counter laughing this deep, weird sort of cackle as something rattled around in his arms."

"Uh-oh." Aladee nibbled her bottom lip.

"Now, Nevan," Edwina went on, "you know I'm a sane, reasonably unflappable woman, right?"

"Sure. Red always says he doesn't know what he'd do without you. Tell me what happened?"

"The rattling I mentioned? I-I couldn't see anything. I mean, there Alfred was, talking and laughing and cursing to himself, and apparently cradling something that was...well, I know it sounds insane, but it seemed like something *invisible*."

Nevan swallowed hard.

"But," Edwina went on, "it sounded heavy, like metal."

Sucking in a gasp, Aladee ran behind the front counter with Nevan and Edwina following behind her. She got on her knees, ducked her head, and felt all around.

"Oh no...oh no, no, no!"

"Don't tell me," Nevan said, gritting his teeth. "Please don't tell me."

"They're gone, Nevan! My bow and arrows are gone!"

"Bow and arrows?" Edwina said, clearly bewildered.

"Shit," Nevan couldn't help uttering, much to Edwina's dismay. "Where's Alfred now?" He clasped Edwina's shoulders, gazing into her eyes.

"Gone."

"As in gone home?" Nevan asked hopefully.

"I don't think so. Alfred jumped around behind the counter, then danced around the shop like...like he was on drugs, cheering and blurting variations on the F-word until I thought he'd lost his mind. Alfred's usually so meek and quiet. With a maniacal grin, Alfred told me he was quitting to go on a mission to find true love."

"Aw, shit," Nevan muttered again, before something Aladee did caught his attention. "What are you doing?"

In reply, Aladee held up a finger, motioning for him to wait. He watched as she dipped her fingertip into one of the small vials in her purse, and then pressed it on Edwina's cheek, next to her nose.

"Breathe..." Aladee instructed Edwina. "Breathe..." And she did.

Edwina looked blank for a moment, blinked a few times, then made eye contact with Nevan. "Oh, hello, Nevan. I must have been daydreaming," she said with a tranquil smile. "I didn't even hear you come in. Did you see Red off on his trip? I do hope he has a good vacation. He really does work too hard."

Nevan just stared at Edwina, mouth agape.

"Nevan?" Edwina looked at him curiously. "Are you all right?"

"Is...is Alfred around?" he asked cautiously.

"I'm afraid not, Edwina said with that same calm smile. "Alfred tendered his resignation and won't be working here any longer. I see your lovely fiancée is here with you. It's a pleasure to meet you, Aladee." Edwina extended her hand. "I've heard so many nice things about you."

"Thank you so much, Edwina." Aladee pumped her hand. "I've heard wonderful things about you too. I look forward to working with you."

"If you don't mind," Edwina said, "I'll just go back to putting that new shipment of supplies away."

After she went in the back room, Nevan turned to Aladee, aghast. "We can do that?" he asked, tapping the side of his nose. "Make people forget and change stuff around in their memory?"

"Quite easily, with experience." Aladee nodded. "It's in chapter eight of our new manual. Needless to say, we must be prudent when using it."

"Holy shit," Nevan said.

"What does excrement have to do with this?" she asked with a tsk.

"Plenty," Nevan answered.

"What are we going to do about Alfred? If Lonan finds out, he'll be so disappointed. And Cupid will be furious. If the council learns I was so careless with the academy's property, they might withdraw my minor goddess status and separate us."

Nevan sucked in a sharp breath...and laughter rushed out. He couldn't help it. He had a feeling this was just the beginning of many such crises he'd encounter in his never boring life with Aladee.

"Looks like we gather our gear, sweetheart, and find Alfred before he wreaks all sorts of havoc with your bow and arrows."

"Oh, Nevan. I'm so sorry." Aladee leaned her head against his chest. "I'm such a...what is the term? A screwball," she said mournfully.

"The word you're looking for is *screwup*," he replied without thinking. Actually, his lovely fiancée was both a screwup *and* a screwball—but he was crazy about her regardless. "No you're not," he gallantly lied, wrapping his arms around her, kissing the top of his capricious little nymph-fiancée's head. "It's okay, Aladee. We'll take care of it before anyone finds out what happened."

"Thank you, Nevan. I promise nothing like this will *ever* happen again."

Nevan heaved a sigh and chuckled.

"Nevan?"

"Hmmm?"

"I love you."

"I love you too, sweetheart."

Nope, no doubt about it. Life with his darling Aladee would never be dull or boring.

~<>~

Thank you so much for choosing to read The Nymph's Heartwish. I hope you got as much enjoyment out of the story as I did writing it. Creating and getting to know each of the six Malone siblings and their mom, Astrid, has been satisfying and rewarding for me...well, except when one of them wakes me up at 3:00 a.m. to let me know they disagree with something I had them think, say, or do.

In the Heartwishes books I've created the sort of loving, close-knit, caring, and supportive family and friends that I wished I'd had growing up. For me, one of the best perks of being a writer is creating fictional worlds, populating them with a large cast of characters, then "living" in that world for hours on end as I tell their stories. Being so thoroughly immersed in a fictional world I've created, the pretend people and their hangouts soon seem to become real. My favorite part is getting to hang out with everybody.

I can't imagine not writing. I write to make myself and my readers happy, which means you're very important to me and I appreciate you! If you enjoyed this book I'd be delighted if you left a positive review or rating on the site where you purchased it. Your review can be long or short, or even just a star rating.

Good reviews tell me that readers enjoy my books, which helps encourage me to continue writing. They help new readers make decisions about whether or not to read my books. Reviews also help my books to be seen so they don't get lost in a site's complicated algorithms. The more reviews a book gets, the better chance it has of readers finding it. You can also help other readers find this book by recommending it to your friends.

As you can probably tell, I'd be exceedingly happy if you left a positive review for my book. Thank you!

I really enjoy connecting with my readers. Visit DaisyDexterDobbs.com[1] to sign up for my newsletter and mailing list to get notifications for my new book releases, contests, and more.

You can also find me here:

Facebook: DaisyDexterDobbs[2]

Instagram: DaisyDexterDobbs[3]

TikTok: @daisydexterdobbs[4]

Twitter: DaisyDDobbs[5]

Goodreads: daisydexterdobbs[6]

Email: DaisyDexterDobbs@gmail.com

---

1. https://www.daisydexterdobbs.com/contact.html

2. https://www.facebook.com/daisydexterdobbs/

3. https://www.instagram.com/daisydexterdobbs/

4. https://www.tiktok.com/@daisydexterdobbs

5. https://twitter.com/DaisyDDobbs

6. https://www.goodreads.com/daisydexterdobbs

Thanks again!
—*Daisy Dexter Dobbs*

~<>~

Don't miss out!

Visit the website below and you can sign up to receive emails whenever Daisy Dexter Dobbs publishes a new book. There's no charge and no obligation.

https://books2read.com/r/B-A-MIIB-QPUWB

BOOKS 2 READ

Connecting independent readers to independent writers.

Also by Daisy Dexter Dobbs

Heartwishes
The Viking's Heartwish
The Genie's Heartwish
The Firefighter's Heartwish
The Knitter's Heartwish
The Nymph's Heartwish
The Psychic's Heartwish

Watch for more at www.DaisyDexterDobbs.com.

About the Author

Long dedicated to providing the magic of escapism through her books, Daisy Dexter Dobbs started writing happily-ever-after stories when she was five, often reading them aloud to her guests, using a toilet plunger as a microphone.

Today, Daisy's books transport readers on wondrous voyages of the imagination. Infused with positivity, hope, joy, humor, friendships, family, and romance, her stories often include a touch of magic and fantasy—and always a happily ever after.

Daisy has ghostwritten speeches for politicians; been an art director; a weight loss counselor; mayor's executive secretary; a Realtor; travel agent; editor; she even worked as a butcher's meat wrapper, quitting on the spot when she saw a big eyeball coming toward her on the conveyor. Having worked at more than 40 different jobs provides Daisy with a bottomless pit of...questionable experience she draws from for her books.

A Chicago native now residing in the Pacific Northwest, Daisy is happily married to her soul mate, the man who is the inspiration for every hero she creates. They have a wonderful daughter, son-in-law, and rescue granddog. Happily for her family and friends, Daisy no longer feels the need to use a bathroom plunger as a microphone when entertaining guests.

Read more at www.DaisyDexterDobbs.com.